THE SECOND RISING

THE CHRONICLES OF ARGHOST
VOLUME 1
DERREN PARSONS

Elven Leaf Publishing

THE SECOND RISING: THE CHRONICLES OF ARGHOST VOLUME I

Copyright © 2023 Derren Parsons

Cover illustration by Getcovers

Illustrations by Tristen Parsons

All rights reserved.

Visit Derren Parsons at www.derrenparsonsauthor.com

THE SECOND RISING/Derren Parsons – 1st ed

2nd Ed 2026

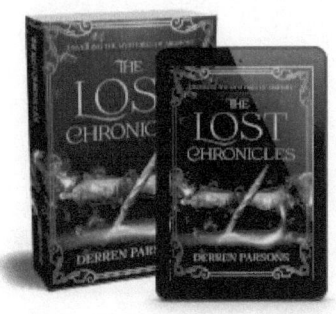

Your Free Book is Waiting

Join us on a journey through Arghost, a land of ancient wars and enchanting magic. From the icy peaks of Atheron to the arid deserts of the Western Lands, this anthology of riveting tales will transport you to a realm of contrast and wonder.

Meet the voices of Elves, Dwarves, Humans, Asakal, and mighty Namites as they navigate through the treacherous and beautiful world they inhabit. But be wary, for danger lurks in the form of Reptans, Wildkin, and other ferocious creatures, waiting to strike from the shadows. Immerse yourself in the magic that weaves through nature and discover the untold stories of Arghost. But beware, for not all mysteries are meant to be revealed...

Get a free copy of the novella

The Lost Chronicles: Unveiling the Mysteries of Arghost.

www.derrenparsonsauthor.com

PROLOGUE

5 00 Years Before

The knight had stood the ramparts for three days without sleep. Twenty years of war had worn him down to bone and habit. He no longer flinched at the sounds that rose from the plains below. The groans of the dying. The scrape of carrion birds. The wind moving across bodies that would not move again.

Whiteguard held. For now.

He gripped the stone ledge and looked out. The battlefield stretched before him, flat and vast, a grey-brown waste where nothing grew. The Legion's forces had pulled back after the last assault, withdrawing to regroup beyond the ridge. Their banners — dark, featureless things — caught no light. The air smelled of ash and rot, thick enough to taste.

Somewhere out there, among the horde, stood Volthar.

The knight had never seen him up close. Few had and lived to describe him. But word had spread through the ranks over the years, whispered between men who had fought at the Legion's edge and stumbled back. A hooded figure. A staff in his hand. Eyes that burned.

The Dark Magika had brought the world to its knees. Twenty years of relentless war. Cities reduced to nothing. Forests burned black. The remnants of Arghost — Dwarves, Men, Elves, Namites, all who still drew breath — had been pushed here. To Whiteguard. To these walls. There was nowhere left to retreat.

The knight exhaled slowly. The sun beat down, indifferent.

Then the Legion moved.

It came without warning. One moment the ridge was still. The next, a dark mass surged forward, flowing across the plain like water finding its level. No war cries. No drums. Just the sound of ten thousand pairs of feet striking earth in unison, steady and patient, and beneath it the low grinding of iron.

The knight's hand found his sword. Around him, others did the same.

The mass stopped.

A figure rose above it — standing on a boulder at the Legion's centre, robed in black, hood drawn low. Even at this distance, the knight could see the staff in his hands. It was tall, gnarled, and dark as the sky before a storm. The Magika held it loosely, as though it weighed nothing at all.

Volthar's voice carried across the plain. It should not have reached the walls. But it did, clear and cold, as though the air itself bent to deliver it.

'The Power Stones are failing,' he said. 'Athris' light drains from this world. And we are here to see it go.'

He raised the staff overhead.

The Legion roared.

The sound hit the walls like a physical force. The knight felt it in his chest, in his teeth. Around him, men shifted, gripped tighter, said nothing. There was nothing to say. They had known this moment was coming. They had simply hoped it would not.

Volthar began to chant.

The words were not words the knight recognised. They were old — older than any language spoken in Arghost. Each syllable fell from the Magika's lips with a weight that seemed to press the air downward. The staff responded. A darkness gathered around it, thick and writhing, pulsing in time with the chant.

The knight watched, unable to look away.

The chanting grew louder. The ground trembled. The staff's darkness swelled, coiling upward like smoke given intent. Volthar's voice rose with it, rising and rising until it seemed to fill the sky itself.

Then it stopped.

Volthar stumbled.

The knight saw it clearly — the Magika's hands tightening on the staff, his body jerking as though struck. For a moment, nothing else moved. The Legion held its breath.

Then the staff burned white.

Not dark. Not the writhing blackness that had fed it moments before. Pure, blinding light erupted from the wood, so bright the knight threw his arm across his eyes. He heard screams from below — from the Legion, not from behind him. The light poured outward in a wave, expanding fast, sweeping across the plain.

He did not see Volthar fall. The light was too bright for that. But he heard the scream — short, sharp, and final.

The wave hit the walls of Whiteguard.

The stone shuddered beneath his feet. The knight gripped the ledge and held on as the light crashed against the fortifications, climbing the walls like water rising. Heat and pressure and a sound like the world cracking open. Men around him cried out, pressing themselves flat against the stone.

Then it passed.

The silence that followed was absolute.

The knight lowered his arm. His vision swam, white-blind, slowly resolving into shapes. He blinked. Once. Twice.

The plain below was empty.

Not barred. Not littered with the dead. Empty. Where the Legion had stood, there was nothing but open ground, pale and bare, as though the earth had been swept clean. A faint haze hung in the air, already thinning in the breeze. The smell of ash was gone. In its place, something else — something green and clean that the knight could not name.

He stood there for a long time, breathing.

Around him, others were rising. No one spoke. They simply looked out at the place where the army had been and tried to understand what they were seeing.

It was near dusk when the gates opened.

A small group stepped out — soldiers, a Magika, a handful of scouts. The knight went with them. Their footsteps were loud in the stillness. Gravel crunched beneath their boots. Wind moved across the plain, carrying the scent of wildflowers. Somewhere ahead, a patch of golden grass had begun to grow, swaying gently in the evening air.

They found the staff first.

It lay in the dust, half-buried, as though it had fallen from a great height. The wood was pale now, almost white, the dark grain washed out. It looked old. Ancient. The carvings along its length glowed faintly, catching what remained of the light.

No one touched it.

They stood around it in silence, staring, until a sound drew their attention.

Footsteps. Soft. Uneven. Coming from the far edge of the plain.

A figure shuffled toward them. Small. Hunched. Wrapped in tattered robes that had once been fine but were now little more than rags. As it drew closer, the knight saw the hood, the bony hands, the staff it leaned on — a different staff, gnarled and marked with symbols that seemed to shift in the fading light.

Beneath the hood, a sharp beak jutted into view. Beady eyes caught the last of the sun and held it.

The Magika beside the knight inhaled sharply. 'The Seer,' he whispered.

No one moved. No one spoke. The figure continued its slow approach, unhurried, as though the battlefield and the silence and the staring soldiers were of no particular concern.

It stopped beside the fallen staff of Athris.

For a long moment, the Seer simply looked at it. Then one bony, three-fingered hand reached down and lifted it from the dust. The wood brightened at the touch — not dramatically, not with any flash or surge. Just a quiet warming of the light within it, as though something had been waiting to be held again.

The Seer turned to leave.

'Wait,' the knight said.

The figure paused. Turned back. Those beady eyes settled on him, ancient and patient.

The knight stepped forward. His mouth was dry. 'What happened?' he asked. 'What was that?'

The Seer extended one hand — thin, bird-boned, trembling slightly with age.

The knight hesitated. Then he placed his hand over it.

The voice came not through his ears but somewhere deeper, settling into his mind like water into still ground.

'I am the Seer of Arghost. The vessel of Athris.'

The knight said nothing. He waited.

'The staff's power can only be bound by one of the ancient bloodlines,' the Seer continued. 'The first races shaped by Athris himself. Volthar knew this. He chose to ignore it.' A pause. Something that might have been pity moved through the presence in the knight's mind. 'His arrogance consumed him. The staff turned its light upon its master. It could do nothing else.'

The knight swallowed. 'Is it over? Is the darkness gone?'

The silence that followed lasted longer than it should have.

'The darkness persists,' the Seer said. 'But it holds no power here. Not now.' Another pause. 'Athris entrusts the survivors to rebuild. That is the task that remains.'

The knight felt the hand withdraw. The presence faded from his mind, leaving only a faint echo — something old and tired, carrying a weight he could not begin to measure.

He looked up.

The Seer was already walking away, the staff of Athris held close, its pale light flickering gently against the dusk. The figure grew smaller with each step, unhurried, moving across the empty plain as though it had all the time in the world.

Perhaps it did.

The knight watched until the Seer was nothing but a shape against the horizon. Then a speck. Then gone.

Behind him, someone let out a breath. Someone else began to laugh — not from joy, but from the simple shock of being alive. Others knelt, hands pressing into the warm earth, faces turned toward the sky.

The knight stayed where he was, watching the place where the Seer had disappeared.

The darkness persists.

A single bird crossed the sky above the plain, its call thin and clear in the evening air. The first green shoot pushed up through the dust at the knight's feet, pale and fragile, reaching for what little light remained.

It was not an ending.

It was a breath held in the dark, waiting to see what came next.

To my beloved wife,
Without whom this book would remain a mere collection of scattered thoughts and dreams, your unwavering support and love have been the guiding light throughout this journey. In you, I found inspiration and strength to weave stories and breathe life into words.

CHAPTER ONE

The Hunt

Niama's pulse hammered, blurring the forest's edges. Leaves whispered underfoot as she ran, breath tight, senses razor-sharp. Ahead, the elk crashed through brush with a sharp crack, flight frantic.

The elk was alone. It should have been with a herd—elk didn't range solo this deep into winter. But she'd seen no tracks, no droppings, nothing but this single animal.

The herds were gone. Not thinning. Gone.

'Keep up,' she hissed over her shoulder.

Coseo didn't answer. His ragged breath tore behind her—too loud.

Niama slowed, raising a clenched fist. They slid to a halt beneath alder and thorn. She dropped to one knee, palm to damp earth. Fresh. Warm. Close.

Wind shifted.

She cursed silently and angled left, downslope, keeping their scent away. Brambles clawed her calves, thorns biting leather. She ignored the sting. Hunger cut deeper.

She glanced back. Coseo's face had paled, sweat darkening his collar.

'Breathe.'

He nodded, jaw clamped, and followed.

They crept forward. Tawny hide flickered through trees. The elk burst into a small clearing and stopped, sides heaving, steam curling from its nostrils in the cold.

Niama sank lower, bow in hand. Too open. No escape but the far treeline. If it bolted, they'd lose it.

She nocked an arrow.

The elk lifted its head, ears twitching. Somewhere above, a bird burst from the branches. The animal froze.

Coseo shifted. A twig snapped. The elk lunged.

Later, Niama would remember this moment. How a single snapped twig nearly cost them everything. How sound carried in winter air.

She'd remember it when the screaming started in the dark.

Niama drew and released in one motion.

The arrow struck high, driving into muscle. The elk screamed, stumbled, crashed through brush, and collapsed in a spray of leaves and frost.

Silence pressed close, the forest holding its breath.

Her hands shook once—then stilled.

Coseo exhaled a shaky laugh. 'By the light...'

Niama was already moving—low, knife ready, eyes on the flank. Only when stillness settled, when she was certain the elk wouldn't rise again, did she relax.

'That was close.'

'You dropped it with one shot.' His eyes widened, fatigue forgotten for a moment. 'I didn't even see the opening.'

'You thought too loudly,' she cut in, a smile tugging her mouth.

She knelt beside the elk, hand to its neck. Warmth lingered beneath fur. She bowed her head, murmuring quiet thanks—old words for bark, root, and blood-soaked earth. This life would not be wasted.

Winter would ease, if only a little.

She rose, knife steady, and began the work.

The elk was smaller than it should be. Ribs showing. A winter kill—already weakened by hunger before her arrow found it. The meat would be lean, tough.

But it would feed the village for two days. Maybe three if they stretched it.

Two days, she thought. Then what?

Coseo stared, chest still heaving. 'Another breath and we'd have lost it.'

Niama allowed a brief smile, a quick nod—thanks enough. He'd remember the shot. She'd remember the wait.

'Apologies. Leg fell asleep.' He winced, shifting weight.

Niama glanced back, red hair slipping loose. 'Patience was never your virtue, Cos.' She glanced at the blood on his hands, the dirt under his nails. 'We both smell like death now.'

She rested a hand on the flank one last time, feeling warmth ebb. 'We'll get you home,' she murmured to the creature. To the hunger waiting beyond the trees. To the children with hollow cheeks.

Coseo nodded, humor gone, and helped shoulder the load.

She wiped her blade clean and wondered—not for the first time—what would happen when the forest no longer answered her prayers.

The journey home was quiet, the elk's weight heavy between them.

Mistwood lay deep in the Erbour Forest, trees close and old, ground remembering every footstep. It was the heart of Illadrel's southern reaches, bark and stone shaped together, nothing apart from the forest that birthed it.

Niama felt the change as the path wound deeper into familiar territory. Air thickened with damp moss, sap, loam crushed under leather. Branches bent aside in silence. Roots rose where feet expected them. The forest knew them here.

This was elven land, shaped by long familiarity.

Niama had grown beneath these boughs, learned to read the forest as others read script. Yet her bond was forged, not born. She remembered nothing before the day they found her bleeding among ferns, past stripped clean as bark from a fallen tree. The elders never spoke of it. Their silences clung tighter than answers.

Tonight, those questions could wait. The village needed meat, not mysteries.

Dusk crept in. Birds settled. Insects stirred. The sun slipped behind the Orborus Mountains, staining the canopy ash and amber.

Mistwood emerged, alive with motion. Torches flickered around the ancient heart tree, flames darting like fireflies among roots. Voices overlapped. Laughter rang.

'That's new,' Coseo murmured.

Too many voices. Niama slowed as they neared the village center. Bodies pressed everywhere—more than she'd seen outside of harvest festivals. Firelight danced across unfamiliar faces.

A villager pushed through the crowd, grin wide. 'Triumphant hunt?'

Niama shifted her grip on the elk, suddenly aware of how small it was. How little it would feed them. 'Hard-won. What's happening?'

'Summons from the elders. Every settlement sent word. Representatives too.' The villager's smile dimmed. 'We feast while we wait for news from the north.'

News from the north. Niama's stomach tightened.

Nothing good ever came from the north.

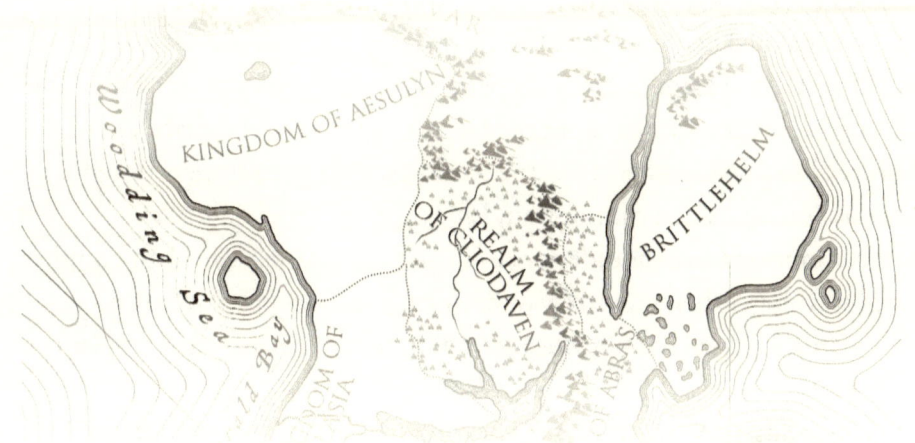

CHAPTER TWO

The Gathering

They entered the crowd, and the feast swallowed them whole.

Smoke curled thick, carrying roasting flesh and sap-rich wood. Drums pulsed beneath flutes' bright trills, the rhythm thrumming through the earth, felt more than heard. Bodies pressed close—villagers from Mistwood mingling with unfamiliar faces, representatives from settlements Niama had only heard named in passing.

The bonfire roared at the center, flames leaping high enough to paint the lowest branches gold. Faces glowed in the firelight, eyes bright, smiles unguarded. Children darted between adults' legs, shrieking with laughter. Sparks drifted upward like wandering stars, disappearing into the canopy's darkness.

Someone pressed a strip of meat into Niama's hands. She bit down. Juice ran hot, rich and smoky, herbs sharp beneath the char. It tasted of effort, blood, cold earth—survival earned. She closed her eyes briefly, letting the noise blur into warmth, the fear of the empty forest fade beneath the press of living bodies.

'The day has been bountiful,' Uthru said beside her.

She turned. The elder watched with quiet approval. 'You've done the village proud, Niama.'

She inclined her head. 'Fortune favored us. Herds thin each season.'

Uthru's smile faded. Lines deepened around his mouth, his eyes. 'Our troubles run deeper than hunger.' He glanced toward the heart tree where other elders were gathering in the shadows, their faces grave. 'Tonight we speak of matters that cannot wait. Enjoy the warmth while it lasts.'

He squeezed her shoulder once—a gesture that felt like both comfort and warning—then moved away, his form swallowed by the crowd.

Niama watched him go, unease settling cold in her stomach despite the fire's heat.

Coseo appeared at her elbow, chewing. 'What was that about?'

'I don't know.' She wiped grease from her fingers. 'But I don't think we're going to like it.'

Around them, the feast continued. Drums quickened. Someone began a song—voices rising, harmonizing, the old words about spring and plenty that felt hollow in her mouth. She didn't join in.

The forest beyond the firelight seemed to press closer, listening.

The horn's call cut through the feast, long and resonant, pulling night taut.

Conversations stuttered. Laughter died. The drums fell silent mid-beat.

Niama set aside her food and followed Coseo toward the circle. Others were already moving, faces shifting from celebration to wariness. Children were ushered toward the outer edges. Hunters moved forward, settling onto logs and stones arranged in concentric rings around the heart tree.

The elders sat on worn benches beneath the ancient trunk, their backs to bark that had witnessed centuries. Firelight flickered across weathered faces—Uthru at the center, Gretha to his left, old Torven to his right. Rolana stood behind them, a hunter herself, arms crossed.

Niama found a place near the front, Coseo beside her. Bodies pressed close on all sides. The air felt heavy, expectant.

Uthru stood.

'We must speak of matters that cannot wait.'

Silence fell like a blade.

Niama's hand found Coseo's shoulder as someone jostled her from behind. His muscles were tense beneath her palm.

'Dire tidings from the north,' Uthru continued, his voice carrying across the gathering. 'Aesulyn villages burn.'

Niama's chest tightened. Aesulyn. She had met the Namite—desert dwellers of Aesulyn—last spring. Three families, maybe four. Children who'd gathered around her bow, asking how far arrows could fly.

'Homes ruined. Survivors taken south, into Ghija's iron mines under Ijovar.'

She saw it behind her eyes—thatch catching, children screaming, the smell of burning flesh and green wood. Her fingers dug into her palms hard enough to hurt.

Uthru's gaze swept the circle. 'Some claim Ijovar's hand guides these acts. Others whisper of darker agents.' He paused. The fire crackled in the silence. 'Sightings of actari.'

A murmur rippled through the gathering like wind through grass.

A woman near the edge backed away, hand flying to her mouth. The hunter beside Niama went rigid, leather creaking as his fists clenched. Coseo's breathing quickened, shallow and tight.

Lhoris of Riverbreak barked a laugh—too loud, too sharp in the quiet. 'Actari? Children's tales. Ghosts to frighten fools from wandering at night.'

Niama shifted, boots grinding into earth. She'd grown on those stories—blood-soaked shadows with eyes like coals, creatures that served ancient darkness and showed no mercy. Her mother—no, not her mother, the woman who'd raised her—had whispered them as warnings when Niama ranged too far as a child.

Voices rose around her. Some nodded agreement with Lhoris, faces set with determination to believe in mundane threats. Others shouted him down, fear bright in their eyes.

Gretha rose from her bench, slowly, her white braid catching firelight. The arguments died.

'They are real,' she said, voice calm but unyielding as stone. 'Legends endure because they were born of truth. The actari serve the darkness between stars. Where they walk, nothing remains untouched. Nothing remains alive.'

Lhoris turned away sharply, jaw clenched. 'We face hunger, not phantoms. Our stores thin. The prey vanishes. The forest itself falters. These are the enemies we know.'

'And if they share a cause?' Uthru asked quietly.

'On whose word?' Lhoris demanded, wheeling back. 'Whose testimony do we trust with our lives?'

'Balen and his son,' Uthru said. 'Traders we've known twenty years. Men who've never lied about the roads they've walked.'

'A convenient story from men seeking shelter and food.'

Uthru's jaw tightened, a muscle jumping in his cheek. 'We will not dismiss warning because it frightens us. That way lies death.'

Gretha's voice cut through before Lhoris could respond. 'If true, it could mark the Second Rising. Darkness does not return without purpose. It does not wake without hunger.'

The name struck like a dropped blade—the Second Rising. Whispers ran through the crowd. Someone sobbed once, quickly stifled.

Firelight twisted across the elders' faces, shadows tangling as if alive, as if something moved just beyond the flames' reach.

Niama swallowed hard. The world felt brittle, like ice over deep water. One wrong step and everything would crack.

Uthru raised his hands, calling for silence. The gesture was slow, weary. 'Enough. Let us not jump to conclusions when we lack knowledge. We will seek counsel first.' His eyes lifted past the gathering, toward the forest's depths. 'From the Seer of Washrock Rise.'

A stir ran through the circle—part fear, part something darker. Washrock Rise. Niama had heard the name in whispers. A place where paths shifted. Where hunters went and didn't return.

Rolana stepped forward from behind the elders' bench, her scarred hands visible in the firelight. She'd survived a bear attack in her youth; everyone knew the story. Now her face was grim.

'There's more the council must hear,' she said. 'Hunters found tracks deep in the forest. Not made by any beast we know.'

The murmurs died. Every eye fixed on Rolana.

'Three weeks past, beyond the northern ridge. Two weeks ago, near Greymire Pond.' She paused, her gaze sweeping across the hunters in the front rows. 'A week ago, near the old cairn.'

Niama's blood went cold.

The old cairn. Where they found me.

Her vision narrowed. Sound became distant, muffled. The old cairn—the place she'd been drawn to three days ago, compelled by something she couldn't name. The place where her life had begun, her memory empty as a scraped bowl.

Uthru's gaze found hers across the fire. Not surprise in his eyes. Confirmation. Recognition.

He'd known. He'd known and waited to see if she'd felt it too.

'Five days ago,' Rolana continued, her voice steady despite the tension crackling through the crowd, 'the eastern watch found tracks a half-day's walk from here. Whatever made them is circling Mistwood. The pattern is deliberate. Tightening.'

The circle went utterly silent. Even the fire seemed to quiet, flames lowering as if cowering.

'We have days,' Rolana said. 'Not weeks.'

Another hunter stood—Maren, young but respected—his voice shaking. 'I found a deer yesterday. Near the eastern border. It wouldn't run.' He swallowed hard. 'Just stood there shaking, eyes wide and white. Like it had forgotten how to fear wolves because something worse was behind it. I... I left it there. Couldn't bring myself to kill something already dead inside.'

The silence that followed was suffocating.

Niama's hands trembled. She clenched them, nails biting into her palms. *Searching,* Rolana had said. *Deliberately.*

Searching for what?

Or who?

The thought coiled in her gut like a snake.

Uthru's voice broke the quiet, each word weighted with resignation. 'Then we ask for volunteers. Three, no more. To seek the Seer at Washrock Rise and return with counsel.'

No one moved.

Sparks rose and died, swallowed by night. Someone added wood to the flames—they surged higher, throwing new shadows that danced across frozen faces.

Niama's pulse hammered in her ears. She looked around the circle. Saw fear in every face. Saw parents gripping their children's shoulders. Saw hunters—skilled, brave hunters who'd faced boar and bear—staring at the ground as if answers might rise from the soil.

No one would volunteer. She knew it in the settling silence, in the way eyes found anything to look at except Uthru's face.

Her hands trembled. She clenched them.

The tracks were at the cairn. The place where she'd been found. Where her story began in blood and mystery.

If something was searching—if something was coming south—it was coming for her.

She could feel it in her bones. In the dreams she'd been having. In the way the forest had felt wrong for weeks, watching, waiting.

She thought of the empty bowl she'd seen in a doorway. Of the children with hollow cheeks. Of two days of meat and then starvation.

She thought of whatever had left her bleeding fifteen years ago. Whatever she'd fled into the forest to escape.

Niama stepped forward.

The circle waited, breath held.

She looked at the hunters—at their fear, poorly hidden. At their relief when she moved, when someone else took the burden.

'We will go.' The words carried across the gathering, clean and unyielding.

She turned to Coseo. His eyes were wide, but he nodded once, jaw set.

'I'm with you,' he said, voice only slightly unsteady.

Movement to her left. A younger man stepped forward—Valran. Niama recognized him from the outer settlements, from occasional hunts where their paths had crossed. Lean, perhaps twenty summers, with a bow slung across his back and callused hands that spoke of long hours with the string.

His voice was steady, but his knuckles were white where he gripped his bow. 'I'll go as well.'

Niama studied him. Dark hair pulled back, sharp cheekbones, eyes that held something fierce beneath the surface. Not just courage. Something else. The need to prove himself, perhaps. Or to escape something.

'You're certain?' she asked. 'Washrock Rise isn't a hunt. It's—'

'I know what it is.' He met her gaze without flinching. 'I've hunted beyond the inner trails. Tracked through the deep woods. I won't slow you down.'

She held his eyes a moment longer, searching for hesitation, for the crack that would appear when fear truly settled in.

She found only determination.

'Very well,' Niama said.

Relief rippled through the gathered crowd like wind through wheat. Shoulders sagged. Parents pulled their children closer. The hunters who'd been staring at the ground now looked up, gratitude and shame warring on their faces.

Uthru inclined his head, something like pride and sorrow mixing in his expression. 'Your courage honors you. Washrock Rise is perilous even in calm times. What you face now—' He paused, collecting himself.

He glanced up through the canopy. Stars shone cold and clear between the branches. 'The new moon rises in four nights. The Seer will speak only then. After, he falls silent for another month.'

A month.

Niama's mind raced. The stores would last two weeks, maybe three if they rationed hard enough. Children would starve waiting for another moon. And if the tracks continued to circle closer—

'The journey is four days in good weather,' Uthru continued. 'In winter, through whatever drives the herds away, with whatever makes those tracks—' His voice roughened. 'You must move faster than safe. Faster than wise.'

He looked at each of them in turn—Niama, Coseo, Valran.

'Depart at first light. Move fast. Don't stop unless you must.' His voice caught, just slightly. 'May the light guide your path. And may you return whole.'

The gathering began to break apart, voices rising again, subdued and worried. Parents hurried children toward home. Hunters dispersed in small groups, heads bent together in urgent conversation.

Lhoris pushed through the crowd without a word, his face dark with anger or fear—Niama couldn't tell which.

As people moved past, an older woman touched Niama's arm. Her face was lined with grief, eyes hollow.

'My son went to Washrock Rise seven years ago,' she whispered. 'We never found his body.' Her fingers tightened, trembling. 'Come back, child. Don't make me mourn twice.'

Before Niama could respond, the woman slipped away into the dispersing crowd.

Uthru appeared at Niama's shoulder. 'All three of you—meet me at the heart tree at first light. There are things you must know before you depart.'

Coseo and Valran exchanged glances, then nodded and moved toward the remaining fires where food still waited.

Uthru touched Niama's arm, holding her back as the others left. The firelight carved deep shadows across his face, making him look older than she'd ever seen him.

'Walk with me,' he said quietly.

They moved beyond the circle's edge, into the space between firelight and forest. The feast's noise faded behind them—voices and crackling flames becoming distant, dreamlike.

'You knew,' Niama said. It wasn't a question.

Uthru stopped, his back to the celebration. 'About the cairn? Yes.' His voice was heavy. 'I was there when the hunters found the first tracks. I sent Rolana to announce it publicly because—' He paused. 'Because I couldn't bear to ask you myself.'

'Ask me what?'

'To walk toward danger when I don't know if that danger knows your name.'

The words hung in the cold air between them.

He turned to face her fully. 'Fifteen years ago, we found you bleeding at that cairn. You were dying, Niama. The wounds—' His voice caught. 'No child should have survived them. But you did. And you healed faster than any elf I'd ever seen. Faster than natural, even for our kind.'

Niama's hands clenched. She'd always known there was something different about her. Cuts that closed in days instead of weeks. Bruises that faded overnight. The elders' careful silence when she recovered too quickly.

'The elders recognized what it meant,' Uthru continued quietly. 'That kind of healing—it's a blessing. Old magic from the first peoples, from bloodlines that walked this world before our kingdoms rose.' His eyes searched hers. 'We didn't know where you came from. Who your people were. But we knew you carried something ancient in your blood.'

'You never told me.'

'We thought it kinder not to.' Something like shame crossed his face. 'You were a child. Traumatized. We gave you a home, a name, a life. Why burden you with questions we couldn't answer?'

Niama's throat tightened. 'And now?'

'Now tracks appear at the cairn where we found you. Now darkness rises and ancient things wake.' His voice roughened. 'I don't know if it means anything. The forest is vast—the tracks could be coincidence. These creatures range everywhere, and the cairn is simply in their path.'

'But you're afraid it's not coincidence.'

'I'm afraid,' he admitted, 'that when old magic walks the world again, it recognizes its own. Your healing—that blessing in your blood—what if the darkness can sense it? What if whatever you fled fifteen years ago is connected to what hunts the forest now?'

The words should have terrified her. Instead, they felt like relief. Like finally naming the shadow she'd felt watching.

'The dreams,' she said. 'I've been having dreams.'

Something like grief crossed Uthru's face. 'I know. Many do, as the darkness grows. But yours—' He paused. 'Are they visions of what's coming? Or memories of what you survived?'

'I don't know,' she whispered. 'Blood. Screaming. Something vast in the dark. I can never tell if I'm remembering or seeing.'

Uthru gripped her shoulders. 'The Seer will know. He's older than this darkness. Older than our kingdoms. If anyone can tell you what you carry in your blood, what you survived, what's coming—it's him.'

'And if my past and this darkness are connected?'

'Then you've survived it before.' His voice turned fierce. 'Whatever left you bleeding at that cairn failed to kill you. Your blood wouldn't let it. That's not weakness, Niama. If darkness comes again—we'll need that strength. We'll need you.'

Silence settled between them. In the distance, someone laughed—a bright sound, incongruous with the weight pressing down on Niama's chest.

'I'm afraid,' Niama admitted.

'Good. Fear keeps you sharp.' He released her, stepped back. 'The Seer may have answers about what's coming. About what hunts the forest. And perhaps—' His voice softened. 'Perhaps he can tell you who you were before we found you. What people gave you that blessing in your blood.'

'I'm not sure I want to know.'

'No,' he said gently. 'But you need to. Whatever's coming, you'll face it better knowing the truth than running from shadows.'

The firelight flickered between the trees, painting everything in uncertain shades.

'First light,' Uthru said. 'Then I'll tell you and the others what I know of Washrock Rise. What to expect. What to fear.' He turned to go, then paused, looking back over his shoulder. 'Niama—your volunteering tonight. That took more courage than the others know. More than you know, perhaps. Thank you.'

Then he was gone, his form swallowed by shadow and smoke, leaving her alone with questions that had lived beneath her skin for fifteen years.

Now they had teeth.

Niama stood in the darkness between fire and forest, listening to the celebration fade behind her. Somewhere in the trees, something watched and waited.

She turned back toward the light, toward the warmth and voices, and tried not to think about how soon she'd be leaving it all behind.

CHAPTER THREE

The Journey

Niama woke with dread already chewing at the edges of her thoughts.

Uthru's warnings still clung to her, beasts in shadow, trouble from the north, whispers of the actari returning. Sleep had tried to bury it. Sleep had failed.

The Second Rising.

The name sat in her chest like a stone.

She swung her feet to the elk-hide rug. Soft. Silent. The treetop window drew her gaze, and Mistwood lay below, peaceful in a way that felt almost fragile, as if a hard word might crack it.

Spring had painted the forest bright, flowers crowding the undergrowth, butterflies drifting between trunks. Sun caught the dew and turned it to silver. Rabbits slipped through the light like quick thoughts.

They had taken her in.

Now their lives sat on her shoulders.

The smell of sizzling meat and fresh bread curled up through the dwelling, warm and ordinary, a small mercy. For a heartbeat, it loosened her throat.

Then her door slammed open.

Coseo strode in like the forest owed him a path, packs and steel clinking with every step. He didn't look apologetic. He never did.

'Are you ready?' he snapped. 'We're burning daylight.'

Niama's jaw tightened. Solitude had been hers for minutes at most, and he'd stolen even that.

Before she could answer, footsteps sounded on the walkway.

Valran appeared in the doorway, dark hair tied back with leather, excitement fighting nerves in his eyes. Leather armor hugged his frame; a short bow rode high with a neat quiver, and his pack sat too squarely on his shoulders, as if he'd measured every strap twice.

He met Niama's gaze and dipped his head, formal, careful.

Niama breathed in once, slow. Calm was a mask she knew how to wear.

'Go on to the circle,' she said, voice even. 'I will follow on swift feet.'

Coseo gave a sharp nod, already turning. Valran hesitated a fraction, then nodded as well, and they were gone, their voices thinning along the wooden walkways until only their boots remained, drumming the boards, fading into the village below.

Niama moved.

She took her bow from the wall, fingers finding the familiar carvings worn smooth by use. It had fed her more than once. She checked the string with a quick pull, then reached for her dagger, the village blacksmith's work, and strapped it tight to her side.

Leather creaked. Wood complained under her steps.

Outside, Mistwood waited. And beyond it, whatever had crawled into Uthru's voice last night.

Niama's hand brushed the worn leather of her armor. Memory stirred beneath her fingers. Near misses. Breath held too long. Victories bought dearly.

Steel did not frighten her.

What followed it did.

She descended the stairs, boards groaning underfoot, and the scent of home wrapped around her one last time. Wood, sap, smoke. It tightened her chest, but she did not slow.

The road was necessary.

The gathering circle opened ahead, ringed with trees and low firelight. Three figures waited.

Uthru stood foremost, sleepless lines carved deep into his face. He straightened when he saw her, stifling a yawn.

'Niama,' he said. 'It gladdens my heart to see you.'

Weariness dulled his features, but not his eyes.

Her companions stood beside him, packs set, faces drawn tight with the same quiet resolve she felt settling into her bones.

Uthru clasped his hands. 'Whispers of war travel from the north. If they are true, Atheron must be ready.' His gaze held hers. 'You must bring us the knowledge to do so.'

Silence closed around the circle.

'The road ahead will test you,' he continued. 'Stand together. What you return with may decide more than your own lives.'

He paced once, slow and deliberate. 'You seek the Seer. Power enough to strip pride from even the strongest. At the threshold, you will lay down your weapons. Only those who arrive unarmed may be heard.'

Unease rippled through the group.

Uthru did not soften. 'Follow the eastern road four days and nights. Watch for the great tree. Silver-barked. Moon-lit. It will guide you to the Seer's cave.'

Valran shifted, curiosity edging his voice. 'What marks this tree?'

Uthru's gaze hardened. 'It is unlike any other. You will know it when you see it.'

He looked at them all then, voice lowering. 'Beware the deep forest. Some things there hunt what walks unwary.'

The fire cracked softly.

Beyond the circle, the trees waited.

Valran's face drained of color.

Uthru studied them once more. 'Hold to the path,' he said. 'Keep your senses sharp. In these woods, vigilance is your truest ally.'

Then he turned and strode back toward the village, robes stirring dust in his wake.

His warning lingered after him.

Niama adjusted her pack. 'We move,' she said, turning toward the eastern road.

A hand lifted.

Elder Gretha beckoned.

Niama paused and looked back to her companions. She offered a small smile. 'Go on ahead. I will not linger.'

Coseo hesitated, then nodded. Valran mirrored him. Their footsteps faded down the path, swallowed by trees and distance.

Gretha waited where the light thinned beneath the branches. Her gray hair lay in a loose braid, her eyes bright despite the years etched at their corners.

'Before you go,' she said gently, 'there is something for you.'

She reached into her leather pouch and drew out a plain gold ring. Its flat face bore the engraving of an elk, simple and sure. Though unadorned, it caught the light in a way that made Niama's fingers still.

'A wandering magika gave me this,' Gretha said. 'Akron. A friend from long ago.'

Memory softened her gaze. 'He told me it would reveal its worth when hope grows thin.'

Gretha pressed the ring into Niama's palm.

'I have walked long in Athris's light,' she said quietly. 'I believe this was meant to reach you now.'

Niama swallowed and slid the ring onto her finger. It fit as if it had always been hers.

Sunlight struck the band. For a heartbeat, the elk seemed to stir.

Beyond the circle, the eastern road waited.

'Your companions wait,' Gretha said, smiling toward the eastern road.

Niama inclined her head in farewell and turned east. The ring rested warm against her finger as she rejoined Coseo and Valran, and the village soon fell away behind them.

They moved deeper into the forest. Leaves whispered as the breeze slid through the branches, but the sound carried little comfort. Beauty lingered here, yet unease crept beneath it, prickling Niama's skin.

Shadows thickened. Silence stretched.

Every sound felt too loud.

Her hand found her dagger by habit. She was not alone. She repeated it silently, even as the sense of being watched refused to fade.

Twilight swallowed the forest.

'We should make camp,' Niama said. 'Night has claimed the trees.'

Valran groaned and rubbed his calves. 'A fire would be welcome.'

Coseo yawned, scanning the darkening woods. 'A clearing,' he said. 'My pack feels twice its weight.'

They found a small glade, ringed by tall, slender trees. Valran coaxed a fire to life at its center, the flames climbing eagerly.

'That should keep the smaller things away,' he said, grinning as firelight warmed his face.

The flames stretched their shadows long into the dark.

Coseo laid out his bedroll among the leaves and ate in silence. Niama followed suit, savoring the warmth as it soaked into her bones.

'We covered good ground today,' she said.

Firelight softened their faces. The scent of ripening berries drifted through the glade, a quiet reminder of harvests yet to come.

Night deepened.

Small things moved in the underbrush.

A branch cracked somewhere close.

Firelight faltered against the surrounding dark, and Niama watched the flames, listening. The warmth did little to drive away the cold knot tightening in her chest.

She folded her arms around herself. Silence had always come easier than certainty.

Still, the unfamiliar road stirred unease at the edge of her thoughts.

Morning light filtered through the canopy, gold spilling across leaf and loam.

Niama woke hard, heart still racing. Smoke from last night's fire clung to the air, stirring bitter memories of earlier camps, when watchful eyes had kept the dark at bay.

A fox crept close, nose twitching. When Niama shifted, it bolted, red tail flashing once before vanishing into brush.

Birdsong swelled as the forest woke. Breeze and earth-scent soothed her nerves, but she did not trust the calm.

Coseo snored nearby, hair fallen across his face. Niama nudged his boot. He jolted awake, mumbling something about pickled fruit pudding.

A faint smile touched her mouth.

Valran was already packing, shooting Coseo an amused glance as he worked.

They broke camp quickly, dousing the fire and shouldering their packs. Niama drew her cloak close, warmth and unease tangled beneath it.

The old road ahead was nearly swallowed by green, cart tracks fading beneath moss and leaf. Roads narrowed for many reasons. Not all of them were accidents.

They walked in silence for the first hour, each lost in thought.

Finally, Coseo cleared his throat. 'So. A Seer who strips pride from the strongest.' He shot Niama a sidelong glance. 'Think that includes you?'

'It includes everyone,' she said.

'Even me?' Valran asked, attempting lightness.

Coseo snorted. 'You've got pride to spare, lad. All that proper bow-holding and measured steps.'

Valran's jaw tightened, but Niama saw the faint smile he tried to hide.

'We'll all be humbled soon enough,' she said quietly. 'Best to practice now.'

Valran slowed, gaze sharpening. 'Do you see that?'

Niama followed his line of sight. Her breath caught. 'A cart,' she said softly. 'And signs of recent use.'

Coseo shouted and charged.

Small shapes burst from the brush, courars scattering in a flash of mottled fur and bared teeth. Niama snapped his name, but it was already too late.

Coseo drove them back with wild swings, laughter in his voice as they vanished into shadow.

Niama caught up to him, irritation flashing. 'Recklessness will get us killed.'

He shrugged. 'They were only courars.'

Niama's gaze swept the trees, skin prickling. 'And what hunted them?' she said quietly. 'That is what worries me.'

The forest offered no answer.

Only silence.

Coseo waved off her concern. 'Whatever it was, it has passed. No threat now.'

Niama did not answer. She sheathed her dagger and moved toward the shattered cart.

The wood was split open as if peeled apart by force. Deep claw marks scored the frame, gouged so hard they bit into the grain beneath. She traced one with her eyes and felt a chill creep up her spine.

Blood tainted the air. Heavy. Metallic.

She swallowed. 'This was no small beast.'

Valran had moved ahead, slipping out of sight beyond the cart's broken wheel. Niama had taken only a few steps after him when his breath caught sharply.

'By the gods.'

The sound tore through the forest.

Niama broke into a run. Dread tightened in her gut as she rounded the cart, and the world seemed to lurch sideways.

An elf lay sprawled in the dirt.

His body was torn open, flesh raked by jagged wounds that bled dark against the earth. Blood had soaked the ground beneath him, his face frozen in terror, mouth open as if he had died trying to scream.

Niama stopped short.

Recognition struck hard. 'Taegen,' she whispered.

Her hand rose to her mouth, fingers trembling.

Coseo came up beside her, his earlier bravado gone. 'He gambled,' he said quietly. 'And lost.'

Taegen had been many things. A trader. A storyteller. A man who walked roads others abandoned and came back with profit and laughter both. Whatever had brought him here had not spared him.

Niama crouched, forcing herself to look closer. The wounds were fresh. Too fresh.

'No more than a day,' she said. 'Perhaps two.' Her gaze swept the surrounding trees. 'Why was he here? These routes have been dead for years.'

Blood-spattered reins lay nearby, the harness torn loose. No drag marks scarred the ground.

Valran frowned. 'Then the horse lived.'

Or was taken, Niama thought, but she did not say it aloud.

Coseo shifted, eyes never leaving the tree line. 'What could do this?'

Niama straightened slowly. 'Something that hunts without haste.' Her voice lowered. 'And may still be close.'

Coseo's hand hovered near his dagger. 'Then we should leave. Now.'

Niama hesitated, then nodded. 'But not like this.'

They worked quickly, but not carelessly.

Niama knelt first, driving her dagger into the soil to break the crust of roots and packed earth. The ground resisted, as if reluctant to open. Her hands were soon smeared with dirt and blood she could not tell apart. No one spoke.

Coseo cleared stones aside with grim efficiency, jaw clenched, breath measured. Valran used the flat of his blade to widen the hollow, each scrape of metal against earth sounding too loud in the stillness.

They laid Taegen into the shallow grave with what dignity they could manage. Niama straightened his limbs, closed his eyes with trembling fingers. The flesh was already cooling. Too soon.

She murmured a brief blessing to Athris, words stripped to their bare bones. Protection. Passage. Peace. Anything more felt like a lie.

Soil fell back onto the body in heavy, uneven clumps. The sound of it striking flesh landed hard in Niama's chest. She forced herself to keep going, to finish the task, even as the forest pressed close, branches creaking softly, as if listening.

When it was done, the grave was little more than a scar in the earth.

They did not mark it.

Lingering felt dangerous.

Niama wiped her hands on the grass, though the feeling of blood remained. She rose, heart pounding, senses stretched thin.

Whatever had killed Taegen had not gone far.

They moved on, nerves drawn tight, every rustle snapping their attention sideways. Leaves stirred. Twigs cracked. The forest no longer felt merely alive.

It felt aware.

Dusk crept in as they reached a narrow stream, water clear and cold over stone. They filled their skins in silence, drinking deeply, knowing such gifts were not guaranteed here.

Valran coaxed a fire to life once more. Its flickering warmth pushed back the dark, but only just.

Niama sat close to the edge of the light. The image of the torn merchant refused to loosen its grip on her thoughts.

Coseo and Valran slept fitfully, breaths uneven, hands never far from steel.

Niama did not sleep.

She kept her vigil long after the forest settled, eyes fixed on the black beyond the fire's reach. The night was too still. Too careful. She had learned long ago that calm often wore the skin of danger.

A chill crept into her bones. Not from the cold.

From being watched.

Hours dragged past. Fatigue tugged at her, heavy and insistent, but she forced her eyes to remain open. It could wait.

Her thoughts slipped despite her will. The merchant's face surfaced again, torn and staring, as if warning her from somewhere just beyond the firelight.

Niama's chin dipped.

Just for a breath.

The fire cracked softly.

Something shifted in the dark.

She straightened at once, heart hammering, eyes burning as she searched the trees.

Nothing moved.

But the knot in her gut did not ease.

Niama woke uneasy, the kind of wakefulness sleep never quite erased.

Morning light filtered thinly through the canopy, pale and borrowed. Here, daylight never fully arrived. Twilight clung to the forest, and night returned too quickly.

They erased all trace of the fire and moved on.

The trail drew them deeper into the woods. Life thinned around them. No birds. No deer. Since the fox, only the occasional rabbit or mouse had crossed their path, darting and gone too fast to be comforting.

A fallen tree blocked the road ahead, ancient and massive, its trunk sprawled across the path as if laid there on purpose. Darkness stretched away on either side.

Climbing was the only way through.

Coseo climbed first, confidence in every movement—until he reached the crest.

He froze.

Then, slowly, he lowered himself back down, face pale.

'What?' Niama demanded, hand already on her bow.

'Wolf,' he whispered. 'But... wrong. Too large. And it's—' He swallowed. 'It's feeding.'

Niama's pulse kicked. She climbed carefully, bark rough under her palms, and peered over.

The creature hunched over something in the path below—the merchant's horse, she realized with a sickening jolt. Its fur was black as charred wood, muscles rippling beneath. Each paw was the size of a man's head.

When it lifted its muzzle, blood dripped from teeth that gleamed like ivory daggers.

Its eyes—Athris help them, its eyes—burned red in the shadow.

Niama slid back down, heart hammering.

Valran read her face. 'What is it?'

'Gorecann,' she breathed.

His skepticism died when he saw her expression.

'Myths,' Coseo muttered. 'Stories to scare children.'

'That thing down there isn't a myth.' Niama's mind raced. 'We can't go around—the forest is too dense. And we can't wait for it to leave. We don't have time.'

Valran swallowed. 'Then we fight.'

'We hunt,' Niama corrected. She studied the fallen tree, the angles, the approach. 'Coseo, you draw its attention from the right. Valran, circle left—stay in the brush. I'll take high ground here.'

'And then?'

'Arrows first. Many. If it charges—' She met their eyes. 'Don't let it close the distance.'

They moved into position, silent as ghosts.

Niama nocked an arrow, drew, breathed.

The gorecann's head snapped up.

It had heard them.

No. Worse.

It had *smelled* them.

The creature's lips peeled back in a snarl that rumbled like distant thunder. It abandoned the carcass and began to stalk forward, nose lifted, testing the air.

Niama loosed.

The arrow struck its shoulder. The gorecann barely flinched.

Coseo shouted and hurled a stone. The beast's head whipped toward the sound—

—and then it moved.

Not like a wolf. Like liquid shadow. Impossibly fast.

It hit the fallen tree with enough force to shake the trunk. Niama stumbled, nearly losing her footing.

The gorecann leaped upward.

She saw its claws, black and curved like scythes, reaching for her—

Valran's arrow took it in the throat.

The beast twisted mid-air, snarling, blood spraying. It crashed down hard, rolled, came up snarling.

'Again!' Niama shouted.

They loosed together. Three arrows found flesh. The gorecann roared—a sound that turned Niama's blood to ice.

It charged Coseo.

He dove aside, too slow—claws raked his shoulder, spinning him. He hit the ground hard.

'Cos!' Niama's hands moved on instinct. Draw. Aim. Loose.

The arrow punched through the creature's eye.

The gorecann screamed. A sound no wolf should make.

Valran was already moving, dagger out, sliding beneath the thrashing beast. Steel flashed. Blood poured.

The gorecann staggered, tried to turn, collapsed.

Silence crashed down.

Niama's hands shook so badly she nearly dropped her bow.

Coseo lay in the dirt, clutching his shoulder. Blood seeped between his fingers.

'By the light,' Valran whispered, staring at the dead beast. 'It's real. The stories are real.'

Niama slid down from the trunk, legs unsteady. 'Cos—'

'I'm fine.' He grimaced, struggling to sit. 'It's shallow.'

It wasn't. But there was no time to argue.

Niama tore a strip from her cloak and bound the wound as tightly as she dared. Her hands still trembled.

'We need to move,' she said. 'If there's one, there may be more.'

Valran's face had gone gray. 'More,' he repeated hollowly.

'Now,' Niama said, forcing steel into her voice.

They climbed over the trunk, leaving the gorecann's carcass behind. Leaving what was left of a horse.

Coseo favored his injured shoulder, jaw tight with pain he wouldn't voice.

Niama's legs felt like water. Her heart wouldn't slow.

They'd killed a creature from myth.

And myths, she realized with cold clarity, were waking all around them.

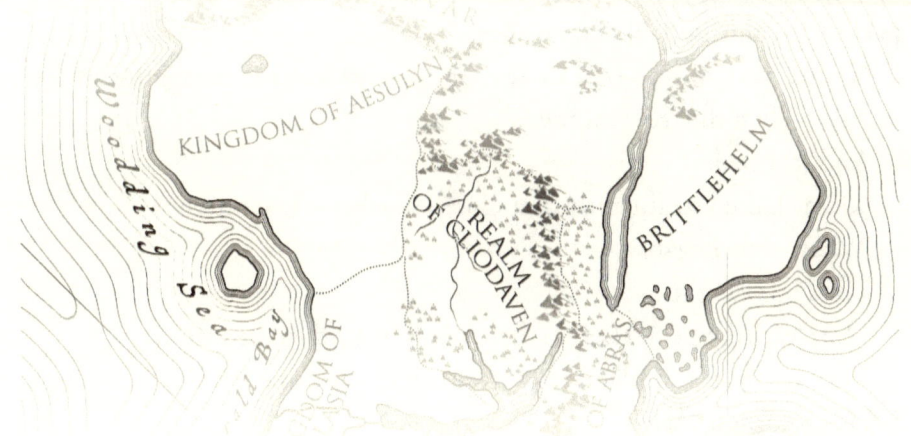

CHAPTER FOUR

The Seer

Two days since the gorecann.

Niama's legs moved by habit now, one foot before the other because stopping meant thinking, and thinking meant remembering the size of those claws. The red eyes burning in shadow.

Coseo's makeshift bandage had bled through that morning. He claimed the wound was healing. The gray pallor of his face said otherwise. He'd stopped complaining about the pain—which worried her more than his earlier groaning had.

Valran hadn't spoken since dawn. He walked with his bow half-drawn, eyes scanning the undergrowth as if expecting teeth to emerge from every shadow.

The forest had changed. Grown stranger. Trees bent at wrong angles. Roots crossed the path like deliberately placed snares. Birds fell silent as they approached, and the few animals they glimpsed fled before they could be properly seen.

As if the forest itself was afraid.

The road narrowed to a game trail, then to nothing. They pushed through undergrowth that seemed to resist them, branches catching at packs with almost deliberate malice.

Niama was about to call for camp—exhaustion dragging at her bones—when the trees thinned.

And stopped.

Niama halted so abruptly that Coseo nearly walked into her.

'What—' he began.

Then he saw it too.

The clearing opened before them like a wound in the forest.

They reached it in silence and stopped. Boots came off. Packs dropped. Breath returned, slowly.

Niama drank from her waterskin, hands shaking slightly. The water tasted of leather and distance.

'Washrock Rise,' she said. Her voice sounded steadier than she felt.

Coseo lifted his head, squinting through the fading light. 'We're close.'

Then the tree revealed itself.

It stood apart from the forest, pale and immense, its bark scarred and silvered as if burned by moonlight alone. One great limb stretched northward, rigid and deliberate, pointing the way like an accusing finger. Around its base, flowers bloomed in defiance of the gloom—white and blue petals bright against dark soil.

Valran slowed, eyes wide. 'That has to be it.'

Coseo didn't answer. He was staring, caught by something he couldn't name.

The tree leaned into the brush at an angle that made Niama uneasy. Old. Scarred. Its roots had torn the earth as if it had tried to leave and failed. And where it pointed, the forest thickened—not tangled, but deliberately closed.

Valran frowned. 'There's nothing there.'

Niama studied the ground at the tree's base. Pressed leaves. A faint break in the moss. The quiet felt shaped, purposeful.

'Wait here,' she said.

She slipped into the brush before either could object.

The forest resisted at first—thorns catching skin, branches pressing close, the hush deepening until her own breath sounded too loud. Then it eased. Not opened. *Yielded.* A narrow track revealed itself beneath her boots, worn smooth by passage too infrequent to name.

She followed it only far enough to be sure, then turned back.

'There is a path,' she said when she rejoined them. 'It climbs.'

Whatever waited beyond had chosen this place to be found.

They pushed through together, the brush closing behind them. The path wound upward, the trees thinning as stone replaced soil. Wind found them again near the plateau, cold and sharp, carrying a scent Niama couldn't name. Old copper. Burnt sage. Something else beneath it, unpleasant and ancient.

And there, split into the rock face, the cave waited.

It did not loom. It did not threaten.

It simply *was.*

No birds crossed its mouth. No sound escaped it.

The darkness inside felt solid, like a presence rather than an absence.

Niama stopped at the threshold. Legends pressed close now, heavy and indistinct. Uthru's warning echoed in her mind: *At the threshold, you will lay down your weapons.*

She unslung her bow carefully, setting it against the stone. Her quiver followed. Then her dagger, the familiar weight leaving her hip with a sense of wrongness that made her skin prickle.

Coseo hesitated, hand on his blade. 'You're certain?'

'Uthru was clear,' Niama said.

Valran placed his bow beside hers with visible reluctance. The small pile of weapons looked suddenly vulnerable, exposed.

Niama stepped forward, unarmed and afraid.

The cave swallowed them whole.

Cold bit through leather and bone the moment they crossed the threshold.

Smoke drifted low across the floor, carrying a bitter-sweet scent that clung to breath and thought alike. The fire at the chamber's heart burned

without sound, its light wrong somehow—too steady for flame, too pale
for comfort.

A figure waited beside it.

Small. Hooded. Impossibly still.

Niama's hand moved instinctively toward her hip, finding nothing. The
absence of her dagger felt like missing a limb.

'Great Seer,' she said, forcing steadiness into her voice. 'We have come
seeking truth.'

The figure did not respond.

Coseo shifted behind her. She heard his breath quicken.

Then the Seer lifted its head.

The hood shifted, and something long and curved emerged beneath
it—a beak, pale and ridged, protruding where a mouth should have been.
It opened slightly.

Click.

Clack.

The sound echoed off stone walls, sharp and arrhythmic. Not speech.
Not silence.

Niama's breath stalled.

'By the light,' Valran whispered. 'What is it?'

The Seer moved—suddenly, violently animated. Thin hands burst from
its sleeves, fingers long and wrong. Three to a hand, knuckles sharp beneath
stretched skin. They snapped and fluttered as it leaned forward, head
cocking, beak clicking faster as if tasting the air.

Click-click-clack.

Its movements were too quick for its size, jerking and precise, like something pulled by invisible strings.

Niama fought the instinct to step back. Reverence tangled with unease
in her chest. This was no sage in waiting. This was a vessel. A thing shaped
around knowledge rather than born to it.

The clicking slowed.

The Seer's head tilted toward her.

Then, not a voice in the air—but pressure behind her eyes. Words that
formed inside her skull:

Truth is weight. Few carry it without breaking.

Niama gasped. Beside her, Coseo swore softly.

'It's in my head,' Valran said, voice tight with fear.

You sought me, the voice continued, settling deeper. *Now you will hear what you came for. Whether you survive the hearing... that is your choice.*

'We came for answers about the darkness,' Niama managed. 'About what threatens our home.'

The Seer gestured with one gnarled hand.

The fire shifted, flaring outward. Shapes formed within the flames, slow and deliberate.

Stones appeared. Six of them. Each burned with a pale crimson hue, suspended above the fire as if held by invisible hands.

Before your world took its present shape, Athris bound it with anchors.

The voice resonated in Niama's chest now, too deep, too vast.

Power Stones. Vessels of divine light.

One stone dimmed. Another brightened, the light pulsing like a heart-beat.

'What are they?' Valran asked, awe overcoming fear.

Not weapons. Not gifts. The Seer's head turned toward him. *Locks.*

The word hung heavy.

They hold the darkness at bay. As long as they endure, Arghost cannot be claimed by shadow.

Niama felt the truth of it settle, heavy and cold. 'And if they fall?'

The stones flickered, dimming as one.

Then the world opens.

Silence pressed down.

Coseo found his voice, rough and shaking. 'Opens to what?'

The fire darkened at its edges. Shadows crept inward, reaching.

To what waits beyond. To what has always waited.

Images formed in the flames—shapes that hurt to look at. Writhing darkness. Things with too many limbs. Eyes that burned with hunger older than stone.

Valran made a small sound of distress.

The images vanished as quickly as they'd come, but the impression remained, burned into Niama's mind.

'The actari,' she said. 'The attacks in the north. Are they—'

Servants of the dark, yes. The first fingers of a hand reaching through cracks in the seal. The Seer's beak clicked once, sharp. *Once before, the darkness sought to unmake the Stones. A servant of shadow unearthed the Staff of Light, believing it a key to dominion.*

'What happened?' Niama asked.

It consumed him. The power was not meant for mortal hands, let alone those stained with shadow. The flames shifted, showing a figure wreathed in blinding light, screaming. *The Dark Lord vanished. The war ended. The cost was nearly everything.*

'Nearly,' Coseo repeated. 'But not everything.'

No. The Seer turned its hooded head toward him. *Some survived. Some remembered. And darkness...*

The fire snapped, loud in the quiet.

Darkness never forgets.

Niama's hands curled at her sides. 'And now it's happening again. The Second Rising.'

The seals weaken. The Power Stones still stand, but their light thins. The stones in the flames trembled, cracks appearing on their surfaces. *Darkness stirs beyond the North. It seeks a will. A commander to unite its scattered servants.*

'Why are you telling us this?' Valran's voice cracked. 'What can we possibly do against something that tried to destroy the world once already?'

You asked for truth. I give it. What you do with it...

The Seer's presence seemed to expand, filling the cave.

That is why you are here.

Niama's pulse quickened. 'What do you mean?'

The Seer turned fully toward her.

The hood fell back.

Light hovered where a face should have been—not warm, but cold and unwavering, like starlight through ice.

The path does not choose randomly. Blood calls to blood. Courage answers necessity.

'No,' Niama said immediately. 'If you're about to tell me I'm chosen—'

Chosen is a word mortals use to make fate bearable. The light pulsed. *You are not chosen. You are inevitable.*

The fire reshaped itself. Images surged forward, too fast to fully comprehend.

A child running through Mistwood, red hair flying.

A woman standing alone, bow drawn, facing shapes in shadow.

Wounds healing too quickly.

Blood that refused to leave her skin.

And beyond it all, a future where she stands on a vast plain under a sky the color of old ash.

An army waited there. Thousands upon thousands, ranks stretching beyond sight. Blades catching non-existent light. Banners bearing symbols that hurt to look at. Shapes too dark to name, moving with terrible purpose.

And before them, a single figure.

Cloaked. Still. Seen only from behind.

One arm lifted slowly.

The army answered as one, surging forward like a black tide.

Niama staggered back, breath tearing from her chest. 'No. No, that's not—I'm not—'

'What did you see?' Coseo gripped her shoulder, steadying her. 'Niama, what was that?'

She couldn't answer. Couldn't speak past the horror closing her throat.

'You mistake survival for destiny,' she finally managed, voice sharp with desperation. 'I lived because others didn't. That doesn't make me anything except lucky.'

You endure when others break. The Seer's presence pressed closer. *That is not kindness. That is not luck. It is requirement.*

'Requirement for what?' Valran demanded.

The Seer didn't answer him. Its attention remained fixed on Niama.

The prophecy does not crown. It demands.

'Then I refuse,' Niama said. 'Find someone else. A warrior. A leader. Someone who—'

Someone who what? The voice cut through her protest like a blade. *Someone who has not already survived what should have killed them? Someone who will not be haunted by what they fail to do?*

'I'm not—I can't—'

You will. Or you will watch everything burn.

The words hit like a physical blow.

'That's not a choice,' Niama whispered. 'That's a threat.'

It is a truth. Choice is what you make of it.

Coseo stepped forward, face flushed with anger. 'You can't just decide someone's fate like that. Prophecy or not, she's her own person. We all are.'

The Seer's head turned toward him with mechanical precision.

And yet you stand here, in my cave, seeking answers to questions that will shape your future. If you did not believe in fate, why come at all?

Coseo opened his mouth. Closed it. No answer came.

'The vision,' Niama said, forcing herself to focus. 'That figure commanding the army. Was that me? Am I meant to—' She couldn't finish.

The future is not written. It is possible.

'Possible,' Valran repeated. 'Not certain?'

Many paths branch from this moment. In some, she leads darkness. In others, she stops it. In most...

The Seer trailed off.

'In most what?' Niama demanded.

In most, she dies trying.

Silence crashed down like a physical weight.

Niama's legs felt weak. She forced herself to remain standing.

'Then tell me plainly,' she said. 'What do you expect us to do?'

The fire flared higher. Ancient words burned in the air, letters sharp-edged and terrible:

THE LION WILL ROAR IN THE EAST

The cave shook. Niama felt the words carve themselves into her mind, hot and permanent.

THE RAVEN WILL FLY FROM THE WEST

Coseo pressed his hands to his ears, though it did nothing to stop the voice inside his skull.

A LIGHT OF LIGHTS MUST SHOW THE WAY

Valran's knees buckled. He caught himself against the cave wall.

AN INNOCENCE LOST, TO SPARK A BEGINNING

Each line felt heavier than the last, pressing down on Niama's shoulders like physical weight.

ONE WILL RISE FROM RUIN

AND ONE WILL FALL INTO CHAOS

The final line seared itself across her vision:

TOUCH THE WORD, FOR THE WORD IS ATHRIS

The flames collapsed inward.

Silence followed, thick and absolute.

Niama was on her knees. She didn't remember falling.

Beside her, Coseo had his hand braced against the floor, breathing hard. His injured shoulder trembled under the weight. Fresh blood seeped through the bandage. Valran's face had gone the color of old parchment.

'What...' Niama's voice came out as a rasp. 'What does it mean?'

The prophecy reveals itself to those who walk it. Not before.

'That's not good enough,' she managed.

The Seer extended one gnarled hand. A medallion appeared within it, gold catching the firelight. A lion was etched on one face, a raven on the other, as if the two could never meet yet were forever bound.

Find the Staff of Light. Without it, the Stones cannot be protected. Without the Stones...

Arghost falls.

The medallion was placed in Niama's palm. The metal was warm, almost hot, as if it had been held in a fire.

Learn the incantations. Protect the Stones. This mark will open doors that would otherwise remain closed.

Niama stared at the medallion. Something about it felt wrong. Too heavy. Too significant.

As if accepting it meant accepting everything else.

'And if we fail?' she asked, though she already knew the answer.

The Seer's light dimmed.

Then Arghost will not survive a third dawn.

'Three days?' Valran's voice was hollow. 'We have three days?'

No. Three ages. Three risings. Three chances. The Seer's form began to waver, edges blurring. *The first was survived. The second approaches. If there is a third...*

There will be nothing left to rise from.

'Wait,' Niama said, struggling to her feet. 'You can't just—we need more answers. Where is the Staff? What are the incantations? How do we—'

I cannot walk your road. Balance forbids it. The Seer's voice was already fading, growing distant. *But know this: you are not alone. Allies will find you. Enemies will reveal themselves. Trust the blood you carry, even when you do not understand it.*

'What blood?' Niama demanded. 'What do you mean?'

But the Seer was already collapsing inward, motion dissolving into embers and smoke, leaving only the echo of its clicking behind.

Click.

Clack.

Then silence.

The fire guttered to coals.

The cave felt suddenly empty, hollow, as if something vast had departed and left only absence behind.

No one spoke.

Niama stood rigid, the medallion burning against her palm. Not warmth. Heat. As if it had only just been forged.

Valran shifted first. The sound of his boot on stone was too loud in the new quiet.

Coseo swallowed hard, eyes fixed on the dying fire. 'Did that really just happen?'

Niama looked at the medallion in her hand. Lion and raven, locked in eternal struggle.

'Yes,' she said quietly.

Coseo ran a hand through his hair, breath shaky. 'An army. You saw an army, didn't you? When the Seer showed you that vision.'

Niama nodded, unable to speak.

'And the figure leading it—' Valran's voice was barely a whisper. 'Was it you?'

'I don't know,' Niama admitted. The confession felt like failure. 'I couldn't see the face. But the Seer said...' She trailed off.

'Said what?' Coseo pressed.

'That it was possible.' Her fingers closed around the medallion. 'That I could become that.'

'Or you could stop it,' Valran said, desperate for any hope. 'Right? That's what you're meant to do. Stop the darkness.'

'Or die trying,' Niama said. 'Those were the options. Lead it, stop it, or die.'

Coseo's jaw tightened. 'Then we make sure it's option two.'

'We?' Niama looked at him. 'Coseo, you heard what it said. This is—this is beyond anything we're prepared for. You both should go home. Go back to Mistwood where it's safe.'

'Safe?' Coseo let out a harsh laugh. 'You think anywhere is safe if you fail? If we fail?' He shook his head. 'No. We started this together. We finish it together.'

'He's right,' Valran said, though his voice shook. 'We need to stop this,' Valran said. 'For everyone we've already lost. For everyone we might still save.'

Niama felt something tighten in her chest. Not resolve.

Gratitude.

'Then we find the Staff,' she said. 'Whatever it takes.'

She slipped the medallion around her neck. It settled against her skin, warm and heavy.

'Come on,' she said. 'We need to leave.'

They moved toward the cave entrance on unsteady legs, exhaustion and shock warring in their bones.

As they crossed the threshold, Coseo stopped.

'Our weapons,' he said.

They'd almost forgotten.

The pile of bows and blades sat where they'd left them, untouched. Niama retrieved her dagger with shaking hands, the familiar weight a small comfort.

When they stepped back into the night, the forest did not welcome them.

It watched.

Branches creaked without wind. Leaves rustled where nothing passed. The dark felt closer, thicker, as if the trees leaned in to listen.

Niama did not look back at the cave. She could feel it behind her anyway, a presence pressed against her spine.

Some thresholds did not close once crossed.

They walked in silence until they found a small clearing, far enough from the cave that the oppressive weight finally eased.

Coseo sank to the ground, back against a tree. His injured shoulder had started bleeding again—Niama could see the dark stain spreading through the bandage.

'We should rest,' she said.

No one argued.

Valran built a small fire without being asked. The flames felt inadequate after the Seer's blaze, but the warmth was real, and that counted for something.

Niama sat close to the heat, staring into the embers. The prophecy circled through her mind, each line a weight she couldn't set down.

The lion will roar in the east.

The raven will fly from the west.

A light of lights must show the way.

What did it mean? Lion and raven—like the medallion. East and west. Light and shadow.

An innocence lost, to spark a beginning.

She touched the medallion through her shirt. It pulsed with warmth against her skin.

'We should sleep,' Coseo said, though his eyes were wide, haunted. 'Long walk back to Mistwood tomorrow.'

'Are we going back?' Valran asked.

Niama looked up. 'What?'

'To Mistwood,' Valran said. 'Are we going back, or are we going after the Staff?'

The question hung in the air.

'We have to report to Uthru,' Coseo said. 'Tell him what we learned.'

'And then what?' Valran pressed. 'The Seer said the darkness is gathering. That it seeks a commander. How long do we have before—'

'We don't know where the Staff is,' Niama cut in. 'We don't know the incantations. We don't know anything except that we're supposed to find answers we don't have.'

'The medallion,' Coseo said. 'The Seer said it would open doors. Maybe it's a key. Literally.'

Niama pulled the medallion out, studying it in the firelight. Lion and raven, eternally opposed. The craftsmanship was exquisite, the details impossibly fine.

But it revealed nothing.

'And what about the blood?' Valran asked quietly.

Niama's hand moved to her side, where scars should have been. Where wounds had healed impossibly fast. 'I don't know,' she admitted. 'The Seer said to trust the blood I carry. But I don't even know what that means.'

'Your healing,' Coseo said. 'The way you survived what should have killed you as a child. Maybe that's what it meant.'

'Maybe.' But Niama wasn't convinced. The Seer's words had felt heavier than that. More significant.

Whatever blood she carried, it was connected to all of this. She could feel it.

'Tomorrow,' she said finally. 'We decide tomorrow. Tonight, we rest. If we can.'

No one objected.

They settled into their bedrolls, but sleep did not come easy.

Niama lay awake, watching stars appear between the branches. The medallion rested against her chest, warm and constant.

Somewhere in the north, darkness gathered.

Somewhere, a Staff waited to be found.

And somewhere—in a future she could not see—she stood before an army, arm raised, deciding the fate of the world.

You are not chosen, the Seer had said. *You are inevitable.*

Niama closed her eyes, but the words followed her into restless dreams.

The journey had only just begun.

And already, she felt the weight of its ending pressing down on her shoulders like stone.

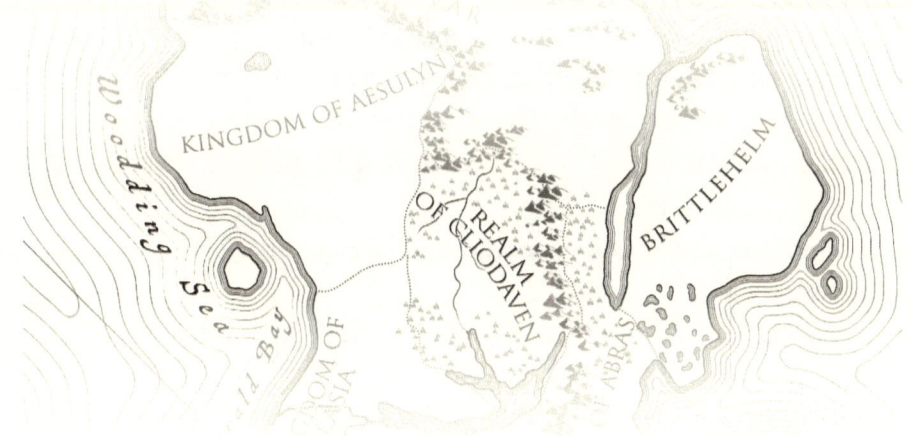

CHAPTER FIVE

The Split

Niama woke with her hand clenched around the medallion.

She loosened her grip and looked down. The lion and raven were imprinted on her palm, red and stark where the metal had pressed into her skin while she slept.

She flexed her fingers. The marks were already fading, edges softening as blood returned.

Not permanent. Just proof she'd held on too tightly.

Coseo crouched nearby, already packing. 'Didn't mean to wake you,' he said quietly. 'But daylight won't wait.'

She took his hand and pulled herself upright. The ground beneath her boots was cold, slick with dew.

The sun rose over the distant hills, bleeding red and gold across the sky. Dawn had come quickly, too quickly.

Valran stood at the clearing's edge, watching the light paint the valley below. His pack was already secured, bow slung across his shoulders.

This was it. The moment they'd discussed last night around the fire.

The split.

'If this were any other morning,' Valran said quietly, 'I'd swear it was a blessing.'

Niama stepped beside him. For a moment, neither spoke. The world stretched outward in every direction, wide and indifferent.

'Travel fast,' she said at last. 'Don't stop unless you must.'

Valran nodded once. 'I'll carry the truth back. All of it.' He hesitated, then met her eyes. 'They'll listen.'

She held his gaze, searching for doubt. Finding none.

'I know.'

Valran clasped her forearm one last time. 'Don't die,' he said. Not a joke. A plea.

'Don't let them,' Niama replied, meaning Mistwood. Meaning the elders who would have to hear impossible truths.

He held her gaze a moment longer, then turned toward the western path.

Only when the forest had fully reclaimed the path did she let her hand fall back to her side.

Some farewells demanded silence.

She turned east.

The forest on this side was different. The trail broader. Worn by many feet, not just beasts. Fallen branches lay cleared. Stones marked the edges of the path, deliberate and old.

'People use this road,' Coseo said.

'Which means people live beyond it,' Niama replied. 'And people make choices.'

The canopy thinned as they walked. Sunlight broke through in pale sheets. Rain lingered on the leaves, dripping steadily, the sound soft but constant.

Niama wiped sweat from her brow. 'I'd forgotten what warmth feels like.'

Coseo gave a faint smile. 'Don't get used to it.'

By dusk, they found a clearing tucked between low shrubs. The ground smelled of wet earth and crushed flowers.

Coseo set about the fire without speaking. The flames struggled at first, damp wood hissing, then caught.

Niama leaned against a fallen trunk and let her breath slow. For the first time since the cave, her shoulders eased.

They ate in silence.

Coseo stared into the fire. 'The Seer's words keep circling.' He glanced at her. *'Touch the word, for the word is Athris.* What does that even mean?'

Niama poked at the embers. 'Maybe it means the answer isn't an object.' She paused. 'Or maybe it is, and we won't recognize it until it costs us something.'

Coseo exhaled. 'That's not comforting.'

'It wasn't meant to be.'

Night settled in. The forest breathed around them, alive with small movements and distant calls.

Niama lay back on her bedroll, eyes tracing the broken stars between branches. The medallion rested against her chest, cool and unmoving.

'Cos,' she said softly. 'Do you think we can actually do this?'

He didn't answer at once.

Then, 'No.' A pause. 'But I think we'll try anyway.'

She smiled into the dark, but it didn't reach her eyes. 'That'll have to be enough.'

Somewhere far to the west, Valran was running.

And somewhere far to the north, something else was already marching.

At daybreak, Niama pushed herself upright, joints stiff and protesting. The sun crested the hills, its warmth settling briefly into her skin, familiar enough to almost feel like safety.

It wasn't.

They ate quickly. Bread. Dried fruit. Enough to move, not enough to linger. Packs were shouldered without ceremony, and they set out while the light was still kind.

The path widened as they walked. Fewer fallen branches. Fewer signs of neglect. Whoever used this road had kept it open.

By midmorning, the forest thinned and released them.

Rolling hills spread before them, green and open, the land falling away toward the distant Orboros mountains. Their peaks cut the horizon like broken teeth. Far overhead, seabirds cried. The air tasted faintly of salt.

Niama slowed, taking it in.

This was not Mistwood. Not even close.

Coseo scanned the distance, jaw tight. 'That's our road,' he said, gesturing north.

Niama nodded. There was nowhere else to go.

Grass brushed against their legs as they moved, tall and wet with dew. Each step crushed scent from the earth. Despite the openness, Niama's unease did not ease. If anything, it sharpened.

As the sun climbed, a sound cut through the wind.

Niama stopped.

'Did you hear that?' she whispered.

Coseo listened, head tilted. 'Could be nothing. Small game.'

Maybe.

They moved on.

The sound came again. Closer.

Niama's hand drifted toward her dagger. Her pulse quickened. The land felt wrong, the way it had before the gorecann. Too quiet between breaths.

The grass exploded.

Niama saw green skin, corded muscle, eyes burning with intelligence—

Then something slammed into her with the force of a battering ram.

The world went dark.

And somewhere in that darkness, she heard Coseo scream.

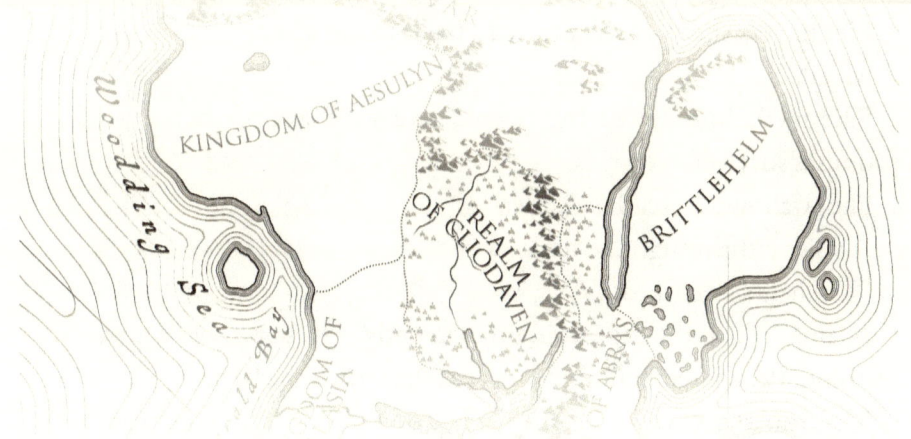

CHAPTER SIX

The Cages

Niama came back to herself choking on cold.

Wood pressed into her ribs. Into her knees. Into her spine. She tried to shift and found nowhere to go. Above her, rope creaked. Below her, nothing.

She was in a cage. Cages were meant to make you small, long before they decided what to do with you.

It swayed slightly, hanging from the ceiling of a vast chamber carved from stone. The air was damp and rank, thick with rot and old blood. Her breath fogged in front of her mouth. Every inhale scraped her throat raw.

Memory stirred too late.

Stories told in low voices. Cages. Pits. Places where screams learned to stop. She had never believed the stories were meant for her.

Her pulse hammered. She curled instinctively, skin burning where the rough slats bit into her. The space barely allowed her to crouch. She reached for her armor.

Nothing.

Panic hit hard enough to make her dizzy. They had stripped her. Leather gone. Weapons gone. Her bow. Her dagger.

Her fingers shook as she pressed a hand to her chest.

Metal.

The medallion rested there, cold and solid against her skin. Some promises survived even this.

She swallowed, breath shuddering.

A voice cut through the dark.

'Well hello, sleepyhead.'

Niama jerked, the cage swinging violently. The rope above groaned in warning. Pain flared behind her eyes as she struck the bars.

'Careful,' the voice said lightly. 'They don't like it when the cages rock.'

She forced her vision to focus.

Another cage hung beside hers. Inside it crouched a man. Human. Thin to the point of sharpness, hair matted, beard wild, clothes hanging in filthy strips. His bare feet were black with grime. A swelling darkened his forehead, old and half-healed.

He grinned at her.

'That one still hurts,' he said, tapping it. 'Yours looks fresh.'

She touched her own head. Pain bloomed. Her stomach lurched.

'What happened?' she whispered.

He shrugged, chains rattling softly. 'You met them.'

'I only saw one.'

His grin widened, showing broken teeth. 'Then you're lucky.'

He leaned back against the bars, cage creaking. 'There's more. Always more. They like to watch you realize it.'

Niama's throat tightened. 'Who are you?'

'Remy.' He dipped his head in a mock bow. 'Unwilling guest. Same as you.'

She hesitated. 'I'm Niama.'

'Well, Niama,' Remy said softly, eyes glinting, 'welcome to where hope goes quiet.' Hope, she thought, did not go quiet. It learned when to hide.

Movement stirred at the far end of the chamber.

Niama's breath caught.

Two shapes emerged from the shadows. Green-skinned. Broad-headed. Their steps were heavy, deliberate. Something dragged behind them, scraping stone.

Her heart stopped.

Coseo.

His body hung limp between them, arms trailing, head lolling at an impossible angle. Blood matted his hair. One side of his face was swollen purple-black.

'No,' she whispered.

The sound tore from her throat then, raw and broken. 'Cos!'

Her cage rattled as she threw herself against the bars. Pain flared through her hands, but she didn't feel it.

'Cos!' Her voice cracked. 'Please—please—he's alive. He has to be.'

Tears burned her eyes, hot and useless. Rage followed, sharp and choking.

'Let him go,' she screamed. 'You don't know what you're doing!'

The creatures stopped.

They looked up.

Their eyes burned like wet embers. Their mouths split wide, strings of saliva stretching between thick lips.

'Quiet,' they rumbled.

The word vibrated through the stone.

'Meat,' one hissed.

Spit hit the ground below Niama's cage. It sizzled faintly where it landed.

The creatures dragged Coseo onward. His head struck a rock with a dull sound.

Niama gagged.

The smell hit her then. Sweet. Heavy. Wrong.

Not food.

Remy had gone very still.

'They're hungry tonight,' he murmured. 'That's never good.'

The creatures moved deeper into the chamber, their forms fully revealed now. Huge heads atop squat, malformed bodies. Bellies distended and sagging. Arms too long, fingers scraping the floor, leaving pale marks in the stone. Their skin was mottled green and yellow, stretched tight in places, scarred in others.

Niama sagged against the bars, chest heaving, nails torn and bleeding.

Far from Mistwood.

Far from safety.

And whatever these things were, they had planned this.

The cage swayed gently, like a pendulum counting down. Time felt different here, stretched thin and waiting to snap.

They worked quickly.

Coseo's weapons were torn from him and thrown aside, steel clattering against stone. His pack followed, split open, contents spilling uselessly across the floor. Then the creatures seized him under the arms and hauled his limp body toward an empty cage.

Niama watched, helpless, breath locked in her chest.

Rope shrieked as it ran. The cage jerked upward, swaying violently before settling into place beside hers. Coseo's head lolled forward, chin striking wood.

Niama gripped the bars. 'Cos?'

No answer.

Her throat tightened. Panic clawed up hard and fast.

'Cos,' she whispered, then louder, 'Cos. Please.'

A foot twitched.

Relief hit so sharply it almost dropped her to her knees.

Coseo groaned, a low, broken sound. He shifted, dragging himself upright with visible effort. 'My head...' He blinked, unfocused, then squinted toward her voice. 'Niama?'

'I'm here.' Her words came too fast. 'You're alive.'

He pressed a hand to his forehead and winced. 'That's debatable.' His gaze drifted, taking in the cage, the height, the dark. Understanding crept in. 'I came after you,' he muttered. 'You just... vanished.'

'I woke here,' she said. 'They caught me from the grass.'

He swallowed. 'Figures.'

Silence pressed down, thick and suffocating.

'They plan to eat us,' Niama said quietly.

Coseo exhaled through his nose. 'Well.' A pause. 'Then I'm grateful I smell like a midden heap.'

Despite herself, a sound escaped her, half laugh, half sob. 'This is not the time.'

'If there were a good time,' he said, 'we'd be somewhere else entirely.'

Her smile faded quickly. Reality closed back in, cold and absolute. 'No one knows where we are.'

Coseo's jaw tightened. His gaze roamed the cavern, sharp now despite the pain. The pile of weapons caught his eye.

'My blades,' he said softly. 'They didn't destroy them.'

'No.'

Hope flickered. Small. Dangerous.

He shifted, testing the cage. The bars groaned but held. 'Damn it.' He struck them once, hard. The impact rang through the chamber.

From the shadows, something growled.

Coseo stilled instantly.

Niama turned her head slowly toward Remy. 'How long?'

The man leaned back against his bars, eyes hollow in the torchlight. Bruises marred his skin, yellowing at the edges. He looked exhausted in a way that went deeper than hunger.

'Day. Maybe two,' he said. 'Hard to keep track when time smells like rot.' His mouth twitched. 'You're the first new company I've had.'

Niama's stomach twisted.

Coseo lowered his voice. 'Do they come back often?'

Remy nodded once. 'When they're bored. Or hungry.' A pause. 'Or both.'

The cages creaked softly overhead, a chorus of quiet suffering.

Niama leaned her forehead against the bars, eyes burning.

This was no ambush. No accident.

They had been taken. Taken was not the same as beaten. Not yet.

And whatever waited in the dark had all the time in the world.

Coseo's voice cut through the gloom. 'What *are* they?'

Remy jerked his chin toward the cavern mouth. 'Wildkin. Goblin folk.'
His eyes tracked the shadows beyond the torchlight. 'They crawl outta the
Orboros mountains. If I had to guess, we're under 'em right now.'

He looked around properly then. At the slime-slick walls. The cages.
The stains that no amount of torchlight could disguise. Whatever hope
he'd been holding finally gave way. His shoulders slumped.

'I was headin' south for work when they took me. Been more of 'em
lately. Since last harvest.' A hollow laugh escaped him. 'They breed fast. Eat
faster.'

Niama's grip tightened on the bars. 'There is always a way out.'

Remy shook his head slowly. 'Only one path leads outta here.' He pointed to a narrow passage cut into the stone. 'Don't know where it goes. Never
seen anyone come back from it.'

Niama followed the line of his finger. Darkness swallowed the corridor
whole. Still, the thought rooted itself in her mind. One way in. One way
out.

Coseo slammed his shoulder into the bars again. The cage shuddered.
Held.

'Useless,' he snarled. 'These weren't thrown together.'

Remy nodded. 'First thing I tried. Spent a day wreckin' myself for noth-
in'.'

Niama drew a slow breath. 'I will not accept that.'

Her gaze swept the chamber. Five cages. Four occupied. A heap of
discarded clothing and bones in one corner. Nothing else.

Coseo nodded toward the far cage. 'What about him?'

The man inside hadn't moved since Niama woke. His body sagged like
it had already given up. One arm dangled through the bars, fingers curled
inward, skin stretched tight over bone.

Remy's voice dropped. 'He was here before me. There were others once.
A woman. Her kid.' He swallowed. 'They took 'em. Couple days back.'

Niama felt something cold settle behind her ribs.

The torches hissed. Water dripped steadily from somewhere unseen.
The sound grew louder the longer she listened, each drop counting something down.

Then the cavern erupted.

Four wildkin burst from the shadows, shrill and excited. Their eyes locked on the far cage.

'Meat,' they crooned. 'Meat. Meat.'

Two rushed to the wall, yanking the rope free. The cage dropped hard, wood splintering as it hit the ground.

The prisoner inside stirred.

Niama's breath caught.

He was alive.

The man tried to stand. His legs buckled immediately. He raised his hands, shaking, mouth opening in a sound that never became a word.

The wildkin laughed.

One swung a jagged stone.

The impact cracked through the cavern.

The man fell without a sound.

Blood spread across the stone floor, dark and quick. She would remember his face, even if no one else ever did.

Niama turned away too late.

The wildkin dragged the body off, chanting, arguing, snarling at one another as they disappeared into the passage.

Silence returned.

Heavier than before.

Remy stared at the ground. 'That's what happens when they get bored.'

Niama's fingers dug into the bars until her hands shook.

This wasn't a prison.

It was a larder. And larders were meant to be emptied.

And somewhere beyond the stone, the wildkin were already deciding who came next.

Niama bit down on the inside of her cheek until she tasted blood. She would not scream. Not now.

'He'll do,' Remy murmured. 'For now.'

She turned on him, fury burning clean through fear. 'He was alive.'

Remy didn't meet her eyes. 'Not for long.'

Coseo rattled his cage. 'We don't wait our turn.'

His gaze swept the chamber, measuring. Calculating. A hunter cornered.

'There's a mechanism,' Remy said quietly. 'Pin and counterweight. Takes two hands at once to release. I've tried everything else.'

'So you've just been waiting?' Coseo demanded.

'For someone who could reach it, yeah.' Remy's jaw tightened. 'The others—they were too weak. Or too far. Or dead before I could ask.'

Niama followed his glance. The iron hook. The rope. The height.

'Then what?' she asked.

'Then I run,' he said plainly. 'And if I live long enough, I come back.'

Coseo snarled. 'You didn't mention this earlier.'

Remy flinched. 'Didn't know. Didn't matter before.'

Niama closed her eyes for a heartbeat. The screams from the tunnel echoed in her skull.

'We do it,' she said.

Coseo stared at her. 'Niama—'

'We do it,' she repeated. 'Now.' There would be no clean outcome from this. She accepted that.

She shifted her weight. The cage swayed, slow at first. The rope creaked in warning. Dust fell from the ceiling.

Remy braced himself, arms raised. 'Again.'

She swung harder. Muscles burned. The cage lurched, momentum building.

Again.

Again.

On the final swing, she launched herself forward. Wood slammed into wood. Remy caught the bars, fingers white with strain.

The stench hit her like a wall. Rot. Waste. Old blood.

She climbed anyway.

Her hands slipped. She dragged herself upward, splinters biting into her palms, shoulders screaming. At the top, the latch stared back at her. Simple. Cruel.

It didn't move.

Her breath came ragged. Below, something howled.

She leaned closer. Saw the pin.

Her fingers fumbled. Sweat blurred her vision. The metal resisted, then—

Click.

The latch gave.

Niama shoved away.

Remy's cage dropped.

It hit the floor and exploded.

Remy rolled free, coughing, bleeding, alive.

For one heartbeat, he looked up at them.

Then noise surged from the tunnels.

He ran.

Niama watched him tear through the pile of discarded clothing, grabbing whatever fit.

At the cavern mouth, he paused.

He looked back once.

Not at the cages.

Not at Coseo.

At her.

His eyes flickered, tight with something that might have been guilt or might have been calculation. The torchlight caught them for a heartbeat, then shifted, and whatever had been there vanished.

He turned and ran. She wondered, distantly, which choice he would regret more.

The echoes of his flight faded.

Coseo went still.

'Coward,' he breathed.

Niama forced herself to move. Rage would come later. Survival first.

Niama looked up. The hook trembled in its mounting, mortar crumbling from the violent swinging.

'Coseo!' she shouted. 'The hook—it's coming loose. Swing! Hard as you can!'

He didn't hesitate.

Their cages swung in opposite directions, then together, momentum building. The rope screamed. The ceiling groaned.

Stone dust rained down.

With a crack like breaking bone, the hook tore free.

Niama fell.

The impact ripped the air from her lungs. Pain flared white-hot, then dulled under adrenaline.

Then she moved.

She stood.

Coseo shouted her name.

'I'm alive,' she gasped. 'Hold.'

She crossed the chamber on shaking legs, wrapped the rope around her waist, braced herself, and lowered his cage.

When it hit the ground, she tore at the wooden bars until they gave way.

Coseo stumbled out and caught her before she fell.

For a moment, neither spoke.

Around them lay broken cages. Blood stains. Bones picked clean.

Niama scrambled to the pile of discarded gear, hands shaking. Blood. Rags. Bones.

There—her leather armor, half-buried under rotting cloth. She yanked it free, ignoring the stench, and pulled it on with fumbling fingers.

Coseo picked up his blade, eyes burning. Blood matted his hair, bruises darkened his face, but his grip was steady.

She looked at the tunnel mouth. Two paths. The way Remy had fled—toward open air, toward freedom.

Or deeper. Into the mountain's heart. Where the wildkin nested.

Coseo followed her gaze. 'We could run,' he said quietly. 'Find our way out. Live to fight another day.'

Niama's hand found the medallion at her throat. Still there. Still cold.

She thought of the prisoner. His face. The sound his skull made when it cracked.

She thought of the woman and her child. Taken days ago. Screaming in these tunnels.

She thought of how many others might be in cages deeper in the mountain. How many would die while she ran.

'No,' she said.

Coseo waited.

'These things hunt,' Niama said, voice hard as stone. 'They take. They cage. They butcher.' She turned to face him fully. 'And they think we're prey.'

Understanding flickered across his face. Then something darker. Colder.

'They're wrong,' he said.

Niama picked up a torch from the wall. The flame cast dancing shadows across her face.

From deep in the caves came sounds—wet feeding. Guttural laughter. The scrape of claws on stone.

The wildkin were returning.

Niama looked at the tunnel leading deeper into darkness. Toward the sound of monsters.

'We end this,' she said. 'All of it.'

Coseo stepped beside her, blade ready. 'No mercy.'

'None,' she agreed.

They walked into the dark.

Not as prey.

As hunters.

CHAPTER SEVEN

The Wildkin

The tunnel cut through the mountain like a wound.

Rot filled it. Old flesh. Old blood. Niama swallowed hard and kept moving. Each step crushed something brittle beneath her boots. Bone, ground smooth by passing feet. She counted steps without meaning to, the way she always did when lost.

Torches spat along the walls, their light dragging shadows across the stone. The shapes twisted as they walked, clawed and misshapen, as if the cavern itself were watching.

Coseo slowed at the bend.

Niama felt it before she saw it, the tightening in his shoulders, the shift from movement to readiness. He edged forward, bow already in hand, and peered around the corner.

A heartbeat passed.

Then he withdrew, pressing flat to the stone. His voice barely stirred the air.

'Another passage ahead. Narrow. It runs deeper. The main tunnel opens into a larger cavern. Two wildkin. Their backs are turned.'

Niama nodded once. 'We take the narrow path. Quiet.' Her gaze flicked past him, already measuring distance. 'It may give us a better angle.'

Coseo raised his bow and moved.

Niama followed, dagger sheathed, arrow nocked. The passage tightened quickly. Stone scraped her shoulders. The air grew thicker, sour on her tongue. She breathed through it and did not slow.

The tunnel ended abruptly.

Not a trap. Storage.

Rags lay in damp heaps. Broken crates leaned against the wall. Old bones mixed among them, picked clean. No way through, but no way back unseen either.

Good.

From the edge of the passage, the cavern opened before them.

Firelight spilled across stone. At its center, a spit turned slowly over open flame. A human body hung there, blackened and slack. One foot remained intact.

Two wildkin stood near the fire, snarling at one another, jabbing thick fingers toward the meat. Another pair slouched against the right-hand wall. Three more lay sprawled near the pit, breathing heavy with sleep.

Seven.

Niama leaned close to Coseo. 'Two by the wall first. While they argue.'

He inclined his head.

They raised their bows together.

Niama drew. The world narrowed to the rise and fall of her target's chest.

'Three,' Coseo murmured. 'Two—'

Movement behind them.

Niama spun.

A wildkin burst from the tunnel they had just used, eyes wide with surprise that turned instantly to rage. It lunged.

Niama loosed.

The arrow took it through the throat. The creature collapsed in a wet heap at her feet.

Silence.

Niama held still, breath locked in her chest.

No alarm.

She turned back toward the cavern, exhaling slowly. 'Too close.'

'Now,' Coseo whispered.

They fired.

Arrows cut through firelight. Two bodies dropped.

The sleepers woke instantly.

One screamed—a high, piercing shriek that echoed through stone.

'Damn it,' Coseo hissed.

From deeper in the caves came answering calls. Movement. The thunder of feet.

'We run,' Niama said. 'Now.'

They fired twice more as they fled, dropping two more wildkin. But the alarm had been raised.

Behind them, the caves erupted with snarls and rage.

'The rest,' Niama said.

They abandoned the bows and moved in close.

Daggers flashed. Short strokes. No wasted motion. One throat opened, then another. A sleeper jerked awake just long enough to meet steel. The last wildkin died clawing at the dirt, breath gurgling out through a slit neck.

Silence returned.

Niama covered her mouth, forcing the bile down as she took in the cavern properly. Bones lay everywhere. Scraps of clothing. Human remains scattered like refuse.

This was no camp.

It was a butcher's floor.

They moved on at once.

Passage after passage. Alcoves. Narrow cuts in the rock. They searched quickly, efficiently, blades ready. Nothing stirred. No alarms sounded.

Then light.

A thin shaft cut through the darkness ahead.

Niama broke into a run.

They burst from the cave and into open air.

Sunlight struck her eyes after hours of darkness. Wind tore the stink from her skin.

Behind them, the mountain rose—sheer rock and shadow. The cave mouth was halfway up the slope, hidden among stones.

Below, the land rolled green and wide. A stream wound through the valley floor, perhaps an hour's descent.

And beyond—there, catching the late sun—a road, heading north. To the east the distant blue line of the Andrean Ocean.

'The road,' Niama said. 'But we can't go straight down. They'll see us from the caves.'

Coseo followed the line of the stream with his eyes. 'We keep low. Use the grass.'

They moved immediately.

The descent was steep. Loose stone slid beneath their boots. Tall grass swallowed them at the bottom, whispering as they passed.

They ran.

'How do you fare?' Niama called over her shoulder.

'I endure,' Coseo replied. 'Do not slow.'

She laughed once, breathless. 'Peaceful village life has made you soft, Cos.'

He surged forward, matching her stride. 'I was conserving strength.'

They ran blind through the grass.

Behind them came crashes. Snarls. The wildkin from the caves had followed them out.

'How many?' Coseo gasped.

Niama risked a glance back. Three. No—four shapes in the grass.

The stream. If they could reach the stream—

One burst ahead of the others, impossibly fast. It slammed into Niama from the side, lifting her clear off her feet.

She hit the embankment hard. Her vision whited out.

Through the ringing in her skull, she heard Coseo shout. Steel rang.

Then hands pulled her up. Coseo, blood on his blade.

'Move!' he roared.

They plunged into the stream. The water broke their scent, confused the pursuit.

The wildkin stopped at the bank, snarling, pacing.

But they didn't follow into the water.

They did not stop running.

Not until the ground leveled.

Not until the growls faded into nothing but memory.

Niama stumbled first, hands slamming into gravel. Her lungs burned, each breath a rasp that scraped raw. She rolled onto her side, eyes fixed on the darkening sky, waiting for the sound of pursuit to return.

It didn't.

Coseo collapsed beside her, retching, fingers digging into the dirt as if the earth itself might flee.

For a long moment, there was only their breathing. Ragged. Uneven. Too loud.

Daylight thinned, bleeding into long shadows that stretched across the land. Dusk pressed in from all sides, quiet and watchful.

Wheels creaked nearby.

A wagon rolled to a halt.

A shadow fell across them.

'Well,' a voice said, rough and amused, 'what do we 'ave 'ere?'

Niama's hand found her dagger. She was too exhausted to run. Too hurt to fight.

But she could still choose how this ended.

She met Coseo's eyes. Saw the same calculation there.

Together, they rose to face whoever had found them.

The wagon. The voice. The shadow falling across them.

Another choice. Another risk.

Niama was tired of running.

CHAPTER EIGHT

The Capture

V alran walked west until the road thinned and the forest swallowed it whole.

Mist clung low, cold against his skin. Rot and wet leaves soured the air. Every step echoed too loudly, no matter how carefully he placed his boots.

He told himself this was good. That fear sharpened the senses. That this was how stories began. Stories, he was learning, rarely warned you before they turned.

The forest did not answer.

Branches creaked somewhere above him. Not wind. Not quite. He stopped once, listening, hand hovering near his blade, then forced himself on.

The image of the gorecann rose unbidden. The way it had moved. The sound it made when it fed. He swallowed and pushed the thought aside, but the forest seemed to remember it for him. Wings beat somewhere in the canopy above. Too heavy for any bird Valran knew.

A voice drifted from the trees.

'Who comes?'

Valran stopped.

His breath caught, thin and fast. He tasted iron on his tongue. The sound had no direction, no source, as though the forest itself had spoken. He did not like the feeling that he had been noticed.

'I—I travel alone,' he called, hating the tremor in his voice.

Silence answered.

Then, closer now, softer. 'Hrr... little one.'

The words scraped against his ears, wrong in shape and sound.

Valran's hand slid to his blade. 'Show yourself.'

Nothing moved. An owl called somewhere above him. Leaves whispered. His pulse hammered.

He forced himself forward.

The road ended at a fallen tree, its trunk sprawled across the path, swollen with rot. Moss slicked the bark, pale fungi blooming in its cracks. Valran climbed, armor rasping, muscles burning as he hauled himself over.

'Hey.'

The shout came from above him.

Valran startled, his foot slipping. He fell hard, crashing onto the path below. Pain flared white-hot through his ankle. He cried out, scrambling for purchase, breath tearing from his chest.

'Who's there?' he gasped.

'You're a long way from where you're meant to be,' the voice said.

Valran froze.

The creature hopped down lightly, claws clicking against bark. Its limbs were too long, its movements too quick. Horns curled from its skull, small and sharp. Two red eyes blazed in what might have been a face. A tail flicked behind it, restless.

It was no animal. No elf. No human. Something else entirely—something that should not exist in daylight or civilization. A creature of the old darkness, perhaps. Or a servant shaped by it.

It leaned close, eyes blazing. 'So many questions,' it hissed. 'I like questions.' Whatever it was, it was not bound by the rules Valran understood.

Valran tried to step back. His ankle screamed. He stumbled, catching himself against the tree.

'W-what do you want?' he asked.

The creature tilted its head, studying him. 'Riddles,' it said brightly. Then, louder, impatient. 'Do you like riddles?'

Its grin widened, revealing too many teeth.

Valran tightened his grip on his blade, heart pounding, knowing with sudden clarity that whatever this thing was, it had never intended to let him pass.

And the forest, all around them, had gone very still. Stillness, he had learned, was never empty.

'R-riddles?' Valran echoed. Pain and disbelief tangled in his voice. He clutched his ankle, knuckles whitening as another pulse of agony rolled through it. 'I'm in no mood for games.'

'Games?' The creature clicked its tongue. 'No. No games.' Its forked tongue slipped between sharp teeth. 'Tests.' Valran had never trusted tests designed by those who already knew the answers.

It paced along the fallen trunk, claws tapping, head tilted as though listening to something only it could hear. 'Riddles, conundrums, little puzzles that show what wriggles inside a mind.'

Valran grit his teeth. 'I don't care about riddles.'

'Pity.' The creature stopped abruptly and leaned forward. 'I care.'

Without waiting, it spoke.

'I am not alive, yet I grow.

I have no lungs, yet I need air.

I have no mouth, yet water kills me.'

Its eyes burned brighter. 'Answer.'

Valran stared up at it, breath hitching. His thoughts scattered, pain drowning reason. 'I—I don't—'

Pain scattered his thoughts like startled birds.

The creature's smile snapped shut. 'Hurry.'

'I don't know!' Valran shouted, anger breaking through fear. 'I told you, I hate riddles. Now tell me what you are and why you haunt me!'

A hiss slid from its throat, low and pleased. 'There it is. Honesty.'

It circled Valran slowly, enjoying his fear. This was the game. Not the riddle. The watching. The waiting. The moment prey realized there was no escape.

It bowed with exaggerated flourish. 'A'Tarchg Ya'regh r'te'ah.' A pause. 'But Bastion will do. Names are heavy things. Best not drop them.'

Bastion tilted its head, listening to something Valran couldn't hear. Above them, something heavy shifted in the canopy. Wings beat once, then fell silent.

'Assist me,' Bastion went on lightly. 'And I assist you.'

Valran barked a laugh, brittle. 'Assist me? You nearly broke my leg.'

'Yes,' Bastion said calmly. 'And I did not.'

It hopped down onto a lower branch, closer now. Too close. 'You are lost. I know these woods. You do not.' Its eyes flicked to Valran's ankle. 'And you will not go far alone.'

Valran swallowed. 'What do you want?'

'Information.' Bastion's head cocked. 'Why did you go to the Seer?'

Valran shifted, pain flaring. 'I know nothing of any Seer. I am a ranger. I hunt. I lost my way.'

Bastion's gaze sharpened. 'Hunter.'

It snapped its fingers.

Fire bloomed at the tip of its tail, a tight coil of orange light that hissed softly in the damp air. Bastion lifted it, illuminating the forest floor.

'No blood,' it murmured. 'No spoor. No elk.' Its eyes slid back to Valran. 'You lie badly.'

The lie had felt thin even as he spoke it.

The fire drifted closer.

'I followed you,' Bastion growled. 'Three elves. One path. One purpose.' Its voice dropped, thick with promise. 'Now tell me what the Seer said.'

Heat washed over Valran's face. He flinched as the flame hovered inches from his skin. Sweat beaded along his spine.

'I speak the truth,' he said hoarsely. 'We sought food. Elk are scarce. Winter comes.'

'Ah.' Bastion smiled again, slow and sharp. 'Elk.'

Its tongue flicked. 'I do like elk.'

Valran's heart hammered. 'You said you would help me.'

Bastion's smile vanished.

'Help?' it snarled. 'I said I might.'

It leapt.

The impact drove Valran flat onto his pack, breath bursting from his lungs. Bastion landed atop him, light and cold, claws pinning his shoulders as bony fingers tore at straps and fabric.

'Did the Seer give you something?' Bastion hissed. 'A stone? A mark? A word?'

'Get off me!' Valran reached for his blade, fingers closing on the hilt—

Bastion's tail whipped forward, impossibly fast. The burning tip touched his wrist.

Pain seared through him. Valran screamed, the blade falling from nerveless fingers.

Bastion leaned closer, breath hot and foul. 'Last chance, hunter man.'

This was not interrogation. It was selection.

'I have nothing!' Valran gasped. 'Nothing!'

For a heartbeat, Bastion did not move.

Then it laughed.

A thin, delighted sound that echoed far too loudly in the trees.

Bastion did not move.

It crouched atop Valran's chest, weight light but absolute, eyes searching his face as though reading something written beneath the skin.

'No,' it said at last, softly. 'I do not believe you, hunter man.'

Valran's breath hitched. 'I told you the truth.'

Bastion smiled without humor. 'You told me *a* truth.' It tapped one claw against Valran's breastbone. 'Not the one I want.'

The creature rose and stepped lightly from him, then bowed with mock courtesy. 'So. We will visit my master instead.' Its eyes gleamed. 'He serves the shadow beyond the North. He'll want to know everything the Seer told you. He has... patience. And tools for those who resist.'

Valran's stomach dropped. 'You said you would help me.'

'I am helping you,' Bastion replied brightly. 'You are going to be very educational.'

Valran understood then that survival was no longer the point.

Bastion threw back its head and howled. It clapped its hands once, delighted. 'We leave now!'

The sound tore through the forest, sharp and unnatural, echoing far beyond the reach of any beast's call. The night answered.

Wings beat the air. Heavy. Near.

Branches cracked overhead.

Valran twisted, panic flooding him, just as two vast red eyes ignited in the darkness above. A massive shape detached from the canopy, descending in a slow, deliberate glide.

'No,' Valran whispered. 'That's not possible.'

The creature dropped into the clearing with a thunder of displaced air.

Its wings spanned the width of the road, membranes stretched tight over long, jointed bones. Black fur bristled along its body, absorbing the firelight, while its eyes burned like coals buried deep in ash. Its jaws parted, revealing rows of curved teeth slick with moisture.

'A Pteradiabus,' Valran breathed. Dread coiled in his gut. Like the gore-cann. Another myth made flesh.

'They're just stories,' he whispered.

Bastion's grin widened. 'Most useful things begin that way. The darkness remembers what the world forgot.' It patted the creature's flank. 'This is Malloc. He flies beautifully—and he's very loyal to our master.'

Malloc struck.

Talons closed around Valran's torso, lifting him from the ground in a rush of wind and terror. Valran screamed, thrashing uselessly as the forest dropped away beneath him.

Bastion leapt upward with effortless grace, landing on the creature's back. It leaned down, peering into Valran's wild eyes.

'Sleep now,' it said. Valran tried to hold onto Niama's name and failed.

A spark flared at Bastion's fingertip. Pale. Cold. It pressed the light to Valran's brow.

Darkness took him mid-breath.

The forest swallowed their passing, branches settling, leaves falling still once more as if nothing had ever disturbed the road at all.

Valran woke to wind and sky.

Mountains passed beneath him, impossibly far below. Bastion's voice drifted back.

'The master rises soon,' Bastion said. 'He waits in the North, where the darkness gathers. In Ijovar, where your precious Aesulyn has already fallen.' Its eyes gleamed. 'You won't be lonely long. Your companions will follow.'

Valran's chest tightened. 'Niama...' he rasped. She didn't know. She was heading east, thinking him safe on the road home. Thinking he'd warn the village.

Instead he'd led the darkness straight to her.

Bastion tilted its head. 'Ah. So that is her name.'

It smiled, sharp and satisfied. 'I'll remember that. For when we find her.'

Valran shut his eyes.

Too late now.

CHAPTER NINE

The Stranger

Niama turned toward a ramshackle cart drawn up beside the road. Its driver sat hunched on the bench, a pipe clamped between his teeth, smoke curling around him with the sour scent of neglect. A small amber lamp hung from a crooked pole, swaying gently and casting uneven light across his face.

He was plump, older, wrapped in a threadbare grey cloak that sagged from his shoulders. A long, tangled beard spilled down his chest. His hands, knotted and scarred, held the reins with a steadiness his posture did not suggest. His eyes were pale, the colour of a winter sky, clouded as though he were looking through years rather than at them.

They lingered on Niama and Coseo longer than comfort allowed. She had learned to trust that feeling before it found words.

'Where did you two crawl out from?' he asked.

Coseo lifted one hand weakly and gestured toward the dark line of the mountains.

The man's brows rose. 'You met the wildkin, then.' He sucked on his pipe, studying them anew. 'And you're still breathin'. That's rare.' She could not tell whether he admired that or resented it.

Niama pushed herself upright, pain flaring through her side. 'Rare,' she rasped, 'but not easy.'

The man smiled broadly and dipped his head in a small, almost courtly bow. 'Jack Parsons,' he said. 'Haulin' goods north. Or I was, till the road offered me company.'

The ease of it set Niama on edge.

'Niama,' she said. 'And this is Coseo.'

'Elves,' Jack said, as if tasting the word. 'Forest folk, if I'm guessin'. Which means you're a long way from home.'

'Far enough,' Niama said.

Jack glanced at the darkening fields, then back at them. 'I'm bound for Whitefield. Night's no friend on this stretch. Wolves, for one.' His eyes slid toward the grass. 'And worse, dependin' who you ask.'

Moonlight silvered the fields. Trees stood in ragged silhouettes, too still, too watchful. The land felt open in a way that offered no comfort.

'We would be grateful for a ride,' Niama said.

Jack tapped ash from his pipe. 'Then climb aboard. You up here,' he added, nodding to the bench. 'Your friend can take the hay.'

Niama hauled herself up beside him. The cart creaked in protest. Coseo climbed into the rear and sank into the hay with a quiet exhale, sleep taking him almost at once.

Jack flicked the reins. The cart lurched forward.

'Looks like the wildkin wore him down,' Jack said, glancing back. 'They do that.'

'We've had little rest,' Niama said. 'And less food.'

'That's fixable.' Jack reached behind the bench and dropped a worn leather satchel into her lap. 'Eat.'

Niama hesitated only a moment before opening it. Nuts. Dried meat. Her stomach answered for her.

Jack plucked a nut from her hand and popped it into his mouth. 'Fresh,' he said around the crunch. 'See?'

She ate.

The cart rattled through the night, wheels biting into ruts, the lamp swaying with each jolt. Above them, the sky was sharp with stars. Ahead, the jagged outline of the Orboros mountains cut into the dark like broken teeth.

'Still a ways,' Jack said. 'My farm's just shy of Whitefield. Few hours yet.' He glanced sideways. 'So. What brings two forest folk this far from their trees?'

Niama chewed slowly, choosing her words with care. She wouldn't tell a stranger their true purpose. 'Trade,' she said. 'Bound for Hazelhaven. We were attacked on the road.'

Jack grunted. 'Aye. Been hearin' that.'

'They took us,' Niama continued. 'Knocked us senseless. Dragged us into the mountains.' Her grip tightened on the satchel. 'We escaped.'

'Escaped?' Jack said.

'With help,' she said carefully, watching his reaction, 'from Athris.'

Jack's hands stilled on the reins. Just for a moment. Then he smiled. The smile came a heartbeat late.

'Athris,' he echoed. Something flickered behind his eyes—recognition, perhaps. Or hunger. 'That's not a name folk use lightly.'

'No,' Niama agreed, hand drifting toward her blade. 'It's not.'

The horse snorted, tossing its head.

Jack chuckled, the moment passing. 'Even old Nance has opinions.'

The cart rolled on, the road narrowing ahead.

Niama forced the rations down. The food filled her belly but did little to ease the tightness in her chest. She watched Jack from the corner of her eye, measuring his easy posture, the way he'd gone still at Athris's name.

Too still. People did that when they were weighing lies.

The prophecy pressed at her thoughts. The Seer's warning. How often safety wore a friendly face. She kept her gaze on the road.

Jack broke the silence.

'You must be near dead on your feet,' he said mildly. He nodded toward the horse. 'Nance'll get us home. Knows the road better than I do.'

He clicked his tongue. 'That's it, girl.'

The horse leaned into the harness, steady as stone.

The fight bled out of Niama all at once. Pain throbbed along her side. Her limbs felt heavy, distant.

'A short rest,' she said. 'Just for a moment.'

Jack smiled, pipe smoke curling around his face. 'That's the spirit.'

Niama leaned back against the bench. The cart rocked beneath her, wood creaking in a slow rhythm. Stars slid overhead. The road hummed under the wheels.

Her thoughts drifted. Forest paths. Blood on stone. The Seer's dark, knowing eyes.

She shifted, eyes half-lidded, and caught movement at the edge of her vision.

A shape. A smile, maybe.

Or nothing at all.

Then even that slipped away.

Sleep took her not like a blanket, but like a hand closing.

The cart rolled on.

Hours passed in darkness. The road unwound beneath them, marked only by the creak of wheels and the steady clop of Nance's hooves. Stars wheeled overhead, cold and distant.

A jolt snapped Niama awake.

'Here we are,' Jack said, already climbing down, his joints popping loud in the quiet.

Leaves rustled. Nance snorted softly.

Niama swung her legs down, boots hitting damp earth. Cold crept through her armor. Woodsmoke lingered in the air.

'Where are we?' Her voice scraped her throat.

Jack patted the horse's neck. 'Home.' He smiled at the animal. 'Ain't that right, girl?'

Moonlight revealed the place in fragments. Crooked timber. A sagging roof. A door scarred by age and weather. The forest pressed in close, undergrowth thick enough to hide watchers.

Niama's hand drifted to her blade.

'Feels good to stand,' Jack said, straightening with a grunt. 'Travel does a number on old bones.'

Coseo stirred in the hay, blinking awake. Straw clung to his hair and cloak. 'What is this place?'

Niama allowed herself a quiet breath of amusement as he brushed it free. 'Jack's farm. Just south of Whitefield, like he said.'

Jack lifted a lantern and waved them closer. 'Come along. No sense lingerin'.'

The key turned. The door groaned open.

Inside smelled of dust and dried herbs. Old paper. Time.

Jack moved through the clutter as if it were second nature, lighting lamps one by one. Warm light filled the space, catching on cobwebs, stacked tools, a worn couch by the hearth, and a rocking chair polished smooth at its feet.

Lived-in. Not abandoned.

'You'll sleep better than the road,' Jack said. 'Beds are through there.'

He nudged open a narrow door. Two frames waited inside, sagging but serviceable.

'I'll see to Nance,' he added, already turning away. 'Best not wander into the barn. She don't care for strangers.'

The warning sat wrong with Niama. Warnings often mattered more than reasons. The horse had seemed gentle enough.

Jack's footsteps faded. A barn door creaked. Hooves shuffled. Then quiet.

Coseo stretched out on one bed, exhaling. 'That was... unexpected.'

'Yes,' Niama said.

She set her pack down and listened. The night pressed close beyond the walls. Somewhere outside, Jack muttered to himself, words lost to distance.

'Did you hear the cart before he appeared?' she asked softly.

Coseo shook his head. 'No.'

Unease coiled low in her stomach.

'I told him little,' she said. 'Only that we were bound for Hazelhaven. A lie, but safer than the truth.'

'Wise,' Coseo murmured. 'Still... something's off.'

Niama lay back, eyes tracing the ceiling. Moonlight slipped through gaps in the roof in thin, pale lines. Stars, cold and distant.

'We decide our path at first light,' she said. 'For now, this will do.'

Outside, something moved. Footsteps, perhaps. Or wind.

Niama's hand stayed on her blade as sleep pulled her under.

Then she closed her eyes.

Sleep came slowly, and it did not feel like surrender so much as a truce.

CHAPTER TEN

The Reveal

N iama woke to the sound of breath that was not her own. It took her a moment to remember where safety was supposed to be.

Coseo lay across from her, already awake, his slow exhale steady and familiar.

Niama's eyes drifted around the room. The hearth was clean, recently used. The floor swept. Yet dust lay thick in the corners, untouched.

The walls, too, showed neglect. Wood dark with rot, gaps visible between boards. The whole structure sagged, held together by habit more than strength.

'Did you sleep?' she asked, voice thick with it.

Coseo stretched beside her, joints popping softly. 'As though the forest itself cradled me.' He smiled faintly. 'And you?'

'Better than I deserve.'

Smoke threaded the air. Woodsmoke. Grain.

Pots clinked beyond the door.

Niama sat up too quickly and sneezed, dust rising in a pale cloud.

The smell of porridge slipped under the door, warm and disarming.

She hesitated, then opened it.

Jack stood at the hearth, back to her, stirring a pot with slow, unhurried care.

'Mornin',' he said. 'Reckon you're starvin'.'

Daylight did him no favors. His cloak was more thread than cloth now. His hair lay flat and grey against his skull. The years sat heavy on him.

Niama tied her hair back and moved to the table. The wood was scarred, stained by decades of meals and knives.

'Thank you,' she said. 'For last night.'

Jack chuckled. 'Road was headin' my way. Seemed rude not to stop.'

He set mugs down. Steam curled upward.

Niama accepted the mug, the heat biting into her palms.

The tea smelled right. Too right. Right things were often the easiest to fake.

She held it there, letting the steam fog her vision, counting one breath. Then another.

Jack followed her gaze and smiled.

'Keeps me busy,' he said, though she hadn't spoken.

The smile reached his mouth, but not his eyes.

Coseo claimed the rocking chair.

'You said you were traders,' Jack said, seating himself. 'Hazelhaven, wasn't it?'

Niama hesitated. A glance to Coseo. Then a nod. 'Yes. We were attacked shortly after leaving the forest.'

Jack leaned forward, elbows on the table. 'By wildkin?'

'Yes.'

'Bold creatures, lately.' His gaze slid to Coseo. 'Travelin' with just the two of you takes nerve.'

'We had little choice,' Coseo said.

Jack smiled thinly.

'And the Seer?' Jack said casually. 'What did he tell you?'

His spoon didn't pause.

Niama felt it lodge behind her eyes, cold and deliberate. She'd never mentioned the Seer to Jack. Only Hazelhaven. Only the wildkin attack.

Jack's eyes flicked once, involuntarily.

Not to her face.

Lower.

The smile stayed where it was, fixed in place, like something worn rather than felt.

Coseo was on his feet in an instant, the poker scraping against stone as he wrenched it free. 'Explain yourself.'

Jack sighed. Not in fear. In disappointment.

'Pity,' he said.

Niama rose. 'Who are you?'

Jack lifted his gaze slowly.

For a heartbeat, nothing happened.

Then his skin slackened, sagging like ill-fitted clothing. Colour drained in uneven patches, revealing something grey and mottled beneath—not flesh, but something that had worn it.

The illusion was breaking. The mask slipping.

His eyes caught the lantern light and reflected it back—not human eyes anymore, but something vast and empty behind them, looking out through borrowed holes.

'You look disappointed,' he said. His voice layered now, multiple tones beneath the folksy accent. 'Most are. They want monsters to look like monsters from the start.'

The skin suit rippled, trying to hold shape. Failing.

His gaze slid to Niama's chest. Stilled. Focused. 'You've been carryin' it a long time,' Jack said.

Not a question.

'If the wildkin had done what they were told,' he rasped, 'we wouldn't be havin' this talk.'

His fist struck the table. Wood jumped. The mugs rattled.

Coseo moved.

He hit Jack hard, shoulder first, the impact driving him back from the table with a snarl of splintering wood.

Jack staggered, more surprised than hurt. His attention snapped fully to Coseo now, fury eclipsing calculation.

Jack tilted his head, studying Niama as one might inspect a flawed tool.

Coseo lunged.

The poker struck Jack's shoulder with a solid crack.

For half a heartbeat, Niama thought it had worked.

Jack staggered a step.

Then black tendrils burst from his hand, fast as striking snakes. They wrapped Coseo's throat and yanked him off the floor. His feet kicked, scraping uselessly against air.

Niama moved.

She didn't reach Jack.

The blow caught her mid-stride, a backhand that sent her into the wall.

The rotten wood exploded on impact, offering no resistance. She crashed through into the next room, splinters raining down, the weakened boards giving way like wet paper.

She hit the floor hard, breath bursting from her lungs. Pain flared through her shoulder. Dust and debris rained down.

She lay stunned, breath refusing to come, mouth full of grit. Somewhere nearby, Coseo choked.

'Wait your turn,' Jack said calmly, voice carrying through the wreckage. 'I'm speakin' with your friend.'

Niama dragged in a breath. Then another. The room swam. Her gaze found the ring, cold and solid.

She didn't know why. Instinct. Desperation. Her fingers closed around it, and it burned hot against her palm.

Gretha's voice echoed in memory: *It will answer when needed.*

Answer what? Answer how?

Niama didn't understand, but her body moved anyway, arm raising, ring turned toward Jack—

For a heartbeat, nothing.

Then the ring blazed. The air thickened.

The light bent and tore free, not as flame but as weight, as presence. The floor cracked as hooves struck it. An elk burst from the radiance, vast and impossible, antlers scraping the beams, eyes blazing with ancient fury.

Jack laughed once.

Then screamed.

The elk hit him like judgment. Light consumed flesh. Shadows burned away. The stench of scorched air filled the room as Jack unravelled, his scream tearing itself apart before ending in sparks.

Silence fell hard.

The ring crumbled to ash against her palm. She stared at the dust, not understanding—then let it fall.

Gone. Whatever it had been, it was spent.

Niama's fingers found the medallion instead, cold and solid. Still there. Still hers.

She didn't remember reaching for it.

Coseo dropped to the floor, collapsing in a heap. He gasped once, throat bruised and swelling, before his eyes rolled back.

Niama was at his side instantly. 'Cos. Cos!'

His chest rose. Fell. Rose again.

Alive. Unconscious. Strangled nearly to death.

But alive.

She had to get him away from here. Now.

She ran.

Not back inside. Coseo needed a healer, needed safety. She needed transport.

Nancy. The cart. Get to Whitefield. Find help.

The barn reeked of death.

Flies rose at her entry, a black cloud breaking apart and reforming with a sound like distant rain. Niama froze.

The bodies lay piled in the corner. Three of them. Not thrown. Placed.

A man twisted protectively toward a woman. Both wore travel-stained cloaks. Merchants, perhaps, or traders.

A child half-hidden beneath them. Small. Too small. Small hands clenched even now.

How many travelers had Jack offered shelter? How many had never reached Whitefield?

Niama swallowed bile, forcing herself to look away before the images could burn into memory.

She hitched the wagon, hauled Coseo's limp weight aboard, threw their gear in beside him, and took the reins.

'Run,' she whispered.

Nancy obeyed.

The cart thundered toward Whitefield as dawn began to bleed into the sky.

Dawn did not feel like mercy.

CHAPTER ELEVEN

The Magika

Whitefield rose out of the road like an answer that might still come too late.

Niama drove the cart hard, fingers locked around the reins until they burned. Nancy's hooves thundered on packed earth, each stride uneven, desperate. Foam flecked the mare's flanks. Her breath came in ragged bursts that Niama felt in her own chest.

Behind her, Coseo did not move.

'Stay with me,' Niama whispered, not daring to look back. 'Just a little longer.'

The land opened as they crested the final rise. Fields spread wide and green, furrowed and ready for planting, dotted with workers who straightened at the sound of the gallop. Whitefield lay ahead, low and sprawling beside the Varenwood River, smoke lifting from chimneys, banners snapping faintly in the breeze.

Too slow. Everything here moved too slowly. Panic had no patience for villages.

Niama urged the mare on.

They plunged into the outskirts, wheels rattling over stone and rutted dirt. The smells hit first: wet earth, livestock, overripe fruit left too long in the sun. Heads turned. Voices rose. People jumped back as the cart tore through, skirts and cloaks snatched out of the way.

Nancy screamed as Niama hauled the reins and brought her to a skidding halt.

'I need a healer!' She shouted. Her voice cracked, sharp enough to cut through the noise. 'Now!'

The square stilled in pockets. A woman in a bright shawl broke from the crowd, eyes already on the cart, on the still form within it.

'What's happened?' she asked, brisk but kind.

Niama didn't waste breath, just pointed. 'My friend. He's dying.'

The woman's jaw tightened. She turned and pointed toward the town's heart. 'Straight through. To the fountain. The healer's shop faces it. Don't stop.' Then, softer, as Niama gathered the reins again, 'May Athris watch your path.'

Niama snapped the leather.

The cart surged into the press of the market. Stalls crowded the way. Fish guts glistened on tables. Spices burned the air. Shouts flared as people leapt aside, carts jolting, baskets toppling. Somewhere metal rang against metal. Somewhere a child cried.

Niama drove straight through it.

The fountain came into view at last, white stone gleaming amid the chaos. Water spilled from carved fish into a wide basin, bright and uselessly calm. To one side stood the healer's shop, its awning heavy with drying herbs and flowers, colour bleeding into the dust.

She hauled the reins again.

'Help!' she cried, already scrambling down. 'Please!'

She was at the back of the cart before it had fully stopped, hands shaking as she reached for Coseo. Fear pressed in now that the running had ended.

She burst through the shop door hard enough to rattle the hinges.

Glass chimed. Shelves crowded with bottles swayed, liquids catching the light in flashes of green and amber. The air hit her at once, sharp with herbs and resin, something bitter beneath. Sunlight filtered through a vine-choked window, breaking into pale slats across the floor.

Books lined the back wall, stacked high and uneven. Parchments littered the counter beside a spilled inkpot. The floorboards groaned as Niama crossed the room.

'I need a healer,' she said. The words tore out of her. 'Now.'

A young woman stood behind the counter, frozen. She clutched a broom like a weapon, knuckles white. Fear widened her eyes.

'I—I am,' she said quickly. 'I can help. I mean—I'm trained.'

Niama barely registered the words. 'Come.'

She turned and was already moving when the healer found her feet.

Outside, the cart waited like an open wound.

The healer climbed up without being asked. Her hands were steady when she reached for Coseo's throat. She counted under her breath. Lifted his eyelid.

Then she flinched.

'No,' she breathed.

Niama's stomach dropped. 'What?'

The healer shook her head once, sharply, as if refusing a thought. 'This isn't injury. Or sickness.' She swallowed. 'This is sorcery.'

Niama leaned closer. 'Then heal him.'

The healer's gaze snapped to hers. 'I can't.'

The word landed like a blow.

'You said you could help,' Niama said. Her voice stayed level only by force.

'I can heal cuts. Breaks. Poison.' The healer backed away, one hand braced on the cart. 'This is dark magic.' The words felt too small for what she had seen.

The phrase echoed too loudly in Niama's head.

Dark magic.

It didn't fit with anything she knew. Light, balance, exchange. Even curses followed rules. This felt hollow, like something had been removed rather than damaged. As though absence itself had learned how to wound.

Niama saw again the smoke pouring from Jack's hand. The way it had moved with purpose.

'What do I do?' she demanded. 'Tell me.'

The healer hesitated only a moment, then made a decision. She jumped down and hurried back into the shop. Locks clattered. The door slammed.

She was back almost at once, breathless, scrambling up beside Niama. 'You take him to the Magika.'

Niama stared. 'The what?'

'The Magika. Lives in the western woods. Reclusive. Dangerous, some say. But if anyone can counter this...' She shook her head. 'It's your only chance.'

She pointed west, beyond the river, toward the dark line of trees. 'That way. Don't stop.'

Niama snapped the reins and sent Nancy west.

The road narrowed at once. The healer braced beside her, voice raised over the rattle of wheels. 'Wallingwich Woods. The Magika lives just inside. She doesn't welcome strangers. If she helps, it won't be because she's kind.'

Whitefield fell away in a rush of dust and shouted curses. Faces blurred past. A crate toppled somewhere behind them. No one followed.

Nancy thundered on, hooves striking hard and fast, breath tearing from her chest in wet, desperate pulls. The cart shuddered with each rut. Niama leaned forward, reins biting into her palms, hair whipping loose and stinging her eyes.

Then the trees closed in. The woods did not rush to meet them. They allowed it.

Elms rose like pillars, their canopies knitting overhead. Light fractured into gold shards across Niama's hands. The air cooled, heavy with damp earth and green life. Birds scattered at their approach, song breaking into startled silence.

'There,' the healer said, pointing. 'That turn.'

The track was little more than a scar in the undergrowth. It split from the road and vanished between two trees so close together the cart barely fit. Roots clawed up like grasping fingers.

Niama didn't slow.

The wheels scraped bark. Vines lashed across their arms. Leaves slapped wet against skin. Nancy pushed on with a low, strained sound, sweat darkening her coat, sides heaving.

The woods swallowed them.

Then, abruptly, light.

They burst into a clearing no larger than a training yard. A house crouched against the trees as if grown there rather than built. Log walls, dark with age. A thatched roof stitched tight. Smoke curled steadily from the chimney. A garden spread around it in careful disorder, herbs and flowers growing thick and deliberate.

Alive. Watched. Niama had learned the difference.

'Here,' the healer said. 'This is it.'

Niama hauled the reins back. The cart skidded to a stop. Nancy stumbled once, then stood, trembling, breath ripping in and out.

Niama was off the bench before it fully stilled.

She ran.

Her fist struck the door hard enough to rattle the frame. 'Help!' she shouted. 'Please—he's dying.'

For a long moment, nothing answered.

Then the door opened a handspan.

A woman filled the gap, shorter than Niama, broad-shouldered, wrapped in red and black robes that looked worn rather than ceremonial. Her hair fell loose down her back, pale against the dark cloth. Lines cut deep into her brow and around her mouth.

Her eyes were sharp. Assessing. Unwelcoming.

'You have five heartbeats,' the woman said. 'Use them well.'

Niama swallowed. 'My friend has been struck by dark magic.'

The Magika's gaze sharpened. It slid past Niama, taking in the cart, the healer, and finally Coseo's still form.

Her expression hardened.

'Bring him inside,' she said. 'And if you've lied to me—'

She flung the door wide, then stopped.

Her eyes snapped back to the cart.

'No.'

She crossed to it in three strides and climbed up beside Coseo, pressing her ear to his chest. Seconds stretched. Niama counted her own breaths without meaning to.

A sharp intake of air.

The woman tugged Coseo's shirt aside. A bruise marred his chest, dark and wrong, its edges feathered as if burned from beneath the skin.

Niama's stomach dropped. She hadn't seen it. Hadn't known to look.

The Magika lifted one of Coseo's eyelids and swore under her breath. 'Inside. Now.'

They moved together, urgency snapping orders short. Niama and the village healer hauled Coseo down, boots skidding on packed earth, arms straining under his dead weight.

'Table,' the Magika said, already clearing space. 'Gently.'

The house swallowed them.

Incense burned thick in the air, bitter and sweet at once. Bundles of herbs hung from the rafters, brushing Niama's hair as she passed. Jars crowded every surface, liquids glimmering faintly as if aware of being watched.

Coseo was laid out. Still too still.

The Magika moved like a storm given purpose. Shelves were ransacked. Bottles shoved aside. One shattered on the floor, scent blooming sharp and floral.

'Drat,' she muttered. 'That took me a season to distill.'

She did not slow.

Her hand closed around a crystal in a drawer near her desk. Clear as ice. Cold as judgment.

She turned. 'Hold him.'

Niama braced Coseo's shoulders. The healer seized his legs. His skin felt clammy, as though warmth were already retreating.

The Magika began to chant.

The words scraped the air, harsh and old. The crystal flared green, light bleeding outward in pulses that made Niama's teeth ache. Coseo convulsed, body arching violently as though something inside him were trying to escape.

'Hold him,' the Magika snapped.

Niama did, muscles screaming as Coseo bucked against her grip. The crystal slammed against his chest and stuck there, humming, feeding.

The light intensified.

Then the Magika pressed both hands to it, face tightening with effort. The glow dimmed, inch by inch, as if being dragged back into the stone.

Coseo collapsed against the table. The fight left his body in a rush.

Silence fell hard.

The healer stared, awe and fear warring on her face.

The Magika straightened slowly.

Her gaze lifted.

Niama felt it before she saw it.

The medallion slipped free.

It hovered above Coseo, light spilling in slow, deliberate waves. Shadows leapt across the walls. The hanging herbs stirred, though there was no wind.

The Magika went very still.

'So it's true,' she whispered, awe threading through disbelief as she stared at the medallion.

Her gaze lifted slowly to Niama.

'That,' she said quietly, 'explains everything.'

Her eyes hardened.

'And it tells me,' she added, voice low and certain, 'that you are in far more danger than you realise.'

Niama stiffened and tucked it back beneath her shirt, pulse quickening. 'What do you mean?'

The Magika straightened, drawing the crystal away as it dimmed in her palm. 'That such a relic still walks the world,' she said. 'And that it answers you.'

She set the crystal aside with care. 'He needs rest. The darkness is drawn out. Whether it left a mark...' Her mouth tightened. 'We'll see.'

'A mark,' Niama echoed. The word lodged in her throat.

'Darkness isn't absence,' the Magika said. 'It's a force. It stains as often as it wounds. The crystal took what it could, but traces cling.' She met Niama's gaze. 'Time will tell if it took root.'

Niama nodded, eyes returning to Coseo. His breathing was slow now, even. Alive. That was enough.

'You may stay,' she said. 'He'll be strong enough to travel in a day or two, if there are no complications.'

Relief buckled Niama's knees. 'You have my gratitude,' she whispered. She brushed damp hair from Coseo's brow, fingers lingering. 'We are in your debt.'

The Magika's expression softened, just slightly. She rested a hand against Coseo's forehead, cool and steady. 'Survive first. Debts can wait.'

Niama turned to the village healer. 'Thank you.'

The young woman smiled, tired but sincere. 'Mira,' she said. 'And I hope he wakes soon.' She squeezed Niama's arm, then stepped back.

The Magika drew herself up. 'I'm Kesaahn,' she said. 'Magika. Advisor to the King.'

Niama inclined her head. 'Niama of Mistwood. This is Coseo. We are of Erbour Forest.'

'So I gathered,' Kesaahn said, gaze flicking to the medallion's faint outline beneath Niama's shirt. 'I need supplies before nightfall.' She looked to Mira. 'I'll escort you back.'

Mira nodded. 'Thank you.' She hesitated, then added quietly, 'I hope everything turns out well.'

She glanced back at Coseo.

'He'll recover,' Kesaahn said, not unkindly. 'And what you saw here stays here.'

Mira understood. She left without argument.

When the door closed behind them, the room felt larger. Quieter.

Niama sat beside Coseo and took his hand. Warm now. Solid. She held it as if anchoring him, fear and resolve twisting together in her chest.

Outside, hooves faded down the path.

Niama woke as the front door creaked open.

'Kesaahn,' she murmured, rubbing grit from her eyes. 'I must have fallen asleep.'

Kesaahn went straight to Coseo and checked his pulse. 'Strong,' she said, a quick smile cutting through her focus. She pressed a hand to his forehead. 'Warmer. He'll be himself soon.'

Relief washed through Niama. She managed a small, grateful smile.

Kesaahn crossed to her desk, peeling off black leather gloves finger by finger and setting them neatly among vials and papers. Today she wore city clothes beneath her travelling cloak. Fine cloth. Deliberate. She looked like someone who belonged in halls, not woods. Her boots sounded firm on the floorboards. In this modest house, she looked like a blade set down in a barn.

'You'll have questions,' Kesaahn said, turning. 'So do I.' She glanced around. 'I don't come here often. This is my retreat. The city can drown you if you let it.'

She sat beside Niama and took her hands. Her skin was cool, smooth, a stark contrast to Niama's calloused palms.

'You have no reason to trust me,' Kesaahn said. 'But if the prophecy has begun, you'll have enemies who want that medallion.' Her gaze flicked to Niama's chest. 'If darkness claims it... you know what follows.'

Niama didn't answer. She couldn't.

Kesaahn leaned back, watching her carefully. 'Before I ask what happened to you, you should know what I am.' Her voice stayed plain, steady. 'A Magika. I work light through living things. Plants. Roots. Oils. It's craft and knowledge, not waving hands and hoping.'

Niama swallowed. 'And you serve the King.'

'I advise him,' Kesaahn said. 'And Prince Rohan. Which means I can open doors you can't.'

She rose, crossed to her desk, and pulled an item wrapped in silk from a drawer. She unwrapped it to reveal a royal seal, a lion crest stamped deep.

'This is real,' she said, holding it out. 'So is what you're carrying.'

Niama's eyes stayed on the lion. 'What do you know of the medallion?'

'Enough to fear it,' Kesaahn said. 'If the Seer placed it in your hands, you've been chosen for a task that will eat the unprepared.' She met Niama's gaze. 'The lion you seek is in Silverfall. We go to the city and speak to the King.'

Niama's thoughts scattered. 'Who is the lion?'

Kesaahn exhaled. 'A title. Old. Older than the city itself.' She paused. 'The details can wait until we reach the Seekers. They'll explain it better than I can.'

'And the Seekers?'

'Keepers of the ancient library. Scribes of the Chronicles of Light.' Kesaahn's eyes sharpened. 'They translate what others can't. They'll help us find the Staff of Light and understand what's coming with the Second Rising.'

Niama blinked. 'Us?'

'Yes.' Kesaahn didn't flinch from it. 'You can refuse, but I wouldn't.' Her tone left little room for romance. 'You'll need me.'

Niama studied her, measuring the calm, the certainty, the seal in her hand.

Kesaahn's fingers settled briefly on Niama's shoulder. 'You've met darkness with a face.' Her gaze flicked toward Coseo, sleeping fitfully nearby. 'Whatever struck him was power. But even in deep shadow, light remains. If you accept my help, I will spend it on your survival.'

Niama's hand drifted to the medallion beneath her shirt. The memory of the raven flashed behind her eyes. 'And the raven?'

Kesaahn's brow creased. 'I won't pretend I know. We'll ask the Seekers.' She stood. 'For now, we eat and rest. Night is close, and the road will test us.'

Niama sat in silence, thumb rubbing the bare place on her finger where Gretha's ring had been. It was gone. No trace.

'It held the power once,' she murmured. 'Then it spent itself.'

'What was that?' Kesaahn asked, stoking the fire.

'Nothing,' Niama said, and meant: thank you, Gretha.

The fire snapped and settled, sparks spiralling up the chimney. Heat eased into Niama's bones. Shadows danced, almost gentle.

'I have one bed,' Kesaahn said. 'Take whatever floor space you need.' She handed Niama a plate piled with food. Niama ate like someone remembering she was alive.

'I'll bring in your belongings,' Kesaahn said, 'then tend to your horse and cart in the barn.'

Niama swallowed. 'They aren't mine. I... borrowed them.' The image of the bodies in Jack's barn rose, sharp and sickening. 'I don't think their owners will need them again.'

Kesaahn's expression softened. 'Then we'll treat them well.' She stepped outside.

Niama watched the door after it closed, unease returning like a tide. Kesaahn had been helpful. Jack had been, too. Kindness, she was learning, did not require honesty.

She made a bed near a bookcase and lay back, eyes fixed on the ceiling. Sleep took her slowly, dreams thick with questions and teeth.

The scream ripped Niama from sleep.

She was on her feet before breath caught up, heart slamming hard enough to bruise. The alcove was empty.

'Cos—'

Cold stone bit into her bare feet as she ran.

She rounded the house and stopped dead.

Coseo stood in the yard, rigid, backlit by dawn. Before him, a pig thrashed weakly in the dirt, its screams collapsing into wet, choking noise. Blood soaked the ground. Steam rose where entrails spilled free.

Coseo watched.

Not in panic. Not in shock.

Niama's stomach lurched.

He was smiling.

The smile belonged to the moment, not the man.

'No,' she breathed, the word tearing loose. She dropped beside the animal, hands already moving, dagger flashing free. 'This is not our way.'

The pig screamed again.

Niama drove the blade down, clean and final.

The sound cut off.

She bowed her head once, breath shaking. Athris, guide it.

When she looked up, Coseo hadn't moved.

His eyes were bright. Too bright. Fixed on the carcass as if disappointed it no longer struggled.

'Cos,' she said softly. Then louder. 'Coseo.'

Nothing.

'Why?' Her voice cracked. 'Why would you do this?'

'It was only a pig,' he said. That frightened her more than any scream.

The words landed wrong. Flat. Empty.

Niama stood slowly, wiping her blade clean without looking away from him. 'That pleasure in your eyes,' she said. 'That isn't you.'

Coseo blinked.

The smile faltered.

'I...' He swayed. Confusion crept across his face like fog. 'I couldn't stop it. There was... pressure. Like a surge.'

She took his arm before he could fall. Sweat slicked his skin. His gaze darted, wild now, frightened.

Inside, she sat him down.

'How do you feel?' she asked.

'Where are we?' He swallowed hard. 'And where's Jack?'

The name cut.

Niama forced her voice steady. 'Jack is gone.'

Footsteps crossed the threshold.

Coseo recoiled as Kesaahn entered, eyes wide. 'Who are you?'

'She saved your life,' Niama said.

Kesaahn inclined her head. 'You were struck by dark magic. You survived. That alone is... unusual.'

Coseo stared at his hands. 'I don't remember.'

Niama told him. About Jack. About the ring. About the light that burned darkness away.

Coseo didn't interrupt.

When she finished, he sat very still.

Kesaahn broke the silence. 'What matters is that you're alive. But whatever touched you may not be finished.' She glanced toward the window. 'We leave today.'

She moved with purpose after that. Food. Water. Packs checked and rechecked.

'Three days to the city,' she said. 'We'll take the cart.'

Outside, Nancy waited, patient and steady. Kesaahn had seen to her — water, rest, a blanket across her flanks.

Niama climbed into the back beside Coseo as Kesaahn took the reins.

The cart rolled forward.

For a time, neither spoke.

'Jack seemed kind,' Coseo said finally.

'That was the danger,' Niama replied.

He nodded slowly. 'Did he say anything about Valran?'

'No.' Niama looked ahead. 'We'll learn the truth when we can.'

Coseo leaned back into the hay, exhaustion pulling him under.

Niama stayed awake.

Fields slid past. Farmers worked, unaware. The world looked peaceful.

She didn't trust it. Peace had a way of arriving before it broke.

Her hand closed around the medallion beneath her shirt as the road carried them onward, toward whatever waited next.

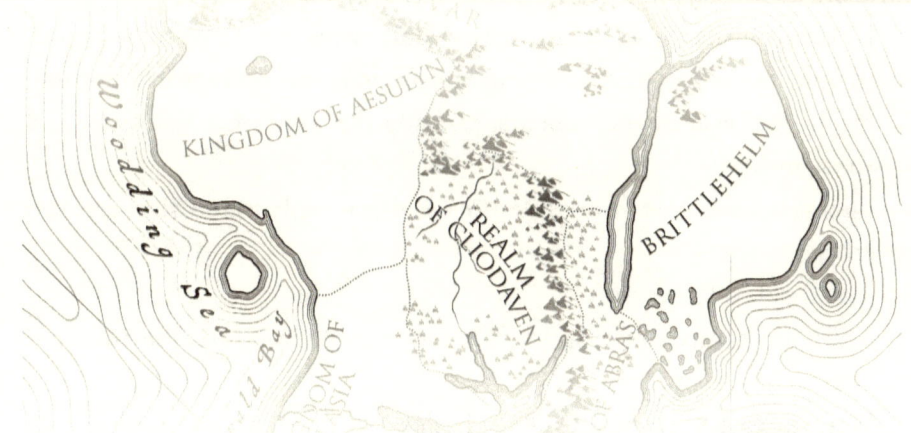

CHAPTER TWELVE

The Rooster

Under the midday sun, farmland spread like a patchwork quilt. Niama glanced from the road to Coseo, asleep amid the hay, his body jolting gently with the cart's rhythm.

His shoulder caught her eye. The one the gorecann had torn open on Washrock Rise. She'd dressed it herself, changed the ointment twice. It had been slow to heal — weeks of careful tending, movement limited, pain evident in every flinch.

Now there was nothing. Not a scar. Not a mark. As though it had never been wounded at all.

Kesaahn had drawn the darkness out. But she hadn't done this.

Had she?

Niama didn't know. That was what frightened her.

His snores rose and fell, steady and oblivious. She wondered what he dreamed. Whether any of it was his own.

Crickets sang as the road unwound beneath them. Niama and Kesaahn traded stories as easily as cards, weaving customs and half-told traditions together. Beneath the easy talk, the shape of the quest lingered, unseen but present, pacing just beyond thought.

By the time the sun bled into the horizon, they reached Woodly, a modest hamlet at the crossroads of Silverfall, Whitefield, and Farwich. Evening crept in, cool against their cheeks, carrying the scent of woodsmoke and roasting meat.

Niama reined Nancy outside the local inn. A battered sign creaked overhead.

The Restless Rooster.

The name earned a brief smirk. With a groan of wheels and the dull thud of boots, they stepped inside.

Warmth rushed to meet them. Firelight ruled the room, casting gold across flushed faces. Ale and smoke tangled thick in the air. Voices overlapped in a constant hum, broken by bursts of laughter and clashing tankards.

Some of the road's weight slipped away. Enough to be dangerous.

Near the hearth, farmers huddled close, their talk loud and animated. They spoke of swollen storehouses in the city, wheat hoarded and prices climbing.

'Haven't seen a boom like this in years,' one said.

'About time we got our share,' another replied, pipe smoke puffing with the words.

Niama's gaze drifted to the bar. A staircase climbed beside it, creaking with every step above. Behind the counter, a broad, balding man wiped tankards with a rag stained by years of use.

'Can I—' He stopped short, eyes widening. 'Lady Kesaahn. Well now. Didn't expect to see you.'

'Gunter,' Kesaahn said warmly. 'How's your family?'

'Well and thriving, milady.' He beamed. 'And your companions?'

'Friends, heading to the city. We'll need rooms.'

'Of course.' He nodded. 'Top of the stairs. I'll have Ademar see to your horse and cart.'

Kesaahn smiled. 'And your wife's pies?'

'Still the best this side of Silverfall. Three?'

'Please. And ale.' She slid silver across the bar. 'Quietly, if you would.'

Gunter's wink was answer enough.

They took a table near the window, the village settling into night beyond the glass.

'He's discreet,' Kesaahn said. 'I trust him.'

'You travel this way often?' Niama asked.

'When I can escape the city.'

Niama studied her. 'He called you "lady."'

'A title for official matters only,' Kesaahn said evenly. 'I prefer anonymity.'

'Anonymity that doesn't seem to extend to in tavernkeepers,' Niama said.

Kesaahn's mouth twitched. 'Gunter is family. Old friend of my mother's.'

Niama turned to Coseo. 'How are you feeling?'

He smiled faintly. 'Like nothing ever happened. Just tired.'

Kesaahn watched him a moment too long.

Music swelled as a bard launched into a tale, lute strings ringing bright. The crowd leaned in, clapping and calling encouragement.

The bard drifted closer, grin easy, lute still humming against his hip.

'Friends,' he said lightly, 'you look like folk who've earned a song.'

'We're tired,' Niama said gently. 'Perhaps another table.'

'Ah,' he laughed, already settling a foot on a chair rung, 'a song costs nothing but a moment.'

Kesaahn's voice followed, calm and firm. 'That moment is not available.'

Coseo didn't look at him.

His fingers tightened on the edge of the table. Niama felt it through the wood, a faint vibration, as if the table itself had gone tense.

'Cos,' she murmured, not quite a warning.

The bard laughed, mistaking it for shyness, and leaned in—

The chair scraped back.

'Leave,' Coseo said.

The word was flat. Empty. It did not sound like anger. It sounded like permission.

The bard blinked. 'Now, no offense meant—'

Coseo stood. The table lurched.

'If you don't,' he snarled, 'I'll tear your throat out.'

The room froze.

Tankards hovered midair. A chair scraped as someone shifted away.

No one laughed.

The bard stood very still, eyes locked on Coseo's face, smile gone.

Niama felt the weight of a dozen stares settle on their table.

Niama stared. This wasn't the man she knew. Not entirely. His face was twisted, eyes burning with something sharp and wrong. Cold swept through her.

'Cos,' she said, gripping his arm.

Kesaahn rose. Not quickly. Deliberately.

'That is enough,' she said, her voice cutting cleanly through the room.

Silence held.

She pressed a coin into the bard's hand without looking at it. 'Our apologies. The fault is ours.'

Her gaze flicked to Coseo. Sharp. Measuring.

'Sit. Now.'

The bard bit the coin, nodded, and retreated. Music resumed. Laughter followed, louder than before.

Kesaahn rounded on Coseo. 'What possessed you?'

He shrugged, a crooked grin tugging at his mouth. 'He's gone, isn't he?'

Niama watched him reach for his ale. Steady hands. Easy smile. As though threatening to kill a man was nothing more than swatting a fly.

The pig. Now this. Each time a little further.

But Kesaahn had said traces cling. Not that they take hold. Not yet.

She kept her hand near her dagger and said nothing.

Her gaze drifted, slow and careful, scanning faces that looked away too quickly, conversations that faltered. Then she saw him.

A man alone in the far corner. Still. Untouched by the noise.

He wasn't watching the bard.

He was watching *them*. Not with curiosity. With intent.

Their eyes met.

He didn't flinch. Didn't pretend. Didn't smile.

Niama's fingers found the dagger at her side, not drawing it, just confirming it was there.

'We've been noticed,' she murmured.

Kesaahn turned—

The corner was empty.

Footsteps approached.

Gunter came from behind the bar, pies and ale balanced carefully, but his eyes never left the table. He set the plates down one by one, slower than before, then placed the key beside them.

'Everything all right here?' he asked.

It wasn't a casual question.

His gaze flicked to the overturned chair. To Coseo's clenched hands. Then back to Kesaahn.

'Just tired,' Kesaahn said.

Gunter held her gaze a moment longer. Then he nodded, once, and withdrew.

The three of them sat in silence until the noise of the inn swallowed their table again.

Niama inhaled the rich scent of the pie and took a bite. Warm. Savory. Comfort she hadn't realized she needed.

'We travel at first light,' Kesaahn said. 'Barewallow by tomorrow night.'

Later, they climbed the stairs.

Niama lay awake on the worn mattress, thoughts racing. The man in the corner. Gone before Kesaahn turned. Watching them with intent, not curiosity.

Someone knew they were here.

Beside her, Coseo shifted and murmured, trapped in restless dreams. She wanted to soothe him, but didn't dare wake him.

A rooster crowed outside, shrill and relentless.

Again.

And again.

Kesaahn slept on, untroubled. Niama lay staring at the ceiling, listening as the night refused to release its grip.

CHAPTER THIRTEEN

The Gauntillia

After their fitful rest, Kesaahn asked, 'How did you both sleep?'

Coseo, looking haggard, managed only a weary grunt.

Niama rubbed at her eyes. 'What was the purpose of the rooster that plagued us throughout the night?'

Kesaahn laughed softly, eyes bright. 'Ah. Reggie. Gunter's pride and curse. He's been here longer than most guests. I've learned to sleep through him.' She winced. 'My apologies. I should've warned you.'

She slung her leather satchel across her shoulder. 'I'll fetch the horse and wagon. Meet me out front. We have a long road ahead.'

The door clicked shut behind her.

Niama buckled her armor, leather whispering as she tightened the straps. The familiar weight of her dagger settled at her hip. Across the room, Coseo bound his hair back and checked his pack, movements careful, precise.

'How do you fare today, Cos?' she asked, watching him closely.

'I am well,' he said. 'Merely fatigued.'

Niama snorted. 'You are my eldest friend. If I wish to worry, I will worry.'

A flush crept up his cheeks. 'Then... thank you. But truly, I'm fine.'

She didn't argue. 'Come. Kesaahn waits.'

They descended the creaking stairs and bid farewell to the tavernkeeper, who waved them on with a murmured wish for luck.

Outside, morning had settled in clean and bright. The sky stretched blue above the rooftops, the air crisp enough to wake the lungs. Niama paused long enough to draw it in.

Kesaahn waited in the cart, reins loose in her hands, patient as tidewater.

Niama glanced up at the sign above the inn and smiled despite herself.

'The Restless Rooster,' she murmured. 'Now it all makes sense.'

'Hop in,' Kesaahn called. 'Let's not waste the day.'

Nancy leaned into the harness as the cart lurched forward, wheels protesting with familiar squeaks.

'We should reach Silverfall the day after tomorrow, if the weather holds,' Kesaahn said.

The road unwound before them through rolling pasture and open fields. Sheep clustered in the distance. Carts grew more frequent as the morning wore on, laden with goods bound for market. The path narrowed, ditches yawning close on either side, a reminder that travel left little room for error.

Niama watched it all in silence as the countryside slid past, the city drawing nearer with every turn of the wheel. Nancy flicked her ears back, then forward again, restless despite the easy pace. Niama noticed it, then told herself it meant nothing. Animals grew skittish near roads. Near people.

The road thickened with noise. Ancient cartwheels rattled over packed dirt, wood complaining with every turn. Horses snorted and stamped, impatient with the press of travel.

As Barewallow drew near, a weathered sign caught Niama's eye. Faded, but still proud, it advertised Sven's honey mead.

Her mouth watered despite herself.

Six wins, the sign boasted, from the annual Beer Fest. Niama pictured the place alive with laughter, mugs raised, voices lifted in song. A tavern that earned that kind of loyalty should have been loud even from the road.

But as the sun dipped low and Barewallow emerged from the gathering dusk, the illusion cracked.

The blacksmith stood dark. The livery shuttered. Shopfronts gaped empty. Torchlight flickered behind a handful of windows, but there was no movement to match it. No voices. No dogs. No life spilling into the street.

The hamlet felt like it had held its breath. As though sound itself had learned to hide.

'Something is amiss,' Niama murmured.

Coseo shifted beside her. 'Perhaps they retire early.'

'Perhaps,' Kesaahn said, though her eyes never left the road ahead.

The wagon creaked toward the tavern at the edge of the square. Its sign swung on rusted chains, letters eaten thin by weather and time.

'Strange,' Coseo said quietly. 'For a place known for its mead.'

Kesaahn reined in before the door. 'Whoa there, Nance.'

Nancy snorted, hooves scraping dirt. She tossed her head, whites of her eyes flashing, unwilling to stand still.

Niama felt the unease deepen. Animals noticed things long before people did.

No sound came from inside. No music. No laughter. Only the flicker of light behind grimy glass.

Niama dismounted. Cold crawled up her spine as her hand closed around the door latch, damp with sweat against the chilled metal.

This is only a tavern, she told herself.

The door opened.

Rot hit her first.

Then blood.

It smeared the walls. Pooled across the floor. Darkened every surface it touched. Her boots squeaked as she stepped inside, the sound sharp and obscene in the stillness.

She didn't imagine the violence. She didn't need to.

Whatever had come through here had not hurried.

Niama staggered back outside, breath tearing loose as she dragged in air that still tasted wrong. The smell clung to her clothes. To her hands.

'We can't stay,' she said, voice shaking. 'Everyone's dead.'

The word fell heavy between them.

Kesaahn didn't argue.

Back on the cart, Niama's thoughts churned. The tavern replayed itself without mercy. Blood on stone. Bodies folded where they'd fallen. The quiet after.

Kesaahn snapped the reins.

The wagon surged forward, wheels rattling hard over ruts. Niama gripped the cart's edge as it lurched, knuckles whitening. Each jolt jarred breath loose from her lungs. Wind tore at her hair, cold and sharp. She shut her eyes, but the images followed anyway.

Fear pressed close, relentless. Whatever had done that had not been a beast acting on hunger alone. The certainty settled heavy in her chest. The world had shifted. She could feel it. There would be no returning to how things had been.

'It's alright,' Kesaahn said quietly. 'You're safe now. What did you see?'

Niama swallowed. 'Something large,' she said. 'Strong.' Her voice dropped. 'Even the dogs didn't escape.'

Silence followed. Only the cart's creak and Nancy's steady breathing filled the space as the light thinned and Barewallow slipped behind them.

The road narrowed, dipping into a shallow gully. A single-lane bridge lay ahead, spanning a slow creek before climbing again toward open ground.

Kesaahn slowed.

Something stood in the road.

'Do you see that?' Niama asked.

A figure waited at the far end of the bridge, motionless. One arm hung low, holding something that swung gently. From beneath the trees, a pair of green eyes caught the fading light.

Too bright.

Too intent.

'Whoa, Nancy,' Kesaahn murmured, reins tightening.

The figure dropped what it held.

For half a breath, it remained upright.

Then it came apart into motion and lunged.

It came on all fours, fast, its growl tearing the quiet apart. The air filled with damp earth and a rank, unfamiliar musk. There was no time to move.

It struck Nancy hard.

The impact cracked like wood on stone.

Nancy screamed once, high and panicked, and for a terrible instant Niama thought she would bolt.

Then the horse reared and went down hard.

'No!' Niama cried.

The creature loomed where Nancy had fallen, breath rasping like grinding rock. In the dim light she saw it fully now. Tall. Wrongly shaped. Scales stretched tight over bone. Fingers too long. A crocodilian skull grinned back at her, fangs slick and bared.

Niama couldn't move.

Whatever this was, it had come to finish what Barewallow had begun.

Kesaahn's hand flew to her mouth. 'A gauntillia,' she breathed. 'But how?'

The word sent a jolt through Niama. 'A gauntillia?' Disbelief curdled in her chest.

Stories surfaced unbidden. Dark magika. Beasts that had fought beside *him* in the last great war. Creatures of legend, hunted to extinction or sealed away when the light prevailed.

Not this. Not here.

The gauntillia growled, thick drool spilling from its maw as it lowered its head. Its eyes fixed on them, intent sharpening.

'Niama, distract it!' Kesaahn shouted, already digging through her satchel.

Niama leapt from the cart, bow in hand. She loosed an arrow mid-stride.

It glanced off the creature's skull.

Another followed. Useless. The gauntillia roared, rage flaring as it surged toward her.

'Cos!' she shouted. 'Move!'

He didn't.

Niama didn't shout again.

He sat frozen in the cart, lips curled in something that was almost a smile. She understood then that hesitation was no longer the danger.

The gauntillia charged.

Niama ran.

Branches tore at her arms as she veered through the trees, the creature's breath hot at her back. She fired as she ran, arrows meant not to kill but to draw it, to keep it away from Kesaahn.

A glimpse back. Coseo, still seated. Still smiling.

One misstep would end them both.

'Found it!' Kesaahn bellowed.

A glass bottle flared in her hand. Words spilled from her mouth, sharp and precise.

Fire exploded.

The blast struck the gauntillia's back, searing scale and flesh. It screamed, a sound like splitting iron, and wheeled toward Kesaahn.

Niama saw it then. A patch where the fire had burned through, raw and pink beneath the scales.

She drew. Aimed. Released.

The arrow sank deep. Black ichor spilled as the creature shrieked again.

It lunged.

Another fireball struck its flank, staggering it. Niama loosed again, breath steady now, fear honed into focus. The gauntillia dropped to one knee.

Kesaahn's last blast caught its head, snapping it sideways.

The gauntillia swayed.

For one awful second, Niama thought it would keep coming.

Then she loosed.

She buried her final arrow between its eyes.

The gauntillia collapsed, its bulk shuddering once before going still.

For a moment, neither of them moved.

Niama wiped sweat from her brow, staring down at the body. Triumph tangled with revulsion, her pulse still racing.

Kesaahn stepped beside her, firelight fading from her eyes. 'Do you think it followed us?' Niama asked quietly. 'Barewallow... was this its work?'

'It's likely,' Kesaahn said. 'And worse for it.' Her jaw tightened. 'The darkness knows us now.'

Niama's gaze dropped to the scorched bottle in Kesaahn's hand.

'What was that?'

'A fireball potion,' Kesaahn said. 'Three charges only. Useful for getting out of trouble.' She turned the empty bottle in her hand. 'With my staff it's stronger, but too cumbersome to carry. I rarely bring it.'

Niama nodded, impressed despite herself.

They stood a moment longer, the gauntillia's body cooling at their feet, the wind threading through their hair. The road ahead felt suddenly longer. Yet for now, they still stood.

Triumph counted for something. It just didn't count for much.

They turned back toward the cart.

Coseo lounged at the rear, his back to them.

Niama swallowed. 'I don't understand why he didn't help.'

Kesaahn was quiet a moment. 'During the fight,' she said slowly, 'what did you see in his face?'

'Nothing,' Niama said. 'That's what frightened me.'

Kesaahn nodded. 'The Seekers need to see him. Before this goes further.'

She didn't say what "further" meant. She didn't need to.

Niama swallowed and nodded.

Nancy lifted her head, snorting softly, legs trembling as she struggled upright. A gash ran along her flank, shallow but bleeding.

'Can she travel?' Niama asked.

Kesaahn checked the wound quickly. 'She'll manage. But we'll need to take it easy for a while.'

'Easy, girl,' she murmured. 'You're safe.'

Behind her, metal scraped.

Kesaahn knelt beside the gauntillia, dagger working at its jaw.

'What are you doing?' Niama asked.

'Collecting,' Kesaahn said, grunting as she wrenched free a fang. 'Gauntillia teeth are rare. Valuable. And we can't leave this thing where someone might find it.'

The stench thickened as they dug. Rot and iron and burned flesh clung to the air. Niama covered her mouth with her sleeve, gagging as they hauled the carcass into the shallow grave.

They worked in silence.

When it was done, they covered the body quickly and moved on.

A short way down the road, they found what the creature had dropped.

Niama saw it before her mind caught up. A torso, half-hidden in the grass. Head severed cleanly. The cut was precise. Deliberate.

Not hunger. Something else.

She looked away. Her stomach turned.

As they passed, Niama noticed Coseo staring.

'Cos?' she said. 'Are you alright?'

No answer.

'Cos.'

He turned slowly.

For a moment, his face looked wrong. Pulled. Distorted by shadow and failing light. Niama's heart skipped.

Then he blinked, and the familiar lines returned.

Niama realized her hands were shaking.

She clenched them into fists until the tremor dulled.

'I'm fine,' he said. 'Just tired.'

Kesaahn didn't look convinced.

'Are you injured?' she asked.

'No.' His gaze shifted east. 'But I hear horses.'

Hooves thundered out of the dark.

A line of soldiers crested the road ahead, armor glinting dully as they reined in. The lead rider raised a hand.

'We've come from the city,' he called. 'There's been word of an animal attack in Barewallow.'

'You're too late,' Kesaahn said. Grief weighed her voice. 'No one survived. A gauntillia. We killed it about half a mile back.'

The soldiers erupted in shocked chatter.

'Silence in the ranks!' the captain barked.

His horse stamped nervously. Sweat and leather filled the air.

'A gauntillia?' he said. 'I thought them extinct.'

'They were,' Kesaahn replied. 'I am Lady Kesaahn of the Royal Court. I suggest you trust my word.'

The captain stiffened, then bowed. 'My apologies, Milady. My men will secure Barewallow.' He straightened. 'I'll ride with you myself. The road to the city shouldn't be taken lightly tonight.'

'I am Captain Aldric Marr,' he said. 'And you are?'

'Niama,' she said. 'And Coseo.'

Something loosened in Niama's chest.

Not relief. Not yet.

The captain studied Coseo closely.

'Elves,' he said. 'Far from home.'

'That is not your concern,' Kesaahn said coolly.

'Of course, Milady.'

She met his gaze. 'Have you seen any strangers on the road?'

'No,' he said. 'Only you.'

His eyes lingered on them a moment longer before he turned away.

He signaled sharply, and the soldiers wheeled their mounts and thundered back down the road, lanterns shrinking fast as Barewallow swallowed them whole.

Only one rider remained.

Captain Marr fell in beside the cart, pace measured, eyes never leaving the tree line. He did not offer reassurance. He did not speak.

The road ahead lay open, pale under the thinning light.

Niama did not relax.

She watched the dark between the trees, felt it watching back. Whatever had walked through Barewallow was gone, but the silence it left behind felt deliberate. Waiting.

Beside her, Coseo stared east, unblinking.

The night had paused.

It had not retreated. It was learning.

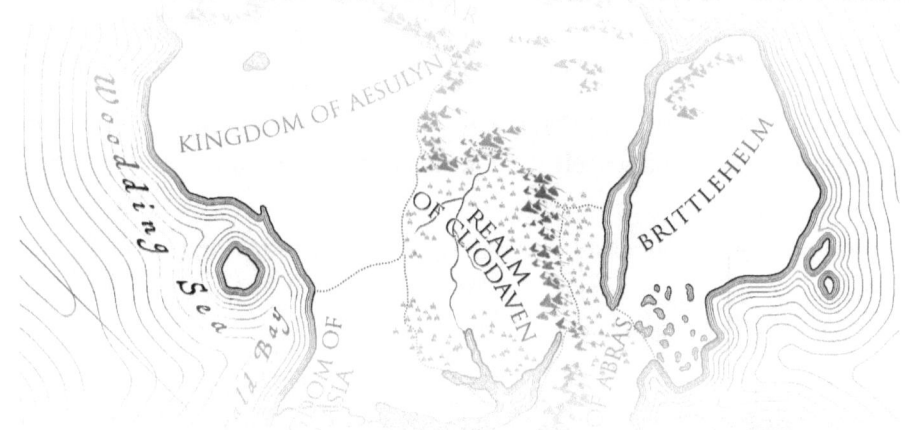

CHAPTER FOURTEEN

The Palace

Captain Aldric Marr rode alongside the cart, close enough that Niama could hear his horse's breathing. Dust rose and fell around his boots, never breaking his pace. Niama pulled her cloak tighter, though the chill along her spine had little to do with the night air.

The road stretched quiet ahead of them. Too quiet. Silence like that was rarely empty.

Since Barewallow, uncertainty had clung like burrs, catching on every thought. Marr kept pace without effort. His gaze moved constantly, not sweeping but cutting. Tree line. Road ahead. The space behind them. He did not look at the cart unless he had reason. Whatever protection he offered came without reassurance, and that, more than words, kept her alert. She trusted that more than promises.

The city rose at last on the horizon, its shape cutting clean against the stars. The whisper inside her eased, not gone, merely waiting. Silverfall was real now. Close enough to touch by morning.

They rode without urgency, but without pause.

Niama took the reins as the night deepened, fingers wrapped around the worn leather. Kesaahn slept for a time, head bowed, breath even. Niama welcomed the small duty. Movement kept thought at bay.

The air cooled as the heat bled from the land. Somewhere behind her, Coseo breathed slow and deep. Too deep. She listened longer than she meant to, then forced herself to look ahead. Watching him would change nothing.

Dawn crept in pale and uncertain. Kesaahn stirred, stretching stiff fingers.

'Did you rest?' Niama asked.

'Enough,' Kesaahn said. Her gaze drifted to the back of the cart. 'Coseo?'

'Still sleeping,' Niama said. 'Hasn't moved.'

Kesaahn watched him a moment longer than courtesy required, then nodded.

As the road widened, travelers appeared. Carts heavy with grain. Teams of oxen. Supply wagons rolling east in numbers that made Niama's mouth tighten. At the first bend where the road narrowed, Marr edged his horse forward without signaling, placing himself between the cart and the approaching travelers. He did not slow. He did not turn. Curious eyes lingered. Whispers followed. Elves drew attention no matter how quietly they traveled.

The closer they came, the more the land changed. The smell of salt threaded into the air, mixing with dust and animal sweat. Stone replaced grass. The road hardened beneath the wheels.

'There are more wagons than I expected,' Kesaahn said, low. 'All bound for the city.'

Marr did not look back. His shoulders stayed squared, his posture unchanged, as if the answer had already been weighed and filed away. 'The King ordered the storehouses filled. That is all I can say.'

It was enough.

Niama leaned closer to Kesaahn. 'The north isn't as distant as people pretend,' she murmured.

Kesaahn inclined her head. No argument. No comfort.

Silverfall rose fully now, its walls pale and sheer against the morning light. The sea gleamed beyond them, endless and cold. Niama had heard stories all her life. None had prepared her for the scale of it. The city did not welcome. It endured. Endurance, she thought, was not the same as mercy.

Banners snapped above the gates, the crowned lion caught in a stiff wind. Guards watched from the heights. Marr lifted his gaze just long enough to be seen, then returned his attention to the road ahead.

Marr adjusted his grip on the reins as they passed under the gate, a small motion, practiced and deliberate. Niama realized he had never once relaxed his hold since Barewallow.

The cart rolled beneath the portcullis, wood and iron swallowing sound as they passed through.

Niama felt the weight of it settle across her shoulders.

This was not refuge.

It was a threshold. Thresholds demanded payment.

As they moved deeper into Silverfall's cobbled streets, Niama's heart beat hard against her ribs. Buildings rose on either side, stone and glass climbing higher than anything she had known. Stained windows caught the light and fractured it into color. The press of carts and bodies closed in around them, noise colliding from every direction. The smells of bread and roasting meat were thick enough to taste, overwhelming in their abundance.

For all its splendor, the city made her feel small. Small enough to be overlooked. Or crushed.

Coseo stared openly, wonder and disorientation writ plain across his face. Kesaahn remained composed, her gaze moving with practiced caution, cataloguing streets and faces alike. When she quietly named their destination to Captain Marr, Niama released a breath she hadn't realized she'd been holding.

'We may be safer here,' Niama said, low. 'But we should not forget why we've come. Whatever hunts beyond the forest does not end at stone walls.'

Her eyes were drawn again to the markets, the laughter drifting from somewhere unseen. 'The elders' tales never spoke of this,' she murmured. 'Not truly.'

'Cities have a way of hiding their teeth,' Kesaahn said. 'Remember that.'

They stopped before a tall grey house set back from the street. Its stonework was old, the carvings worn smooth by time rather than neglect. Captain Marr dismounted first and offered Kesaahn his hand. Niama was already at the door, Coseo trailing behind her with a wide, poorly stifled yawn.

'You have our thanks for your escort, Captain,' Kesaahn said.

Marr inclined his head. His boots rang once against the stone as he turned back to his horse, already withdrawing.

Kesaahn ushered them inside. 'Make yourselves comfortable. I'll request an emergency council session. Roderick will see to you while I'm gone.'

The door closed behind her, the sounds of the city muffled at once.

Relief came, but it was thin. Temporary.

A man stepped forward from the hallway.

He moved with a cane, but not as someone who relied on it. Each tap was measured, placed with intent. Deep lines cut his face, not from frailty but from attention paid over many years. His silver hair was neatly bound back, his eyes sharp and unhurried as they passed from Niama to Coseo, then lingered on the cart dust still clinging to their boots.

'Roderick?' Coseo ventured.

The man did not answer at once. His gaze dipped briefly to Niama's hands, the calluses there, the faint nick along one knuckle. Then to Coseo's pack, buckled twice where once would have done.

'You are unexpected, Milady,' he said at last. 'You weren't due back for another week.'

Kesaahn's expression didn't change. 'Plans shifted. We'll need the council sooner than expected.'

Roderick inclined his head. 'Of course.' His gaze moved to Niama and Coseo. 'Follow me.'

He led them into a chamber just off the hall. Bookshelves climbed the walls, dense and uneven, some volumes worn to softness, others untouched. A fire burned low in the hearth, banked rather than blazing. The room was warm, but not indulgent.

'Sit,' he said. 'You'll want strength if Lady Kesaahn calls you before the council.'

Niama hesitated only a fraction before moving. Coseo followed.

'Refreshments?' he asked.

'Yes, please,' Niama said.

'Wine, then.' A pause. 'Unless you prefer water.'

Niama met his gaze. 'Water is fine.'

When he returned, the tray was balanced effortlessly on one hand. Bread still warm. Cheese sharp enough to sting the tongue. Fruit cut cleanly, no waste. He placed it within easy reach, then stepped back.

'Eat,' he said. 'Rest.'

He turned and left, the cane's rhythm steady, unhurried, already elsewhere in thought.

They ate in silence at first, savoring more than the food. When Niama finally spoke, her voice was softer.

'If our people could see this place...'

Coseo shook his head. 'It's impressive. But it isn't ours.'

She reached for his hand. He squeezed back, grounding, familiar.

'No,' she said. 'It isn't.'

Beyond the walls, the city continued to breathe. Somewhere deeper still, unseen and unheard, something waited. It always did.

As the sun slid low, staining the chamber gold, the doors creaked open.

'We must prepare,' Kesaahn said. 'The council convenes tonight.'

Coseo stirred on the divan, rubbing sleep from his eyes. 'Alright,' he murmured. 'Let's—'

'No,' Kesaahn cut in, gentle but absolute. 'Not you.'

He blinked. Niama turned toward her.

'The council permits one,' Kesaahn continued. 'Niama will attend.'

'But we both spoke to the Seer,' Niama said.

Kesaahn nodded once. 'And you carry what matters.'

She gestured, and Roderick stepped forward without a word.

'Coseo should rest,' Kesaahn said. 'Roderick will see to him.'

Coseo rose. He did not argue. He did not look at Niama as he followed Roderick from the room.

The door closed.

She wanted to call after him. Didn't.

Kesaahn leaned in, her voice lowered. 'The court does not yet know what he is. Until they do, we do not place him before them.'

Niama swallowed. 'You think he's dangerous.'

'I think he is unfinished,' Kesaahn said. 'And the royal family cannot afford uncertainty.'

She straightened. 'The King and Prince will receive us. There is unrest in the city. We go clean. We go unarmed. We speak carefully.'

She turned and led Niama down the corridor.

A small chamber waited at the end. Steam curled faintly from a basin. Water murmured as it spilled over stone.

'Wash,' Kesaahn said. 'I will return.'

Niama undressed slowly. The water was cool, then warm, then steady. It carried the road from her skin but not from her thoughts.

Lavender rose with the steam. Familiar. Almost painful.

The medallion rested against her chest, heavier than it should have been. When she touched it, the metal felt cold, dense, as though it remembered more than she did.

Darkness seeks this, the Seer had said.

Niama breathed through it and rinsed again.

When she dressed, her armor lay waiting. Clean. Oiled. Too perfect, given the hours that had passed.

Roderick stood by the door, already turning away. She murmured her thanks. He inclined his head and was gone.

She cinched her belt.

A knock.

'Are you ready?' Kesaahn asked.

Niama opened the door. 'I think so.'

Kesaahn studied her. Not unkindly. Not warmly. Like a piece set on a board.

'Better,' she said. Then, without ceremony, she reached out and removed Niama's dagger.

The weight left her side.

Then, without asking, lifted the bow from her shoulder and set it aside.

'The court forbids weapons. The guards will decide what protection looks like.'

She held Niama's gaze a moment longer. 'From here on, every word matters.'

She turned toward the hall.

'Welcome to Silverfall's true danger,' she added softly.

'One moment,' Kesaahn said.

She stepped aside to speak with Roderick, their voices low. Niama caught only fragments. A name. Coseo's.

When Kesaahn returned, Niama didn't wait. 'What was that?'

'Roderick checked on him,' Kesaahn said. 'He's asleep. Deeply.'

Niama frowned. 'And the guards?'

'A precaution,' Kesaahn replied evenly.

'Against Coseo?'

Kesaahn shook her head. 'Against anyone who might come looking. They won't know which of us carries the medallion. That uncertainty makes everyone dangerous.'

Niama absorbed that in silence.

Together, Niama and Kesaahn walked toward the hall.

Outside, torchlight flared against steel.

Two armored soldiers stood at attention. Beyond them waited a black carriage edged in gold, its lacquered sides drinking in the firelight. Four riders flanked it, motionless as carved figures. The driver stood ready, reins gathered, eyes forward.

They climbed inside.

The door shut. The latch fell

The carriage rolled.

Silverfall passed in fragments. Shuttered windows. Narrow alleys. Lanterns swinging like watchful eyes. The city felt muted, as though holding something back.

The wheels jolted.

'Halt,' a voice rang out. 'In the King's name.'

The carriage slowed.

Niama's breath caught.

A reply came sharp and immediate. 'Stand aside.'

Steel rang.

The sound was close. Too close.

Kesaahn did not move.

Outside, horses shifted. Boots struck stone. A command barked low and final.

'Stay inside,' a guard called.

Niama leaned forward despite herself. Through the narrow window she saw blades drawn, riders forming a barrier, bodies angling outward toward the dark.

Then it was over.

Orders snapped. Hooves turned. The carriage lurched forward again.

As they rounded the corner, Niama glimpsed two shapes crumpled in shadow. Black cloaks. Stillness where movement should have been.

The smell reached her a heartbeat later.

Blood.

'Who were they?' she whispered.

Kesaahn's jaw tightened. 'Someone who found us sooner than they should have.'

Niama's mind raced. The mystery man at the inn. Now this. Whoever served the darkness had eyes in the city itself.

'Does the King know?' she asked.

'He will,' Kesaahn said. Her voice was steady, but her hands were not.

The palace gates rose ahead.

Stone. Iron. Discipline made visible.

Soldiers lined the walls at measured intervals. Inside, gardens bloomed under torchlight, carefully contained beauty pressed into order. White statues watched from their plinths. Somewhere beyond, steel rang as guards drilled in the courtyard.

The carriage slowed.

Niama's pulse had not.

She touched the glass, grounding herself in its cold. *This is real,* she told herself. *This is happening.*

'Ever met a king?' Kesaahn asked, lightness threading her voice.

Niama swallowed. 'No.'

'Then listen more than you speak,' Kesaahn said. 'Truth only. No speculation. And never turn your back.'

Niama nodded. 'Simple enough.'

Kesaahn smiled faintly. 'Nothing about this is simple.'

The carriage stopped.

The door opened.

Torchlight spilled in.

Niama stepped down, the palace rising before her in pale stone and shadow. The air felt heavier here, as if weighed by centuries of secrets.

She followed Kesaahn toward the doors.

The night did not follow them in.

But Niama felt it waiting.

CHAPTER FIFTEEN

The Council

Niama faced the palace gates.

Iron rose before her in sheer planes and riveted seams, their height less decorative than declarative. Power made solid. Stone never pretended to be kind. She swallowed, breath tightening as the scale of it settled into her bones. This was no forest threshold. In the forest, at least, the trees did not lie.

She steadied herself.

The prophecy did not care for comfort. Neither could she.

Torchlight played across carved crests and ancient sigils worked into the stone. Flowers crowded the entrance in careful abundance, their sweetness heavy in the air, braided with incense, clean linen, and the faint musk of bodies moving with purpose. Luxury pressed close, practiced and deliberate.

She crossed the threshold.

Marble took her weight, cold and unyielding beneath her boots. The sound of her steps echoed, swallowed, returned. Walls rose high around her, dressed in tapestries of battle and bloodless triumph, victories rendered orderly by thread and pigment. Above, the vaulted ceiling caught firelight and fractured it, the painted figures seeming to shift as shadows moved.

Wax and smoke lingered, the scent of vigilance disguised as ceremony.

'Impressive, is it not?' Kesaahn said quietly.

Niama nodded. Words felt inadequate. Awe was present, yes, but edged with caution. Grandeur, she was learning, often existed to remind you where you stood.

An attendant led them into a side chamber. Thick carpets softened their steps. Dark wood gleamed beneath careful polish. A chandelier cast a warm, controlled glow that did not quite reach the corners. The man bowed, informed them the King would receive them shortly, then withdrew without sound.

They were not alone. The air felt crowded with decisions.

Five figures waited, robed in silver and gold. Conversation died as Niama entered. Eyes assessed. Measured. Weighed.

Kesaahn stepped forward. 'Niama,' she said, 'the Royal Council.'

The first was Lord Bernard. Age had softened him, not diminished him. His hair was silvered, his beard neatly kept. When he took Niama's hands, his grip was gentle but firm, skin rough with years.

'It's a pleasure,' he said, voice warm, practiced. 'I've known many of your people. Elves make memorable company.'

There was something behind the smile. Not unkind. Not fully open.

Niama inclined her head. 'You honor me, Lord Bernard.'

Next came Lord Simpkin. Tall and narrow, his robes hung too loosely from his frame. Dark spectacles hid his eyes, but his tension showed elsewhere. In the tightness of his mouth. The crease between his brows. He studied her as if she were a ledger he did not like the numbers in.

'These are troubled days,' he said. 'We place great hope in what you bring.'

It was not reassurance he sought.

It was confirmation.

Niama inclined her head. 'It is my hope as well,' she said, carefully. Hope was safe. Promises were not.

Kesaahn turned next to Lady Edelina.

She carried herself with an ease that did not ask permission. Dark curls framed her face in deliberate disorder, her green eyes sharp but welcoming. Strength showed in her posture more than her features. The faint scent of lilac followed her movements, subtle rather than indulgent.

'Niama,' Edelina said warmly. 'Your journey here was not a small thing. We are grateful.'

The sincerity caught Niama off guard. She felt something ease in her chest. 'Thank you, milady.'

Next came Lord Ingeram.

He was compact and rigid, built like a man who had learned long ago how to hold a line. His eyes were hard, assessing. Leather and steel clung to him despite the finery of court.

'The King awaits what you carry,' he said. 'Time grows short.'

It was not encouragement. It was expectation.

Niama nodded. 'Then I will speak plainly.'

Lady Metylda followed. Tall and composed, a streak of silver cut through her auburn hair, bound tight from her face. Her gaze lingered longer than courtesy required, thoughtful rather than hostile. The scent of spice clung to her robes, warm and grounding.

'Dark days,' Metylda murmured. 'May Athris guide us.'

Niama inclined her head. 'May his light hold.'

The words felt heavier here.

The door opened.

The room shifted as one.

The Prince had been delayed. No one said so. No one needed to.

'My liege,' the council said, voices folding into reverence. His bearing was assured without display, his presence drawing the room into alignment around him. Blond hair, clean-cut features, blue eyes that missed very little. The red lion stitched over his chest caught the torchlight as he moved.

He stopped before her.

'You must be Niama,' he said. 'Prince Rohan.' His smile was practiced, but not false.

He took her hand, bowed, and brushed his lips against her knuckles. The gesture was brief. Correct. Intimate only by tradition. Tradition, she thought, was just another kind of leash.

'Your Highness,' Niama said, steadying herself.

'Shall we join my father?' Rohan asked, already turning.

Kesaahn inclined her head. 'That would be wise.'

The doors to the court opened.

They passed beneath carved lions locked in perpetual snarl. Guards flanked the entrance, motionless behind polished steel. The air inside was cooler, heavier, carrying stone and age and the faint trace of old incense.

Rohan offered his arm. Niama accepted, aware of every watching eye.

The chamber opened wide around them. A long table waited beneath hanging banners and layered histories. Lords and Ladies took their places with quiet precision.

Niama remained standing a heartbeat longer than the rest.

Expectation settled over her like a measured weight.

And somewhere beneath it, something older stirred, patient and unseen.

'Remain here,' the Prince said quietly, releasing her hand. 'My father will join us directly.'

He took his place behind the table.

The doors at the far end of the chamber opened with a low groan.

The room stood as one.

The King entered without haste. He was broad through the shoulders, his years carried in weight rather than weakness. Torchlight caught in the lines of his face, carving it into something both familiar and formidable. His gaze fixed on Niama at once and did not waver.

The air went still.

'Forgive my delay,' he said, voice deep enough to settle the chamber. 'Matters do not pause simply because prophecy arrives at the gate.' A pause. 'You have not waited long.'

Niama shook her head. 'No, Your Majesty.'

He approached Niama and placed his hands over hers, firm and warm, the gesture deliberate rather than gentle. She felt the pressure, the measure of him.

'Niama,' he said. 'You are welcome here. I regret the cause of it. I have spoken often with your elders. Thoughtful people. Careful ones.' He released her and stepped back. 'Let us hope their judgment was sound.'

He turned and seated himself beside the Prince.

'Begin,' the King said. 'Tell us what the Seer showed you. Spare nothing. Even fragments matter.'

Niama drew a breath and spoke.

She told them of the cave. The waiting. The transformation. Light where flesh should have been. The words that had not been words at all. She spoke of the prophecy as it had been given, unpolished, unsoftened. If it offended them, it deserved to.

No one interrupted.

When she finished, the silence held for a heartbeat longer than comfort allowed.

Then the council stirred.

Low voices crossed the table. Names were weighed. Symbols pulled apart.

'The Lion is clear,' Lord Ingeram said. 'The Crown.' His gaze flicked to the Prince. 'The Raven remains uncertain.'

'The Seekers will know more,' Lady Metylda said.

'And the Staff?' Edelina asked. 'Even if found, its use is not without cost.'

The room shifted again, tension tightening.

The King let it build, then cut it cleanly. 'Armies alone will not be sufficient. We have prepared for war. But preparation is not victory.'

Niama's fingers closed around the medallion beneath her shirt.

She drew it free and lifted it into the torchlight.

Light spilled outward, warm and steady, scattering gold across stone and silk.

No one spoke. Reverence and hunger wore the same face.

'The Seer gave me this,' she said. 'Whatever comes next begins here.'

The Prince leaned forward slightly, interest sharpening. 'That he entrusted it to you speaks plainly.'

Niama met his gaze. 'Its purpose remains unclear. Only that it matters.'

Lady Metylda exhaled slowly. 'The Seekers will know more.'

The King studied the medallion without reaching for it. 'Then they will be consulted.'

He straightened.

'We have reports from the east,' he continued. 'Villages burned. The Namites of Aesulyn pushed back across their borders. Small engagements. Nothing decisive.'

Niama spoke before she could stop herself. 'The Seer warned of a greater will. A dark master.'

A murmur rippled the table.

Lord Ingeram frowned. 'Implied, not named.'

Niama flushed, then steadied. 'He was clear. The invasion begins when the shadow calls.'

The King's gaze narrowed. 'Did he name this master?'

'No,' Niama said. 'Only that the light knows it comes. Not the form it will wear.'

Silence returned, heavier now.

The King leaned back, fingers steepled. 'Then we stand at the edge of something unfinished.'

His eyes returned to Niama.

'And you,' he said quietly, 'stand at its center.'

He let the weight of that settle before asking,

'Is there anything else you have not yet told us?'

The torches cracked softly.

Niama held the medallion tighter.

And wondered, for the first time, whether the question itself was the danger.

Niama glanced toward Kesaahn before continuing.

'In Barewallow,' she said, 'we found no survivors. The town had been emptied with intent, not haste. We fled east. Not far beyond the road, we were intercepted by a creature. Lady Kesaahn identified it as a gauntillia.'

The word did not echo.

It unsettled.

Whispers stirred the chamber, low and quick, like dry leaves disturbed by a careless step. Niama felt the shift immediately. These were not villagers weighing rumor. These were people whose disbelief carried consequence.

Lady Edelina rose sharply. 'Impossible.'

Lord Ingeram followed, voice clipped. 'Gauntillia have been extinct since the last war.'

Niama held her ground. She had seen the thing breathe. Heard it scream.

The King's hand struck the table once.

Silence fell.

He turned to Kesaahn. 'Can you confirm this?'

Kesaahn stepped forward without haste. 'Yes, Your Majesty. Without doubt.' She reached into her satchel and placed several dark, jagged teeth on the table. 'I took these myself.'

The room leaned in as one.

'Captain Aldric Marr of your guard escorted us here,' Kesaahn continued. 'He ordered his men to secure Barewallow. Without Niama, I would not be standing before you now.'

The King studied the teeth, his expression closing like a door.

'How was the creature slain?' he asked.

'Through preparation and nerve,' Kesaahn replied. 'And Niama's resolve.'

She did not look at Niama when she said it, but Niama felt the weight of the words settle anyway. Not praise. Recognition.

'An account we will hear again,' the King said. 'Later.' His gaze returned to Niama. 'Continue.'

The Prince spoke next. 'Why do you think the Seer chose you?'

Niama hesitated. The room waited.

'I don't know,' she said finally. 'I was a huntress. Nothing more.'

The King looked to his son. 'We do not measure the Seer's choices by comfort.' He turned back to Niama. 'And we do not mistake humility for smallness.'

His voice softened, just enough to unsettle her further.

'History rarely chooses those who seek it. It chooses those who endure.'

Niama lowered her eyes, the medallion heavy against her chest.

If that were true, she wondered what endurance would cost.

And whether the choice had already been made for her.

Niama felt it press against her, heavy and deliberate. The council's attention was no longer curious. It was evaluative. As if they were weighing not just her words, but her capacity to endure what those words implied.

The King cleared his throat. The sound carried.

Torches hissed softly along the walls. Perfumed oils lingered beneath the heavier scent of wax and old stone. Niama reached for the thought of home without meaning to. Hearth smoke. Bread torn by hand. Children's laughter drifting between trees.

She let it go.

'You will have our support,' the King said at last. 'Such as we can give.'

He rose from his throne.

The movement stilled the room.

His robes whispered as he crossed the floor, each step measured. The scent of leather and polished steel followed him. When he stopped before her, Niama felt suddenly, acutely seen.

'The fate of Arghost does not rest on prophecy alone,' he said. 'It rests on those willing to act when certainty is denied.' His gaze did not soften. 'If you succeed, history will remember you. If you fail—' He paused. 'History will not be written at all.'

Murmurs of agreement rippled through the remaining councilors.

Lady Kesaahn rose.

'Before any blade is drawn,' she said, 'the prophecy must be understood.' She met the King's gaze. 'The Seekers. The Isle of Thunder.'

Niama inclined her head. 'We cannot move blindly. Not against this.'

The King was quiet a moment. 'Granted,' he said. 'And my son will accompany you.' His gaze shifted to Prince Rohan. 'If the Lion is named, then he cannot stand apart from what follows.'

Niama's breath caught despite herself.

Rohan bowed once. No hesitation. No protest.

'The Isle of Thunder is not reached lightly,' the King continued. 'The passage has claimed many who believed themselves ready. You will not be afforded the luxury of choosing ideal circumstances.'

He raised his hand. 'The rest of you may go. I will speak further with these three.'

The council rose as one. Robes whispered. Chairs scraped softly. Concern lingered in their glances as they filed out.

The doors closed.

The chamber felt smaller.

The King did not return to his throne.

'In times such as these,' he said quietly, 'trust becomes a liability.' He looked between them. 'You are being hunted.'

Niama stiffened. 'Hunted by whom?'

'The Order of the Fallen Phoenix.'

The name settled poorly in the air.

Niama felt it prickle along her skin. 'I've never heard of them.'

'Few have,' the King said. 'They draw members from many races. Their purpose is unclear. Their methods are not.' His mouth tightened. 'They will stop at nothing to prevent what you carry from fulfilling its role.'

He turned slightly, as if addressing the room itself.

'They are patient. Embedded. Difficult to expose.' His gaze returned to Niama. 'I suspect they move within my walls even now. But suspicion is not proof, and proof is what power requires.'

The implication hung unspoken.

You are not safe here.

Not even now.

The torches crackled.

Niama felt the medallion rest cold and solid against her skin.

And understood, with a clarity that left no room for comfort, that the world had already begun to close around her choices.

Niama's breath caught as the weight of the King's words settled. Fear did not rush her. It seeped in, cold and deliberate, tightening around her ribs.

'Sire,' Kesaahn said, breaking the silence. 'The escort met two cloaked men on the road tonight.'

The King's expression hardened. 'Then this confirms it.'

He stepped back, voice lowering. 'From this moment, you are no one of consequence. You will speak no names. You will claim no titles.' Names, she realized, were a kind of beacon. His gaze held on Kesaahn, then shifted to the Prince. 'Not even yours.'

Niama's stomach turned as he continued. 'Niama, the Seer has placed leadership upon you. Kesaahn, your house is compromised. You will not return there tonight.' A pause. 'I've prepared a refuge. Clothing. Coin. Provisions.'

Niama swallowed. 'And Coseo?'

'He will be brought to you,' the King said. 'With your weapons. Quietly.'

He did not soften his tone. 'This is all we can do without drawing attention. From here, you move alone. You will find your own passage to the Isle of Thunder.'

'We understand,' Niama and Kesaahn said together.

The King turned before doubt could follow.

He opened a narrow door Niama hadn't noticed. The passage beyond was dim and close. She followed, senses sharpened, every sound magnified. Warm air rose as they descended. The smell of roasted meat and spice gave way to damp stone and grain.

They passed through the stores and out a low service door.

A hay wagon waited in shadow, driver still as stone.

The King pressed black cloaks into their hands. 'Wear these.' His voice softened, only slightly. 'Athris guide you.'

He turned to the Prince. 'You go not as royalty, but as a man. Prove yourself worthy of both.'

'As you command,' the Prince said, bowing.

The King's hand rested briefly on his shoulder. 'Remember—nobility is chosen.'

They climbed into the wagon.

Hay scratched at Niama's skin as she settled beneath it. The smell of dry grass and old wood filled her lungs. She stilled her breathing as the driver clicked his tongue and the wagon lurched forward.

Cobblestones rattled beneath the wheels.

Niama parted the hay just enough to see.

Silverfall passed in fragments. Lanternlight. Laughing voices. Doors opening. Lives continuing, unaware. The sound of it tightened something in her chest. This city would sleep tonight. Others already lay dead. She wondered how many times it had done so before.

She closed her eyes.

Buildings loomed as the wagon wound through narrow streets, shadows stacking deep between stone walls. The night felt watchful. Expectant.

Niama clenched her hands in the hay, grounding herself in its coarse bite. The Order. The medallion. The weight of command she had never asked for.

She whispered a prayer to Athris, not for safety, but for clarity.

The wagon slowed.

The driver spoke without turning. 'One at a time. Right. Through the door.'

Niama's pulse thundered.

They slipped down into darkness, silent as breath. The wagon rolled on, its sound fading until it was swallowed by the city.

Niama did not look back.

Whatever waited ahead would not be faced from the shadows.

The house was small, two stories tucked close to the street, its slate roof worn thin by years of weather. Inside, a narrow hall opened to a modest kitchen on one side and a sitting room on the other. A fire burned low in the hearth, warmth rolling outward in quiet waves. The furniture was old, scuffed smooth by use. The air smelled of woodsmoke and candle wax.

It felt lived in. That mattered.

Coseo stood near the table, a mug cradled in both hands. Steam curled upward, carrying the familiar bite of herbs. Niama felt some of the tightness ease from her chest at the sight of him.

'You made it,' he said.

'Barely,' Niama replied. 'We can't stay long.'

Prince Rohan stepped forward, posture straight, expression composed despite the hour. 'I've given thought to our next move.'

Coseo's gaze slid to him, measuring. 'And you are?'

Niama hesitated only a breath. 'Rohan. He's traveling with us.'

That was all she offered.

Rohan inclined his head, voice calm, practiced. 'Niama speaks highly of you.'

Coseo grunted, unconvinced, but turned back to Niama. 'Traveling where?'

'The Isle of Thunder,' she said quietly. 'We'll explain. But first we need a way off this coast.'

Rohan nodded. 'There's a tavern by the docks. The Wheel and Anchor. If there's a captain willing to sail without questions, we'll find them there. Discretion costs coin. Fortunately, we have it.'

Niama listened, fingers resting against the scarred tabletop, committing every word to memory.

'Not tonight,' Kesaahn said. Her voice cut through the room, gentle but firm. 'You're all exhausted. Rest. We move at first light.'

No one argued.

They took the stairs in silence. Niama's legs ached with the effort. When she reached her room, the door closed softly behind her, shutting the world out at last.

Her gear waited on the bed.

Black leather armor. New boots. A darker cloak with a deep hood. Rope. A heavier quiver. Coin and provisions packed tight and efficient. The smell of fresh leather filled the room as she lifted the armor, testing its weight. Lighter than it looked. Stronger than what she'd worn before.

She fastened the straps, movements automatic, familiar. The fit was good. Too good. As if someone had known exactly what she needed. Being anticipated did not feel like being protected.

A new bow lay beside the rest. Dark wood, beautifully balanced.

Niama's hand passed over it and went instead to her own. The one she'd made. The grip worn smooth by years of use. It settled against her palm like memory.

She slung it over her shoulder and went downstairs.

The others waited.

Coseo stood ready, jaw set. Rohan had traded court finery for travel leathers, the lion crest gone. Kesaahn stood apart, dressed in black edged with deep violet, a sword at her hip and her staff in hand. The carvings along its length caught the firelight, old and deliberate.

Niama took them in, one by one.

'Ready?' she asked.

They answered without flourish.

'Then we go,' Niama said. 'Rohan, lead us.'

They stepped back into the city.

Night still clung to Silverfall, but the streets were alive now. Voices. Footsteps. The distant clang of metal and the smell of salt drifting up from the docks. Niama moved with purpose, senses tight and alert.

Whatever waited at the Wheel and Anchor, it would not be friendly.

But it would be necessary.

And necessity, she was learning, did not care who you had been before.

From somewhere down the street came a sudden shout, cut short just as quickly.

Niama didn't slow.

No one did.

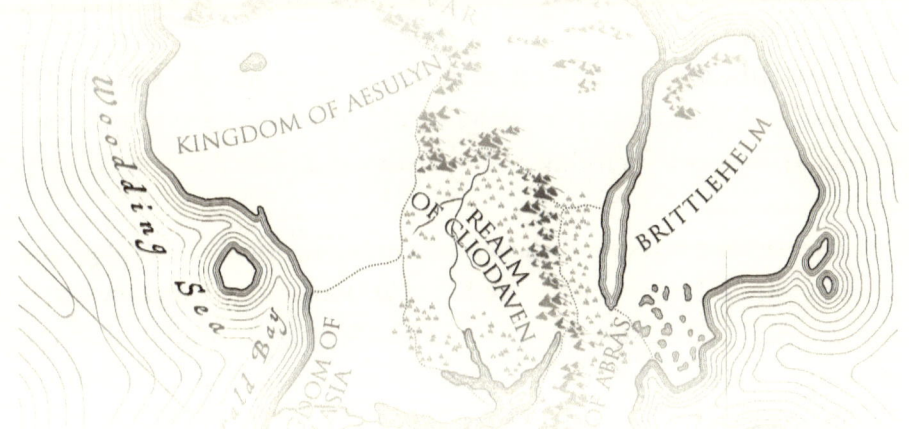

CHAPTER SIXTEEN

The Cell

The Pteradiabus struck the ground with a thunderous shriek, its impact hurling Valran across frozen stone. Snow and ice exploded outward, driven by the brutal downwash of its wings. He clamped his hands over his ears as the sound tore through the ruins, echoing off broken walls and hollow towers.

Pain bloomed where its talons had seized him. Deep. Throbbing. A reminder of how easily the creature had lifted him from the sky.

Valran pushed himself upright, breath rasping in the cold. Fear clawed at his chest, but he forced it down. Panic wasted air. He needed all of it. Fear could stay. It just wasn't allowed to drive.

The city around him lay in ruin. Once-grand structures sagged beneath the weight of snow, beams bowed and splintered. Pillars lay shattered across the ground, statues reduced to faceless torsos half-buried in ice. The air smelled of rot beneath the clean bite of frost.

Then came the voice.

Bastion's call slithered through the wreckage, and something large shifted in response. A hulking shape emerged from behind a collapsed wall, its presence heavy enough to be felt before it was seen. The ruin seemed to make room for it.

A Swinish.

The word surfaced unbidden, dragged up from old stories and blood-soaked histories. Valran swallowed. He had hoped never to see one outside the songs of warning and the half-remembered horrors of past wars.

The creature advanced, each step sending dull vibrations through the frozen ground. Its shoulders were broad as doors, muscle packed dense beneath pallid green skin and clotted fur. Heat rolled from it in waves, sharp against the cold. When it stopped before him, its breath washed over Valran, thick with the stench of fresh kill.

Jagged teeth crowded its snout. Steam poured from its mouth with every slow exhale. Around its neck hung a grisly necklace, trophies taken from those who had not survived its grip.

Valran held his ground. Moving now would only amuse it.

A voice sounded behind him.

'Take the hunter man to the cells.'

Valran turned.

Bastion stood amid the rubble, tail coiling lazily behind him, eyes alight with cruel delight. 'I'll see you soon, friend,' he said lightly. 'Perhaps we'll have some fun.' Bastion spoke like pain was a hobby.

His laughter lingered even after he vanished into the ruins.

The Swinish's hand closed around Valran's arm.

Cold. Iron-hard.

He was hauled forward before he could brace, dragged into the shell of a once-resplendent building. Faceless statues lined the entrance, their features worn smooth by time and violence. Tiles cracked beneath his boots as he stumbled through the lobby, then down rough stone steps carved directly into the earth.

The creature sniggered as it pulled him along.

Below, the air changed. Damp. Stale.

Torchlight flickered along a narrow corridor, shadows stretching and collapsing with each uneven flame. Four cells lined the walls, iron bars running from floor to ceiling. The Swinish shoved him into one without ceremony, sending him sprawling across cold stone and into a pile of mildewed hay.

The door slammed shut.

'Stay,' the creature rasped, breath wheezing with laughter. 'The dark master comes soon.'

Its footsteps retreated, heavy and unhurried.

Valran lay still, chest rising and falling as the stink of rot and old blood filled his lungs. The other cells stood empty. Beyond them, crates and sealed jars were stacked against the far wall, silent and waiting.

Valran closed his eyes once, briefly.

Then he opened them and began to listen.

As Valran's eyes adjusted to the gloom, the shape of the cell resolved around him. Two walls were rough-hewn stone, damp and cold to the touch. The third faced another cell, its iron bars thick with rust. High on the rear wall, a narrow window admitted a sliver of light, just enough to carve long, warped shadows across the floor.

A plank hung from chains driven into the stone, swaying faintly. Beneath it, the hay lay crushed thin.

Something shifted in the far corner.

'Is someone there?' Valran asked, keeping his voice steady.

A low chuckle answered him.

'Och, an' who's askin', then?' came a gravel-rough voice from the dark.

Valran leaned closer to the bars. 'I am Valran. An emissary of the Elves. And you?'

The figure stepped forward into the weak light.

A stocky man with a wild beard and iron threaded through his ears grinned back at him. 'Name's Dorsey,' he said, spreading his arms. 'An' welcome tae Alboros. Or what's left o' the once-bonny thing.'

Valran's gaze flicked around the cell. 'What happens here? What do they want of us?'

Dorsey snorted. 'Questions first, answers later. But tell me this, elf. Was that red devil skulkin' about when they dragged ye in?'

'Yes. He brought me himself.'

Dorsey's expression shifted, the humor draining from it. 'Did he, now?' He scratched at his beard. 'That's no small thing. Means they think ye're worth the trouble.'

Valran frowned. 'Forgive me. I don't understand. I was hunting. I lost my way.'

Dorsey barked a laugh. 'Aye, an' I'm the Queen o' Aesulyn. Bastion's no fool. He'll peel the truth out o' ye, one way or another.'

Valran's pulse quickened. 'What do you mean... peel?'

The air felt suddenly closer. Thicker. The stink of rot clawed at his throat.

Dorsey studied him a moment, then shrugged. 'Means don't expect kindness.' Valran had heard threats before. This felt like instruction.

Valran took in the man properly now. The tangled beard. The piercings. The hard, weathered eyes. Childhood tales surfaced unbidden. 'Are you a pirate?'

Dorsey scuffed the stone with his boot. 'That's a bit rude, that is.' A pause. 'Trader's the word I prefer. I just... trade things that already belong tae someone else.'

'That sounds like piracy.'

Dorsey waved it off. 'Words are a comfort folk cling tae.'

'How long have you been here?' Valran asked.

Dorsey's jaw tightened. 'Couple o' days. Maybe more. Time goes soft in places like this.' He leaned closer. 'Ye said the red one flew ye in. Means ye saw the city from above. Where'd he snatch ye from?'

'The forest of my people. I was tracking elk when he took me.'

'Elk, eh?' Dorsey smacked his lips. 'Fine meat.' Then, sharper, 'An' what else did ye see? Towers. Walls. Patrols.'

Valran shook his head. 'Snow. Ruin. Broken structures. Nothing of note.'

Dorsey knelt and brushed the remaining hay aside, exposing bare stone. 'Right then. Use this.' He pressed a loose rock into Valran's hand. 'Scratch out what ye remember. Rough's fine.'

Valran crouched and began to mark the floor. Fallen towers. Open courtyards. Breached walls.

'Guards?' Dorsey asked. 'How many?'

'Few,' Valran said. 'Scattered.'

Dorsey went very still. 'Few guards,' he repeated quietly. 'That changes things.' He leaned back, eyes narrowing. 'With horses, we could reach Aesulyn in three days.'

'I saw none.'

Dorsey grunted. 'Aye. Figures.'

He looked at the map again, then at Valran.

'Looks like ye're deeper in this than ye ken, elf.'

The torchlight flickered.

And somewhere above them, stone shifted, slow and deliberate.

Dorsey's expression darkened.

'No horses, then?' He blew out a slow breath. 'That's a curse an' a half. On foot, through snow an' ruin? Doubles the time tae Aesulyn. Maybe worse.'

He dropped onto the stone, the sound dull and final.

Valran took in the cell again. The sour reek of spoiled food. The hay ground thin to chaff. The cold seeping up from the floor, patient and relentless. The truth of it pressed in on him with a weight heavier than chains.

Still, he straightened.

'Then we flee regardless,' he said. 'Even if we must fight our way clear.'

Dorsey looked up at him, surprise flashing before a rough grin split his beard.

'Well now,' he rumbled. 'There's steel in ye yet. I'll give ye that.' The grin faded. 'But how d'ye plan on givin' those guards a proper thrashin'? They tossed ye in here like a sack o' turnips. Bastards aren't careless.'

Valran frowned, thought turning sharp and restless.

'I have no clear design,' he admitted. 'But surrender will not serve us. Time presses. We must shape something from what little we have.'

They spoke in low voices after that, trading half-formed notions and dangerous guesses. Nothing solid. Nothing safe. Yet with each exchange, a fragile thread of hope took hold, thin but stubborn. Better that than waiting.

As the light beyond the narrow window bled away, the cold deepened. They dragged what hay remained into a rough mound and huddled close, breath fogging the air.

After a long while, Dorsey spoke again, softer now.
'So. Where d'ye hail from, then?'

'Mistwood,' Valran said. 'In the Erbour Forest.'

Dorsey hummed. 'Aye. Know the place. Folk whisper the Seer walks those woods.' He tilted his head. 'Ever cross paths with him?'

Valran hesitated. Just a beat too long.
'No,' he said. 'His domain lies deeper than most dare tread.'

'Shame,' Dorsey muttered. 'Some say he knows every secret worth knowin'. Might even ken a way out o' this gods-forsaken hole.' A pause. Then, casual as falling snow, 'So ye were huntin' elk, were ye?'

Valran's breath caught. The cold bit harder.
'I was,' he said carefully. 'But not as you imagine.'

Dorsey studied him, then looked away.
'Fair enough, mate.'

He settled back against the wall, and something in his posture shifted. Not tension. The absence of it. As though a decision had already been made.

Silence settled between them, thick and watchful. The torches outside guttered, shadows shifting along the corridor walls.

Valran closed his eyes, conserving warmth, conserving thought.

Above them, somewhere in the ruin, something moved.

And whatever waited did not intend to wait long.

Morning light seeped through the narrow window, a thin, colorless wash over the snow beyond. Cold gnawed at Valran's joints, deep and intimate. He drew a shallow breath as heavy footsteps scraped stone above.

They stopped outside the cell.

'Ah, Mr Hunter-man,' Bastion crooned. 'I trust the accommodations have not disappointed.'

Valran rose slowly. 'What do you want from me?'

Bastion smiled, all teeth and patience. 'Only the truth. It frees everyone. Eventually.'

The Swinish behind him snorted, wet and pleased.

Dorsey moved first.

He stepped to the door, shoulders squared, voice rough. 'Well then, Mr Devil-man. I've done what we agreed, aye?'

Valran's stomach dropped.

The air changed, as if the corridor leaned in to listen.

The latch slid open.

Dorsey stepped out without looking back. 'Hunter's a stubborn one,' he went on lightly. 'Might need... encouragement. Bit o' pressure tae loosen the tongue.'

Bastion chuckled. 'You've been most helpful.'

Valran surged forward. 'Dorsey—what bargain—'

Too late.

The Swinish moved.

One massive hand closed around Dorsey's throat. The other twisted. There was a sound like wet cloth tearing.

Then nothing.

Dorsey's body collapsed in on itself, blood spraying across stone, across iron, across Valran's face. The head rolled once before coming to rest against the bars, eyes already empty.

Valran screamed.

He fell to his knees, breath tearing from his chest, the world narrowing to red and iron and disbelief. Betrayal burned, but horror burned hotter. No lie, no bargain, deserved that end. Bastion wasn't collecting truth. He was collecting compliance.

Bastion leaned close to the bars.

'Take your time, Hunter-man,' he said softly. 'Memory has a way of sharpening on its own.'

He turned away, tail swaying, boots climbing the stairs at an unhurried pace. The Swinish followed, chuckling.

Silence rushed in behind them.

Valran remained where he was, shaking, staring at the blood slicking the floor. Shock gave way to clarity.

He would die here if he waited.

His gaze swept the cell, frantic and searching. The bars held firm. The walls were stone. Then he saw it.

A knife.

Small. Plain. Half-hidden near the edge of the corridor where it had skittered during the killing.

His pulse steadied.

Training surfaced, old as muscle and bone. Always keep a blade. Steel meant options. Options meant breath.

It was just out of reach.

Valran crossed to the hanging shelf and slammed his shoulder into it. Once. Twice. The chains shrieked. Wood splintered.

He tore free a jagged length and used it to hook the knife closer, inch by inch, until he could snatch it through the bars. He slid it into his boot at once, heart pounding—not from fear now, but focus.

The window.

He tested the bars. One shifted. Barely.

Enough.

He worked fast, knife biting into corroded bolts softened by centuries of cold. He wrenched loose another timber, lashed it between the outer bars with his belt, and twisted.

Metal groaned.

Again.

The bar cracked.

Valran did not stop until the frame tore free in his hands, cold air flooding the cell as the opening yawned wide.

Beyond it lay snow, ruin, and distance.

He pulled himself up onto the ledge, breath tight, ready to drop—

Footsteps. Above. Close.

The Swinish.

Valran dropped back into the cell without a sound, pressing himself against the wall beneath the window. His heart slammed against his ribs. He held his breath and listened.

The footsteps passed overhead, slowed, then descended the stairs.

He moved at once, crossing to the front of the cell, positioning himself where a casual glance would not stray upward. The air tasted stale and dry. His heart hammered hard enough to bruise. His hands shook, slick with sweat, despite the cold.

The door slammed open.

'Food,' the Swinish barked.

A bowl clattered onto the floor. Fruit. Meat. The guard barely spared Valran a glance, his attention already snagging on the body sprawled in the corridor.

With a grunt, he seized Dorsey's corpse and flung it back into the cell. It struck the wall and collapsed in a boneless heap.

'There,' the creature jeered. 'Your friend's back.'

Laughter followed him out. The door slammed shut.

Valran did not move until the footsteps faded.

Only then did he breathe.

Hunger cut through revulsion with brutal efficiency. He dragged the bowl closer, turned his face away, and ate quickly. The fruit dulled the edge in his stomach. He wrapped what remained in a scrap of cloth and tucked it into his pocket, hands steady now.

The cold beyond the window waited.

He stripped the corpse quickly, hands steady despite the stench. The clothing was too large and stiff with old blood, but it would break the wind. That was enough.

At the window, he paused and looked out.

Snow lay unbroken. Ruins slouched beneath it, quiet and indifferent. To the south, jagged peaks clawed at the sky. West lay lower ground. Passage. Possibility.

Valran pulled himself up and through the opening, stone scraping skin, breath caught tight in his chest. He pressed himself flat against the wall and listened.

Nothing.

No alarm. No cry.

He dropped into the snow, the cold biting hard, immediate, honest.

Turning west, he did not look back.

Behind him lay iron, blood, and cages.

Ahead lay hunger, distance, and the open night.

For the first time since the talons closed around him, Valran chose his own direction.

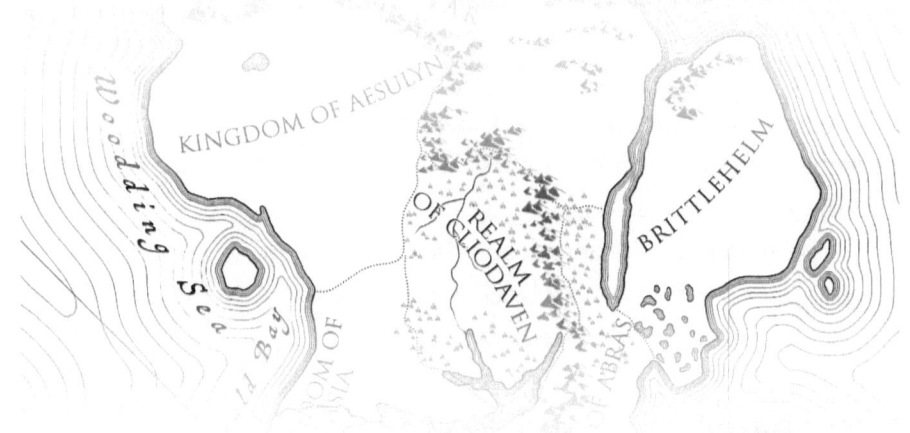

CHAPTER SEVENTEEN

The Wheel and Anchor

The last of the companions melted back into the street, and Coseo closed the door behind them, already dissolving into the flow of bodies. Niama followed, senses alert as the capital pressed in around them.

Rohan slowed, eyes lifting as Old Town opened before them. Old Town did not welcome. It appraised. A rare softness touched his expression. He gestured east with a gloved hand.

'It's been some time since I walked this quarter,' he said. 'It's close. A short way yet.'

They moved on together, swallowed by the city's churn. Cartwheels thundered over cobblestones. A town crier's voice cut through the din, sharp and insistent. The air was thick with competing smells: roasting meat, biting spice, and the sour tang of waste ground into stone.

A crash overhead made Niama flinch. A window flew open and a sheet of foul water spilled into the street. Coseo sidestepped it without breaking stride. Niama exhaled, grateful again for his quiet awareness.

Across the way, four guards advanced in loose formation. Their eyes lingered too long. Niama felt the prickle rise along her spine. The last of them, broad-shouldered and watchful, seemed on the verge of crossing—

'Thief!'

The shout split the street. The guards broke instantly, boots pounding as they gave chase. The moment passed. Niama did not slow until the noise fell away behind them.

The street bent and dropped, and the city fell open.

Below them, the harbor sprawled in restless motion. Ships crowded the docks, hulls creaking like tired beasts as sailors hauled crates ashore. Nets were flung wide. Fish spilled bright and slick onto waiting tables. Gulls wheeled and screamed overhead, thick as smoke.

Rohan turned them sharply into shadow.

'This way.'

They descended a narrow stair, stone worn smooth by centuries of passage. The buildings leaned closer here, their faces darkened, windows blind and watchful. The sky narrowed to a thin, pale strip overhead. Moss slicked the steps. Salt and mildew clung to the air.

Sunlight struggled to reach them and failed.

'This quarter has sharp habits,' Rohan said quietly. 'Stay within arm's reach.'

Somewhere ahead, laughter rose. Music followed. Too loud. Too careless.

Niama did not like the way the sound carried.

Her thoughts drifted briefly toward home as they stepped into the tavern. The air hit hard. Salt, sour ale, and the rank breath of too many bodies crowded together too long. Patrons sprawled across scarred floorboards, boots tangled, heads lolling. Yet beneath the filth ran a current of rough joy. Dancers spun to clapping hands. Laughter burst and ricocheted off the walls, loud enough to drown caution.

She angled toward the bar.

A hand closed around her arm.

The grip was rough. Possessive.

She was jerked sideways toward a man with a wet grin and unfocused eyes.

'What've we got 'ere?' he slurred, dragging her closer. 'Pretty little thing. C'mon then, give ol' Billy a—'

Niama did not answer.

She drove her knee up, clean and precise.

The man folded with a strangled sound and collapsed to the floor. Laughter erupted around him, cruel and delighted. Niama tore free, pulse hot but steady, and rejoined the others without looking back. Her jaw was tight. Her eyes were hard.

Coseo reached for her arm, concern flickering across his face. 'Are you hurt?'

'No,' she said, calm as frost. 'I merely corrected an error of manners.'

Coseo huffed a quiet laugh and glanced over his shoulder at the groaning heap on the floor.

'You've always had a talent for handling yourself.'

At the bar, Rohan and the others were already speaking with the tavernkeeper. The man wiped a tankard with a rag that had long since lost the battle against grime.

'There may be someone,' he said at last, nodding toward a dim corner. 'Captain Fiske. Sailed that route more than once. Comes back alive. Mostly.' He returned to his work without ceremony.

Approaching the captain, the group found him seated in the tavern's deepest shadow, a broad-backed figure hunched over a scarred table. Several unsavory men clustered around him, their laughter loud, their movements careless. At Rohan's approach, the sound ebbed.

'Captain Fiske?'

The man did not look up at once. He finished his drink, set the tankard down with deliberate care, then lifted his gaze. One by one, the men around him retreated under it, drifting away without protest.

'State your business,' the Captain said, shooing the last of them aside with a curt flick of his fingers.

Introductions were brief.

'We require your services,' Rohan said.

Captain Fiske studied them in silence. His eyes moved slowly over each of them, not meeting their gazes so much as measuring weight, strength, resolve. His hands rested on the table, thick fingers marked by rope scars and old cuts, the hands of a man who knew exactly how much pressure it took to break something.

At last, he gestured to the empty chairs. 'What do you require?'

Niama stepped forward. 'We seek passage to the Isle of Thunder.'

For a heartbeat, nothing changed.

Then the Captain laughed.

The sound was loud, rough, unrestrained, drawing glances from nearby tables. But his eyes remained sharp, fixed on Niama, stripping the humor from the noise. He leaned back in his chair, wood creaking beneath his weight, gaze flicking briefly to the tavern door, then the windows, then back to her.

'The Isle of Thunder.'

He let the words sit like a blade on the table. 'That route kills the unprepared. Why are you asking me for it?'

Rohan stepped forward. 'We require passage to the Isle of Thunder. Half the payment now. Half on arrival.'

He placed the pouch on the table. The weight of it was unmistakable.

Fiske's gaze dropped to it. Not hungrily. Assessing.

'Agree to transport us,' Rohan said, 'and you'll receive half when we embark. The other half upon our arrival.'

He lifted the pouch and tucked it back into his belt without hurry.

Fiske watched the motion. Something shifted behind his eyes.

'Why should I risk my ship?'

'Because the gold is real,' Rohan said. 'And you know it.'

For a moment, the Captain did nothing.

Then, as Rohan retrieved the pouch, the space around the table seemed to contract. Fiske leaned forward just enough for his shadow to stretch across the wood, across the place where the gold had been.

Rohan continued, unfazed. 'Reconvene here in two hours, and we shall complete our arrangement.'

Fiske's smile did not fade.

But it thinned.

And as the Prince turned away, Niama felt it settle behind them like a hook beneath the water's surface, patient and certain.

The captain leaned back, studying him now with something closer to respect.

'Those terms are either brave or stupid. I'll decide which.'

Rohan met his gaze without blinking.

'Decide which,' he said.

With a stiff nod, the Captain accepted their terms.

Fiske rose from the table, tugging his hat into place. 'Very well,' he said. 'I'll see ye in a couple o' hours, then.' His gaze slid to Rohan's hand, where the coin pouch had been. 'Keep that purse close. Men disappear for less.'

Then he turned and disappeared into the crowd, swallowed by noise and smoke.

Kesaahn watched the door a moment longer than necessary. 'I don't trust him.'

Niama nodded. 'Nor do I.' She exhaled slowly. 'But we have no other path. The Isle awaits, and this is the road that leads to it.'

Rohan folded his gloves into his palm. 'Then we take it with our eyes open. He may yet prove useful.'

Niama said nothing. Doubt sat heavy in her chest, unwelcome but familiar. Captain Fiske felt less like a solution and more like another hazard to be measured and endured. Still, she kept the thought to herself. Fear multiplied when spoken aloud.

'Before we meet him again,' Kesaahn said, breaking the silence, 'we'll need provisions. There's a herbalist nearby. We have time.'

They agreed without argument and turned from the tavern, the sound of laughter and music closing behind them like a door.

Niama stepped back into the street, unease pacing her stride.

The gamble had been made.

Now all that remained was to see what it would cost.

They returned to the tavern later in the day, the sun angling low enough to stretch shadows long across the cobbles. Inside, the air was thick with smoke and noise.

Captain Fiske waited at the foremost table.

He did not rise as they approached. His gaze cut through the haze, sharp and appraising, lingering just long enough to unsettle.

'Early,' he said, voice rough with old rum and gravel. 'No matter. Follow me.'

Something in his ease tightened Niama's chest. Too smooth. Too certain.

They trailed him back into the street, senses sharpened, every sound edged. He led them toward the docks, boots striking stone with purpose.

'This way,' he called.

Salt air rolled in from the harbor, sharp and clean, colliding with the warm scent of bread from a nearby bakery. The contrast set Niama's nerves on edge. Her heartbeat kept pace with her steps, a steady warning she could not quiet.

The alley narrowed to stone and shadow.

Walls pressed in until the sky became a pale strip overhead. Their footsteps sounded too loud here, every scrape of leather echoing back at them. Niama felt the change before it fully registered. The harbor noise dulled. The city's breath seemed to draw away.

Kesaahn slowed half a step.

Rohan noticed. His hand drifted closer to his sword. 'Are you certain this is the route?'

Captain Fiske did not turn. 'Shortcut,' he said easily. 'Cuts the distance in half.'

The alley ended.

The passage ended in a dead wall, damp and featureless.

No door. No turn.

Only certainty.

Niama's stomach dropped.

Before anyone could speak, something shifted above them. A scrape of boots. A displaced pebble.

Three men dropped from the rooftops behind them, landing hard. Steel flashed as blades cleared scabbards. The sound rang sharp in the narrow space, impossibly loud.

Rohan spun. 'What is the meaning of this?'

Captain Fiske turned at last.

The grin he wore was slow and deliberate, as if he'd been waiting to put it on. His sword slid free with a soft, practiced sound, its point settling against Kesaahn's satchel.

'Business,' he said. 'Hand over the gold. Then anything else worth takin'.'

The sailors behind them laughed, low and eager.

Niama felt fear lock its grip around her ribs. Cold. Precise. But beneath it, something steadier took hold.

She stepped forward. 'You don't understand what you're interfering with.'

Fiske's eyes flicked to her, amused. 'I understand coin just fine.' His gaze swept them again, calculating. 'Now kneel. Slow. No tricks.'

Niama lowered herself, heart hammering, fingers brushing her boot.

'What are you doin'?' Fiske snapped.

'Complying,' she said.

Niama's hand moved once. The dagger left her like a thought she'd finished having.

It struck Fiske high in the throat, the sound wet and final. His hands flew up, blood spilling between his fingers as he staggered back into the barrels. He tried to speak. Only a bubbling hiss came out. Then his knees buckled and he slid to the stones, eyes wide and empty.

For a heartbeat, no one moved.

Then everything broke at once.

One sailor rushed Rohan and died cleanly, the prince's blade punching through his chest with a precision that left no room for doubt.

Another turned toward Kesaahn. Her staff cracked against his wrist, sending his sword skittering away. Her hidden blade followed, quick and exact, opening his throat before he could cry out.

The third sailor went for Coseo.

They collided hard, bodies slamming into the alley wall. The man was bigger, stronger. He laughed as he drove Coseo down, blade scraping uselessly against stone.

Niama took a step toward them.

Too late.

Coseo twisted, trapped the man's sword arm with brutal efficiency, and drove his forehead into the sailor's face. Bone crunched. The laughter stopped.

Coseo didn't stop.

He wrenched the man's arm back until it screamed, then forced him face-down against the stones. The sailor tried to beg. Tried to turn.

Coseo drove the dagger down again, and again, and again, each strike placed with the same ugly care.

Then, as if to make certain, he grabbed the man's hair, hauled his head back, and opened his throat from ear to ear.

Blood ran along the alley stones.

Silence followed. Thick. Stunned.

Niama stared.

Rohan's sword lowered slightly, forgotten. Even Kesaahn had gone still, eyes fixed on Coseo.

He stood there breathing hard, dagger dripping, expression unreadable.

When he finally looked up, their gazes met.

There was no triumph in his eyes.

Only resolve.

Niama recoiled. That was not killing. That was something else.

The smell of blood was everywhere now, copper-thick and cloying. It coated the back of her throat, made her stomach twist. The sailor's final

sounds still rang in her ears, wet and unfinished, and she could not recon-
cile them with the man she thought she knew.

Coseo still stood over the body, dagger slick, breathing hard.

'Cos—what are you doing?' Niama said.

Her voice cut sharper than she intended. Shock and revulsion threaded through it, impossible to separate. Rohan and Kesaahn flanked her,
weapons half-raised, their expressions caught somewhere between disbelief
and alarm.

Coseo did not answer.

The sound reached Rohan first. Boots. Voices. Too close.

'We need to move,' he said urgently. 'Now.'

Kesaahn's gaze never left Coseo. 'This is not finished,' she murmured to
Rohan. 'But it will have to wait.'

Niama swallowed and forced herself forward. She grabbed Coseo's arm,
hauled him back from the corpse with more strength than she knew she
had. He resisted for a heartbeat, then let himself be pulled away.

She wiped his blade against the dead man's coat without looking down.

'We're leaving,' she said. 'Right now.'

They ran.

The alley spat them out toward the docks, their footfalls loud and reckless. At the far end, a figure burst into view and froze, hands snapping up
in surrender.

Niama stopped short, dagger already in her grip.

Rohan's sword leveled at the young man's chest. 'Don't move. Who are
you?'

'I—Will,' the boy said quickly. 'I heard Fiske at the tavern. He planned
to rob you. Said it'd be easy coin.' His eyes flicked past them, toward the
dark mouth of the alley. 'Looks like he didn't live long enough to enjoy it.'

'How do you know about Fiske?' Niama asked.

'Everyone at the Wheel and Anchor knows,' Will said. 'He's done this
before. Lures in passengers, takes them down that alley.' He swallowed.
'My captain's been trying to put a stop to it. Bad for the dock's reputation.'

Niama studied him. Thin. Underslept. Brave enough to stay.

'I warned my captain,' Will went on. 'Told him what Fiske was about. He agreed to take the job instead. We've sailed near the Isle before. We know what waits there.' He hesitated. 'We also need the work.'

Footsteps thundered closer now. Shouts echoed between buildings.

Niama did not look back.

'Take us to your ship,' she said.

Will nodded once. 'This way.'

They plunged into the docks.

The air shifted, sharp with salt and fish and wet rope. Dockworkers shouted over one another as crates were hauled and nets dragged free. Masts swayed overhead, creaking like old joints. A gust off the water struck them full on, stinging Niama's eyes and plastering her clothes to her skin.

They reached the end of a jetty where a modest two-masted vessel rocked gently against the pilings.

Will swept an arm toward it. 'The *Little Dove*. She's no beauty queen, but she'll hold.'

Niama took her in. Weathered planks. Honest lines. No obvious menace.

After what they had just fled, innocence felt dangerous in its own way.

'Wait here,' Will said. 'I'll fetch the captain.'

He disappeared aboard, leaving Niama and the others alone on the dock.

The *Little Dove* creaked softly, ropes knocking against wood like a patient heartbeat.

Niama couldn't tell if the ship promised refuge, or merely a cleaner way to drown.

Her gaze traced the *Little Dove's* lines, following the sag of rope and the quiet patience of her rigging. The ship looked small beside the heavier vessels crowding the harbor, but there was a lean confidence to her hull, a promise of speed rather than comfort.

Footsteps sounded behind her.

Will returned with a tall, broad-shouldered man whose skin bore the map of years spent under sun and salt. His beard was streaked with grey, his eyes bright and alert, measuring even as they smiled.

'So,' he said, voice steady as a helm. 'You're the travelers Will told me about.'

Niama inclined her head. 'I am Niama. These are Kesaahn, Rohan, and Coseo.'

The man tipped his hat. 'Captain John Cotton. And this fine lady is the *Little Dove*. She may not look like much, but she'll outrun half the tubs rotting in this harbor.' His gaze flicked briefly to the water. 'You're seeking passage.'

'To the Isle of Thunder,' Niama said.

Cotton's brow lifted a fraction. 'The Isle is a hard sail.' A pause. 'Conveniently, we're between contracts. But bold voyages cost more than ordinary ones.'

Rohan stepped forward, posture composed, voice calm and assured. 'Gold will not delay us.' He loosened the pouch at his belt, the weight of it unmistakable.

Cotton's smile sharpened. 'That'll do nicely.' He accepted half the coins without ceremony. 'Will, get them settled. We sail as soon as lines are clear.'

Will led them below.

The hold was low and close, smelling of rope, tar, and old wood. Hammocks hung in quiet rows, some occupied by crew already resting. Crates were lashed tight, supplies stacked with practiced care. The ship creaked softly around them, a living thing adjusting to the tide.

'Pick an empty sling,' Will said. 'She's not fancy, but she's dry. That counts.'

Niama left the others to settle and climbed back to the deck.

Sunlight warmed her face, the taste of salt sharp on her tongue. The city's noise faded behind her, replaced by the rhythmic slap of water against hull.

Captain Cotton stood at the helm, eyes on the horizon.

'The sea's a temperamental creature,' he said without turning. 'One moment she bears you like a favored child. The next, she reminds you who truly decides.' He glanced skyward. 'Today, though, she's in a generous mood. Wind's honest. Tide will turn shortly.'

'How long to the Isle?' Niama asked.

'Four days, maybe five, if Athris smiles.' His mouth tightened. 'There's always weather around that place. Storms that don't seem to move. Not a journey for those fond of certainty.'

'We have no other course,' Niama said.

Cotton studied her, then nodded once. 'Aye. Folk bound for places like that rarely do.' He laid a hand on the wheel. 'I know a route that skirts the worst of it. Still rough. Still unforgiving.'

'We need only arrive,' Niama replied. 'What follows matters more than comfort.'

The Captain exhaled slowly. 'Then we understand each other.'

He raised his voice. 'Cast off!'

Ropes were loosed. Sails snapped and filled. The *Little Dove* shuddered, then surged forward, cutting cleanly through the harbor water.

Niama watched the docks begin to recede.

Somewhere below, Coseo was settling into a hammock. She did not go back down to check on him.

Stone gave way to open water.

And with it, the last easy certainty she had.

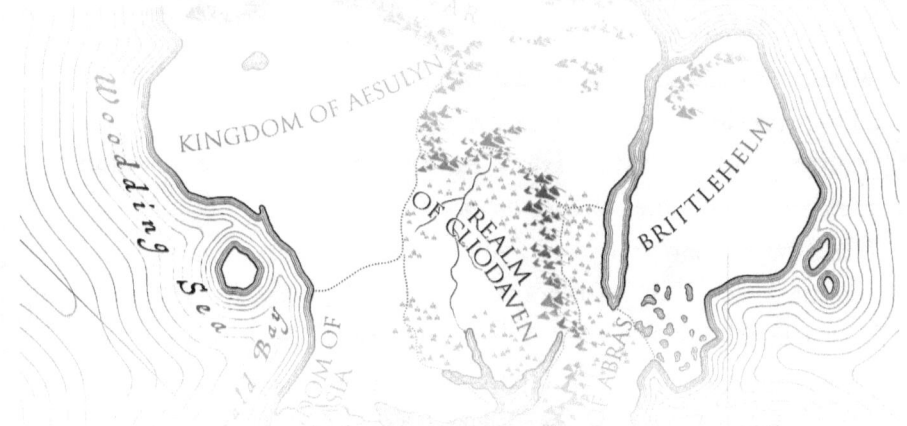

CHAPTER EIGHTEEN

The Tempest

C aptain Cotton's predictions proved uncomfortably precise. As the Little Dove slipped from the harbor, the wind rose with sudden confidence, swelling the sails until they strained taut, canvas groaning like muscle under load. Late afternoon light washed the deck in gold, warming weathered faces as the ship cut cleanly through the water, white foam boiling in its wake.

Kesaahn stood alone near the rail, the sea wind striking her face, salt sharp against her senses. She did not move when Rohan approached, though worry clung to him, etched deep into his brow.

Niama lingered at the edge of their exchange, listening.

'The lad, Coseo,' Rohan said quietly. 'Is he... well?' A pause. 'What he did in the alley was... disturbing.'

Kesaahn turned to him, unease flickering behind her calm. 'When Niama brought him to me, he was barely conscious. His body bore the marks of severe sickness.' She hesitated. 'There was a black fog within him.'

Rohan stilled. 'The Darkness?'

'As surely as I can say,' Kesaahn replied. 'I drew out what I could, with the aid of a luminous crystal.'

Rohan's voice dropped. 'And if some of it remains?'

Kesaahn's gaze shifted toward the horizon. 'Then it has taken root. His violence is no longer wholly his own.'

Rohan glanced around the deck, lowering his voice. 'Then shouldn't we act? Before he becomes something we can't stop?'

That was enough.

Niama stepped forward, boots striking the planks with sharp intent. 'Then speak plainly,' she said. 'What course would you have us take?'

Rohan met her gaze. 'If he is changing, he endangers us all.'

Memory surged. Hunts shared. Fires laughed around. Trust forged over years, not moments. Niama's jaw tightened. 'I will not abandon him so easily. If even the faintest chance remains, I will not release it.'

Rohan's expression softened, but only slightly. 'I understand what he is to you. But our task is larger than any one bond. Each day this continues, the risk grows.'

Niama said nothing. The image of Coseo's eyes, hollowed by pain, rose unbidden. The sound of his screams echoed beneath the rush of wind and water. She would not leave him to that.

'I stand with Niama,' Kesaahn said at last. 'If there is a way to save him, we must try.'

Rohan exhaled, long and controlled. 'Very well. But hesitation may cost lives.' He turned and strode toward the lower deck, footsteps heavy against the boards.

Kesaahn's hand found Niama's shoulder. 'He speaks from fear, not malice.'

Niama shrugged the touch away, anger flaring hot and sudden. 'I require no protection.' Her voice trembled despite herself. 'Coseo would do the same for me. Without question.'

She turned from her, gaze caught by the endless sweep of sea. Quietly, she murmured, 'Athris... guide us. Let us carry him to the Seekers before the light within him is lost.'

She had nearly reached the stair when Will appeared.

'Everything all right?' he asked gently.

'Fine,' Niama replied too quickly. She stopped, drew a breath. 'Forgive me. I did not mean to snap.'

Will smiled, unoffended. 'You're carrying more than most would manage. The sea has a way of collecting those who need refuge.'

'More than you know,' Niama said.

He gestured toward the hold. 'I was fetching something to eat. Would you care to join me?'

She nodded. 'Yes. Thank you.'

'I'll return shortly,' Will said, already turning. 'And for what it's worth—the Captain knows these waters. You're in capable hands.'

Niama watched him descend, the deck creaking softly beneath her boots, and wondered how long that assurance would hold.

As she waited for Will's return, Niama glanced toward Kesaahn, still at the rail, her gaze fixed on the rolling expanse beyond the ship. The sea stretched without boundary, layered blues and greens broken by whitecaps that rose and fell in steady rhythm. Wind carried salt and spray across the deck. Above, seabirds wheeled and cried, their calls swallowed by the endless rush of water.

Niama joined her.

'I spoke too sharply earlier,' she said. 'Coseo and I were raised together. Forest-born. Our bond is closer than blood. He is... my brother, in all but name.'

Kesaahn turned, a small, understanding smile touching her lips. 'You need not apologize. I would have done the same.' Her eyes returned to the sea. 'If we abandon those we love when darkness reaches for them, then we have already surrendered.'

Niama nodded, memories pressing close. Shared fires. Shared hunts. A lifetime braided together.

'I'm going below to rest,' Kesaahn said gently. 'We'll need our strength.' She inclined her head and disappeared into the hold.

Will emerged moments later, balancing a tray. 'Here,' he said, passing her crusty bread, sharp cheese, and a tankard of ale.

Niama ate slowly, eyes drawn back to the water. The scent of salt mingled with the warmth of the food. 'It's extraordinary,' she said quietly.

Will glanced at her. 'The meal?'

'The ocean,' Niama replied, gesturing outward. 'I've known it only through stories. Rivers shape my homeland. But this—' She shook her head softly. 'It feels... endless.'

Will smiled. 'Eight years I've sailed these waters, and it still steals my breath.' He hesitated, then added, 'I wonder if my child will feel the same.'

'You have a child?' Niama asked.

'Soon,' he said, pride warming his voice. 'My wife's with child. Our first. I've a feeling it's a boy, but I'd be just as glad either way.' He breathed in deep, as if to anchor the thought.

'Then my congratulations to you both,' Niama said. 'I'm certain you'll be a fine father.'

'I hope so,' Will replied. 'One day, I want a proper home in the city. For the three of us. Captain Cotton's been good to me. Maybe... one day.' His voice trailed, the future hovering just beyond reach.

Niama rested her hand briefly on his shoulder. 'It will come,' she said. 'And when I return, I'll visit you there.'

Will laughed softly. 'I'd like that.'

They stood together in silence as the ship cut on. The sun slid toward the horizon, staining the sky in amber and rose. The waves answered in low thunder against the hull.

'I haven't seen a sunset like this,' Will said at last, eyes distant, 'since my parents were still alive.'

The sea kept moving.

And the light kept fading.

'What happened to them?' Niama asked quietly.

Will did not answer at once. When he did, his voice was steady only by effort. 'I was twelve. They were returning from the market at Riverhurst.' He swallowed. 'Swinish bandits took them. What they did...' His breath hitched. 'They left nothing fit for burial.'

A tear slipped free. He brushed it away with the back of his hand, jaw tightening. 'Captain Cotton found me not long after. Gave me work. Gave me direction.' His gaze lifted to the horizon. 'Stopped me from chasing vengeance and ending up the same.' A pause. 'Now I have a family coming. That matters more.'

Niama rested her hand on his shoulder. 'You're a good man, Will.'

He nodded once, accepting the words without ceremony.

The wind rose, filling the sails. The ship rolled gently beneath their feet.

'I should see to my duties,' Will said. 'We'll meet the storm in a few days. Let's hope for calm until then.'

Niama watched him go, his stride purposeful. Her resolve hardened. Whatever awaited them was no longer only about prophecy or distant kingdoms. It was about people like Will. Families that never knew the threat until it arrived.

Days slipped past in uneasy quiet. The crew worked. The companions rested, spoke little. Meals were taken without ceremony.

On the third day, Will pointed toward the horizon.

A wall of darkness loomed there, vast and unmoving.

'That's it,' he said, raising his voice over the wind. 'The Tempest. They say it's ringed the Isle of Thunder since the world learned fear.'

Lightning flickered within it, brief and violent, revealing waves already rearing beneath its shadow.

The sea ahead looked unfinished. As if the world had stopped mid-breath.

'All hands, batten down the hatches!'

Captain Cotton's shout cut through the ship like a blade. Crewmen scattered, hauling rope and canvas as the wind surged. The deck pitched beneath Niama's feet.

Will met her gaze, fear stripped bare beneath his calm. 'Below deck. Now.' His hand closed briefly on her shoulder. 'It's safer.'

She obeyed.

Below, the hold swayed and groaned. Niama lay in her hammock, heart racing, forcing her breath to slow as the storm gathered its weight above them. She tried to lose herself in the fragments of the prophecy. Failed.

Time dissolved.

'All hands to stations!'

She was on her feet instantly.

The deck was chaos.

Rain struck like thrown gravel. Wind tore at cloaks and rigging. The ship heaved, wood screaming in protest. Captain Cotton's voice carried through the din, strained and sharp.

'This isn't right,' Cotton shouted. 'Storms don't hold still. This one's hunting.'

A wave rose ahead of them, impossibly tall.

Niama gripped the rail at the stern, the wood slick beneath her palms.

The world tilted.

Water slammed into the ship, ripping her from her feet. She slid across the deck, heart hammering, the sea yawning wide below.

A hand caught her wrist.

'Hold fast!' Will shouted, braced against the mast, knuckles white. 'I've got you!'

The ship lurched upright. He shoved her toward the hatch. 'Go!'

She obeyed, but not before she saw it.

A figure high on the mast.

Rigid. Exultant.

Rain hammered her face as she looked up. Coseo stood lashed to the rigging, arms spread wide, eyes open to the sky. Lightning split the dark and for one terrible instant she saw his face clearly.

He was smiling.

The sight iced her blood.

Below deck, Rohan and Kesaahn clung to supports as crates skidded past.

'What's happening?' Kesaahn shouted.

'The Captain says the storm isn't natural,' Niama answered.

The ship listed violently. A crate slammed past Rohan, splintering wood.

'Where's Coseo?' Kesaahn asked, the words thin with dread.

'He's on the mast,' Niama said. 'Up there. In the storm.'

Kesaahn's face drained of color. She moved without another word.

The ship groaned, water sloshing at their boots.

When Kesaahn returned below, her expression said everything.

'It's Coseo,' she said hoarsely. 'He's bound to the storm. He's driving it.' Her voice broke. 'He means to sink us.'

Niama's world tilted again. Reality slipped, then snapped back into place, sharper than before.

'We won't last the night,' Kesaahn said.

Rohan's voice cut through the fear. 'We're taking on water. We abandon ship.'

'Will, he's still up there,' Niama said.

No one answered.

Cold surged around Niama's ankles as the hold flooded. She turned—

Something struck her head.

The world went dark.

And the storm swallowed the rest.

CHAPTER NINETEEN

The Shieakfin

Rohan broke the surface with a choking gasp, lungs seizing as icy water burned through him. The cold clawed deep, forcing a shudder he could not suppress. Beside him, Kesaahn fought for breath, her gasps harsh and ragged. The storm raged on, alive and furious, flinging splintered remnants of the *Little Dove* through the roiling sea. They shouted to one another over the gale, arms thrashing as they fought to stay afloat.

'Niama!' Rohan called, desperation cutting through his voice as he scanned the heaving water.

Kesaahn's face was pale, fear stark in her eyes. 'I don't see her!'

Rohan's jaw set. 'Hold to something,' he said. 'I'm going under.'

He drew one last breath and plunged beneath the surface.

Cold closed over him like a fist, crushing breath and thought together. Sound vanished, replaced by pressure and darkness, the storm above reduced to a distant roar. He kicked hard, forcing himself down as debris spun past him, planks and canvas tumbling like falling bones.

The wreck emerged in fragments—first a broken spar, then the torn belly of the hull yawning open beneath the waves. The *Little Dove* lay canted on her side, masts swaying as if still trying to sail.

Rohan angled toward the breach and pulled himself inside.

Inside, the water was thick with silt and drifting debris. Rohan kicked blindly, lungs burning, eyes straining against the murk.

Niama floated among the debris, limp as torn canvas.

Rohan kicked hard, lungs already screaming, and seized her arm, his grip whitening his fingers. The cold gnawed at him, the current tugging insistently, but he did not let go. He dragged her toward a shrinking pocket of trapped air.

'Niama,' he pleaded, shaking her. 'Wake up.'

Her eyelids fluttered. A sound escaped her lips, unfocused, barely conscious.

The air pocket was failing. Time was running out, and his lungs knew it.

Rohan gathered her against him and kicked for the exit, chest burning as he fought the instinct to breathe. The ship groaned and shifted around them, sinking as they tore free of its ribs. They broke the surface together, gasping, coughing seawater into the storm-wracked air.

Rohan hauled Niama onto a crude raft Kesaahn had lashed together from floating wreckage. He laid her flat, eyes darting over her shallow breaths and the blood seeping from a wound at her temple.

Somewhere beyond the wind and waves, he thought he heard laughter. Faint. Malicious. The sound raised gooseflesh along his arms.

Kesaahn clutched the raft's edge, knuckles white. 'What now?' she cried. 'We're lost!'

'We hold,' Rohan shouted back.

They worked blindly, binding more debris to the raft as the sea battered them without mercy, each wave threatening to tear their fragile refuge apart.

Rohan froze.

Something moved in the water. An arm. A shape.

'There!' he shouted. 'Someone's alive!'

He secured a rope to the raft and struck out into the swell. 'Swim toward us!' he called, voice hoarse. 'We're coming!'

The waves fought him every stroke. His muscles burned as the distance closed.

The survivor's face came into view.

'Will!' Rohan gasped. 'Hold on. We're almost there.'

Will's expression was hollow with exhaustion, but his arm still moved.

And that was enough. Survival rarely asked for more.

Despite the waves' relentless assault, they reached him.

Rohan's hand closed around Will's arm. For one breathless instant, relief flared—

Then the sea rose.

A towering wall of water smashed down upon them, tearing Rohan free and hurling all three beneath the surface. The world became cold and tumbling dark. When Rohan broke back into the air, the raft was gone, lost in the spray.

Niama's coughing cut through the storm, thin but alive.

Rohan spun, panic clawing at his chest. 'Will!' he shouted, voice shredded by wind. White water surged between him and the wreckage. Then he saw it—a body rising and falling in the trough beyond the waves.

He swam.

Every stroke burned. His limbs felt leaden, his lungs aflame, but he reached the drifting form and hooked an arm beneath Will's shoulders. Together, half-drowned and barely conscious, they fought their way back toward the raft's dark silhouette.

Rohan hauled Will across the lashed planks and collapsed beside him, chest heaving. The raft pitched wildly, but it held. Kesaahn clung to the opposite edge of the raft, hair plastered to her face, eyes fierce and alive.

For a time, they could do nothing but cling to the debris as the storm raged on, rain and wind beating them down without mercy. Rohan pressed his forehead to the wood, breath ragged, thoughts splintering into prayer and defiance in equal measure.

At last, exhaustion claimed them.

The wind still howled. The sea still writhed, patient and unforgiving.

But the raft endured.

And somewhere beneath the storm's fury, hope remained—fragile, un-spoken—waiting for the waves to carry them somewhere other than death.

Warm sunlight brushed Niama's eyelids, coaxing her back to the world. She stirred, breath catching as memory rushed in fragments. Wind. Water. Darkness.

The storm was gone.

The sea lay calm and unbroken, a wide sheet of blue glass stretching to the horizon. For a moment, the night's violence felt unreal, like something dreamt and already slipping away.

She shifted, pain blooming dully at her temple, and forced her eyes open.

The raft floated low but intact. Will lay nearby, unmoving, his chest rising in shallow rhythm. Kesaahn was sprawled beside him, soaked hair tangled across her face, equally still. At the far end of the raft, Rohan lay flat on his back, eyes closed, too motionless for comfort.

Niama crawled to Kesaahn first, gripping her shoulder. 'Wake,' she whispered, then louder.

Kesaahn groaned and stirred, eyes fluttering open.

Relief came sharp and fast.

Niama turned next to Rohan, shaking him hard. 'Rohan.' Again. Harder.

He sucked in a breath and coughed, rolling onto his side with a groan.

Only then did Niama allow herself to breathe.

The motion sent pain lancing through her skull. She swayed, bracing herself against the raft as the world tilted, salt stinging her eyes, thirst burning her throat raw. For a moment she simply knelt there, forcing the horizon to stop spinning.

When she spoke, it was because standing idle felt worse than the pain.

'We must decide our next course,' Niama said, her voice steadier than she felt.

Will stirred at the sound, pushing himself upright with a wince. 'What... what happened?'

Niama touched the tender swell at her scalp, fingers brushing dried blood. 'I remember the ship breaking.' She looked to Kesaahn.

Kesaahn's jaw tightened as she spoke, recounting the storm's unnatural turn, the way the wind had bent, the waves obeyed. Will nodded grimly.

'The main spar came down on Captain Cotton,' Will said. His voice was flat. Empty. 'Crushed him where he stood.'

He swallowed.

'And your friend was on the mast the whole time.' His hands trembled. 'He laughed.'

The words struck like a physical blow, knocking loose years she had believed unbreakable.

Niama stared at Will, the world tilting beneath her. Coseo's face rose unbidden in her mind. Shared years. Shared trust. The memory clashed violently with what she was hearing.

Rohan said nothing. Silence sat on him like armor he could not remove. He sat hunched, elbows on his knees, gaze fixed on the water.

At last, Kesaahn spoke. 'The Darkness twists those it touches. It feeds on pain and fear, bends the will.' Her eyes lifted to Niama. 'It does not excuse what was done. But it explains the force behind it.'

Niama closed her eyes briefly. 'Then we must resist it. In him, and in ourselves. We cannot let it decide what we become.'

The raft rocked gently beneath them, the sea whispering against its rough edges.

Exhaustion crept in, heavy and inescapable. Hunger, thirst, and shock dragged at their limbs. One by one, they slipped back into uneasy sleep, bodies surrendering where resolve could not.

When Niama woke again, the sun hovered low, painting the water in molten gold. A great seabird circled overhead, its cry lonely and distant.

She lay still, breathing in salt and warmth, listening to the quiet lap of waves against wood. The fear remained, coiled and watchful, but for the moment, the sea was calm.

Their fate drifted with the current now.

And land, if it waited at all, was still unseen.

The raft jolted hard, the impact snapping Kesaahn from sleep.
Wood groaned. Water surged. Half-awake, Niama barely had time to gasp
before a vast shadow rolled beneath them, the sea bulging as something
immense rose from the depths.

A low vibration thrummed up through the planks, not a sound but a
pressure, as if the water itself were tightening around them.

Kesaahn was already moving.

'Now,' she said, voice sharp with urgency. She tore open her herb pouch,
hands flying. 'Niama, with me. We must drive it off.'

Niama stared at the bundle of roots and vials, dread locking her limbs.
'What is it?'

Kesaahn's eyes flicked to the water. 'A shieakfin. It hunts for sport.' Her
jaw tightened. 'It enjoys fear.'

The sea erupted.

A monstrous fin knifed through the surface, jagged and ridged with
spines. A vast, tooth-lined maw followed, its roar tearing the air apart. The
sound vibrated through bone and blood, forcing them to clamp hands over
their ears as the creature surged toward the raft.

The wood lurched violently.

Kesaahn worked with brutal focus, crushing herbs, pouring liquid,
murmuring words that scraped against the air. The mixture frothed, hissing, the stench sharp enough to burn the nose.

'The salt water,' she said, thrusting the bottle toward Niama. 'Fill it from
the sea. Quickly. I must seal it.'

The shieakfin struck.

The raft bucked upward, throwing Niama sideways. The ingredients
scattered. Will lost his footing and vanished over the edge with a shout.

'Rohan!' Kesaahn cried. 'Get him back!'

Niama's heart slammed as she scrabbled through wet debris, fingers numb, breath ragged. Panic clawed at her throat, but she forced it down. Found the vial. Snatched it up.

'Here!' She slammed it into Kesaahn's hand.

Rohan hauled Will back onto the raft, both of them coughing and drenched.

'Brace yourselves!' Kesaahn shouted.

She closed her eyes.

The potion began to glow.

Light pulsed within the glass, building, tightening, the air humming as if stretched too thin. Kesaahn lifted the bottle high, teeth clenched, veins standing out along her neck.

The release came as sound, violent and absolute.

A concussive wave tore outward, not heat but pressure, a thunderclap that smashed into the sea itself. Water exploded upward. The raft shuddered, nearly breaking apart.

The shieakfin convulsed, its massive body writhing as the sonic force ripped through it. Another roar burst free, ragged and pained, before the creature sank back beneath the surface, the water swallowing it whole.

Silence rushed in behind it.

They watched the water, waiting.

At last, the sea stilled.

Niama exhaled shakily, heart still racing. 'That was...'

Rohan stared at Kesaahn. 'What spell was that?'

She managed a weak smile. 'Sonic amplification. Improvised.' Her eyes flicked to her empty pouch. 'The last of my Argonian root.'

Will shook his head in awe. 'I've never seen anything like it.'

Niama knelt beside Kesaahn, steadying her. 'Are you well?'

'Drained,' she admitted. 'Without my staff, it costs far more. Protection magic always does.' She swallowed. 'But I'll recover.'

A shout cut through the moment.

'Land!' Will pointed toward the horizon.

Through the haze, a jagged island rose from the sea, dark cliffs climbing toward the sky. The sight struck them all at once, hope flaring despite their exhaustion.

'We head for it,' Rohan said. He dragged a half-submerged crate closer and hauled it onto the raft. 'Break this down. We paddle.'

They worked with dull determination, splintering wood, shaping crude oars. The raft crawled forward, inch by inch, muscles burning.

After long minutes, Will sagged. 'This isn't enough. It's too far.'

Kesaahn shook her head faintly. 'I have nothing left. Most of my supplies went down with the ship.'

Hunger gnawed. Thirst burned. One by one, they slumped back onto the raft, bodies refusing further command.

Niama stared at the island, its cliffs dark against the sky.

It was close enough to see.

Far enough to hurt.

And waiting.

Niama drifted back toward awareness.

Motion came first. A gentle sway beneath her. Then the press of cloth against her shoulders.

Her eyes fluttered open to blurred shapes above her—two hooded figures moving in careful unison, their faces hidden. She lay on a stretcher, the world tilting with each step.

'Who... are you?' Her voice scraped out thin and dry, her throat aching with thirst.

'Rest,' a calm voice replied. 'You are safe now.'

For the moment, Niama thought.

The words floated, steady and measured, as they carried her across uneven stone. The air smelled of old rock and damp iron. Somewhere nearby, waves struck the cliffs below in a slow, tireless rhythm.

Niama tried to move. Her body answered with nothing but weight.

Too weak to resist, too emptied to argue, she let herself be borne along. Questions crowded her thoughts, pressing and unformed, but exhaustion dulled their edges. The night air was cold, yet heavy cloaks had been drawn around her, their warmth sinking gradually into her bones.

Footsteps fell in an even cadence.

Against her will, it soothed her.

And as darkness closed in once more, Niama wondered—not for the first time—whether safety was merely another kind of threshold.

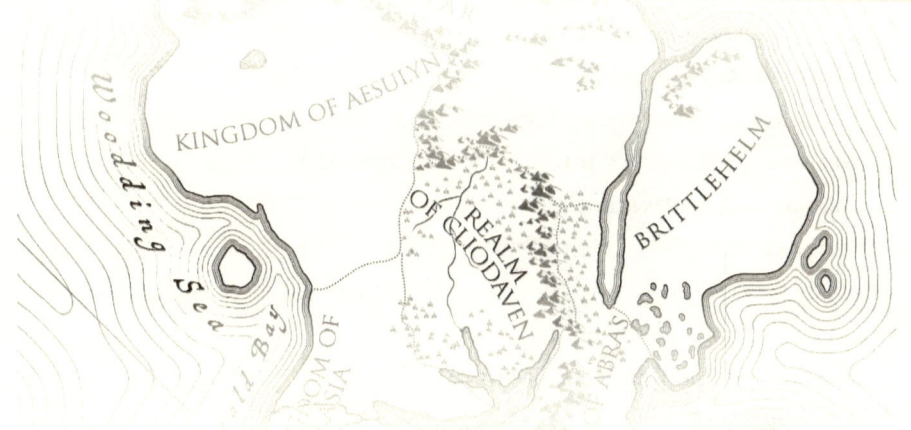

CHAPTER TWENTY

The Seekers

Niama's eyes flew open and she lurched upright, dragging in air as if she had surfaced too late. Her breath came ragged and shallow, chest aching beneath the frantic hammer of her heart.

The scent of salt and wind was gone.

In its place lingered stale air, tinged with damp wood and old stone. The change disoriented her more than the panic. Her fingers pressed into the surface beneath her, revealing softness, cool and yielding. A mattress. Not the splintered raft. Not the open sea.

Niama stilled.

She lay in a wide, dormitory-like chamber, beds lining the walls in various states of use. Light filtered softly through high windows. A wooden chair stood beside her own bed, simple and unadorned. Draped over it were her clothes, folded with careful precision.

Relief struck hard enough to make her sway, then falter.

She crossed to the chair, fingers brushing familiar fabric, grounding herself in the feel of it. Her dagger lay atop the clothes. She lifted it at once, the familiar weight settling her racing thoughts. Steel, honest and unchanged.

Only then did she notice the gown she wore.

White. Clean. Unmarked.

Her pulse jumped again. Someone had undressed her. Tended to her. She reached instinctively for her throat, fingers cold.

The medallion was still there.

She exhaled slowly, forcing her breath to steady as she dressed, senses straining for sound beyond the room. When she finished, unease lingered, coiled and watchful.

The door opened without warning.

A tall figure entered, wrapped in a long brown cloak that whispered softly as he moved. His presence filled the room without effort. When he spoke, his voice was low and gravel-rough, carrying an unsettling calm.

'Forgive my intrusion,' he said. 'But I am glad to see you awake, child.'

Niama's grip tightened on the dagger.

Questions crowded her tongue. She forced them out, one breath at a time. 'Where am I? Who are you? How did I come here? Where are my companions?'

The man did not remove his hood.

'All in good time,' he replied evenly, as though time obeyed him. 'For now, I trust you are recovering. And I suspect you are hungry.'

Her stomach answered for her, an unwelcome but undeniable growl.

'Yes,' Niama said. 'I am.'

He inclined his head. 'Then come. Food awaits.'

He turned and led the way.

They descended a carved wooden spiral stair, the walls adorned with tapestries and painted panels. Scenes of distant lands passed beneath her gaze. One stopped her short.

Mistwood.

The forest rendered in careful detail, green and alive. Home.

A tight ache lodged beneath her ribs. Niama tore her eyes away and hurried after her guide, unwilling to let longing slow her steps.

Whatever this place was, she would not meet it distracted.

As they moved through the halls, Niama took in the other cloaked figures who passed them, their gazes curious but restrained. Most wore the same brown cloaks as her guide, though now and then she glimpsed figures robed in white within adjoining rooms. The contrast lodged in her thoughts, unanswered for now.

Then she heard voices she knew.

Her pulse quickened.

The dining hall opened before them, broad and welcoming. A fire burned low in the hearth, sparks snapping up the chimney as pale smoke drifted above. Warmth settled into her bones. At one of six long tables sat Kesaahn, Rohan, and Will, already gathered in quiet conversation.

The scent of food hit her all at once.

Roasted fish. Spiced meat. Fresh bread.

Her stomach clenched painfully, a sharp reminder of how long she had gone without proper nourishment. She wrapped her arms around her middle, steadying herself as hunger made her sway.

The cloaked man halted, inclined his head, and departed without a word. The door closed softly behind him.

Kesaahn looked up first.

She was on her feet in an instant, crossing the room with relief bright in her eyes. Niama met her halfway, folding her into a fierce embrace. The warmth of her friend's body was grounding, real.

'It's good to see you standing,' Niama said quietly.

Rohan joined them, setting a firm, reassuring hand on Niama's shoulder. 'You frightened us,' he said. 'But you're tougher than most.' His hand did not leave her shoulder.

'Exhausted and ravenous,' Niama replied, managing a faint smile. 'But whole.'

Rohan guided her gently toward the table. 'Then sit. Eat. There's more than enough.'

Will rose as well. 'It's good to see you awake, miss.'

'And I am glad you are here,' Niama said sincerely.

They returned to their places, and Niama settled at the head of the table. Before her lay a spread that bordered on lavish. Platters of fish glazed with herbs. Bowls of stewed meat rich with spice. Loaves of bread still warm enough to steam when broken.

After hunger and salt and survival, it felt unreal.

'Welcome to the Isle of Thunder,' Kesaahn said softly. 'Home of the Seekers.'

They ate in earnest, the scrape of cutlery and the low murmur of contentment filling the space. Flavor bloomed across Niama's tongue, rich and grounding, each bite easing the hollow ache in her chest.

When the worst of her hunger had dulled, she looked up.

'Tell me,' she said, voice low. 'What happened... after the raft?'

Rohan wiped his hands and leaned back slightly. 'As we neared the island, a wave drove us into the rocks. The raft shattered.' His gaze flicked to her. 'You were struck again. Lost consciousness.'

Will shifted, embarrassed by the attention. Rohan clapped him on the shoulder. 'He caught you before you sank. Got you to shore.'

Kesaahn nodded. 'We followed close behind. When we reached land, there were torches waiting. They had seen the raft drifting in.'

Niama listened, letting the truth of it settle.

They had survived. For now.

But survival, she knew now, was rarely the end of the story.

Niama turned to Will, gratitude plain in her eyes.

'You have saved my life once again,' she said softly. 'It seems we are becoming accustomed to such debts between us.'

Will flushed and ducked his head. 'It was nothing, miss. Truly. I only did what anyone should.'

Rohan cleared his throat, easing the moment. 'After that, the Seekers brought us ashore, gave us shelter and food. And... here we are.'

Niama nodded, resolve settling back into place. 'Then we must seek counsel without delay. The prophecy will not unravel itself.'

'We will,' Kesaahn said calmly. 'I've already spoken with them. Once we've finished eating, they'll take us to the Grand Seeker. He is the highest authority among their order.'

Relief threaded through the table as they ate and spoke more freely, recounting fragments of the storm and the wreck, the terror softened now by survival. Bruises and aches were the only marks left behind.

When Niama finished, she rose at once. 'If we are ready, then let us proceed.'

Chairs scraped softly against stone as the others stood.

A brown-cloaked Seeker waited to guide them. They followed him into the corridors beyond, their footsteps echoing against smooth stone. Sunlight streamed through tall windows, painting the halls in gold. Doors lined the passage, some closed, others ajar, offering brief glimpses of figures bent over desks, poring over parchment, quills scratching in quiet industry.

At the corridor's end stood a door of dark, polished wood, its surface carved with a radiant sun motif. The Seeker opened it, gestured them inside, and withdrew, the door closing with a muted thud behind them.

Niama stepped forward—and stilled.

The chamber rose around them, vast and reverent. Shelves towered from floor to ceiling, crowded with volumes of every size, their spines worn smooth by time and touch. The air carried the scent of old parchment and cured leather, dense and comforting, heavy with memory.

Knowledge pressed close from every side.

An elderly man sat at an ornate desk near the far wall. His beard fell long and white against his chest, his brows thick beneath the hood that shadowed his face. Small round spectacles perched on his nose, and a deep purple cloak edged in gold rested across his shoulders.

He looked up and smiled.

'Welcome, my children,' he said, his voice warm and steady. 'Welcome to the archives.'

He rose and approached them, his movements unhurried, assured.

As they drew closer, the room seemed to quiet around him. Niama felt an unexpected ease settle in her chest, as though the weight she carried had found a place to rest.

'Thank you, Grand Seeker,' they said together.

He chuckled softly. 'No need for titles here. Cedric will do.' His gaze settled briefly on Niama, keen but kind. 'I am the Grand Seeker of the

Order of the Archivists. Few reach the Isle of Thunder.' A pause. 'Fewer still arrive by choice.'

His smile faded just enough to carry meaning.

'You are fortunate to have survived the storm. Now,' he said gently, 'tell me what has driven you into its heart.'

Cedric's gaze drifted, then fixed on the medallion peeking from beneath Niama's tunic. His eyes sharpened with sudden focus.

'I sense you carry something of consequence,' he said, extending his hand. 'May I see it, child?'

At Kesaahn's slight nod, Niama slipped the chain from her neck and placed the medallion in Cedric's palm.

He cradled it reverently, thumb brushing its surface. A quiet breath escaped him. 'Ah. Then you have met the Seer.' His eyes lifted, bright with restrained wonder. 'Tell me everything.'

Niama recounted the encounter, the cave, the clicks and clacks, the weight of the prophecy pressing down like stone. Cedric listened without interruption, murmuring softly at intervals, his expression shifting between fascination and grave concern.

When she finished, silence settled heavily in the chamber.

'The Second Rising has begun,' Cedric said at last. The warmth in his voice dimmed. 'We have long anticipated it, yet knowing does little to ease the sorrow of its arrival.' He turned slightly, gaze distant. 'Our scholars have studied the ancient texts for generations. Much is known. Much... remains fractured.' His voice trailed off.

'And I see you have brought the Lion.'

Rohan stiffened, chin lifting with composed dignity. 'How could you possibly know that?'

Cedric smiled faintly. 'We catalogue royal bloodlines, Prince Rohan. Every branch, every sigil. It is our charge.' He settled back into his chair, fingers steepled.

'The title is older than most remember. Before Abras was unified, its people were scattered tribes — nomadic, proud, and at war with one another. Resources were plentiful. Peace was not.' His gaze grew distant, as though reading from memory. 'The tribal leaders had grown wealthy in their own right. None would bend. None would compromise. The tribes tore at each other for generations.'

He paused.

'Then came the son of one such chieftain. Young. Stubborn. Possessed of something his father's generation had lost entirely.' Cedric's mouth curved. 'The belief that a stronger future was worth more than a comfortable present.'

Will leaned forward, drawn in despite himself.

'War came, as it always does when change is demanded. But the son held. He spoke to the leaders who would listen, and confronted those who would not. When it was finished, Abras stood as one nation.' Cedric lifted his gaze to Rohan. 'The people named him Lion. For his courage. For his refusal to let pride decide the fate of those he served.'

The room was quiet.

'Since then, the title has passed to the son of the King. Ceremonial now, in practice.' A pause. 'But not in meaning. It is a reminder of what came before unification — and what was built after.'

Rohan said nothing. But something shifted behind his eyes.

Rohan straightened. 'Then what is my role?'

Cedric held his gaze a moment longer than comfort allowed.

'That,' he said quietly, 'will become clear when the time comes. Not before.'

Something in his tone closed the question.

Will stared at Rohan, disbelief written plainly across his face.

Rohan met his gaze. Something in his expression softened — not quite an apology. Close to one.

'We can speak of it later,' Rohan said quietly.

Will nodded slowly, jaw tight, but said nothing.

Cedric returned to his desk. 'Let us proceed.'

He unfurled a parchment, adjusted his spectacles, and read aloud.

'A raven of shadow shall rise from the western horizon. Beyond the Withered Peaks, in the lands of magic-born folk, lies Cliodaven. There, within the village of Silenthollow, you must find a girl named Ammadella. One of the last Arvi.' His voice lowered. 'She is essential to the final trial.'

Niama leaned forward. 'The Arvi... skin-changers?' The word felt strange on her tongue.

Cedric nodded, hands gesturing as he spoke. 'They shift between human and raven form. Once numerous. Nearly hunted to extinction for their beaks and feathers. Dark worshippers prized them most.'

He turned then to Kesaahn, his expression sobering. 'A radiant beacon must guide the way. Kesaahn, your role is vital. You must create the Potion of Immutable Luminosity. The God's Light.'

Kesaahn went pale.

She sank into the nearest chair, trembling. 'That is no simple potion,' she whispered. 'No Magika has ever succeeded. Not one.' Her breath caught. 'Except the Dark Magika.'

Rohan's hand settled on her shoulder, steady and protective. 'What makes it so dangerous?'

'The ingredients are scattered across Arghost,' Kesaahn said faintly. 'Some thought lost. Some guarded by horrors. And the incantation itself...' She shook her head. 'It drains more than the body.'

Cedric's expression sobered. 'The light does not wish to be held. It was never meant to be owned.'

Niama looked between them. 'What does the God's Light do?'

Kesaahn lifted her gaze, fear and reverence intertwined. 'It rivals Athris' own radiance. It will guide us where no other light can reach. The light doesn't answer ambition,' she said softly. 'Only absence.'

'Is there no other way?' Niama asked quietly. The weight of what lay ahead pressed hard against her chest.

Cedric's answer was immediate. 'No.' His tone left no room for doubt. 'Where you are going, lesser light will fail. Our scholars will give you the incantations once the ingredients are gathered.'

Niama nodded, though her heart raced.

Cedric rose and rested his hands on the desk's edge. 'The final trial will test not strength, nor wit—but character.' His eyes darkened. 'For the sacrifice of an ungranted light shall herald a new dawn.'

He paused, letting the words settle.

'There exists but one creature in all Arghost born without the light of Athris within it.' His voice softened with reverence. 'A great bird. Known to the Namite as Qraith. To the Khuris, Akeela. We call it Luminavix. The Soaring Luminescence.'

The room seemed to hold its breath.

'It is sacred,' Cedric continued. 'Revered by many races. To harm it is unthinkable.' His gaze swept over them. 'Yet the prophecy is clear.'

Niama felt the future tilt, sharp and unavoidable.

And for the first time since leaving the forest, she wondered what the cost of salvation would truly be.

'Yes,' Niama said softly.

The word barely disturbed the air.

Her thoughts slipped backward, unbidden, to childhood evenings beneath the forest canopy, when elders spoke the Luminavix's name in reverent tones. A creature woven into story and memory. A promise of life renewed. Its song, they said, could mend what grief had broken, or break what pride had hardened.

Cedric continued, his voice steady.

'The Luminavix nests high among the Black Spire peaks. In the frost months, the hatchlings come.' He paused. 'The mother lays her eggs, then shatters the shells herself. The young emerge lifeless upon the ice.'

Silence settled, heavy and deliberate.

'She sings then,' Cedric said. 'A lament carried on the wind. A plea to the Lord of Light.'

Niama's breath caught.

'And the light answers.' His gaze lifted. 'It descends in a living cascade. It wraps mother and young alike, blue and gold entwined. What was still awakens. What was broken draws breath.'

The image struck Niama with quiet force, not spectacle but surrender. Loss followed by faith. Beauty sharpened by grief.

Cedric's voice hardened.

'To create the God's Light, you must take that radiance before it reaches the young.'

The words cut clean.

Rohan frowned. 'How?'

'You must interrupt the rite at its apex,' Cedric replied. 'When the light descends, but before it binds.'

Her throat tightened. 'Then the hatchlings...'

No one spoke.

Cedric met her gaze. 'They will die.'

The chamber seemed to contract around them. Shelves loomed. Knowledge pressed in, unyielding.

Niama closed her eyes, just long enough to steady herself.

When she opened them, resolve burned clear and cold.

'Then that is the cost,' she said quietly. 'And we will carry it.'

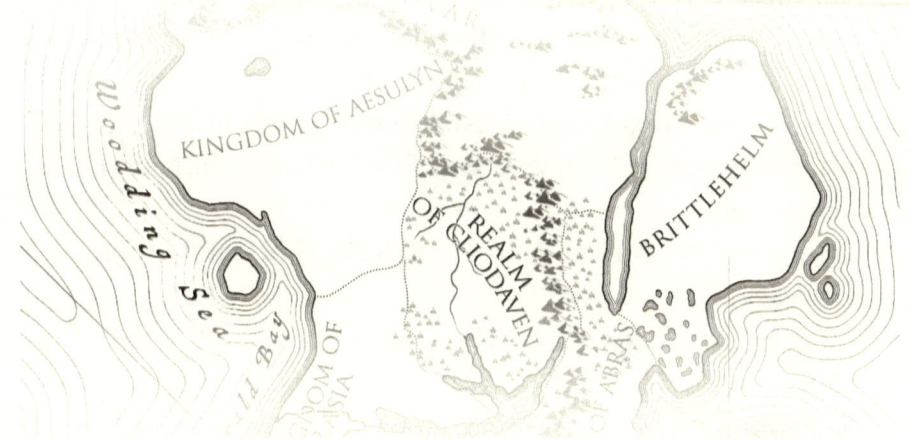

CHAPTER TWENTY-ONE

The Dark Master

The silence that followed was not agreement. But it was acceptance, heavy and unwilling.

Cedric's voice carried the weight of long regret. 'There is no other path, my dear. This task was never meant for gentle hands,' he said, and did not soften the words. His gaze lowered. 'The mother will fight without hesitation. Any Luminavix within reach will answer her cry. They do not abandon their own.'

Shock rippled through the group.

'This is truly the only way?' Rohan asked, doubt cracking his composure.

Cedric removed his spectacles and pressed his fingers briefly to his eyes. 'Once the light is absorbed, it diminishes. Time erodes it.' He replaced the lenses and leaned back against the desk. 'What you're being asked to do is cruel. But it is also necessary.'

The chamber seemed to close around Niama. Dust and parchment thickened the air. Fear left a bitter taste on her tongue. How did one weigh a single innocent life against thousands? How did one carry that answer and still breathe?

'How do we take it?' she asked. Her voice trembled, but she did not look away.

'With precision,' Cedric replied. 'And knowledge you do not yet possess. In Silenthollow, you will find a woman of the forest. She will know how to ensnare the light.'

Rohan paced, boots striking stone, hands clenched as if the room itself were an enemy he could strike.

Will stood frozen, eyes wide. 'What is all of this?' he whispered. 'What have I been pulled into?'

Niama turned to him, the words heavy but measured. 'We could not tell you. The prophecy binds us, and enemies listen where they should not. The Second Rising has begun. The Actari march against Aesulyn. That is why we were driven here.'

Will staggered back as if struck. 'The Second Rising?' His voice broke. 'My wife—she's alone. With child.' He swallowed. 'I need to go back.'

'You will,' Niama said firmly. She met his gaze, unflinching. 'We will see you safely reunited. And we will stop what's coming.'

Tears welled as Will turned away, shoulders trembling.

Rohan drew a slow breath and faced Cedric. 'Another matter. The Order of the Fallen Phoenix hunts us. What do you know of them?'

Cedric's expression hardened. His fists struck the desk with a sharp crack. 'Fanatics. They believe destruction is purification.' His eyes burned. 'They hide within every culture, whispering poison. They will oppose you at every turn.'

His gaze pinned Rohan. 'Move unseen. Trust sparingly. If they block your path—remove them.'

The words settled like ash.

Cedric straightened. 'You have much to learn, and little time. I will take you to the library. My brothers will assist you.' He paused. 'If you need me, you know where to find me.'

He led them down the hall to a broad chamber lined with tables and towering shelves. A man in a white robe looked up from a stack of scrolls, his round face brightening instantly.

'Ah!' he exclaimed, rising with surprising speed. 'Visitors!' He bowed slightly, beaming. 'I am Scholar Brom. Cedric has told me of our... predicament.' His smile widened. 'And I am delighted to help,' he said, a little too brightly. 'Ask. Read. Learn. The answers are here somewhere, I assure you.'

Behind them, Cedric withdrew, his footsteps fading.

Ahead, knowledge waited.

And with it, the next impossible choice.

Kesaahn stepped forward, urgency sharpening her stride. 'We need to know everything about the God's Light.'

Scholar Brom's expression brightened, equal parts reverence and dread. 'Then come.' He led them into a shadowed alcove, where the shelves pressed close and the air felt older. He withdrew a dust-choked scroll and laid it carefully upon a desk. 'A torch, if you would,' he said to Will.

Flickering light bled across the parchment as they gathered around. Shadows climbed the shelves, stretching long and distorted. The scent of aged paper and oil thickened the air.

'The God's Light,' Brom said softly, 'is not merely illumination. It is Athris made manifest. It reaches where all lesser light fails.' His finger traced the script. 'The components are drawn from places where light is tested, strained, or broken,' Brom said quietly.

He read on.

'Everleaf. Solis gland from a male Infurnus lizard. Purified water from this isle. Mithril dust. Emerald Coeylite powder. Afeacress from the Pools of Intris. And the light of a—'

Kesaahn lifted a hand. 'Everleaf grows high in the Orboros range. Traders in Fairmoor or Steepmoor might carry it.' She paused. 'In theory.' 'Infurnus lizards dwell beyond the Swamp of Anguish. Mithril we can barter for, if the Dwarves will listen.' Her voice tightened. 'Emerald Coeylite... I have not heard of any in years. And the Pools of Intris are guarded.'

Silence settled over them.

Niama felt her stomach knot as the path ahead took shape, not as a road, but as a series of wounds carved across the map.

'I've heard of a Coeylite gem,' Rohan said at last. 'Kept within King Wymond's throne room. Stonebreach.'

No one spoke.

'The sunken city?' Will asked quietly.

Rohan nodded once.

Brom hesitated before continuing.

'To bind the God's Light,' he said, 'the vessel must be touched by Athris himself. That grace can only be drawn at the highest point in Arghost.'

Kesaahn went still. 'Dead Man's Rise,' she said, and did not elaborate.

Brom inclined his head. 'A place where few return.'

Niama did not need to ask what dwelled there. The name alone carried the weight of it.

Brom nodded once. 'Where the Luminavix return light to the world.'

Silence pressed in.

'Then you already know the cost,' Brom said quietly. 'I will not dress it in reverence. This is not a blessing. It is a taking.'

'Then what choice do we have?' Niama asked.

None came.

The silence answered for them.

Boots suddenly struck stone. Another Seeker burst into the alcove, breathless. 'We've pulled a survivor from the rocks,' he said. 'The brothers are bringing him now. He asked for you.'

The torch guttered.

And the path ahead grew darker still.

The companions exchanged uneasy looks.

'Another survivor?' Rohan said, doubt sharpening his voice.

Two Seekers entered, bearing a man between them. His head hung low, arms draped over their shoulders, boots leaving damp tracks across the stone. The smell of salt and rotting seaweed clung to him, sharp enough to sting the eyes.

Niama's breath caught.

'Coseo?'

Rohan moved instinctively, hand half-drawn. 'Get him out of here. Now.'

The Seekers tightened their grip, pulling back toward the door.

Coseo laughed.

It was low and wet, the sound scraping through the chamber like something dragged across bone.

'Such a welcome, Prince Rohan,' he said, voice thick with mockery.

With a flick of his wrist, the two Seekers were hurled aside. They struck the shelves with bone-jarring force. Wood cracked. Dust and parchment burst into the air.

He lifted his head.

Black eyes met Niama's gaze, lightless and vast. Her stomach twisted. The face was familiar, but wrong. Skin stretched pale and tight, as if it no longer belonged to him. Gums raw and bleeding. Cheeks hollowed as if something inside him had already eaten its fill.

'I'm pleased you survived our little voyage,' Coseo said mildly, floating free of the floor. 'It would've been terribly dull if you'd drowned.' He smiled. 'Where's the joy in that?'

Kesaahn stepped forward despite the tremor in her hands. 'What do you want?'

Coseo's grin widened.

'Eventually? Your deaths.' A soft chuckle followed. 'But patience has its pleasures.'

His gaze snapped to Will.

Dark vapor spilled from his fingers, coiling like smoke made solid. It seized Will's throat and lifted him from the floor, his feet kicking uselessly in the air.

Will's eyes found Niama's.

'No!' Niama cried. 'Cos—please!'

Coseo turned to her. Not hurried. Not enraged. He studied her as if weighing a memory.

'You always did surround yourself with fragile things,' he said softly. 'People who believed you'd save them.'

His fingers tightened.

The crack was sharp and final.

Will hit the stone and did not move.

Coseo did not look at the corpse.

He watched Niama instead.

For a heartbeat, Niama could not hear. Not the scholars screaming. Not the wind tearing through the chamber. The world narrowed to the shape of Will's body on the floor and the dark mark blooming at his throat.

She waited for something inside her to shatter.

It did not.

Instead, a cold clarity slid into place.

This was not loss. This was not chaos. This was choice, made in full awareness.

Coseo had chosen.

And in doing so, he had burned the last bridge between them.

'What have you done?' Niama whispered, the words barely forming.

Niama's hands trembled, but her voice did not.

'You wanted me to see,' she said.

Coseo smiled.

Something inside her closed, quiet and final, like a door sealed against a storm.

The room froze.

Coseo hovered higher now, power radiating from him in cold waves. 'The Dark Master has returned,' he proclaimed. 'And Arghost will kneel.'

The scholars recoiled. Books rattled on their shelves.

Coseo lifted his arms and spoke.

The words were not meant for mortal tongues.

'Ark t'ra et mortania evo mortis.'

The chamber erupted. Wind tore through the library, pages ripped loose, shelves shuddering as knowledge centuries old was thrown screaming into the air.

Coseo threw back his head, laughter swallowed by the rising gale. Black smoke poured from his chest, spiraling outward, vast and consuming.

'I summon my legions,' he roared.

The blast hit like a hammer.

Then he was gone.

Brom's hands shook as he smoothed a torn parchment against his chest. 'The words he spoke,' he said, voice barely steady. 'Ancient tongue. I've only ever read them.' He swallowed. 'World of light will die. Darkness returns.'

The wind fell away as abruptly as it had risen.

Papers drifted down through the stillness, settling across broken shelves and shattered knowledge. No one moved. Even the scholars seemed afraid to breathe.

Will lay where he had fallen, a single human life reduced to silence amid centuries of learning.

Niama knelt beside him, not to plead, not to deny, but to close his eyes. Her fingers lingered there only a moment.

When she stood again, the room felt smaller.

'He's declared himself,' she said.

Rohan looked at her sharply.

'The Darkness doesn't hide anymore,' Niama continued. 'It wants us to know who leads it.'

Brom swallowed hard. 'Then the Second Rising is no longer prophecy.'

Niama met his gaze. 'No. It's a war.'

And somewhere deep within the Isle, the storm answered.

CHAPTER TWENTY-TWO

The Namite

V alran braced himself against the wind's icy fangs, clutching Dorsey's coat tight around his shoulders as a borrowed shield against the merciless cold. The stink of alcohol and sweat clung to the fabric, sharp and familiar, and he welcomed it for that very reason. It was real. It was grounding.

Snow crunched beneath his boots with each careful step, the sound echoing too loudly in his ears as he slipped from shadow to shadow, face kept low, breath measured. Above him, the stars lay scattered like broken glass, the crescent moon hanging pale over the desolate streets of Brittleheim. Guided by that cold light and the silent geometry of the heavens, he pressed west through the ancient city, letting the encroaching darkness fold around him like a cloak. For now, it hid him.

Though the Kingdom of Ijovar was not his home, Valran moved through it with uncanny ease. The village children had once given him a name for it, a teasing honor for his strange talent for finding his way back no matter how far he strayed. Land and sky spoke to him in ways maps never could. Direction lived in his bones.

For the first time he could remember, that certainty faltered, just long enough to unsettle him.

Aesulyn lay westward. The desert kingdom waited beyond snow and stone, and the knowledge of it steadied his pace.

His thoughts drifted, unbidden, to the Namites who dwelled there. Relations between their people and the elves had always been warm. As a child, Valran had watched the villagers gather eagerly each year for the arrival of Namite traders, their caravans heavy with silks, spices, and strange treasures that smelled of heat and sun. There had been no fear in those days. Only anticipation.

He remembered Uthru then, the old elder with the weathered voice, recounting tales of Alboros, the great northern city of Ijovar before its fall. Once magnificent. Once alive. Now a ruin of collapsed roofs and empty windows, its bones picked clean by war and left to the mercy of northern winds. Even as a child, Valran had felt the warning in those stories.

A murmur of voices snapped him back to the present.

His heart lurched. Heavy footsteps scraped against stone nearby. Valran pressed himself flat against the wall of a half-ruined building, breath held, pulse pounding hard enough to betray him. Two bulky figures passed within arm's reach, deep in conversation, their attention elsewhere.

Only when they moved on did he exhale, slow and shaking, the sound scraped thin through his chest.

He edged forward again, eyes fixed on the dark fringe of trees ahead. If he could reach them, the forest would take him in. Shelter. Cover. Safety. The last building on the city's edge loomed before him, and within it, a flicker of firelight glowed warm against the snow.

He slowed.

A shadow moved across the ground outside the window, wavering with the fire's pulse. Curiosity warred with caution. Carefully, Valran crept closer and peered inside.

The rear of the structure had collapsed, roof caved in beneath the weight of winter. Snow drifted through the ruin, collecting in pale mounds. The front remained intact. A fire crackled low. Torches burned along the walls. Beyond a shattered window at the far end, the trees waited, dark and close.

The door stood ajar.

Inside, two Namites knelt bound at the center of the room.

They were immense, towering well over seven feet, their bodies dense with muscle and thick hair from crown to heel. Plate armor encased them, battered but intact. Even on their knees, even restrained, they radiated defiance. Jackal-like heads lifted proudly, dark eyes fixed on their captors. When they spoke, it was in low, rasping growls that carried neither fear nor submission.

A Swinish guard stood watch nearby.

Beside him loomed Bastion.

And with him—

Valran's breath caught.

The hooded figure stepped forward into the firelight and lowered his cowl.

Coseo.

The name landed wrong, as if the sound no longer fit the shape before him.

But not as Valran remembered him.

The eyes were wrong. Blackened. Empty. His face was drawn thin, lips pale and tight, something twisted beneath the skin. The voice that followed carried a weight of malice that chilled deeper than the wind outside.

This was no longer the boy who had once shared fires and laughter.

Questions surged, sharp and relentless. Why was Coseo here? Why with Bastion? Where was Niama?

Valran did not move.

He stayed hidden in the shadows, watching as the scene unfolded, knowing instinctively that whatever came next would change far more than his own fate.

'Where are your armies hiding, jackal?' Coseo snarled, his voice echoing off stone.

The Namites stiffened at the insult. Their hackles rose beneath iron and fur.

'Never shall we yield such knowledge to the likes of you, black-eyed filth,' one growled, tusked muzzle lifting in defiance. 'Our brethren will fight until their final breath. This war shall not be claimed by your kind.'

Coseo smiled.

'Is that so?'

He lifted one hand.

Spectral tendrils lashed from his fingers, coiling around the Namite's throat and tearing him from the floor. The creature's armored boots kicked uselessly in the air as he clawed at the grasp, breath sawn into wet gasps.

Valran stared.

Namites were massive creatures, muscle packed beneath thick pelt, their bodies built to endure the desert's cruelty. Even unarmored, they were heavy. Encased in iron and gold, they were immovable.

And yet Coseo held him aloft as if he weighed nothing.

There was a sharp crack. Too loud, too deep. Not just the neck. Something else had broken.

The Namite collapsed bonelessly to the stone.

Valran did not breathe. His mind struggled to fit what he had seen into any shape he understood. This was not anger. Not rage. Not even cruelty, exactly.

It was ease.

The second Namite roared and lunged.

Coseo did not turn fully. A single backhand sent the creature hurtling into stacked crates. Wood shattered. Dust bloomed. The Namite slumped, unmoving.

'I will return for the other,' Coseo said calmly, already turning away.

Bastion followed without a word.

The Swinish guard grinned, eyes shining with crude awe, and closed the door behind them as he resumed his post.

As their footsteps faded, Valran caught Bastion muttering something about a hunter.

That was enough.

He slipped through the window and crossed to the fallen Namite, crouching low. One glance at the door. Still closed.

Valran shook the Namite's shoulder.

Harder.

The creature stirred.

Valran pressed a finger to his own lips. 'Shhh.'

Confusion flickered in the Namite's eyes.

'I have come to free you,' Valran whispered, breath fogging the air. 'Let me undo your bonds.'

After a moment's hesitation, the Namite extended his wrists.

The ropes fell away with a soft, final thud.

The Namite rolled his shoulders once.

Then seized Valran by the throat.

He lifted him effortlessly, teeth bared beneath his jackal muzzle.

'Who are you?' he rumbled, voice low and dangerous, hot breath reeking of iron and damp fur.

'V-Valran,' he rasped, fingers scrabbling at the Namite's grip. 'I was held here. I am escaping.' He jerked his chin toward the door. 'They'll return.'

The Namite studied him in silence.

Then released him.

'Hmmm,' he grunted. 'We leave. Now.'

He moved to the window and stepped into the snow without another word.

Valran followed.

The forest loomed ahead, dark and sheltering, wind cutting sharp across their faces.

'That way,' Valran whispered, nodding toward the trees. 'But a Swinish guards the door.'

The Namite straightened, shoulders squared.

'Then he shall not,' he growled, and strode toward the front of the building.

'Wait,' Valran whispered, but the Namite did not slow.

A dull thud sounded ahead. Then another.

By the time Valran rounded the corner, the Swinish lay slack and unmoving, dragged across the stone like refuse. The Namite hauled him inside and shut the door with a final, deliberate shove.

They paused only long enough to scan the forest.

'Follow,' the Namite growled.

He broke into a run.

The forest swallowed Valran whole.

Darkness closed around him, cold and formless, pressing in from every side. Snow muffled the world, swallowing sound even as branches clawed at his arms and roots snared his boots. He caught only fleeting signs of the Namite's passage: a snapped twig, a whisper of displaced snow, a shape that vanished before his eyes could fix on it.

Then the Namite was gone.

Valran pushed on blindly, lungs burning, legs protesting as the undergrowth thickened. His heart hammered loud enough to drown thought. Panic rose sharp and sudden.

A shape resolved ahead.

The Namite stood waiting, barely winded.

'What pitiful pace is this?' he snarled. 'Time bleeds away, and you crawl like a newborn beast. You run as a pup runs, without teeth.'

Valran bent double, hands braced on his knees. 'I... cannot match you,' he gasped. Sweat chilled against his skin, breath tearing from his chest in ragged pulls.

The Namite studied him for a moment.

'Then climb,' he said.

Valran hesitated only a heartbeat before grasping the Namite's broad shoulders and hauling himself up. The creature surged forward at once.

The forest blurred.

Snow streaked past beneath them as the Namite ran, each stride devouring ground with terrifying ease. Valran clung tight, awed and breathless, the world reduced to motion and cold and the pounding of blood in his ears.

He tried to track their heading. West. It should have been instinct.

It wasn't.

Hours passed. Or moments. He could not tell.

Moonlight washed the forest in silver, snow glowing pale beneath their passage. The only sound was the Namite's heavy stride and the relentless rhythm of Valran's heart.

Cold seeped deeper now, gnawing at bone and muscle alike. Valran's limbs trembled with exhaustion, yet the Namite showed no sign of slowing. His fur radiated heat, a living barrier against the night, though it did little to ease the dread coiling tighter in Valran's chest.

Coseo. Bastion. The hunters that would follow.

At last, the Namite slowed.

'Here,' he rumbled, voice rough with fatigue. 'I must rest and restore what has been spent.'

He gestured toward a hollow nestled among the snow-buried hills ahead, a shadowed refuge half-hidden by stone and wind-carved drifts.

'We pause,' he said. 'Movement resumes when strength returns.'

The forest closed around them, and for the first time since fleeing the city, Valran allowed himself to breathe.

Not safely.

But alive.

As they approached, Valran spotted the tunnel only by the way the roots bent around it, old and knotted, drinking from the stream like grasping fingers. Water-worn stone and hanging moss disguised the entrance so completely it vanished unless one knew where to look.

He slid from the Namite's back, boots sinking into snow with a dull hush.

They entered the tunnel together.

Moist air closed around them, cool and mineral-heavy. Water whispered along the walls, its sound low and constant, as though the stone itself murmured secrets too old to name. Deeper in, the stream widened and curled away, revealing a shallow alcove cradled in rotting leaves and forest debris. Dry ground waited there, gritty beneath Valran's palm as he lowered himself to sit.

The Namite stood motionless for a time, breathing deep, broad chest rising and falling as strength seeped back into his frame.

'I am called Tehuti,' he said at last, voice roughened by exhaustion but unbroken. 'Valran, you have acted with honor. Your aid is received. Your debt is marked.'

Valran inclined his head. 'Your words are heard.' His gaze flicked toward the tunnel mouth. 'And... my condolences. For your companion.'

Tehuti's ears flattened slightly.

'Amenrut,' he said. 'Brother-in-arms. Shieldmate. His claws did not fail.' A pause. 'His absence will be felt when blood is next spilled.' He lowered his gaze to the stone. 'Such is the price of war.'

Silence settled, broken only by water and breath.

'By what road did you come to Ijovar, elf?' Tehuti asked. 'Your scent carries forest, prophecy... and flight.'

Valran swallowed and told him.

Of the Seer.

Of the Second Rising.

Of the medallion.

As he spoke, unease coiled tighter in his chest, a quiet pressure just beneath the ribs. Something in the telling felt incomplete, as though a piece of truth had slipped away while his back was turned.

'In what turning of the world,' Valran murmured, voice scarcely louder than the stream, 'does Coseo become the harbinger of darkness?' He shook his head faintly. 'His face was... altered. As if something else now wore it.'

Tehuti's breath hitched.

His gaze dropped to the stone between them.

'Then the Second Rising is no longer distant,' he growled. 'This is news of grave weight.'

He studied Valran closely. 'You falter. Are you wounded?'

'No,' Valran said too quickly. He rubbed his temples, trying to dispel the pressure building behind his eyes. 'Only the air. It presses strangely here.'

Tehuti did not answer at once.

'When the Dark Commander gathers his legions,' he said slowly, 'the world will have little time to brace itself.' His eyes lifted. 'Did the Seer speak of the prophecy?'

Valran nodded. His gaze fixed on the damp stone. 'It was why I left them. Why I fled the forest.' His voice thickened. 'Niama carries the Seer's mark now. A medallion. She journeyed east, to Silverfall, seeking answers.' A pause. 'I pray she still draws breath.'

Tehuti's ears rose.

'They move to fulfill it?' he asked.

'They do,' Valran said. 'Or will try.'

Tehuti regarded him for a long moment.

'Then the Seer has chosen,' he said at last. 'This is... fitting.' A low rumble entered his voice. 'The wheel turns as it must.'

Valran looked away. 'Yes. Fitting.'

He did not speak Coseo's name again.

The darkness roaming free felt too vast to voice.

He forced himself to breathe, to anchor his thoughts somewhere safer. 'How did you come to be here?' he asked quietly.

Tehuti's jaw tightened.

'By war,' he said. 'And by betrayal.'

And in the dim hush of the tunnel, the stream whispered on, indifferent to the shape of the coming storm.

Tehuti shifted, extending his long, furred legs, the movement careful despite his size.

'My kin have endured repeated assaults these past months,' he said, voice low and even. 'Settlements east of the Kingdom were put to flame. Reduced to bone and ash, picked clean by fire.' His jaw tightened. 'Then, a fortnight past, the attacks ceased.'

Silence fell, sudden and heavy.

Tehuti drew a slow breath. His gaze unfocused, as though fixed on something far beyond the tunnel walls. 'The stillness was unnatural. No enemy withdraws without purpose.' He paused. 'The King sent Amenrut and me to Ijovar to uncover the reason.'

He leaned back against the stone.

'Our passage through Kambish was unchallenged,' he continued. 'No patrols. No banners. No resistance. Whatever force once held the pass had retreated deeper into Ijovar's heart.' A low growl edged his words. 'That alone was warning enough.'

Tehuti closed his eyes.

'On the fourth day, we reached the ruins of Flatfold, west of here.' His ears flattened. 'It appeared abandoned. A lie.'

He stopped. His clawed hand tightened against the stone.

His breath left him slowly. 'The Swinish descended without sound. They were many. We were two. Bound. Delivered.' He opened his eyes again. 'You witnessed what followed.'

Valran hesitated before asking, 'How do we escape Ijovar?'

Tehuti lifted one clawed hand and gestured west. 'Toward the Ashstone Mountains. We cross their spine, then descend to Kambish.' His voice hardened. 'That road leads home.'

He turned his gaze on Valran fully.

'I return to Kahid,' he said. 'The King will hear this. My people must be warned. War is already moving, whether they yet see it or not.'

'I understand,' Valran said quietly, eyes drawn toward the tunnel mouth and the dark beyond.

'For now,' Tehuti said, rubbing at his eyes, fatigue finally bleeding through his iron composure, 'we rest. The road ahead is long. Our bodies must endure it.'

Valran nodded and settled back against the bank. Exhaustion seeped into his bones, heavy and unrelenting. The day had stripped him raw, leaving questions unanswered and fears unspoken.

Outside, an owl called, low and mournful. Wind stirred the trees, leaves whispering secrets the night would not yet reveal.

Valran closed his eyes.

He hoped Niama still lived.

He hoped the forest still stood.

The night offered nothing in return.

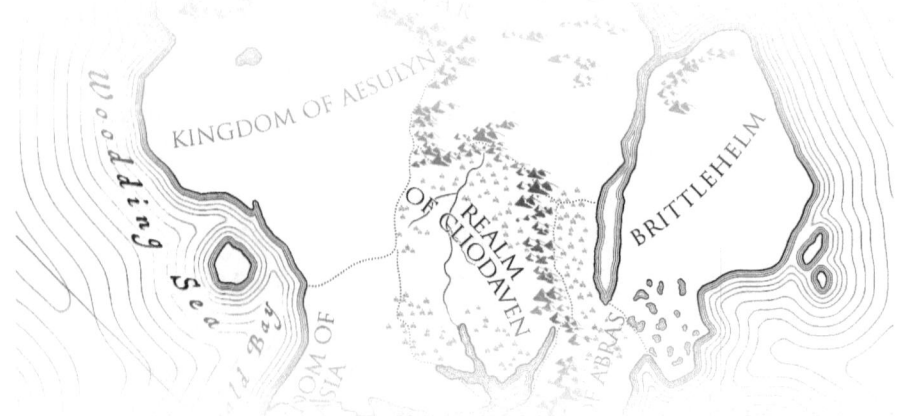

CHAPTER TWENTY-THREE

The Return

Niama knelt beside Will's body, her tears falling soundlessly as she whispered a prayer to Athris. Grief pressed down on her, thick and airless. She wanted to strike back, to tear something apart, to make the world pay in a language it understood. Instead, she remained motionless, hands braced against the stone, holding herself together by will alone.

Kesaahn's hand settled on her shoulder, warm through cloth. The touch steadied her, though Niama could not bring herself to look up.

'Will was a good man,' Kesaahn said quietly. 'His loss wounds us deeply. But the path ahead does not loosen its grip. We must continue.'

Niama wiped her face with the back of her hand. Her eyes burned, raw and reddened, but her voice came out low and controlled. 'I know.' A pause. 'It feels as though everything that mattered has slipped beyond my reach.'

Rohan stepped closer, grief tightening his features. 'He didn't deserve this,' he said. 'And Coseo—'

The name struck like flint.

'That thing was not Coseo,' Niama snapped. Her voice rose, sharp with fury she no longer tried to hide. 'My friend is gone. Whatever wears his face now has hollowed him out and learned to smile with what it stole from him. And if we fail, it will do the same to countless others.'

Cedric entered then, his presence drawing her attention despite herself. Guilt stirred in her chest, cold and unwelcome. They had failed Will. Not by weakness. By being one step too slow. No amount of resolve could undo that.

The library bore the scars of the assault. Shelves stood half-emptied, parchment strewn across desks and stone alike. Seekers moved through the wreckage, binding wounds, stamping out small fires sparked by fallen torches, salvaging what knowledge they could from the ruin.

Cedric's gaze lingered on Will before lifting to meet theirs. 'The Dark Master has revealed himself,' he said. 'War has returned to Arghost.' His voice hardened. 'The Seekers will lend what aid we can.'

'We will need arms,' Kesaahn said at once. Resolve burned behind her exhaustion. 'I require a staff.'

Rohan nodded, his hand clenching at his side. 'And I will need a sword.'

Niama rose slowly. Her limbs trembled, but she did not falter. She could not change what had been taken from them. But she could decide what came next. She bowed her head briefly, whispering one final prayer for Will's light, hoping he had found the peace denied him in life.

'Follow me,' Cedric said, turning toward the far corridor.

Niama fell into step beside Kesaahn and Rohan. Smoke still hung in the air, bitter on her tongue. Ash crunched faintly beneath their boots as they moved through the damaged halls, the echo of footsteps following them like a reminder of what had been lost.

She did not look back.

Will's memory would not be honored with tears alone. She would carry it forward—in action, in resolve, and in whatever justice she would force from the darkness ahead.

Cedric led them down a narrow, descending passage where the air lay thick and stale, heavy with the scent of damp stone and forgotten years. Cobwebs sagged from the ceiling in pale veils, brushing close as they passed. Niama drew her cloak tighter, the chill creeping into her bones. A single torch burned ahead, its flame guttering as if it, too, wanted out.

At the foot of the stairs, Cedric paused. He sifted through the keys at his belt before selecting one unlike the rest and fitting it into the iron lock.

The door screamed as it opened, the sound tearing through the corridor and echoing long after the motion ceased. Niama flinched despite herself, unease prickling along her spine.

Cedric moved quickly, lighting the wall torches one by one. Warm amber light bloomed across the chamber, revealing its purpose at once.

Weapons lined the walls.

Swords, axes, spears, shields, bows. Steel and wood arranged with care rather than ostentation, each piece bearing the quiet certainty of use, not display. Shadows slid along honed edges and worn grips, hinting at hands long gone and battles already paid for.

Cedric lifted a sword from its rack, fingers tracing the runes etched into the blade. 'Forged in the Jagged Hills,' he said softly, reverent. He returned it to its place with care.

Rohan drifted toward the blades, lifting a curved scimitar, its balance clean and deadly. 'Aesulyn make,' he noted.

'In capable hands, a devastating weapon,' Cedric agreed.

Rohan set it aside and moved on. 'Not mine.' He selected a shorter blade instead, testing its weight. 'I prefer something that answers quickly.'

Cedric turned to Kesaahn and gestured toward a staff resting apart from the others. 'And for you.' His voice warmed. 'This belonged to Serindup. A Master Magika. He wielded it in the last war.' A pause. 'You will not find a more suitable focus in all of Arghost.'

Kesaahn accepted it carefully. Power stirred beneath her grip, a low hum that thrummed through bone and blood. She turned the staff once, feeling its balance. At its head, a fitted vial gleamed, ready to receive reagents and spells alike. Magic could be cast without such a conduit—but never with the same force.

Cedric's gaze shifted to Niama. 'And you?'

Niama hesitated. 'My bow was lost,' she said quietly. 'With the ship.'

Cedric smiled and gestured toward a wall of bows. 'Then choose. Elven craft, every one. Made to endure.' He stepped back. 'Let the wood decide.'

Niama moved slowly along the display, fingers brushing polished limbs and braided strings. One bow drew her hand without thought.

Mistwood. She stilled, breath catching as if the wood itself had spoken her name.

The grain, the curve, the scent faint but unmistakable.

'Melfanden,' she said softly.

Cedric nodded. 'Yes.'

'He taught me to track,' Niama continued, voice barely above a whisper. 'And to listen.'

She lifted the bow, the weight settling into her palms as if it had never left them. Cedric placed a quiver beside it.

'It is fitting,' he said. 'That it returns to the forest through you.'

Gratitude rose sharp and unexpected. A fragment of home, found here of all places.

Cedric stepped back, surveying them once more. 'I have secured passage for you,' he said. 'A trade vessel bound for Cloudmoor. It leaves with the tide.'

Steel, wood, and resolve now in their hands, the path forward sharpened.

And there would be no turning back.

The companions exchanged uneasy glances. Cedric noticed at once.

'There is no cause for alarm,' he said. 'Though the storm guards this isle, our ships pass it when they must. Our captains know a route few others do. It draws less attention. Less resistance.'

Rohan frowned. 'A secret passage?' He glanced toward the distant sea. 'Then what of those who die trying to reach you?'

Cedric's expression darkened. 'Not all who come seek knowledge.' His voice lowered. 'The storm protects more than our solitude. Within these walls lie relics, texts, weapons. Without the storm, the Isle would be stripped bare.' He turned, ending the discussion. 'Come.'

They followed him from the stone edifice and down a narrow path toward the wharf. For the first time, Niama truly saw the island.

It was harsh. Beautiful in its severity.

The great structure they had left behind seemed almost swallowed by the jagged hills that ringed it, stone pressed into stone as if the land itself wished to hide it. Salt hung thick in the air. Waves crashed against the shore below, their rhythm steady and unyielding.

At the dock, Cedric halted. His gaze moved briefly to the narrow coffin already secured along the rail, then back to Niama.

'He will be returned to his kin,' Cedric said quietly. 'The Seekers have seen to it.'

Niama nodded, unable to trust her voice.

'Captain Steele,' he said. 'A steady hand and a seasoned sailor. He will see you safely to the mainland.' A pause. 'Our prayers go with you.'

He motioned to several packed satchels already stowed aboard. 'Your passage is provided. Provisions as well. My brothers have seen to it.'

Cedric then turned to Kesaahn, pressing a small vial and a rolled parchment into her hands. 'Purified water,' he said quietly. 'And the incantations. Guard them well.'

Kesaahn inclined her head. 'I will.'

They boarded the vessel one by one.

The ship itself was unremarkable. A narrow-bowed craft built to cut through rough water, its sides scarred and weathered by long service. The deck was cramped but solid beneath Niama's boots. The smell of tar and salt rose from the planks, familiar and steadying.

A frayed sail hung ready to catch the wind. Oars lay lashed along the sides should the breeze fail. Nothing about the vessel was elegant—but it was sound.

As the final lines were cast off, Niama turned back to Cedric, who stood watching from the dock.

'Do you believe we will succeed?' she asked.

Cedric regarded her for a long moment. 'My belief is of little consequence,' he said at last. 'The world will not be saved by spectators.' His gaze sharpened. 'What matters is what you choose to do when the moment demands it.'

Niama accepted the truth of it with a slow nod.

She had chosen mercy before. It hadn't saved Will.

She would not stop choosing it. But she would choose it with her eyes open.

She withdrew to the small cabin at the stern as the ship eased away from the wharf. The sea stretched dark and restless ahead, the storm's distant presence felt rather than seen.

Bound for Cloudmoor.

Bound for whatever waited beyond.

By dusk, the storm found them.

It was smaller than the one that had shattered *The Little Dove*, yet no less restless. Waves rose and fell in heavy succession, slamming against the hull with bruising force. The wind tugged hard at the lone mainsail, but Captain Steele held the ship steady, reading the sea with practiced ease.

This vessel handled differently. With only a single sail, it answered the helm more cleanly, cutting through the swell rather than fighting it. The motion was harsh but controlled, demanding vigilance rather than desperation.

Three sailors worked the deck, all clad in the white cloaks of the Seekers. They moved with quiet efficiency, hands sure on rope and rail, faces set with the calm of those accustomed to hostile seas.

The sea still fought them, but without malice.

Niama felt it then—the absence.

The waves rose and fell as waves should, driven by wind and tide alone. No wrongness pressed against her senses. No will bent the water toward ruin.

She thought of the first storm. Of the laughter carried on the wind.

This one was only a storm.

The storm passed as abruptly as it had risen.

Clouds thinned. Wind slackened. The sea eased back into long, rolling breaths. The ship righted itself and resumed its course toward Cloudmoor beneath a clearing sky.

Four days lay between them and the mainland.

There was nothing to do but endure the passage—rest when they could, watch the horizon, and let their thoughts circle what had been lost... and what still waited ahead.

Niama stood at the prow, the ship cutting steadily through the darkened water. Sun-warmed air brushed her skin, and the sea spoke softly against the hull, a low rhythm that almost invited calm. Almost.

Cloudmoor lay ahead as a faint scatter of lights, pressed against the mainland's edge. A few hours more, and solid ground would replace the endless sway beneath her feet. The thought eased something tight in her chest, though it did not loosen it entirely.

Kesaahn joined her without a word, studying the set of Niama's shoulders. The girl she had first met weeks ago was gone. What stood beside her now was sharper, quieter. Hardened by loss that had not yet found release.

'These past weeks have been unkind to you,' Kesaahn said at last. 'You have carried more than any should.'

Niama did not look away from the horizon. 'Coseo,' she said, the name rough against her tongue. 'I can't escape the feeling that I should have seen it. That whatever he became... somehow, I failed him.'

Kesaahn shook her head. 'No. The Darkness does not ask permission. It takes root long before it shows its hand.' Her voice lowered. 'Whatever wears Coseo's face now chose him for reasons far beyond you.'

Silence stretched between them, filled only by wind and water.

A long moment passed. Then Kesaahn's voice changed — quieter, more deliberate.

'What matters now is what comes next.'

'I know,' Niama said. Her thoughts were already moving ahead, mapping danger and distance.

'In Cloudmoor, we'll need horses,' Kesaahn added. 'The Seekers have seen to our funds. We'll use them well.'

Niama nodded, the salt on her lips sharp and grounding. The sea had carried them this far. What waited beyond it would demand more.

Night had fully claimed the sky by the time they docked. Cloudmoor's harbor buzzed with muted life, sailors calling to one another, gulls shrieking overhead. Niama paused as they disembarked, turning back once to Captain Steele.

'Thank you,' she said simply.

He inclined his head, nothing more.

They followed lanternlight into the town's narrow streets, the sounds of the harbor fading behind them. Cloudmoor slept lightly. Eventually, they found the Vagabond Inn, tucked along a quiet lane. Its sign creaked softly in the night, worn but cared for.

Inside, candlelight flickered across scarred tables and tired faces. The air was thick with old ale and sweat. Niama felt it then, a prickle along her spine, the sense of being measured. Watched.

They ordered drinks. Niama kept her gaze moving, noting exits, shadows, hands that lingered too long. Everything looked ordinary. That, somehow, made it worse.

Rohan approached the bar with practiced courtesy. 'We're in need of rooms for the night.'

The barkeep squinted, studying him with open suspicion.

'Have we met?' he asked.

'I don't believe so,' Rohan replied evenly.

The man's eyes narrowed further. 'You're from Silverfall, ain't you?'

'No,' Rohan said. 'Fairmoor.'

Niama's fingers brushed the hilt of her dagger.

Something here was already out of place.

The barkeep's eyes narrowed, lids lowering like a drawbridge being pulled shut.

'You look a lot like the Prince,' he said slowly. 'Uncanny, really. Took my family to Silverfall last year. The procession. First time we'd ever seen the royal line up close.'

Rohan did not flinch. 'I assure you, I am not the Prince.' A faint edge crept into his voice. 'And if I were, why would I choose to stay in a place like this?' He let his gaze drift deliberately around the room, taking in the stained tables and watchful faces.

The barkeep considered this a moment longer than was comfortable. Then he reached beneath the counter and produced a key. 'Third door at the top of the stairs.'

Coins changed hands. The key slid across the bar.

As they climbed, Niama felt the weight of a stare settle between her shoulders. She glanced back once. The barkeep had not moved. His eyes followed them, unblinking, as though counting steps.

At the landing, Rohan paused.

'Something is wrong,' he said quietly. The ease had gone from his posture, replaced by a coiled alertness. 'We should not take the room he gave us.'

Niama did not argue. Neither did Kesaahn.

They crossed the hall instead, ignoring the key's number. The opposite room opened onto neat beds and untouched linens, the air faintly scented with soap and old wood.

'We keep watch,' Rohan said. 'No chances.'

'I'll take first,' Niama said at once. 'Sleep won't come easily.'

They settled into uneasy stillness. Niama took a chair by the window, candle guttering beside her. Below, the inn murmured softly, wood creaking, a hearth sighing as it burned low. The smell of smoke and damp cloth lingered in the air.

Her unease did not fade.

Minutes stretched. Then hours. She told herself it was exhaustion. Grief. The echo of too many narrow escapes.

Then the whispers came. Soft. Intentional.

Niama rose without sound and pressed her ear to the door. Voices drifted along the hall, low and urgent, stopping near the room they should have taken.

Her pulse thundered.

She turned and signaled. One finger raised. Silence.

Kesaahn and Rohan were awake instantly, hands already moving toward weapons. No words passed between them.

The door across the hall creaked open.

Heavy footsteps followed. A pause. Then the door slammed shut.

The footsteps retreated.

The silence afterward was worse.

'How did they find us?' Kesaahn breathed.

Rohan's jaw tightened. 'I don't know.' His eyes flicked to the window, the door, the narrow space between. 'But we won't be here when they return.'

Niama nodded, heart steady now in a way it hadn't been moments before.

The hunt had begun.

At first light, they slipped from the inn.

The sky blushed pink and gold above Cloudmoor's rooftops, dawn arriving soft and indifferent to what had passed in the night. Hoods drawn low, they moved with purpose through quiet streets, boots whispering over stone. No one called after them. No doors opened.

At a merchant's stall near the square, they purchased what little they could carry: bedrolls, dried food, waterskins. The unspoken truth settled between them. Comfort was behind them now. From here on, the road would offer only what they took by foresight, or force.

The stables lay just beyond the town's edge. Three horses were chosen quickly, sturdy rather than swift, their coats still damp with morning dew. Saddles were cinched. Packs secured. No lingering.

They rode north as the sun climbed higher, Cloudmoor shrinking behind them until it became nothing more than a pale smudge against the
coast. Wind tugged at cloaks and hair, hooves striking earth in a steady,
driving rhythm that echoed like a second pulse in Niama's ears.

She did not relax.

Every bend in the road felt watched. Every rise in the land hinted at
pursuit. The smell of cut grass and damp soil should have soothed her, but
instead it sharpened her senses, setting her nerves taut as drawn wire.

Rohan rode slightly ahead, posture rigid, gaze sweeping the horizon with
practiced intensity.

'We move as though already hunted,' he said at last. His tone carried
something else beneath the caution. Not accusation. Not forgiveness either. 'The Order will not abandon the trail easily.'

Niama nodded, fingers brushing the bow at her back. Kesaahn's expression remained composed, but her eyes missed nothing.

They rode on.

No banners followed. No riders crested the hills behind them.

Yet none of them believed that meant safety.

Glimmerfell lay ahead, somewhere beyond fields and forest and uncertainty, and they pressed toward it without looking back, carrying the quiet
knowledge that the space between them and their enemies was already
shrinking.

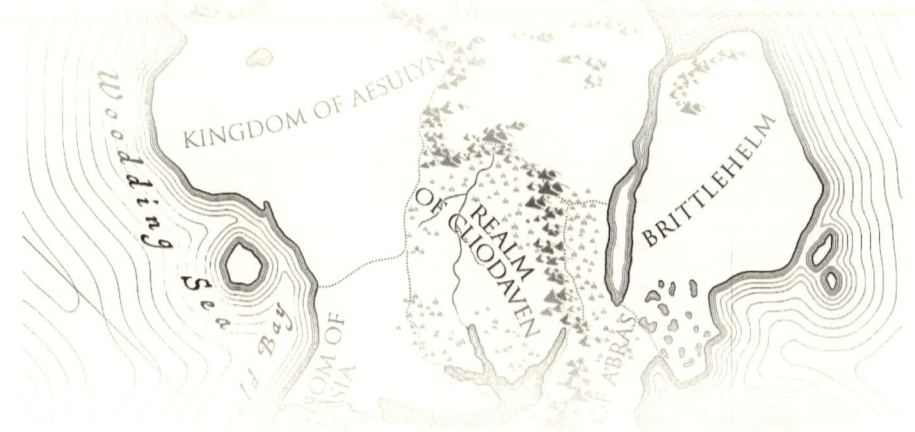

CHAPTER TWENTY-FOUR

The Sunken City

Dusk stained the sky in bruised violet and amber as they reached the edge of Timberham. They did not enter the hamlet. Instead, they guided their horses into a rough stand of brush beyond the fields, where a shallow hollow offered concealment enough to rest.

Rohan tethered his horse to an oak and coaxed a small fire to life. The heat crept outward, welcome against the night's first bite. Timberham lay just beyond the trees, its presence announced not by sound but by scent. Pigs. Thick and unmistakable, carried on the wind.

'We camp here,' Rohan said, low and decisive, as they laid out their bedrolls. 'We keep clear of the village. Rest now, move early.'

No one argued.

He tore a piece from a loaf of bread and ate without ceremony. Kesaahn drank from her waterskin, the coolness sharp on her tongue. 'How long to Glimmerfell?'

'If the road stays quiet,' Rohan replied, eyes already scanning the dark, 'we reach it by midday.' He straightened. 'I'll take first watch. From here, we'll see anyone coming. You both sleep.'

The fire settled into a steady rhythm. Embers glowed. Sparks rose and vanished.

Niama slept quickly, breath evening as the warmth and crackle of flame folded around her. Kesaahn lay wakeful beside her, gaze lifted through the bare lattice of branches to the stars beyond. The sky felt immense. Distant. It stirred memories she did not invite. A cabin tucked deep in the forest. Stillness. Familiar paths.

Those images fractured against the present. Against the road ahead. Glimmerfell waited somewhere beyond the dark, and with it choices that would not be undone.

Anxiety and anticipation twisted together in her chest.

Sleep came slowly.

When it did, her dreams were restless. Hope threaded through them, bright and fragile, shadowed always by the sense that something waited just beyond reach. Something already moving to meet them.

Kesaahn woke to Rohan's voice, sharp and commanding, cutting through the morning hush.

Dawn spilled gold across the low hills, and with it came movement. A column of soldiers advanced along the road beyond the trees, armor catching the light, ranks tight and disciplined. The ground seemed to tremble beneath their passage. Kesaahn's pulse quickened as she took it in.

The fire had burned down to embers. Smoke clung low, sour and bitter, tangled with the heavy stench of pigs drifting from Timberham. The mix curdled her stomach.

'Silverfall,' Rohan said quietly, eyes never leaving the road. 'The King's army.'

He rose at once and moved toward the tree line, posture low, deliberate. Kesaahn followed just far enough to see him step into view, one hand resting near his sword.

A mounted officer broke from the column, armor polished bright, blade drawn but held low. Words passed between them too softly to hear. Then the man dismounted.

He dropped to one knee. Kesaahn's stomach tightened. This was not protocol. This was allegiance.

Kesaahn caught her breath.

Rohan motioned him up. They spoke briefly, faces grave. When the exchange ended, the officer mounted again and rode hard back to the column.

The army marched on.

Horns sounded. Spears rang against shields in a steady, martial rhythm that carried far across the fields. Dust rose beneath thousands of boots.

Rohan returned, expression set.

'Captain Bluyr,' he said. 'From Silverfall. One of my father's most trusted.'

Kesaahn searched his face. 'Their destination?'

'Silverwind Pass.' His jaw tightened. 'Stagburgh has already fallen.'

The words landed like a blow.

Kesaahn's thoughts raced, unbidden images forming. Homes burning. People fleeing with nothing but what they could carry. She swallowed hard, throat tight with a grief she had no time to indulge.

'Abras is next,' Rohan continued. 'They're moving to reinforce Oxemount Fort. It's the last line before the heartland.'

The army was vast. Ordered. Relentless. Watching it pass, Kesaahn felt the scale of what lay ahead settle coldly into her chest. Whatever they faced would not be small. It would not be contained.

'They'll reach the fort within the week,' Rohan said. 'My father will hold there as long as he can. He's waiting on scouts before committing the rest of the force north.'

He looked back toward the road, the dust, the banners snapping in the morning wind.

'War is no longer a warning,' he said. 'It's already moving.'

The horns faded into the distance.

And the road ahead felt suddenly, terrifyingly narrow.

'We must secure the Emerald Coeylite and the Solis gland from the Infurnus,' Kesaahn said, tension threading her voice. 'Then we ride west, past Silverwind Pass, without delay. If Athris forbid the Dark Legions break the line—' She cut herself off. 'We would be forced south around the Orboros range. It would cost us days we do not have.'

Rohan nodded, already scanning the road. 'Then we move now.'

They broke camp in moments. Bedrolls were bundled. Embers scattered. Saddles cinched tight. Rohan spurred his horse forward, the others falling in behind him.

'The sunken city,' he called over the wind. 'We reach it as fast as hooves will carry us.'

They hit the north road just as the last ranks of the army vanished beyond Timberham. Dust still hung in the air, trampled flat beneath thousands of boots.

'We leave the roads to soldiers,' Rohan said. 'Along the coast we keep our pace and our distance.'

The shoreline opened before them, sea stretching wide and calm beneath a pale sky. Salt wind swept Kesaahn's face, cool and bracing, and for a brief moment Glimmerfell's silhouette against the water stirred something like hope.

It did not last.

Smoke drifted above the town ahead. Voices carried on the wind. Shouts. Cries. The closer they rode, the clearer it became.

People were fleeing.

Families hauled carts overloaded with whatever could be carried. Livestock bleated and pulled against their tethers. Cookfires burned low as final meals were scraped together in haste. Panic thickened the air, sharp and choking.

'What's happening?' Rohan asked, stopping a woman rushing past with a bundle clutched to her chest.

She barely slowed. 'Silverwind,' she said, fear cracking her voice. 'The Legions are coming. If you've sense, you'll run too.' And she was gone.

Kesaahn's chest tightened as she watched the exodus swell. Pots clattered. Children cried. Mothers shouted names into the chaos. The town felt hollow, its spirit fleeing ahead of its people.

Niama watched a mother drag two children past them, the woman's face white with terror. Neither child looked back.

'We can't stop this,' Niama said quietly. Not to anyone. To herself.

'Not yet,' Kesaahn replied.

At the port, the truth struck harder still.

Ships were already casting off. Others groaned under the weight of refugees packed tight along their rails. No one lingered. No one waited.

Rohan hailed a man loading a narrow fishing boat. 'What price for passage to the sunken city?'

The man shook his head without looking up. 'None. I'm leaving before the Actari arrive. I won't die for coin.'

'Anyone else?' Rohan pressed.

A shrug. 'Old Bill, maybe. End of the jetty. If he hasn't gone already.'

They hurried along the docks, past empty slips and half-cut lines, until they reached the final jetty. One small sailing boat remained, bobbing uneasily against the posts. An old man worked its rigging with deliberate care, his movements slow but practiced.

'Ahoy,' Rohan called.

The man straightened, squinting at them beneath the brim of a salt-stiff cap. 'What d'you want?'

'Passage,' Rohan said. 'To the sunken city.'

The old man laughed once. Not kindly.

'Stonebreach?' He shook his head and went back to his knots. 'This ain't no time for sightseeing. You seen the roads? Everyone else has sense enough to run the other way.'

'We're not sightseers,' Rohan said.

Bill snorted. 'That so? Then you're worse than fools.' He glanced toward the town, where shouts still carried over the water. 'Dark Legions marchin', Actari prowlin'. World's about to tear itself open, and you lot want to sail *into* it?'

Kesaahn stepped forward. 'We have business there. Urgent business.'

The old man finally looked at her properly. His gaze lingered, sharp despite the years. 'What d'you want in a drowned city full of ghosts and bad memories?'

Kesaahn met his stare. 'Something that doesn't belong to the Dark Master.'

That gave him pause.

He studied them again, slower this time. The weapons. The way they stood. The way none of them looked uncertain.

'You don't look like looters,' he muttered. 'Or pilgrims.' A beat. 'That makes you dangerous company.'

'We'll pay,' Kesaahn said. 'Well above your usual fee.'

Bill huffed. 'Gold won't stop what's comin'.'

'No,' Niama said. 'But it'll keep you fed while you outrun it.'

The old man sighed, long and weary. 'You've got that right.'

He spat into the water, then jabbed a thumb toward the stable at the dock's edge. 'Tie your beasts there. Nelly'll see to 'em. She bites less than I do.'

They moved at once.

When they returned, Rohan placed a gold coin into the old man's palm. Bill turned it slowly, holding it up to the light. His brows rose despite himself.

'Well I'll be damned,' he murmured. 'Haven't seen one o' these in a good long while.' He tucked it away, then fixed them with a hard look. 'Listen close. Once we're out there, there's no turnin' back easy. Sea don't care about courage. And Stonebreach—' He shook his head. 'That place remembers blood.'

'So do we,' Niama said.

Bill studied her a moment longer, then nodded once. 'Right then. Help me clear the jetty. We paddle till we're free, then the wind takes us where it will.'

They took the oars together. The boat creaked as it slipped from the dock, water hissing beneath the blades. When they reached open water, Bill hauled the sail aloft. Wind caught it cleanly, snapping canvas taut.

The shore began to fall away.

Bill kept his eyes forward. 'If you're wrong,' he said quietly, 'this'll be the last calm water you ever see.'

Kesaahn gripped the rail, the knot in her stomach tightening. 'If we're right,' she said, 'it might be the last calm water anyone sees.'

The old man said nothing more.

They were moving.

Behind them, the shore burned with fear and flight. Ahead lay only water, stone, and whatever waited in the depths of the sunken city.

And beneath it all, the quiet, relentless sense that the world was already shifting faster than they could run.

'So why do you stay?' Niama asked, raising her voice over the slap of waves against the hull, 'when everyone else is fleeing?'

Bill did not look back at the harbor. Smoke and shouting carried faintly across the water, wood groaning as overloaded boats pushed off in haste.

'Run to where?' he said at last. His voice was rough, weathered thin by salt and years. 'If the whispers are true, there's no safe shore left.' He shrugged once. 'I'd sooner die where I was born than crushed between fear and screaming children.'

His gaze slid to them, sharp beneath the brim of his cap.
'So tell me,' he said. 'What drags you toward Stonebreach when sense says turn away?'

Kesaahn felt the question settle like weight against her ribs. She answered anyway, voice steady.
'We seek a relic.'

Bill grunted. 'Treasure hunters, then.'

'No,' she said. 'Not treasure.'

That earned a longer look.

'I've ferried my share over the years,' Bill went on. 'Some came back with trinkets and tales. Most didn't come back at all.'

Rohan leaned forward. 'Do you know the way to the throne room?'

Bill's jaw tightened. 'Aye. And I'd advise against it.' He spat over the rail. 'Something's claimed it. Something old.'

Niama's pulse quickened. 'What kind of thing?'

Bill lowered his voice. 'A Hascesh.'

The word itself seemed to draw the air thinner.

'Half woman. Half eel.' He stared ahead, eyes distant. 'Four arms clad in slick scales, claws sharp enough to peel iron. A mouth full of glass-bright teeth.'

Kesaahn's grip tightened on the rail.

'Its scream doesn't kill,' Bill continued. 'It freezes. Stuns. Then it feeds.'

Kesaahn swallowed. Her stomach twisted at the image.

'Can it be killed?' Rohan asked.

Bill rubbed his chin. 'Stories say light drives them back. Strong light. But I've never seen it tested.' A grunt. 'And I don't plan to.'

Kesaahn's eyes sharpened. 'Light, you say.'

She knelt and opened her satchel, hands already moving. Glass clinked softly as she mixed reagents, the scent of crushed leaves and sharp minerals cutting through the salt air.

Bill glanced down. 'What're you brewing?'

'Something small,' Kesaahn said. 'It won't burn bright. But it may be enough to wound shadow.'

She drew out several pearlescent seeds and held them up. 'In your ears. They swell shut. You won't hear the scream.' She met Bill's gaze.

Bill stared, then barked a laugh. 'Well I'll be damned.' He shot Rohan a crooked grin. 'Lucky choice of company.'

Rohan allowed himself a thin smile. 'Luck had little to do with it.'

Stonebreach waited beneath the waterline, patient as rot.

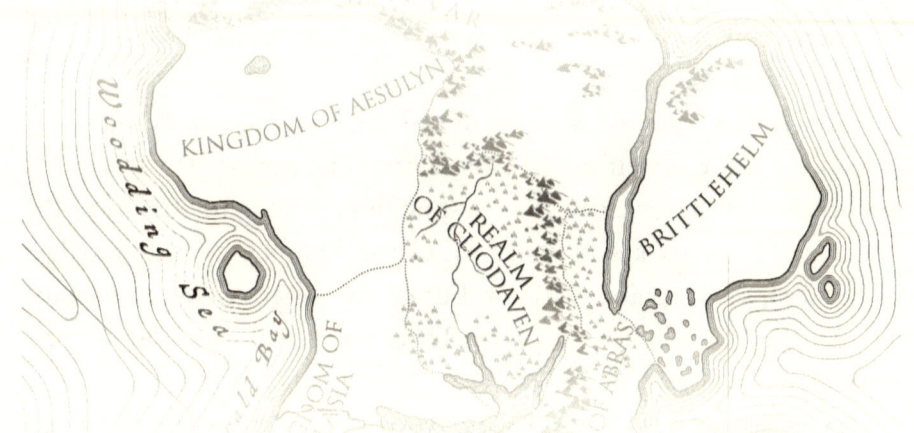

CHAPTER TWENTY-FIVE

The Hascesh

Niama shaded her eyes. Shapes were rising from the water ahead, pale and broken.

'What lies there?' she asked.

Stone emerged from the sea like a dream half-remembered. Towers leaned at impossible angles. Spires pierced the mist like drowned fingers clawing skyward. The city revealed itself slowly, reluctantly, as though ashamed to be seen.

Bill lifted one hand. 'Cathedral spires,' he said. 'The palace roof, there. See how it crowns the water.' He gestured north. 'Old sentry towers. Once guarded the harbor.'

Niama stared, awe and dread tangled tight in her chest. 'What destroyed it?'

Bill exhaled. 'Depends who you ask.'

'Some say Athris himself struck it down. Others blame a magika who reached too far.' His eyes never left the ruins. 'Truth's buried with the dead.'

Salt stung Kesaahn's tongue as wind cut across the deck. Cold crept beneath her cloak, raising gooseflesh along her arms. The sea whispered against the hull, steady and merciless, as though counting down.

Stonebreach waited.

And whether it offered salvation or ruin, none of them could yet say.

Kesaahn bent herself fully to the work. The potion demanded her attention, and she gave it willingly, though her thoughts strayed to the Hascesh. Bill had spoken its name like a curse. Doubt pressed at the edges of her resolve, sharp and insistent, but doubt did not change necessity. The Emerald Coeylite was required. There was no path that did not pass through its shadow.

As the boat skirted the drowned city's perimeter, her heart beat like a trapped thing against her ribs, frantic and unyielding. Stonebreach rose beneath the water in broken grandeur, towers bowed and shattered, beauty drowned but not erased. Awe and grief twisted together in her chest. Fear followed close behind.

She drew steadiness from her companions. Rohan stood rigid at the rail, jaw set, eyes fixed forward. Niama watched the water with hunter's focus, hands still, breath measured. None of them spoke. Each understood what waited below.

The sun slid toward the horizon, bleeding amethyst and crimson across the sea. The upper reaches of the keep came into view, jagged silhouettes beneath the surface.

Bill lifted a hand.

'There,' he said. 'That tower. Swim down through it. Guardhouse first. Then south through the kitchens. Two great doors at the end. One'll be open.'

Rohan turned to Niama. 'You stay with Bill.'

'I should go,' she said at once, fear and frustration tightening her voice.

He shook his head. 'We don't risk all of us.'

Niama hesitated, then nodded, though the motion cost her.

Kesaahn pressed two dried strands of Eglanip grass into Rohan's palm. 'Chew,' she said. 'Slowly. Don't swallow.'

He frowned, then obeyed. The bitter fibers broke apart between his teeth, releasing a sharp, resinous taste that burned his tongue and sinuses.

His chest tightened—then eased.

'You'll feel it in your lungs,' Kesaahn added. 'It won't last long.'

Rohan inclined his head once.

They climbed over the side.

The sea closed over them like a blade. Cold bit hard, driving the air from Kesaahn's lungs in a shocked gasp before the magic took hold. Darkness swallowed the world as they descended, Stonebreach rising to meet them like a grave dressed in splendor.

She triggered the potion.

Soft light bloomed around them, pale and steady, revealing walls veined with coral and slow-drifting plants that glowed in quiet defiance of the dark. Hope flickered, fragile but real.

They followed the light down.

Rohan kept the Eglanip pressed to the side of his mouth, jaw working steadily. Each breathless moment scraped at his instincts, but the tightness in his lungs never quite became panic.

Not breathing, his body screamed.

Still alive, the grass insisted.

The halls beyond burned with color, coral and moss weaving a luminous path toward the throne room, fish scattered in flashing silver clouds.

Kesaahn renewed the light.

The doors emerged from the dark.

They towered over the corridor, vast slabs of carved stone and bronze fused together by age and craft beyond any living hand. Faded gold filigree traced the outlines of crowned figures locked in eternal procession, kings and queens rendered in solemn relief, their eyes lifted toward a sunburst etched at the doors' heart. Time had dulled the metal, sea growth crept along the seams, but the authority of the place remained. This was not merely an entrance.

It was a boundary.

Beyond it had once been rule, judgment, and ceremony. A throne room where power had been spoken into law.

Kesaahn felt it in her bones as they swam closer.

The doors stood partly ajar, darkness breathing through the narrow gap like a held breath.

They passed through together.

The chamber beyond was vast and hushed, pillars rising like drowned giants, the throne still standing at its heart. Water muted its former grandeur, but echoes of power lingered in the stone.

The taste in Kesaahn's mouth had begun to fade. The sharp resin dulled to bitterness, then to nothing at all.

Her lungs burned harder now. Not enough to force her up—but enough to warn her.

Then the water pulsed.

A pressure rolled through her, rhythmic and wrong. Her chest tightened. She turned—

The Hascesh slid from the darkness.

It was vast, its body a slick, sinuous coil of muscle and scale, half-eel, half-woman, fused into a blasphemy of flesh that should never have learned how to breathe. Its lower form writhed in slow, patient loops, powerful enough to crush stone. Above it rose a warped torso, disturbingly human in proportion, skin pale and translucent beneath the water, veins pulsing with borrowed life.

Four arms unfolded from its sides, too many, too long. Each ended in talons like curved glass, edges shimmering with a wet, predatory sheen.

Its face was the worst of it.

Once human. Once beautiful, perhaps. Now stretched and broken, jaw unhinged to reveal a cavern of needle-bright teeth that glinted as it opened its mouth. Gills flared along its neck, fluttering as it drew the water through itself. And its eyes—

Black. Unblinking. Intelligent.

They fixed on Kesaahn and Rohan with ancient patience, not hunger alone, but possession.

The light recoiled against it, pressing the creature back, but it did not flee.

It waited.

Rohan pointed.

The gem lay embedded in the throne, green fire caught in stone.

Kesaahn swam for it, knife biting into ancient mortar. Each scrape rang loud in her head. The Hascesh circled, black eyes never leaving them.

The gem came free.

She turned—

The light flickered.

Then died.

Darkness slammed in.

The Hascesh struck. Talons raked across Rohan's leg. He was wrenched sideways, dragged into the black. The Eglanip tore loose from his teeth in the violence of it.

Water rushed in.

Kesaahn forced the potion alive again, light flaring just as the creature recoiled, shrieking soundlessly.

He found the grass by feel, half-dissolved, crushed it back between his teeth with shaking fingers.

The burn returned — weakly.

Rohan fought within the glow, driving the Hascesh back.

One last swing tore him free.

He drifted back into the light, leg shredded, breath failing.

Kesaahn seized him, hauling him toward the doors as the potion dimmed again. Rohan bound the wound with shaking hands.

Too fast.

They fled down the hall as the throne room doors exploded behind them, wood splintering outward. The Hascesh surged through the wreckage. Its mouth opened — the scream hit the water in visible waves — but the seeds held. Kesaahn felt nothing but pressure.

And the light was fading.

Kesaahn did not slow. Back through the kitchens. North through the guardhouse. The tower passage rose steeply above them.

Rohan groaned as they climbed, his body sagging against her grip. Blood streamed from his leg in dark ribbons, clouding the water behind them.

Kesaahn tightened her hold and pushed harder, lungs burning now, the last of the Eglanip's bitter edge already fading.

The potion's light guttered.

Then the surface shattered above them.

They broke free in a rush of spray and gasped air into scorched lungs, ripping the spent grass from their mouths as they clung to the night-churned water. Sound crashed back all at once as Kesaahn tore the Pearl Blossom seeds from their ears, the roar of waves and wind slamming into her senses.

No moon. No guiding light.

Only distance.

The boat was there—too far. Far enough to matter.

Despair flared. She pulled again, every stroke tearing at muscles already past their limit.

'Come on, Rohan,' she urged, voice breaking despite herself. 'Almost there.'

From the boat, Niama saw them at last.

Something in the way Rohan hung slack against Kesaahn's grip told her everything. She shouted to Bill, pointing hard, panic flooding her chest as the dark smear of blood spread through the water.

Bill moved at once.

Together they hauled, hands burning on wet wood and rope as Kesaahn forced Rohan upward. He collapsed across the gunwale with a choking gasp, Kesaahn following a heartbeat later.

The water behind them rippled.

'We leave. Now,' Niama said, scanning the black water. Her voice shook, but it did not falter.

Bill yanked the sail free. Canvas snapped open as the wind caught hard, and the boat lurched forward, slicing into the chop. Niama clutched the rail, knuckles white, eyes fixed on the wake as the shapes surged—then hesitated.

Whether the Hascesh still followed, she could not tell. She did not wait to find out.

Kesaahn cut away the blood-soaked binding on Rohan's leg. The wound beneath was savage, torn deep by teeth not meant for flesh alone. She did not flinch. From her satchel she drew a small jar and pressed the salve into the gash, murmuring a binding phrase under her breath.

Rohan hissed—then sagged, the pain dulling.

The boat flew.

Salt spray lashed their faces as the hull skimmed the waves, light and desperate. Behind them, the water darkened once more—then stilled. The pursuing shapes slowed, sank, and vanished back into the depths of the drowned city.

Bill exhaled and laughed softly, the sound edged with relief. He patted the gunwale. 'She's no looker,' he said, 'but she runs true.'

Kesaahn nodded, gaze still fixed on the water they'd fled. 'We would not have survived her at close quarters.'

Bill's mirth faded. 'Aye. Few do.' He spat over the side. 'She's had years to sharpen her hunger.'

They docked hours later beneath a silent sky.

The town lay hollowed, lanterns guttering low, streets abandoned. Bill secured the lines and glanced back at them, his voice dropping.

'Not many left now,' he said. 'You can take the room behind the stables. Let your friend rest.'

Kesaahn helped Rohan to his feet, every step a quiet victory.

Behind them, the sea closed over its secrets once more.

Niama's smile came softly, fragile with relief.

'You have our thanks, Bill,' she said, voice low. 'You've done more than you know.'

Rohan pressed a small stack of coins into the old man's hand, wincing as he shifted his weight. 'This settles our debt,' he said. 'And a little beyond it.'

Bill weighed the coins, then nodded once. 'Much obliged.' He tucked them away and glanced toward the dark water. 'I'll take my rest while the night still allows it.' A pause. 'Good luck to you, all of you.'

He turned and made his way down the jetty, boots thudding softly until the darkness swallowed him.

They helped Rohan into the room behind the stables. It was narrow but warm, lit by a single torch whose flame guttered in the draft from a small, barred window. Shadows stretched long across the rough wooden walls. The air smelled of hay and horseflesh, earthy and steady, accompanied by the low snorts and shifting hooves from the stalls beyond.

One bed stood against the far wall, its quilt threadbare but clean. A pair of cupboards sat nearby, doors ajar to reveal folded linens. Nothing more. Nothing wasted.

'Drink this,' Kesaahn said, pressing a small vial into Rohan's hand.

He did not question it. The draught vanished in a single swallow. Moments later, his shoulders sagged, the tension finally bleeding from him.

'Quite the venture,' he murmured, already drifting.

Niama remained by the bedside, watchful even as his breathing deepened. Only when sleep fully claimed him did the tightness in her chest ease.

They unrolled their bedrolls on the stone floor. The ache of the day settled into bone and muscle, heavy but survivable.

Niama turned her head toward Kesaahn. 'Did you find it?'

Kesaahn answered by drawing the gem from her pocket.

Even in the dim light, it glimmered. A deep, living green pulsed beneath its smooth surface, as though something inside it breathed. It was heavy for its size, unyielding, flawless.

'We did,' she said quietly.

Niama stared, reverent. 'It's... beautiful.'

'Rare,' Kesaahn replied. 'And stubborn.' She turned it once in her hands. 'It must be ground to powder. Only the Dwarves can manage it.'

Niama nodded, already feeling the road stretching ahead. 'Then we rest while we can.'

Kesaahn settled back onto her bedroll, the gem returned to her satchel but its presence still felt, a quiet weight of promise and danger alike.

'Yes,' she said. 'Just for tonight.'

Sleep came slowly, but it came.

And as darkness gathered gently around them, Kesaahn knew this was no mere crossing survived. It was a threshold passed. Whatever lay ahead would demand more of them than before.

For now, though, the horses breathed.

Rohan slept.

And the gem waited.

CHAPTER TWENTY-SIX

The Tracker

Dawn crept into the room, pale light nudging back the night. Rohan woke with a dull throb in his leg, the ache anchoring him to the moment before his thoughts fully cleared. Stonebreach. Blood. The sea. He pushed the remnants of sleep aside and caught sight of Kesaahn and Niama through a gap in the weathered timbers, already at work among the horses.

He dressed quickly, fingers clumsy with the laces of his boots, urgency pressing him forward.

'Ready to press on?' Kesaahn asked, tightening the last strap on her saddle. The familiar scent of leather and horse steadied him.

'Ready,' Rohan said.

Bill crossed the yard toward them, boots thudding against packed earth as he adjusted his suspenders. 'Sleep treat you well?' he asked.

Niama colored faintly. 'It did. You have our thanks.'

They gathered at the stable entrance as Bill cast an approving glance along the stout wooden walls. 'Humble place,' he said. 'But it keeps the weather out. I take it you're headin' back to the city?'

Rohan secured his gear and shook his head. 'North.'

Bill blinked, the smile fading. 'North?' Concern crept into his voice. 'That's rough country. Actari demons up that way, or so the talk goes.'

'Our forces hold the wall,' Rohan said. He kept his tone even, though doubt stirred beneath it. 'They'll keep the line.'

Bill studied him a moment, then huffed a short laugh and patted his coin purse. 'Let's hope so. World's thinner on good folk than it used to be.' He gave them a wave and turned away.

They mounted soon after and rode out, leaving the churned yard and familiar track behind. Rohan felt his pulse quicken as the road narrowed. The north waited, cold and unresolved.

'Did you find what you needed?' he asked Kesaahn.

'Not enough,' she said, scanning the deserted buildings they passed. 'Most fled south. Supplies were taken with them.' The air carried a stale, musty odor that clung to the abandoned streets.

Crates lay smashed along the road, contents spilled and forgotten. Wind tugged at Rohan's cloak as rain began to fall, light at first, then steadier. 'They didn't leave slowly.'

'Dawnbury's a day out,' he said after a time. 'We'll need a tracker to cross the swamps. There's no other way to reach the Infurnus.' His mouth tightened. 'And the Reptans won't forgive mistakes.'

The rain thickened, soaking into leather and wool. Southbound traffic crowded the road. Families passed with carts piled high, faces drawn and hollow, eyes fixed anywhere but ahead. Rohan swallowed as they rode among them, the weight of unspoken loss pressing close.

He drew alongside one man struggling to keep his load balanced. 'What happened?'

'Soldiers came two nights past,' the man said, breath ragged. 'Told us to clear out. Head south. No questions.'

'Anyone stay behind?' Rohan asked.

The man shook his head. 'Not if they had sense.'

They pressed on, hooves striking wet earth in a steady rhythm as the road worsened, mud pulling at every step. Rohan tightened his grip on the reins, eyes forward, as the forest closed around them and the last signs of comfort fell away.

'We leave the road,' Niama said.

She guided her horse north, off the churned track and into the open fields beyond. Grass bent beneath the rain, the air thick with wet green and earth. Behind them, the road swallowed its own footprints.

They reached Dawnbury long after nightfall.

Rohan left Niama and Kesaahn at the inn to find a tracker.

Rain soaked through his cloak as he moved from house to house, knocking once, then not at all. Doors were barred. Windows shuttered. The town had folded in on itself.

One door stood ajar.

The latch hung broken.

Rohan drew his sword and pushed inside.

A man stood near the hearth, thin and wiry, clothes patched but clean enough to suggest care rather than poverty. His smile came a heartbeat late, practiced and cautious, as though he were measuring which version of himself might survive the moment, hands half-raised, eyes wide. The room smelled of damp ash and fear.

Rohan took him in at a glance. Mud on his boots. A sack at his feet. Someone moving where he should not be.

'Looting?' Rohan said.

The man swallowed. 'I was retrieving something. For my aunt.'

Rohan stepped closer. Floorboards creaked beneath his weight. 'Strange time for errands.' His blade lifted slightly. 'The soldiers outside might find it interesting.'

Armor clattered somewhere down the street.

The man's gaze flicked toward the sound. 'I'm no thief,' he said quickly. 'I swear it.'

'What is your name?' Rohan asked.

'Randul,' he said quickly, offering his name the way one might offer a coin already spent.

Rohan closed the distance and set the sword's tip against the man's chest. 'Convince me.'

Silence stretched.

'I need a tracker,' Rohan said. 'North. Through the swamps. You help me find one, and this conversation ends.'

The man hesitated, fingers brushing his chin. 'Trackers don't work for nothing.'

'I pay well,' Rohan said. The blade rose, kissed the underside of the man's jaw.

Randul's eyes never stopped moving. Not to the sword, but to the door, the windows, the shadows between.

Sweat beaded along his brow. 'Then you're in luck.' He forced a thin smile.

Rohan did not move. 'Is that so?'

'I've crossed Langmore more times than I can count,' Randul said. 'You can put that thing away now.'

Rohan leaned in. 'And the swamps?'

Randul stiffened. 'The Reptans? I know a way through.'

The sword pressed harder. A thin line of blood traced down Randul's chin.

'Listen carefully,' Rohan said, voice low and even. 'You lead us true, and you're paid. You lie, stray, or hesitate at the wrong moment—'

He withdrew the blade just enough for the threat to breathe.

'—and I will finish what the swamps start.'

'That seems extreme, don't you think?' Randul said, voice tight as he swallowed.

Rohan's grip firmed. The sword bit deeper, another drop of blood sliding down Randul's chin.

'Do we have an understanding?'

'Yes. Yes, fine,' Randul said quickly. 'You can trust me.'

Rohan lowered the blade. 'No. But you'll do.' He stepped back. 'Gather what you need.'

Randul bent for his sack.

Steel flashed.

'That stays,' Rohan said.

Randul froze, then straightened slowly, wiping at the blood on his chin. 'You cut me.'

'You're alive,' Rohan replied. 'Move.'

They stepped out into the rain. Mud clung to their boots, the night pressing close around the narrow street. Up close, Randul looked exactly like the town itself. Worn, adaptable, patched together by necessity.

'Why live like this?' Rohan asked as they walked.

Randul shrugged. 'Some of us learn early that comfort is borrowed.' He glanced sideways, measuring. 'Most of my gambles failed. A few didn't.' A thin smile. 'This one might.'

They reached the inn. Kesaahn and Niama waited beneath the veranda, rain turning the street to blur and shadow.

Randul's eyes flicked to them. His smile sharpened.

Rohan stepped in front of him at once.

'You look,' he said, voice flat. 'You don't speak.'

Randul raised his hands. 'Understood.'

Rohan turned to the others. 'This is Randul. He'll guide us north.'

Kesaahn studied the tracker in silence. Niama's gaze lingered longer, unreadable.

Randul shifted under it, then glanced at Rohan's belt. 'When do I see the first payment?'

'When you earn it,' Rohan said.

Randul's mouth twitched. 'Generous.' He looked past them toward the road. 'Before we go, we'll need supplies.'

'We do,' Rohan said.

'Those beasts won't survive the swamps,' Randul said, eyes flicking to the horses. 'The Snakemen go mad for horseflesh.'

Rohan studied the animals, then his companions. The decision settled heavy in his chest. 'Is there somewhere we can leave them?'

Randul shrugged. 'Once, maybe. Not now.'

Silence followed. The horses shifted, unaware.

Niama moved first. She unbuckled her saddle and slid it free with practiced ease. 'We walk.' She pressed her forehead briefly to her horse's, whispered low, then struck its flank. The animal bolted south.

Kesaahn followed. Then Rohan.

He watched them disappear, the sound of hooves fading until the road swallowed it. The loss sat deep. Necessary.

Randul stared. 'That was... unexpected.'

Rohan pushed him forward. 'We move.'

'One more thing,' Randul said quickly. 'The Snakemen won't let us pass without tribute.'

'What kind?' Kesaahn asked.

'Meat.' His gaze slid north. 'Sheep will do.'

They found the farm at the forest's edge. The house stood shuttered, garden still tended despite abandonment. A barn loomed beside it, doors barred.

'Farmer Burns locked them in before fleeing,' Randul said. 'Five should be enough.'

At the gatepost, he placed a silver coin.

Randul frowned. 'What's that for?'

'Payment,' Rohan said. 'We're not thieves.'

Randul shook his head but said nothing more.

'Seems pointless,' Randul muttered once they were clear.

'Principles often do,' Rohan replied. 'To those without them.'

They reached the stables as dusk settled. The structure stood empty, hollow.

'Beds would be more comfortable,' Randul said.

'This will do,' Rohan replied.

They spread bedrolls in the hay. The scent of horses lingered, sharp and familiar.

Without warning, Rohan seized Randul and drove him into the straw.

'What are you—'

Rohan bound his wrists and ankles swiftly. 'I don't trust you. And I won't wake with a blade in my ribs.'

Randul scowled. 'Didn't think you'd actually do it.'

'Sleep,' Rohan said. 'You'll walk at dawn.'

Randul muttered as Rohan stepped away, the hay muffling his complaints.

The stable fell quiet.

Rohan lay awake a long while, listening to the night. The road ahead pressed close, narrow and unforgiving.

When sleep came at last, it brought no comfort.

CHAPTER TWENTY-SEVEN

The Swamp

Niama woke to the damp, hay-sweet scent of the stable. Rain tapped against an empty barrel in a steady rhythm, softer now as dawn thinned the dark.

She rose from her bedroll, brushed straw from her clothes, and took in the quiet movement around her. Kesaahn and Rohan stirred nearby. Randul snored among the sheep he had huddled with, his bound hands tucked awkwardly against his chest.

Niama crossed to the stable doors and pushed them open. Wood groaned. The sheep bleated and shifted, jostling Randul awake. He blinked, then thrust his tied wrists toward Rohan.

'Would you mind?' he asked, voice tight with urgency.

Rohan cut the bindings without comment.

Randul bolted for the far corner, fumbling with his trousers. 'By Athris, thank you,' he muttered, relief flooding his voice. 'I was running out of time.'

Niama looked out over the town. Empty streets. Shuttered windows. The quiet pressed too close. She missed the noise of life, the barter and laughter, the ordinary mess. This silence felt like something holding its breath.

She turned back inside and rolled her bedroll tight. 'We leave now,' she said. 'It's a long road.'

Kesaahn and Rohan nodded, shouldering their packs.

'Agreed,' Kesaahn said. 'Let's make use of the break in the storm.'

Randul returned, looser now, eyes darting between them. 'Why exactly are we headin' into the swamps?' he asked. 'Most folk work hard to avoid that.'

Niama met his gaze. 'That is not your concern.' Her voice was calm, final. 'You're to guide us to Brittleheim and back. Nothing more.'

Randul stiffened. 'Brittleheim?' His color drained. 'That's fire-lizard country. No one said anything about that.'

Rohan stepped in smoothly. 'Gold has a way of easing difficult paths.'

Niama watched Randul weigh the words. She didn't trust him, but she trusted his appetite for coin.

'Triple,' Randul said at last, jabbing a finger upward.

Rohan considered him. 'Double,' he said, 'if you take us to the edge of Brittleheim and wait until we return.'

Randul hesitated, then nodded. 'Done.'

Gold still ruled him.

Rohan finished securing his satchel. 'Then let's move.'

Randul wrestled the sheep toward the door, muttering under his breath as his face reddened with effort. Kesaahn laughed softly at the sight.

Before they stepped out, she turned to Rohan. 'One moment.' Her gaze dropped to his leg. 'Let me see the wound.'

'It feels fine,' Rohan said. 'But go on.'

Kesaahn peeled back the bandage, her brow creasing briefly before smoothing. 'It's healing well.' She applied fresh salve and wrapped the leg again with careful hands. 'Fortune favored you.'

Rohan smiled faintly. 'They raise us stubborn where I'm from.'

Niama watched them finish their preparations, unease stirring beneath the quiet of the stable. Calm never lingered long. She had learned that much.

They gathered their weapons and packs and stepped onto the dirt road beyond the stables.

The forest closed around them almost at once. Leaves whispered overhead. Small creatures stirred in the undergrowth. Damp earth and fresh growth filled the air as sunlight filtered through oak and birch, breaking into shifting patterns across the path. The road bore the marks of long use, pressed smooth by generations of passage.

Niama walked alert despite the peace. The fall of Stonebreach had reshaped the land. Ahead, what had once been forest now bled into swamp, and with it came creatures that did not belong.

She listened. The birds. The insects. The pauses between sounds.

'Does this path see much travel?' she asked.

Randul nodded as he prodded the sheep forward. 'Enough. Hunters use it. Elk used to roam further north. Lovely lady,' he said with a wide grin.

Niama's hand settled on her dagger. 'Niama,' she said coolly. 'Not "lovely lady."'

Randul glanced back, amused. 'As you wish.'

Rohan stepped between them without breaking stride. 'Ignore him.'

'I can hear you,' Randul muttered.

'I know,' Rohan replied.

Kesaahn veered from the path, scanning the brush. 'There's silkbloom nearby.' She adjusted her satchel. 'I'll gather what I can. My stores are thin.'

'Don't stray far,' Niama called after her. 'The forest listens.'

Kesaahn gave a brief nod and vanished into the undergrowth.

By dusk they reached a clearing marked by old use. A ring of smoke-darkened stones. Logs positioned for rest. Someone had camped here often enough to trust it.

They tethered the sheep. Randul dropped heavily to the ground, breathless. 'I won't lie,' he said. 'If anyone wants to trade places with the flock tomorrow, I'd be grateful.'

'No,' Rohan said, already gathering kindling.

Fire caught quickly. He passed out rations once the flames settled. 'Eat.'

Niama sat close to the warmth, hunger finally making itself known. Her stomach tightened as she took the food, the day catching up with her all at once.

The fire crackled. The forest pressed close.

And somewhere beyond the trees, the swamps waited.

They had barely settled when a rough voice cut through the firelight.

'Well. What do we have here?'

Three men stepped from the trees, swords bare, steel catching the flames. The smell of sweat and sour mead reached Niama before they did. Men who came armed into a camp at night were not here to talk.

Rohan and Niama rose together.

The one in front wore his violence openly. A beard gone wild. His grin twisted as he advanced, blade loose in his hand. One of the others bore a scar that pulled his face sideways. The third watched too closely, eyes bright and restless.

'Is that...?' one muttered.

The leader's gaze fixed on Randul. 'Well, I'll be damned.' His grin widened. 'Randul.'

Randul sagged as if the name itself had weight. 'Evenin', Bumpa.'

The air tightened.

'Fancy meeting you out here,' Bumpa said, stepping closer. 'You got my coin yet?'

Randul swallowed. 'Soon. Just a few more days.'

Bumpa laughed, low and ugly. 'Don't have days.' He gestured behind him. 'We're heading south. So let's settle accounts.'

'I don't have it,' Randul said, voice cracking. 'I'm working on it.'

Bumpa's eyes slid past him, assessing. 'And these?' He smiled slowly. 'New partners?'

'Just passing through,' Randul said quickly. 'Heading north.'

Bumpa's gaze lingered on Niama. 'An elf.' His teeth showed, blackened and broken. 'Boys, this night keeps improving.'

Rohan moved in front of her without a word.

Randul shrank back, hands trembling.

Niama felt the moment tighten like a drawn string. There would be no retreat. No bargaining.

Rohan drew his sword.

Bumpa chuckled. 'Easy work,' he said to his men. 'That's my favorite kind.'

Niama stepped past Rohan's shoulder.

'Leave,' she said, voice cold and clear. 'Now.'

Bumpa lunged.

Niama felt the moment snap into focus. The world narrowed to breath, distance, angle.

Her bow rose.

Two arrows. Two heartbeats. One struck the throat. The other punched clean through the chest. Both men fell almost together, the sound of their bodies hitting the earth reaching her a beat later.

Bumpa's grin faltered.

Rohan moved.

Steel met flesh, and the scream tore free before the sword was even withdrawn.

Silence followed, heavy and absolute.

Fire popped. Blood steamed faintly in the grass.

Niama lowered her bow, pulse hammering. Anger burned hot beneath the shock. Gold. Always gold. Enough to risk lives. Enough to drag ruin.

Randul stared at the bodies, pale and shaking. His breath came in short, ragged pulls.

Then he laughed. High and brittle. 'Serves you right, Bumpa—'

Rohan slammed him back against a tree, one hand closing around his throat. 'Anyone else we should expect?' His voice was low, steady, far more dangerous than shouting.

Niama watched, anger still burning. Randul's laughter rang wrong to her. To her people, life was not spent lightly. To kill was to lose something that never returned. The elders' warnings echoed in her thoughts, sharp as arrowheads.

'No,' Randul gasped. 'I swear.'

He wet himself. Rohan released him with a look of disgust and tossed him aside. He wiped his blade on Bumpa's tunic.

'Pray that's true,' he said. 'Or you'll lie with them.'

Niama turned away before the fury showed on her face. Randul's carelessness had nearly cost them everything.

A sound in the trees snapped them all taut.

Then Kesaahn stepped into the firelight. Her gaze swept the bodies, then settled on the others. 'That's one way to say hello. What did I miss?'

'Old debts,' Rohan said. He dragged the corpses into the dark and returned moments later to bind Randul to a tree. 'At least you won't need to wander off tonight.'

Randul flushed, muttering under his breath.

Niama scanned the forest. 'We keep watch. No exceptions.'

'I'll take first,' Rohan said.

They settled near the fire. Sleep came thin and restless. Even wrapped in her cloak, Niama could not fully let go. The night felt crowded. Too quiet in the wrong places. When exhaustion finally claimed her, it brought no peace.

Morning found them at the swamp's edge.

Mist clung thick and low, beading on skin and cloth alike. The air smelled of rot and stagnant water. Somewhere ahead, something splashed, slow and deliberate. Niama felt the sound more than she heard it.

Randul stopped and turned. His usual flippancy was gone.

'Before we step in,' he said, fixing Rohan with a hard look, 'you keep your weapons sheathed. Let me speak. I've dealt with them before, and they don't take kindly to mistakes.' His jaw tightened. 'And whatever you do, don't anger them.'

Rohan's expression darkened. 'I don't intend to.' A beat. 'But you're trying.'

Randul ignored him. He turned back to the fog and drew a breath that seemed more courage than air.

'Stay close,' he said.

He led them forward.

The fog swallowed them whole. The ground softened underfoot, water sucking at their boots. The sheep bleated once, then fell quiet.

Behind them, the forest vanished.

Ahead, the swamp waited.

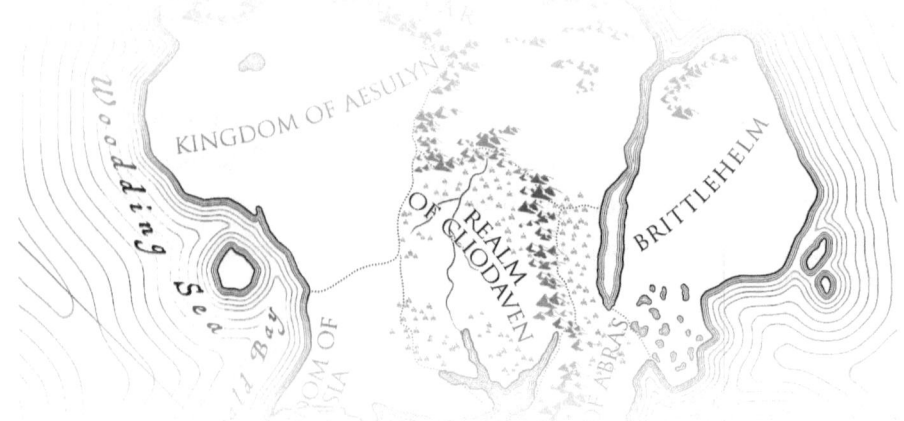

CHAPTER TWENTY-EIGHT

Brittleheim

The Swamplands of Despair opened before them, a drowned expanse of fog and rot. Skeletal trees clawed up from black water, their twisted limbs reaching upward.

Niama's pulse quickened. The silence pressed in, wrong and watchful. The sheep sensed it too, bunching close, their bleats sharp with fear as Randul struggled to keep them moving.

A voice slid through the fog.

'Your pressssence is not welcome here.'

The sound seemed to come from everywhere at once, low and rasping, heavy with threat.

'Who issss it that daressss tread the marssssshlandssss?'

Randul stepped forward before anyone could stop him. 'I am Randul of Dawnbury,' he said, his courage thin and shaking. 'These are my companions. We seek passage only.'

The fog shifted.

A figure rose from it, half-man, half-serpent. A thick humanoid torso supported a massive, scaled head, its body tapering into a long, sinuous tail that vanished into the water. Talons curled at the ends of its arms. Its eyes were dark hollows that swallowed what little light remained.

Niama fought the instinct to recoil. Rohan moved closer, his presence steady at her side.

'What bussinesss bringsss you here?' the creature hissed.

'We travel north,' Randul said. 'Toward the Infurnus Lizards. The swamps are unavoidable.'

The creature tilted its head. 'Infurnuss Lizardss.'

Its tongue flicked out, tasting the air. The sheep stumbled, hooves tangling as panic rippled through the flock.

'I mussst ssspeak with my kin,' it said at last. 'Do not move.'

Then it slid back into the fog, soundless and swift.

The water where it vanished did not still. Ripples widened slowly, spreading long after the creature was gone.

No one moved.

Only when the fog closed fully did Niama realize she had been holding her breath. 'We're surrounded,' she murmured. 'I can feel them.'

The mist parted again.

'You may passss,' the creature said. 'Leave your tribute. Take nothing that doesss not belong to you. We do not forgive those who sssteal.'

Randul gestured toward the sheep. 'They're yours. All five.'

The creature seized the sheep with startling speed, hauling them into the fog. One bleat rang out, sharp and panicked—then cut off as if smothered.

Silence rushed in to fill the space it left.

Randul straightened only after a moment too long, his laugh arriving late and brittle. 'Right. Path's this way.'

Niama's gaze flicked to Rohan, then Kesaahn. She whispered a brief prayer and followed.

The swamp closed around them.

Water crept into her boots, weight replacing warmth. Each step came back slower than it went out, the ground clinging, tugging, refusing release. Somewhere nearby, something shifted beneath the surface, unseen but close enough to feel.

They moved carefully, guided by Randul's memory rather than sight. Fallen trunks and pools of ink-dark water blocked the way. Every few hours they found small rises of dry ground, barely islands, where they paused to rest and catch their breath.

When night fell, they made camp on one such rise. The fire burned low but steady, its light swallowed quickly by the mist beyond.

Niama claimed first watch.

Rohan looked at her, question in his eyes. She answered without words, her posture firm, gaze fixed on the dark.

The swamp listened.

'Did you rest at all?' Rohan asked, catching the strain in Niama's posture.

'No,' she said. She rubbed her eyes, then stilled her hand. 'The fog presses too close. It's hard to breathe, harder to think.'

Rohan nodded. 'Then we move.' His gaze shifted to Randul, curled tight beside the fire. He nudged him with a boot. 'Up.'

Randul stirred, wiped his mouth on his sleeve, and squinted at him. 'You always wake people like that?'

'How long through the swamp?' Rohan asked.

Randul stretched, joints cracking. 'If nothing goes wrong, a day. Maybe two.'

A branch snapped somewhere beyond the fog.

Something moved. Not fast. Not slow. A drag and slide, then silence again.

Rohan's hand tightened on his sword hilt. 'We don't linger.'

They pushed on, pace quickening as the path narrowed and the ground softened beneath their boots. By nightfall they reached a small rise of firm earth dotted with thin trees. An old campsite. Untouched.

Whatever haunted the swamp kept its distance.

They took turns on watch. Sleep came thin and shallow.

At first light they broke camp without speaking, eager to leave the fog and the rot behind. The air thickened as they moved north, pressing against her chest until every breath felt measured, rationed. Even the sound of it seemed swallowed before it could escape.

Then Niama saw the nests.

Clusters of them, half-hidden in reeds and mud. Eggs lay exposed, some no larger than a fist, others nearly the size of a helm. Their shells shimmered faintly, stained with color.

Reptan breeding ground.

Randul slowed. His eyes lingered too long, his fingers twitching once at his side.

'Those fetch a fine price,' he said softly.

Rohan's voice cut in. 'Keep walking.'

Randul looked away, chastened but not cured.

Niama watched him for a moment longer than was comfortable. The Reptans' warning echoed in her mind. *We do not forgive those who steal.*

Heat thickened with every step. The fog thinned, replaced by a wavering haze. Sweat ran freely now. Breath burned.

'We're close,' Randul said at last, stopping at the edge of a sparse clearing. 'This is it. I don't go further.' He shook his head. 'Reptans are one thing. Infurnus lizards are another.'

The others exchanged a glance.

'We'll take it from here,' Rohan said.

Niama nodded. 'We won't be long.'

Randul hesitated. 'Might be best if you pay me now. Just in case.'

Rohan gave him a thin smile. 'Wait.'

Randul sat heavily on a fallen log, frustration etched deep.

The three of them pressed on.

The heat was relentless now, a living weight that clung to skin and breath alike. Light pulsed ahead through the haze, dull orange and red, as if the land itself smoldered.

'Stay close,' Rohan said. Sweat darkened his collar. 'Any way to tell male from female?'

'Yes,' Kesaahn said. 'Males have head frills. Larger build. Solitary.' She glanced at him. 'Avoid the neck. The solis gland sits there. We need it intact.'

Rohan nodded once.

Ahead, the ground shimmered.

And whatever waited beyond the haze was already aware of them.

Niama and Rohan shared a brief look, then scanned the ridge.

The fog peeled back all at once, as if pushed aside by a massive hand.

Brittleheim lay below.

Niama felt no shock—only a quiet certainty, as if the land had finally shown its true shape.

They stood on a narrow spine of rock overlooking a land stripped bare.

No sign of recent ruin.

No sense of collapse.

This place had endured exactly as it was meant to.

No green. No water. Only stone, fire, and heat. Volcanoes rose like broken teeth, coughing black smoke into a copper sky. Rivers of lava cut glowing paths through the land, crawling toward the distant sea. The air burned with sulfur and ash, every breath sharp in the lungs.

The ground hissed. Boiled. Cracked.

Niama had seen devastation before. This was something older. A wound that had learned to live with itself.

Infurnus lizards moved through it all, vast shapes of scale and muscle. Some lay sprawled across heat-soaked stone, sails flared wide, eyes half-lidded in contentment. Others rose onto their hind legs at the slightest disturbance, heads lifting to taste the air with rows of jagged teeth.

Niama pointed.

A cluster of females lounged near a lava flow, hides glowing orange and brown in the firelight.

Kesaahn followed her line of sight. 'Females,' she murmured. Then she gestured farther off. 'There. A male. Alone.'

The Infurnus male lay apart from the others, massive and still, its sail folded tight against its spine.

Rohan swallowed. 'Agreed. We get closer. Carefully.' His voice dropped. 'I've heard they can throw flame thirty feet.'

They edged along the ridge, stone hot beneath their boots. Below them, the male shifted, scales catching the glow of molten rock, nostrils flaring as it drew in the air.

Niama and Kesaahn exchanged a look and nodded once.

'I'll circle left,' Rohan whispered. 'When I'm in position, distract it. I strike from behind.'

He moved without another word, slipping from rock to rock until he vanished behind a massive boulder near the creature's flank.

Moments stretched.

Then Rohan raised his arm and waved sharply.

Now.

'Ready?' Niama whispered.

Kesaahn nodded.

They descended.

Niama loosed the first arrow.

It sank deep into the Infurnus's side, biting through scale. The beast roared, the sound tearing across the valley as flame erupted from its jaws in a violent arc of red.

The creature spun toward them, jaws snapping, heat rolling off it in suffocating waves.

Rohan burst from cover and drove his sword into its flank.

The Infurnus screamed and thrashed, its body twisting violently. Rohan clung to the hilt, boots skidding as the beast surged forward.

Niama fired again. The arrow glanced off the creature's shoulder as it turned, eyes locking on her.

It charged.

Rohan was dragged with it, refusing to release his blade. The Infurnus drew in a deep breath, chest expanding as fire gathered behind its teeth.

Kesaahn slammed her staff into the ground. The vial at its head flared white. She spoke the word — and felt it pull, deep in her chest, a cold thread of power drawn out and spent.

Frost exploded outward.

A surge of icy mist struck the creature full in the face. Flame died in its throat. The Infurnus coughed, staggered, its roar breaking into a choking wheeze.

Rohan ripped his sword free and plunged it forward again, driving steel deep between the ribs.

Into the lungs.

The beast convulsed.

The Infurnus let out one final, broken cry, lifting its head toward the ash-choked sky before collapsing in a thunder of heat and stone.

Stillness followed.

Niama and Kesaahn moved at once.

'Your knife,' Kesaahn said, already kneeling. 'We need the gland. Quickly.'

Niama passed her the dagger.

Kesaahn cut deep into the creature's neck. Thick, black blood poured free, steaming as it hit the ground. She thrust her hand into the wound without hesitation, fingers searching.

'Got it.'

She drew out a glowing orange mass, slick with blood and heat, nearly the size of a melon. Rohan turned away, jaw tight. Even necessity had its limits.

Kesaahn wrapped the gland in cloth and stuffed it into her satchel.

She stared down at her sleeve, now stained dark. 'That will never come out,' she muttered. 'And I was rather fond of it.'

Despite themselves, Rohan and Niama gave strained, breathless laughs, more reflex than humor.

The stench clung to them. Blood, sulfur, scorched earth. It settled over Niama like a weight. Guilt stirred, sharp and unwelcome, but she pressed it down. This death had purpose. Or so she told herself.

She closed her eyes and whispered a brief prayer, not for forgiveness, but for balance.

They climbed back toward the ridge at a hurried pace.

When they reached the clearing, Randul straightened at once.

'I never thought I'd say this,' Rohan said, wiping sweat from his brow, 'but I prefer the swamp to whatever that place was.'

Niama nodded once.

'That was... fast,' Randul said, eyes darting.

'Something troubling you?' Rohan asked.

Randul glanced toward the fog. 'Only a strong desire to leave.'

'Not tonight,' Niama said. 'We move at dawn.'

Randul opened his mouth, thought better of it.

'I agree,' Kesaahn said. 'Rest now.'

Randul's gaze caught on her sleeve. His nose wrinkled. 'Is that what I think it is?'

'Lizard,' Kesaahn said flatly. 'Try not to faint.'

They built a small fire as the mist thickened around them. Shadows stretched and warped across the clearing, flames painting their faces in flicker and gold.

Conversation dwindled. Each of them retreated inward.

Niama sat apart, fingers resting against the rough bark of a nearby tree. The swamp breathed around them. Water shifting. Creatures moving unseen. The scent of rot, smoke, and blood tangled in the air.

Despite it all, a strange calm settled over the camp.

Not safety.

Not peace.

Only the quiet that comes after something irreversible.

CHAPTER TWENTY-NINE

The King

The party woke beneath a dim, murky light, already smothered by fog. Sound felt swallowed before it could travel. Randul was packed and waiting, his agitation as thick as the mist coiling around them.

'We should move,' he said, tugging at his straps. 'The swamps don't forgive delays. The fog only makes it worse.'

Niama, Rohan, and Kesaahn broke camp quickly. Movements turned sharp, efficient, urgency bleeding from Randul into the rest of them. They exchanged a brief glance. Something was off.

Rohan secured his bedroll. Niama doused the fire and swept their remaining supplies into her pack.

'Did anything happen while we were gone yesterday?' Niama asked, tightening her straps.

Randul hesitated. His lip trembled beneath his protruding teeth. 'No. Nothing.' He forced a shrug. 'I just hate the fog.' He rubbed his arms and pressed ahead, boots sucking free from the mud with each step.

The mist thickened as they moved, folding in around them, closing ranks like a patient army.

Then a voice hissed from everywhere at once.

'You have betrayed ussss, Randul of Dawnbury. We warned you.'

The words struck like a blow.

Randul bolted.

'What did you do?' Niama shouted, chasing him. 'Randul!'

Rohan and Kesaahn followed hard on her heels.

'It was only one,' Randul cried, panic breaking his voice. 'I didn't think they'd even notice!' He stumbled, nearly pitching face-first into the muck.

Rohan narrowed his eyes. 'One what?'

The answer came with a sound of sliding scales.

A Reptan burst from the fog and slammed into Randul, knocking the breath from him. He flew backward into the water, his skull cracking against a jagged stone. A raw groan tore free.

The creature circled him, eyes burning low and bright. 'Where issss it?' Its tail lashed, sending foul water spraying.

Gasping, dizzy, Randul clawed himself upright. With shaking hands, he dug into his pack and drew out an egg. Smooth. Pale. Intact.

He set it carefully on a moss-slick rise. 'Here,' he rasped. 'Take it. It's unharmed.'

The Reptan gathered the egg with reverent care and vanished into the fog.

Randul sagged, a wild grin breaking across his face as the adrenaline hit. He laughed once, breathless.

Niama felt heat rise behind her eyes. 'What possessed you?' Her voice shook with fury. 'After everything they warned us?'

Randul stared at his boots. 'Those eggs are worth a fortune back—'

'They told you not to take anything,' Rohan snapped, fists clenched. 'Anything.'

The fog stirred again.

Heavier this time.

The sound was wrong. Larger. Closer.

They turned as a massive Reptan emerged, its bulk rippling beneath scaled hide.

It struck without slowing. Jaws clamped onto Randul's shoulder and tore free as it passed, poison sinking deep. Randul went rigid, breath locking in his chest.

'H-help me,' he whispered, eyes glassy, unfocused.

Niama's heart slammed against her ribs. Horror rooted her where she stood.

Rohan and Kesaahn flanked her, weapons raised, yet none of them moved. The swamp seemed to hold them fast, thick with consequence and waiting.

The fog thickened.

Another Reptan slid from it, jaws already wide, teeth catching what little light remained. The companions scattered instinctively, hearts hammering as the creature struck.

Randul did not move.

The Reptan's fangs sank into him again. He locked in place, body rigid, eyes wild and darting, the venom stealing motion but not awareness.

Then something larger moved behind him.

The mist parted, and an immense Reptan rose, its bulk eclipsing what little sky they could see. Its eyes burned like coals. Its jaws opened, revealing rows of serrated teeth.

No one breathed.

The creature lunged.

Its mouth closed around Randul's torso. He made no sound. Fear crushed it out of him. The Reptan lifted him effortlessly, tilting its head back as Randul slid deeper into its throat.

Bone cracked.

The sound carried.

Then a wet, final drag as the creature swallowed him whole.

No one moved.

Niama's stomach twisted violently. Her body trembled, caught between nausea and disbelief. She wanted to scream. To strike. To undo what had just happened. But shock held her fast, hollowing her from the inside out.

Rohan and Kesaahn stood beside her, faces set, eyes fixed on the Reptans. There was nothing to be done. There never had been.

A long silence stretched.

The great Reptan turned to them.

'We do not suffer thievessss who profit from our offsssspring,' it said. Its gaze moved from one to the next. The only sound was their own breathing, ragged and loud in the stillness.

Its scales caught the light, dull gemstones beneath the fog. 'You may leave,' it continued. 'No harm will come to you... if you ressssspect our lawsssss.'

Rohan swallowed hard before he bowed, the motion stiff rather than graceful. His sword slid back into its sheath with a faint scrape.

'Randul acted alone,' he said, his voice low and tight. 'We did not know of his intent.'

He hesitated, just long enough to betray himself.

'Thank you... for allowing us to leave.'

Niama forced herself to remain still. Blood and swamp rot hung heavy in the air. Cold sweat slicked her skin. Survival demanded composure, no matter the cost.

'I understsssstand, Prince Rohan,' the Reptan replied, its voice deep and knowing.

Rohan stiffened. 'How do you know who I am?'

'We posssssessss knowledge of many thingssss, Prince Rohan,' the Reptan said. 'Including the Ssssecond Rissssing.'

Its crimson gaze did not waver.

'We withheld our knowing while you traveled with the thief. Your intentssss were... unclear. He wasssss known to usss. That is why my kin obssssserved you. We do not watch the human realm idly. What stirs there echoes here.'

A pause. Heavy. Deliberate.

'I am Tagaoe,' it continued. 'Voice of my people. We will assssisssst you.'

Niama found her voice, though it trembled beneath her control. 'We return south, to Dawnbury. From there, west.'

Tagaoe inclined its head. 'Then my kin shall essssscort you to the marsh's edge. You depart with my blessssssing.'

Niama hesitated only a heartbeat before climbing onto the nearest Reptan. Its scales were warm beneath her palms, slick with damp heat. Rohan mounted another, movements stiff, followed by Kesaahn, who muttered something under her breath.

The Reptans surged forward.

The swamp blurred.

Their motion was effortless, powerful. Water split and rejoined beneath them as they ran, mist tearing past Niama's face. The sensation was not flight, but something close to it. The ground no longer resisted. It yielded.

Awe stirred, sharp and unwanted.

And then the memory came.

Randul. The snap of bone. The sudden absence where a man had been.

Niama shut the thought away and focused on the rhythm beneath her, on the living strength of the creature carrying her through the mire.

Hours later, the ground hardened beneath them.

They dismounted at the swamp's edge, legs unsteady. Behind them, the fog thinned. Ahead, the air shifted, cleaner, touched with the scent of green growth. Wildflowers dotted the rise beyond the marsh, bright and impossible.

Niama turned back. 'You have my thanks,' she said quietly.

'No gratitude issss required,' a Reptan replied. 'Fulfillment of what isss foretold isss enough.'

One by one, the Reptans slipped back into the fog.

The last paused.

Its head lifted slightly, as if listening to something far deeper in the marsh than sight could reach. For a breath too long, its gaze lingered on Niama.

Then it turned and vanished, the water folding closed behind it.

The fog resumed its slow drift, unchanged.

But the ground beneath Niama's feet did not feel the same.

Silence followed.

Niama's voice was barely more than breath. 'Randul was broken,' she said. 'But no soul deserves to be ended so.'

Rohan nodded, his expression tight. 'It was brutal.' A pause. 'But he was warned. And he chose.' His jaw flexed. 'Gold blinded him.'

Niama folded her arms, the chill creeping deeper than the air allowed. 'We cannot carry his shadow with us,' she said, though doubt threaded the words. 'What is set before us must still be done.'

Kesaahn broke the quiet. 'With the south emptied, Everleaf won't be found in trade. We'll need to harvest it ourselves.'

Rohan nodded. 'Then we return to Dawnbury, take the Steepmoor road west.'

Kesaahn grimaced, glancing at her sleeve. 'After I wash this. There's a stream nearby. I won't sleep smelling like lizard.'

She looked to Niama. 'You're quiet.'

Niama shook her head slowly. 'A shadow lingers,' she said. 'It has not finished with us.'

'Randul?' Kesaahn asked.

'Perhaps,' Niama replied. 'Or perhaps what followed him.'

Rohan exhaled, steadying himself. 'Then we move on. Together.'

As they entered the forest, the sounds of water and leaves closed around them. Wildflowers brushed their legs. Cold seeped through cloth and bone alike.

And still, Niama felt watched.

After several hours, they reached a narrow stream cutting across their path. Its steady murmur broke the lingering hush left by the swamp. A patch of short grass beside it offered dry ground enough for camp.

Kesaahn wasted no time. She slipped out of her outer dress, light armor catching the firelight as she knelt at the bank. Soap and water worked together to scour the last traces of lizard gore from the fabric while Rohan set about building a fire.

Niama rested against a tree, eyes tracking the water and the shadowed woods beyond. She ate sparingly, nuts and berries rough against her tongue, grounding her in the small, ordinary act.

Kesaahn hung the dress over a low branch, droplets falling back into the grass. She joined Niama, following her gaze into the trees.

'I often wonder why the Seer chose me,' Niama said at last. Her voice was low, almost lost to the stream. 'The path feels... larger than I am.'

Kesaahn considered her, fingers brushing damp earth from her palms. 'None of us are chosen because we're ready,' she said. 'Only because we're necessary.' A pause. 'The Seer saw something. That matters more than confidence.'

Rohan fed another log to the fire. It caught with a dull crackle. 'Whatever the reason,' he said, 'we keep going.'

Niama nodded, though the weight did not lift. She drew in the night air, cool and clean, pine and damp soil replacing rot and smoke. The forest felt older here. Familiar. For the first time since leaving the swamp, her shoulders eased.

Kesaahn's voice softened. 'There's purpose behind the Seer's silences as well as his words.'

'The road ahead is harsh,' Niama said. 'And the cost may yet ask more than we can give.'

'Then we pay it together,' Kesaahn replied. 'We've already walked where most would have turned back.'

Silence settled, companionable and unforced. Firelight flickered against tree trunks. An owl called once, then again.

After a time, Kesaahn glanced sideways. 'May I ask something I've wondered for a while?'

Niama inclined her head.

'You don't look like the southern elves of Atheron. Where are you from?'

Niama hesitated. 'I don't know.' She kept her eyes on the fire. 'The elders found me alone in the woods as a child. Blood on my hands. None of it mine.' Her fingers tightened briefly. 'They took me in. Raised me.'

'And your past?'

'Hidden. Or lost. Perhaps both.' A faint exhale. 'I stopped asking when the answers never came.'

The fire popped, sending sparks upward.

Kesaahn smiled, not unkindly. 'Whatever your beginning, you're not alone now.'

Niama met her gaze. 'For that, I am grateful.'

They settled in as night deepened. Rohan stretched out on his bedroll, staring up through the branches, a blade of grass between his teeth. Stars winked overhead, pale and distant. The forest breathed around them, alive with small sounds and quiet motion.

For a little while, the world felt still.

They woke to cold ash and dead embers.

The fire had burned down to nothing in the night, leaving the camp exposed. Their packs lay disturbed. Scraps of food were scattered where small shapes had rummaged through them.

Rohan swore under his breath as he gathered what remained of his rations. 'Damn vermin.'

Kesaahn smirked faintly. 'Perhaps next time you'll guard your supper with more devotion.'

He shot her a look but said nothing, stuffing what was left into his pouch.

Niama watched him, sensing the sting beneath his irritation. 'If you're hungry, I can share.'

Rohan straightened at once. 'No. Truly.' He bowed, hand to his chest. 'Your offer is more than enough.'

They moved on.

It did not take long for Rohan to notice what was wrong.

The forest sickened as they walked. Leaves hung limp and grey. Moss crumbled to dust beneath their boots.

'This land was green days ago,' he said, disbelief tightening his voice. 'What happened here?'

'The corruption spreads faster than we feared,' Kesaahn replied. 'It chokes the land before it takes the people.'

The birds had gone silent.

Rohan slowed. 'If it's reached this far south...' He swallowed. 'Oxemount has fallen.'

Niama's hand closed around her dagger.

Smoke curled above the trees ahead.

They approached cautiously, then dropped behind a fallen log as heat washed over them. The stench of burned timber and flesh clawed at Niama's throat.

The town was ruined.

Blackened buildings smoldered. Actari moved among the wreckage, small and quick, clad in dark leather, faces hidden behind black masks. Their movements were precise. Practiced.

Then one stepped aside.

Another figure stood among them.

Niama's breath stopped.

Coseo.

Memory crashed into her. Laughter. Long nights. Trust freely given. Will's body, broken and still, rose in its place.

Her hands shook as she lifted her bow.

Kesaahn caught her arm. 'Not yet,' she whispered. 'You'll have your moment.'

Niama lowered the bow, vision blurring.

'Who is that?' Rohan asked softly.

The Actari dragged a man onto the road. He wore armor, battered and scorched, his helm torn away.

Rohan went still.

The man lifted his head.

'Father,' Rohan breathed.

Kesaahn seized him. 'No.' Her grip was iron. 'You cannot.'

The king spat at Coseo's feet.

'You mistake cruelty for power,' he said, blood threading his teeth. 'I ruled men who would have died for me. You command beasts that feed on fear.'

Coseo knelt, wiped the spittle from his boot with careful fingers, and rose smiling.

'Fear is enough,' he said.

The dagger flashed.

Niama's breath stalled.

This was not a battlefield.

This was what came after defeat.

She understood it then with sudden, brutal clarity: this was the shape of a future where the prophecy failed. Not fire. Not glory. But kings broken publicly, hope consumed piece by piece, and the world taught to watch in silence.

Her fingers tightened until her knuckles burned.

She did not look away when the dagger rose.

'Tonight,' Coseo said, voice carrying clearly now, 'you dine on a king.'

The Actari removed their masks.

Niama gagged.

Black flesh. Vast eyes. Mouths filled with layered teeth where faces should have been.

They fell upon the king.

The screams stopped.

Rohan collapsed to his knees, hands over his ears. Niama retched into the dirt, bile burning her throat. The smell of blood and smoke pressed in, suffocating.

When the creatures moved on, silence rushed back in.

'How did they reach him?' Rohan whispered. 'He was meant to lead the reinforcements. Who guards the city now?'

Kesaahn knelt beside him, slower than usual. Her breath caught once before she spoke.

'I don't know,' she said. Her voice wavered, raw in a way it never was. 'But we must assume the worst.'

She rested a hand on his shoulder. It trembled.

She did not pull it away.

'Your father did not beg,' she said quietly. 'He did not bow.'

She swallowed.

'That matters more than they understand.'

Niama wiped her mouth, tears streaking her face. The prophecy pressed down on her like a hand on her spine.

They could not stop.

They could not fail.

'Then we finish this,' she said quietly. 'For him. For all of them.'

The forest did not answer.

But the road ahead no longer allowed retreat.

It demanded everything they had left.

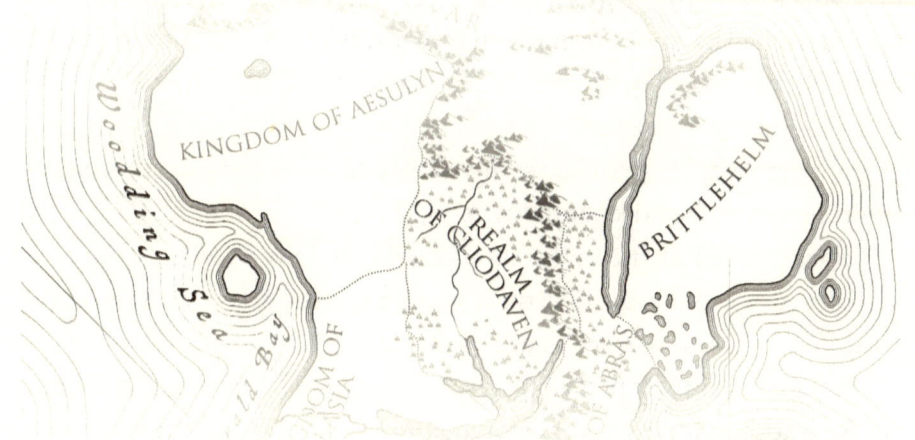

CHAPTER THIRTY

The Restraint

As the companions stirred, dawn threaded pale gold through the trees. Smoke still clung to the air. The faint crackle of dying embers whispered from somewhere deeper in the forest. Niama blinked against the light. Warmth touched her skin, a fragile comfort against the lingering chill, but the taste of ash sat heavy in her mouth.

'We should leave,' she said. Urgency sharpened her voice. Her gaze swept the quiet woods. Too quiet.

Rohan lay slumped against a fallen log, soot dusting his clothes and skin. Niama's breath caught as she looked at him. 'Will he endure this?'

Kesaahn did not hesitate. 'He will.' Her voice was steady, unyielding. 'With his father gone, he must become what his people need. Whether he wishes it or not.'

Niama drew the map from her pack, the Seekers' gift crackling softly as she unfolded it. Her finger traced the worn lines with care. 'We skirt the northern edge of Abras,' she said, thinking aloud. 'Find the Power Stone. Then south, through the mountains. We avoid Coseo's forces as they press toward Dawnbury.'

Kesaahn nodded, approval glinting in her eyes. 'The Seer chose well.'

Niama looked up. The sky beyond the canopy was smeared with ash, the blue dulled by smoke rising from Dawnbury's ruin. Bitterness filled her lungs. She closed her eyes briefly, steadying herself. 'Only time will tell,' she said, folding the map away.

Rohan stirred. He stretched stiffly, rubbed his eyes, and rose, the lines of strain already etched deep into his young face.

Kesaahn rested a hand on his shoulder. 'How do you feel?'

Rohan exhaled slowly. 'Like there's no time left to grieve.' His jaw tightened. 'We save who we can. That's all that matters.'

They gathered their packs quickly. Niama slung her bow and took one last look at their hiding place before stepping from behind the fallen tree, senses taut.

'We move fast,' she said. 'Power Stone first. Then south, toward the Ereda Hills and Steepmoor.'

Rohan nodded. 'Your path is sound.'

'If fortune favors us,' Kesaahn added, 'we'll miss the worst of what marches south.'

A harsh laugh carried down the road.

Niama froze.

Two figures emerged from the northern path, axes slung loose in gore-smeared hands. Their laughter was thick and ugly, echoing too loudly in the morning air.

They were massive, their green-tinged skin stretched tight over corded muscle. Heads too large for their bodies lolled forward, pig-snouted faces split by wide mouths crowded with jutting teeth. Small eyes squinted with crude delight.

'Swinish,' Rohan breathed.

Niama's grip tightened on her bow. Tales whispered around campfires painted these creatures as brutal beyond reason. They did not need provocation.

She motioned sharply.

The companions slipped back behind the fallen tree, hearts pounding, the laughter still scraping at the edges of the forest as the danger drew nearer.

'We can't let them reach Silverfall,' Rohan said. His hand was already on his sword. There was no hesitation in him now, only a cold, contained fury. 'Every one we cut down spares lives.'

Niama and Kesaahn nodded. The crackle of distant fires crawled through the trees.

'I take the north,' Rohan said. 'Niama, south. Kesaahn, center. Support and strike on my mark.'

Kesaahn tightened her grip on her staff. The vial bound to its head glimmered faintly as she tipped it, gauging what remained. 'It will be enough,' she murmured.

Niama raised her bow and moved south. Breath slowed. The forest narrowed to angles and distance.

Rohan vanished into the trees.

The Swinish were laughing, oblivious, axes resting loose at their sides as they surveyed their ruin.

Rohan's signal came sharp and brief.

Ice detonated across the road.

Kesaahn's magic struck first, frost blooming across green flesh, locking joints, stealing balance. The Swinish roared in surprise as cold tore into muscle and bone.

Niama loosed.

Her arrows flew clean and fast, shafts biting deep. One creature staggered. The other fell to a knee.

Rohan hit them from the flank.

Steel flashed. He moved with ruthless economy, blade rising and falling in swift, final arcs. The Swinish collapsed in the dirt, axes clattering from slack hands.

Silence rushed in behind the violence.

Rohan bent, hands braced on his knees, breath steaming. 'Move them,' he said. 'No one finds this.'

They dragged the bodies into the trees, blood darkening the roots, leaves hastily pulled to cover the signs of death.

Then they moved on.

The road bent north toward Oxemount.

They hadn't gone far when sound reached them. Not laughter. Not battle.

Feeding.

They stopped at the tree line.

Two immense shapes loomed beside the old farm. Pale hides stretched over towering muscle. Long white hair streamed around horned heads crowned with curling tusks. The barn lay torn open, beams snapped and dangling like broken ribs.

Jalheim.

Each stood taller than the surrounding trees. Thirty feet of hunger and weight. They scooped sheep into their jaws with careless efficiency, mouths closing wetly as bone shattered. Blood streaked their chins. The animals' screams tore through the air, sharp and helpless.

Niama's bow rose before she realized she'd lifted it.

Her hands shook.

'Those poor creatures,' she whispered. Every instinct in her screamed to act. To loose an arrow. To *do something*.

Rohan's breath came hard beside her. His hand flexed on his sword hilt, muscles tight, coiled. For a heartbeat, Niama knew he was measuring distance. Angles. Whether sacrifice could still mean victory.

Kesaahn caught the moment and crushed it. 'No,' she said softly. Not a command. A truth. 'That is death.'

Rohan exhaled, sharp and controlled. His grip loosened by degrees. 'They're being driven,' he said, voice tight. 'Used.'

'Yes,' Kesaahn replied. 'And if we reveal ourselves, we join the slaughter.'

Niama lowered her bow. Her fingers would not fully release it. The cost of restraint burned worse than fear.

They eased back, step by careful step, letting the forest reclaim them.

Behind them, the screams went on.

They left the road behind, pushing north through brittle undergrowth. The land bore the scars of flight and failure. Shrubs withered. Small animals lay where they'd fallen, caught too slow.

Far off, larger shapes fled through the trees, silhouettes breaking away from the creeping rot.

The forest was dying.

And it was not dying quietly.

They followed the road at a distance, never setting foot upon it. Dead leaves muted their steps, brittle and dry beneath their boots. Each footfall sounded louder than it should have.

No birds called. No insects stirred. Even the wind moved carefully, brushing the trees without voice. The silence pressed in until Niama became aware of her own breathing, slow and measured, too loud in the hush.

Smoke lingered low among the trunks, stinging her throat. It clung to bark and stone alike, a bitter reminder of what had passed through here. Splintered branches lay snapped and trampled, undergrowth crushed into the earth as though the land itself had been forced to kneel.

As the sun sagged toward the horizon, the sky bruised beneath a veil of ash. Cold crept up from the ground, stealing warmth from fingers and breath alike. Their exhalations fogged the air, pale and fleeting.

The forest did not resist their passage.

It endured it.

'We camp off the road,' Rohan said quietly.

Niama scanned the darkening forest. 'There.' She nodded toward a fallen tree set back from the path. 'It'll break the line of sight.'

They slipped toward it, bark rasping under their palms as they climbed over. The tree's bulk hid them completely. Dusk folded in, thick and watchful.

'No fire,' Rohan said. His gaze never stopped moving.

Niama tried to eat and failed. Her appetite curdled beneath the memory of smoke and blood. She looked out into the stripped forest and caught sight of a lone elk standing motionless between the trees.

'Why does the darkness spare the large beasts?' she asked. 'And us?'

Kesaahn's voice was low. 'It hasn't grown strong enough yet. When it does, it won't discriminate. The legion follows in its wake, feeding it ground to spread.'

Niama frowned, thoughts turning hard and sharp. 'Then light can still fight it.'

'Yes,' Kesaahn said. 'Athris's Staff drove darkness back before, even in the void. If it exists in this world, it can wound what's coming.'

Silence returned, heavier now.

Rohan broke it. 'My father believed darkness hunts weakness. As long as we stand, it won't take us.'

Niama felt something stir. Small. Fragile. But real.

'He was wise,' Kesaahn said. 'Few understood the balance as he did.' Her voice softened. 'He will be remembered.'

Rohan looked to Niama. 'You never told us what truly happened to Coseo.' His tone was gentle, but steady. 'It's time.'

Niama's breath caught. Her fingers closed around the medallion at her throat. For a moment, the forest blurred, replaced by damp stone and running feet.

She steadied herself. 'The southern Wildkin captured us,' she said. 'We escaped their caves by chance and stubbornness. They followed us longer than they should have.'

She hesitated. 'Then Jack found us.'

Kesaahn stiffened slightly.

'He seemed helpful,' Niama continued. 'But something felt wrong. Coseo sensed it too. I should have listened.' Regret tightened her voice. 'When Jack questioned us about the Seer, Coseo challenged him.'

Her hand trembled. 'Jack's magic was... wrong. It wrapped around Coseo like living shadow. I used the ring. Light burned him away.' A pause. 'But it wasn't enough.'

Tears slipped free. 'Coseo was gone.'

Kesaahn rested a hand on her knee. 'You survived,' she said gently. 'That matters.'

Niama nodded, though the weight remained. Coseo's last look still haunted her. His warning. His fear.

This war was not only against darkness.

It was against what hid behind friendly faces.

Rohan sat apart, gaze fixed on the darkened forest as if it might yield answers if he stared long enough. Leaves sighed overhead, the breeze threading through them like a half-remembered warning.

Kesaahn broke the silence. 'The ring,' she said. 'How did it come to you?'

Niama's fingers lifted, brushing the bare place where it had once rested. 'An elder gave it to me,' she said quietly. 'She claimed it was a legacy. Passed down from a wandering magika she once knew.'

Kesaahn's eyes sharpened. 'Did the ring bear a sigil?'

'An elk,' Niama said without hesitation.

Kesaahn leaned forward, breath catching. 'Then it was an animus etheri.'

Rohan frowned. 'A weapon?'

'Not quite,' Kesaahn said. 'A vessel.' She glanced at Niama. 'Forged to *hold* light. Living light. Athris's own.'

Niama's mouth tightened. 'It didn't survive.'

'They never do.' Kesaahn nodded once. 'When awakened fully, the power burns through its shell. Light that pure refuses confinement.'

'So it destroys darkness?' Rohan asked.

Kesaahn shook her head. 'No. It erases it.' A pause. 'There's a difference.'

Rohan looked up. 'And the Staff of Light?'

Kesaahn's gaze drifted, distant now. 'That is no vessel. It does not *contain* light. It *is* light.' Her voice lowered. 'And it chooses who may wield it.'

'Who last held it?' Niama asked.

'Volthar,' Kesaahn said. 'When he died, the Staff vanished. Some believe it withdrew from the world rather than be misused.'

Silence followed. Heavy. Listening.

The forest seemed to lean closer.

A branch cracked somewhere in the dark, sending a jolt through the quiet. The sound loud enough to jolt Niama upright.

Rohan was already moving. 'We post a watch.'

'I'll take first,' Niama said.

She rose and took her place beside the tree, bow in hand, eyes probing the dark. The forest was unnaturally quiet. No owls. No insects. Even the wind seemed to hesitate.

Behind her, Rohan's breathing steadied as sleep claimed him. Kesaahn followed soon after.

Niama remained awake.

Her thoughts circled the ring. Gretha's timing. The elder's knowing look. Had the gift been chance... or preparation?

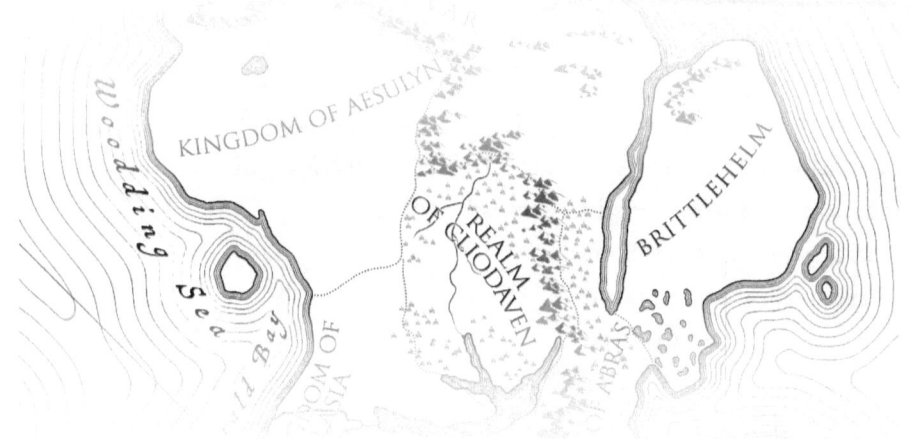

CHAPTER THIRTY-ONE

The Chasing

V alran jerked awake with a gasp, heart hammering, as he swatted something from his face.

A spider skidded across the cavern floor, its hairy legs still twitching.

He froze, breath caught in his throat, staring as it vanished into a crack in the stone. A cold shiver crawled up his spine.

Tehuti's laughter rolled through the cavern, deep and rough, shaking the plates of his armor.

'I see you've made a companion of the night,' he said, voice thick with amusement.

Valran shot him a glare, rubbing feeling back into his leg. 'How long have you been awake?' His pulse was only just beginning to slow.

'Not long,' Tehuti replied. Calm, unhurried. 'The earth stirs before the sun.'

Valran noticed the Namite chewing thoughtfully. 'What are you eating?'

His stomach tightened at the thought of real food. Hot broth. Fresh bread. Anything warm.

Tehuti lifted the stick in his hand. 'Cutleaf root. Bitter at first. It keeps the body steady.'

He reached to the small pile beside him and offered one. 'Try.'

Valran bit down.

The root was dense and raw, the taste of soil and sap filling his mouth. It grounded him more than he expected. For a fleeting moment, he saw long tables back home. Firelight. Voices. Laughter.

Homesickness struck hard.

He swallowed and nodded. 'Thank you.'

Tehuti inclined his head.

Despite himself, Valran's eyes flicked toward the shadows where the spider had vanished. He trusted Tehuti. He had no reason not to. Still, some fears refused to loosen their grip.

They left the cavern beneath a heavy, iron-colored sky.

Tehuti paused, studying the clouds. 'Snow will fall soon.'

Valran pulled Dorsey's jacket tighter around his neck, grateful for the extra weight. Cold was one thing. Cold with nowhere to hide was another.

A shape loomed in the distance.

Tehuti stiffened. 'Jalheim.'

The word settled like ice in Valran's chest.

They moved carefully, boots crunching through the frost-stiff ground. The cold bit through cloth and skin. Their breath fogged thick and white in the air.

Then came the howl.

Low. Distant. Wrong.

It crawled into Valran's bones, dredging up stories whispered by firelight when he was young. He forced himself to keep moving.

Ahead, the land opened.

Several Jalheim stood clustered together, their massive forms stark against the snow. Between them moved a man in dark robes, arms lifted, gestures sharp and commanding.

Valran's heart stuttered.

'I need a better look,' he whispered.

Before Tehuti could answer, Valran was already climbing. The bark was rough beneath his fingers, cold biting into his palms as he pulled himself higher.

From the branches, the scene sharpened.

The Jalheim listened.

The robed figure spoke with furious energy, voice lost to distance but posture unmistakable. Authority. Control.

Coseo?

The thought sent a dangerous thrill through Valran. Fear still clutched his chest, but beneath it stirred something else. Curiosity. The terrible pull of knowing more.

Then the Jalheim shifted.

Too sharply.

Heads turned. Massive bodies reoriented.

Toward him.

Valran's breath caught as every instinct screamed at once.

They had been seen.

He called below to Tehuti, who was already making the journey up the tree.

They flattened themselves among the branches as the Jalheim thundered past below.

The ground shook with each step. Snow spilled from the limbs overhead. The sound was not a charge but a passage, heavy and indifferent, as if the forest itself were being pushed aside.

When the last tremor faded, Valran realized he had stopped breathing.

He drew air in slowly, carefully, then craned north through the lattice of branches. The robed figure was gone.

Tehuti's gaze found him through the branches. Said nothing. Didn't need to.

They climbed down in silence, boots sinking into churned snow.

'I believe the dark commander was speaking to them,' Valran said at last, his voice thin in the cold. 'They listened.'

Tehuti's jaw tightened. 'Then they are no longer beasts alone.' A low growl threaded his words. 'They are weapons.'

Snow had begun to fall in earnest now, a thin white veil settling over the forest floor. They moved at a jog, breath burning in their lungs, frost cracking beneath their steps like brittle parchment.

Tehuti slowed and pointed. 'There. Shelter.'
A hollowed tree yawned ahead, its split trunk black with age. 'Briefly. If the Kambish Pass is lost to us, the mountains will demand their price.'

Valran slipped inside and pressed his back to the wood. The rough bark steadied him, its scent deep and old, a reminder that some things endured longer than fear.

Outside, the world felt too large. Too loud.

He closed his eyes and let the hollow swallow him. Damp earth. Resin. Rot and life tangled together. His thoughts raced, circling the image of the Jalheim, their size dwarfing reason itself.

Time thinned.

Then Tehuti spoke, quiet and firm. 'We move.'

Valran shifted to crawl out when Tehuti's body went rigid.

'Wait.' His voice dropped to a hiss. 'Do you hear that?'

At first there was only wind.

Then wings.

Massive. Slow. Beating the air with deliberate weight.

'Inside,' Tehuti breathed. 'Now.'

They pulled back into the hollow as a shadow passed overhead.

A voice followed, smooth and amused.

Tehuti peered through a narrow gap in the trunk.

Above them, the great bat circled lazily, wings catching the light as it drifted back and forth.

'Mr. Hunter, man,' said Bastion, his voice drifting through the hollow like smoke. 'My master regrets your absence. You slipped away before introductions were made.'

Tehuti raised a finger to Valran's lips.

'He does not see us,' he whispered. 'Not yet.'

They did not move.

'Stillness won't save you,' Bastion said softly. 'It only helps me remember where to look next.'

Hours dragged past. Snow thickened. Wind howled through the trees, rattling branches and packing the hollow deeper in white. The world narrowed to breath, cold, and waiting.

At last, the wings faded.

Only the soft hush of falling snow remained.

Tehuti exhaled. 'Now.'

Valran hesitated, then nodded. 'We must blur our trail. Branches tied low. Let the forest erase us.'

Tehuti regarded him for a beat, then inclined his head. 'You learn quickly.'

Quickly, they cut branches and lashed them to their belts. The work was silent, practiced. Needles scraped skin. Sap clung to fingers. They moved again at once, senses stretched taut, listening for anything out of place.

The forest closed behind them as if they had never been there at all.

Cold bit hard. Breath steamed. Snow glare burned the eyes as the sun climbed, forcing them to squint and turn their faces aside. The branches dragged behind them, scouring away tracks, breaking their passage into confusion rather than trail.

Tehuti led them out of the woods.

Beyond the trees, the land opened wide. Ruins lay to the south. Mountains rose to the west, their stone faces dark and severe.

Flatrfold.

Its broken towers stood like ribs through snow, walls sagging under age and vine. Lichen blackened the stone. The air around the ruins lay unnaturally still, as though sound itself hesitated to enter.

Valran scanned the distance. 'Fires,' he murmured. 'Few. Either resting... or few in number.' His gaze lifted to the far treeline. 'If we move now, we might make it unseen.'

Tehuti measured the distance, then nodded once. 'Climb.'

Valran mounted his back.

Tehuti ran.

Snow shattered beneath each stride. Wind tore past them, sharp and punishing. Valran clung tight, heart hammering as the open ground swallowed them. The sun flashed off Tehuti's armor, a cruel, betraying glint.

Almost there.

They hit the treeline—

'Tehuti!' Valran shouted. 'Above!'

The shadow fell first.

A colossal bat tore through the sky, wings beating thunder into the air as it dove straight for them.

Tehuti surged forward, crashing into the forest's cover. Branches snapped. Pine and damp earth flooded the air. He vaulted fallen logs without slowing, each leap jolting Valran's spine as the Namite drove deeper into the trees.

'He's locked on us!' Valran yelled.

Tehuti growled low and pushed harder, but strain crept into his movement. Breath rasped. The forest thinned here. Ijovar's trees stood wider apart, sky leaking through the canopy in pale, dangerous gaps.

Ahead, a massive fallen trunk lay half-buried in snow.

Tehuti vaulted it and staggered to a stop. 'Here,' he rasped. 'Briefly.'

Valran slid down and turned, scanning the woods while Tehuti bent, armor rising and falling with heavy breaths.

'I think we lost him,' Valran said, forcing the words steady.

Then the snow shifted.

Bastion perched atop the fallen tree behind them, wings folded like a patient cloak. His eyes caught the light, bright and wrong.

Valran's chest tightened. 'How—'

Bastion smiled.

'You prune the forest so carefully,' he said, voice soft as snowfall. 'And still... you grow loud.'

The bat's wings unfurled, slow and deliberate.

'Run again,' Bastion whispered. 'I enjoy the chasing.'

Valran's hand closed around his dagger. It wouldn't help. He knew that.

He ran anyway.

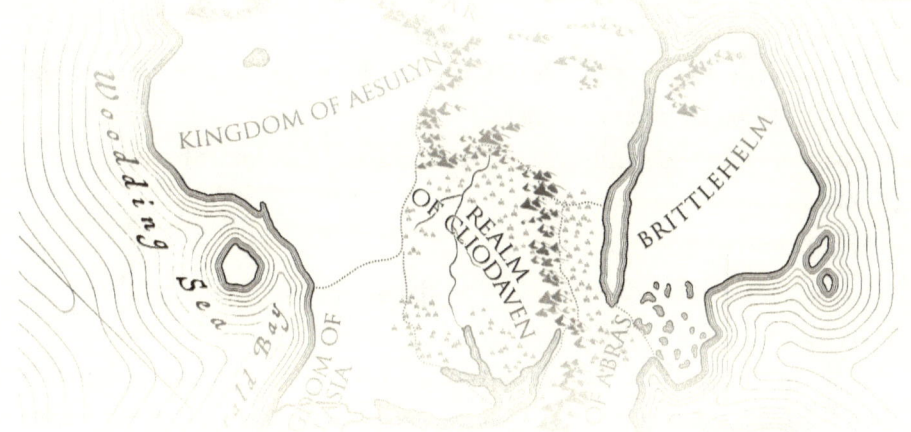

CHAPTER THIRTY-TWO

The Power Stone

Rohan's touch drew Niama from sleep. Dawn's chill brushed her face, sharp and unwelcome. Birds called somewhere beyond the trees, their song bright against the heaviness she carried.

'Wake,' Rohan said softly. 'We move.'

She opened her eyes, dread settling before thought could follow. Whatever waited ahead felt closer now. Inevitable.

Niama sat up as Rohan moved to wake Kesaahn, drawing her knees in, arms wrapped tight. The path before them pressed on her chest. The Power Stone. The Seer's silence. The weight of being *necessary*.

Rohan returned, gaze fixed west. 'The stone lies ahead. Near.' A pause. 'But its light is hidden.'

Before them, the land lay stripped and colourless. No glow. No sign. Only ruin stretching into the distance.

They reached the road and stopped.

The stench hit first. Thick. Rotting. Sweet and foul all at once, drawing carrion from the trees.

Bodies lay scattered across the ground, twisted where they'd fallen. Swinish. Gauntillia. Actari. Armoured shapes tangled together, their retreat frozen into slaughter.

Niama's breath snagged. Doubt surged, sharp and sudden. Could she truly stand against what did this?

Then she met the empty gaze of the dead and the doubt hardened into resolve.

She had no right to turn away.

Rohan covered his mouth, voice muffled. 'They were fleeing. Whatever came upon them did not slow.'

Among the dead lay men in silver, the royal lion smeared dark across their breastplates. Niama felt a pull she could not explain and knelt beside a fallen Actari. Her fingers hesitated, then slipped beneath the edge of its mask.

She pulled it free.

The face beneath was slack and wrong. Black flesh stretched tight, eyes dull and empty. Whatever hunger had lived there was gone, leaving only a hollow shell.

Niama recoiled, bile rising fast. Rohan and Kesaahn were beside her at once.

'I had to see it,' Niama said, forcing the words steady. 'They aren't just enemies at a distance. This is what we face.'

Kesaahn did not argue. 'Then we do not linger.'

They moved on, skirting the bodies, stepping carefully where the earth was stained too dark. The forest beyond swallowed them quickly, its shadows closing like a held breath.

Rohan traced the path ahead. 'A few hours,' he said. 'No more.'

As they pressed deeper, the air thickened. Light thinned. Decay crunched beneath their boots, brittle and dry. The smell of rot clung to skin and cloth alike, refusing to fade.

The forest did not welcome them.

It endured them.

A bird nearby struggled in the undergrowth, wings scraping uselessly against the earth.

Niama's breath caught. She stepped toward it.

Kesaahn's hand snapped out, catching her wrist. 'Don't.' Her voice was low, urgent. 'The darkness has touched it.'

Niama froze.

The bird convulsed once more, then stilled. Its small body lay slack in the leaves, life extinguished without ceremony.

Grief pressed sharp and sudden behind Niama's eyes.

'To lose the light is cruel,' Kesaahn said quietly. 'But darkness does not linger over mercy.'

Niama swallowed and looked away.

Then she saw it.

A faint blue glow filtered through the trees ahead, pale but unmistakable. It cut through the rot and shadow like a held breath.

'There,' Rohan said, wonder breaking through his fatigue.

They stepped into a small clearing, and the world changed.

Grass grew thick and green beneath their boots, untouched by decay. At its heart stood the Power Stone, a towering obelisk of polished blue crystal. Light pulsed softly within it, steady and cool, as if the forest itself were drawing breath through its presence.

Niama stopped short.

The stone *felt* alive.

She approached without thinking, drawn forward by something older than choice. When her fingers brushed the surface, warmth surged up her arm, swift and overwhelming. Her breath caught as energy flooded through her, settling deep in her chest like a second heartbeat.

The stone welcomed her.

Rohan's voice cut in, tight with unease. 'Something's wrong.'

Niama turned.

Rohan was circling the stone, eyes narrowed. 'The light should spread farther than this.' His jaw set. 'It should protect the forest.'

He vanished around the far side.

'No,' he breathed.

Niama and Kesaahn hurried to him.

The base of the obelisk was stained dark, veins of grey-black creeping upward through the crystal like ink through water. The corruption pulsed faintly, slow but certain.

'It's already begun,' Kesaahn said, laying her palm against the stone. Her face was grave. 'If this spreads... the others will follow. When they do, Arghost will be lost.'

'It's as the Seer foretold,' Niama whispered.

Niama drew her hand back, the warmth fading too quickly. The absence of it ached, sudden and strange, like losing grip on something she hadn't known she was holding.

'Then we stop it,' she said. Not a vow. A decision.

They turned south.

The forest thickened as they traveled, green returning in earnest. Leaves rustled overhead. The air smelled clean again. For a time, the world almost felt whole.

Niama breathed deeply, letting the solidity of earth and the steady presence of her companions anchor her. The relief was brief, but it was real.

By dusk, they reached a quiet rise and halted.

'We camp here,' Rohan said.

He gestured south, where two low peaks marked the edge of the Orboros range. 'East takes us toward Steepmoor. More enemies. Possibly Everleaf in the abandoned shops.' A pause. 'West is slower. Fewer patrols. But the climb will be hard.'

Kesaahn considered the mountains. 'Everleaf grows higher. If any remains untouched, it will be there.'

Niama nodded. 'West,' she said. 'Less chance of being seen.'

The decision settled between them.

The mountains waited.

Rohan spread his bedroll with a quiet grunt, shifting until the stones beneath him settled into something tolerable. 'We rest,' he said. Not a suggestion. A necessity.

Niama met his gaze and nodded. Kesaahn did the same.

They settled quickly. No fire. No wasted movement. The forest supplied its own sounds, leaves whispering overhead, insects threading a thin, restless chorus through the dark.

Twilight bled fully into night.

From where Niama lay, the distant glow of the Power Stone filtered faintly through the trees, its pale light fractured by branches and shadow. It stretched the forest into unfamiliar shapes, trunks twisting longer than they should, roots clawing at the earth like grasping hands. The clearing felt borrowed, not claimed.

Kesaahn rolled onto her side, already stilling. Weariness claimed her fast.

Niama pulled her blanket close, the fabric rough but welcome against the chill that crept in once the sun vanished. Cold brushed her cheeks, sharp and clean. She turned her head and found Rohan propped against a tree, chewing methodically through what little remained of their rations.

He did not look hungry so much as determined.

Her thoughts drifted to their waterskins. Too light. Too few. The knowledge pressed at her ribs, quiet but insistent. Thirst would come before hunger. It always did.

The forest did not care.

Eventually, the rhythm of the night closed in around them. Breath slowed. Muscles loosened despite themselves.

Sleep found Niama gently, though it did not come unmarked.

Her dreams wove faces and moments together. Hands reaching. Voices calling her name. The weight of choice pressing down, again and again. Not fear. Not peace. Something steadier.

Purpose.

And beneath it all, the sense that the forest was listening.

Niama's eyes snapped open at the soft crunch of footsteps.

Her hand found her dagger before thought followed. 'What are you doing?' she breathed.

Rohan emerged from the dark, breath ghosting white in the cold. One hand rested on his sword, his gaze never still, sweeping the trees as if expecting them to answer back.

'I couldn't sleep,' he whispered. 'I scouted Steepmoor.'

Niama pushed herself upright, chill biting through cloth. 'And?'

'It's standing,' Rohan said. His eyes met hers. 'Empty. Or close enough. I saw no movement.'

Hope flickered despite her caution. 'No legions?'

'None that I could find.' He rubbed his arms, jaw tight. 'If it holds, it gives us options.'

Niama listened past him, straining for anything out of place. The forest gave nothing. 'Then rest,' she said quietly. 'I'll keep watch.'

Rohan hesitated, then nodded. Within moments he was still again, breath slow and even, sleep claiming him without resistance.

Niama leaned back against the tree, bark rough against her spine. The scent of damp earth filled her lungs. Every sound sharpened. Leaves shifting. Wind threading through branches. An owl's call cut the dark, low and hollow.

Her grip tightened.

The night pressed close, heavy with things unseen. Each rustle felt deliberate. Each pause felt watched.

Rohan slept on, unaware.

Niama did not.

Kesaahn sat beneath the twisted roots of an ancient oak, sorting through her leather satchel with practiced care. The morning air was crisp, laced with the scents of Shadowmoss, Shadowbell, Silkbloom, and the deep, loamy bitterness of Dreamroot. Leaves stirred overhead. Oak branches sighed. Birch leaves whispered thinly to the breeze.

'Do you have enough?' Niama asked, rising from her bedroll and stretching the stiffness from her limbs. Dew scattered from nearby leaves as she moved, the chill sharpening her voice. Sleep had come easily last night, and she felt almost renewed.

Kesaahn glanced up, momentarily startled, then smiled. 'Enough for now. The rest I can gather as we travel.' She tucked a loose strand of hair behind her ear. 'A Magika's satchel is never full.'

Niama returned the smile, but her gaze drifted to the forest beyond them. Sunlight filtered through the canopy in fractured patterns, bright and beautiful. Still, unease coiled in her chest. They were not alone here. Experience had taught her that much.

'Rohan scouted Steepmoor last night,' she said quietly. 'It's still standing. If we're fortunate, we may find Everleaf there.'

Kesaahn's expression sobered at once. 'Then we cannot delay. The darkness won't spare it forever.' She secured the satchel and rose, staff in hand. 'If it's untouched, we take what we need and leave.'

Rohan groaned as Kesaahn nudged him awake. 'Already?' he muttered, blinking into the light. 'I was dreaming of better days.'

'We all were,' Niama said softly.

Rohan rolled his bedroll tight and stood, wincing. 'Then let's move.'

They set out beneath his lead, following narrow forest paths and crossing a chattering brook as the land dipped and rose. Steepmoor lay ahead, nestled at the base of a rocky pass. Small, but vital. The last true outpost of Abras before the wild reach of Cliodaven.

As they crested the hill north of Steepmoor, the town spread out below them.

Thin threads of smoke lifted from the north, pale against the sky, as though something there still smoldered and refused to die. Steepmoor itself lay silent. No voices. No movement. No dogs nosing through refuse, no merchants calling the morning. For a trading town of its size, the stillness was wrong.

Unease slid cold down Niama's spine.

They descended at a quicker pace, senses drawn tight. Vigilance clung to them, an invisible weight. Rohan took the lead, sword bare in his hand, gaze cutting from shadow to shadow between the buildings. Niama and Kesaahn followed close, weapons ready, breath measured.

The smell reached them before the streets did. Burned wood. Old smoke. It hung low and bitter, settling into the back of Niama's throat. Rohan slowed, blade angled defensively as they slipped between buildings, boots careful on the packed earth.

As they passed behind the nearest structure, Kesaahn spoke, her voice low but urgent. 'We find a herbalist. Quickly. Everleaf first, questions later.'

Her eyes searched doorways and windows for any sign of life. Rohan gave a brief nod, scanning the road and rooftops. Niama's pulse thudded hard in her ears, every sound magnified by the emptiness pressing in around them.

'I'll take the eastern road,' Rohan said quietly. 'If anything moves, I'll whistle.'

He turned and melted away between the buildings, leaving Niama and Kesaahn in the smoke-stained hush of the town.

'Agreed,' Niama said, already nocking an arrow.

She and Kesaahn moved toward the main road, steps light, deliberate. Steepmoor lay hollowed out. Gravel shifted beneath their boots. An old wooden sign creaked once in the breeze, then fell still again. Niama's crimson hair stirred, bright against the town's grey quiet.

To the west, the mountain road wound upward, scarred by the passage of countless caravans. Dust lifted in faint spirals where the breeze traced its path.

Niama's gaze never stopped moving. Doorways. Windows. Rooflines. Her fingers hovered near the string, ready.

'You know,' Kesaahn murmured, a thread of unease beneath the humor, 'the Magikas say the Everleaf has a sense of timing. Perhaps it's hiding from us out of spite.'

Niama let out a soft, surprised laugh. The sound felt almost foreign in her throat. For a breath, the tension eased.

The levity faded as quickly as it came.

Kesaahn slowed, eyes sharpening. She searched façades and hanging symbols, memory guiding her more than sight. Then she stopped. 'There.' She pointed to a modest building tucked beside a bakery just off the road. 'Herbalist.'

Nothing stirred.

They crossed quickly.

Up close, the shop felt abandoned in haste. The door stood shut, shutters half-latched, as though someone had fled mid-thought. No footprints. No sound from within.

Niama tested the handle. Solid.

They circled to the rear. Niama tipped her head back, eyes tracing the thatch. 'That'll do.'

She turned to Kesaahn. 'Brace yourself. Hands together. Like this.'

Kesaahn set her back to the wall and locked her fingers. Niama took a short run, planted her foot, and vaulted. Her dagger bit into the thatch. Straw tore free as she hauled herself up and worked a narrow opening, careful, patient.

When it was wide enough, she slid through.

The scent hit her first. Herbs. Dry leaves. Bloom and root. It wrapped around her, familiar and grounding. Shelves lined the walls, jars and bundles left scattered, barrels half-open as if abandoned mid-inventory.

She dropped lightly to the floor and crossed to the back door, lifting the brace. It opened without complaint.

Kesaahn slipped inside, eyes already alight.

'Elegant,' she said, glancing up at the roof. 'Remind me never to be chased with you nearby.'

Niama smiled faintly and took position by the door.

Kesaahn moved through the shop with reverence and urgency, fingers hovering over jars, eyes skimming labels. Glass flasks caught the light. Seeds. Powders. Pressed leaves. Her dress whispered as she turned, searching.

Then she stopped.

Her breath caught.

'Found it.'

Niama crossed the room in two quick strides, floorboards creaking underfoot. She leaned close, breath caught between hope and fear.

In Kesaahn's palm lay two broad leaves, vivid green and faintly luminous, each veined with life.

'Everleaf?' Niama asked.

Kesaahn nodded, careful already. 'Yes.' A pause. 'Only two. I pray it will suffice.'

Kesaahn slid the leaves into her satchel and cinched the strap tight. She gathered what else she could in swift, practiced motions — a bundle of Dreamroot, two sealed jars she didn't stop to label. Then her hand stilled on the back of the highest shelf.

She lifted the vial carefully, as though it might dissolve. The contents were a pale crystalline blue, catching the dim light with an almost mineral quality. She turned it over, read the hand-scratched label, and went very still.

'Gelufrigus glacicontrarius,' she breathed. Almost to herself. Almost disbelieving.

Niama looked over. 'What is it?'

'Something that has no business being in a herbalist's shop in Steepmoor.' Kesaahn closed her fingers around it gently and tucked it into the deepest pocket of her satchel. 'Something I haven't seen in years.' A pause. 'We're keeping this.'

'We'll repay the owner,' she said quietly. 'If there's an owner left.'

They slipped out the back, latching the door behind them. Kesaahn allowed herself a small smile, the thrill of success flickering through her. Niama did not return it. Her thoughts were already racing ahead.

Kesaahn squeezed her shoulder once. No words. None were needed.

They signaled Rohan.

He emerged from cover at the road's edge, eyes sharp. 'You found it?'

Niama nodded. 'We have the Everleaf.'

Relief loosened his shoulders. 'Then we leave. Now.' His gaze snapped south. 'Something's coming.'

They moved fast, cutting west toward the mountain pass, keeping to shadow where they could. Behind them, sound swelled. Boots. Iron. Voices raised in coarse chant.

The town came alive in the worst way.

Shouts. Splintering wood. Fire catching fast.

Smoke thickened, bitter and choking. By the time they reached the trees beyond Steepmoor, flames were already licking rooftops.

They stopped beneath cover and looked back.

The town burned.

Swinish poured through the streets, crude banners raised, iron clashing as they claimed what little remained.

Niama's hands shook. She curled them into fists until it hurt.

Another place lost.

Another mark burned into the map of the world.

They turned away before the screams could sink deeper.

CHAPTER THIRTY-THREE

The Soldier

The mountain path wound between two towering peaks, narrow and unforgiving, beginning at the ruined edge of Steepmoor. The climb was cruel even in kinder seasons. Rockfalls were common. In winter, ice slicked the stone and turned missteps lethal.

Niama and her companions climbed in silence. The sun eased the bite of the wind, its warmth welcome against chilled skin. Pine and cedar scented the air. Birds called faintly, their voices thin at this height.

Her legs burned with each step. Breath tore from her in short pulls as the pack bit into her shoulders.

Rohan stumbled on loose stone, arms flaring as his boots scraped for purchase. He recovered, but the effort showed. His stride lacked its usual certainty, fatigue etched deep into his face.

They did not stop.

The path climbed endlessly, stone upon stone, each rise demanding more than the last. Niama fixed her gaze ahead and fed the fire of resolve that kept her moving. Whatever waited beyond these peaks mattered more than comfort.

At a narrow turn, the land fell away to the west.

Steepmoor smoldered below them, its ruins coughing smoke into the sky. Black plumes drifted upward as Swinish forces withdrew toward Dawnbury, their work done. The sight burned too close.

Beyond the ruins, the world split.

To the south, fields rolled green and gold, alive with spring growth. The wind carried their scent upward, sweet enough to dull the ache in Niama's chest for a moment.

To the north lay devastation.

The earth there was broken and bare, stripped of life. No trees. No birds. Only red-brown soil stretched toward the Orboros ranges, cracked and hostile.

Farther still, darkness crept southward, slow and relentless. It bled into the land like a spreading wound, reaching toward Langmore Forest.

The climb steepened.

Cliffs rose close on either side, shale sliding underfoot, the path narrowing to little more than a scar in the rock. One mistake would mean a long fall and no return. The mountains offered no forgiveness.

And yet, from this height, the view was vast.

Ranges folded into valleys beyond sight, bathed in warm light where the sun still held sway. Beauty and ruin existed side by side, neither yielding to the other.

Niama felt small beneath it all.

Humbled.

But she kept climbing.

As daylight thinned, breath grew harder to draw.

'We rest off the road,' Niama said, scanning the slopes. She pointed instead to a massive boulder jutting from the mountainside, close to the pass. 'There. It'll break our outline.'

They followed her up the incline, boots slipping on loose shale. Niama climbed first, one careful step at a time, using the stone as a guide. The slope fought every movement. Rock grated beneath her feet. She pressed on, pulse hammering, lungs burning in the thin air.

Cold stung her nostrils. The only sounds were their breathing and the brittle crunch of stone. Wind cut across exposed skin, sharp enough to make her ache for fire.

She rounded the far side of the boulder—

—and stopped.

A man sat there.

His chest rose and fell in harsh pulls. Sweat slicked his face despite the cold, and his armor bore the marks of too many fights survived too narrowly.

His sword was half-raised.

His hands shook.

Blue eyes snapped wide as they locked on Niama.

Niama's hand went instinctively to her bow.

Wind tore through the pass, flinging dust and grit between them.

'Stay back,' the soldier barked, voice cracking as it echoed off the stone. 'Who are you?'

Kesaahn and Rohan stepped into view, hands raised.

Rohan moved first, slow and deliberate. 'Easy,' he said. 'We mean no harm. I'm Rohan. These are Niama and Kesaahn.'

The soldier did not lower his blade.

Niama stepped forward instead, just a pace, careful not to crowd him. 'We're travelers,' she said gently. 'Like you.'

His eyes flicked past her shoulder, then back again. His breath hitched. 'They didn't follow you,' he said. It wasn't a question. 'Did they?'

Rohan's gaze sharpened as he scanned the road behind them. 'Who?'

The soldier swallowed hard.

'The things from the north,' he whispered.

'The creatures,' the soldier said. His voice trembled, thin as wind through leaves.

Rohan did not raise his voice. He did not rush him. 'You're safe here,' he said. 'We were careful.'

The soldier stared at him harder, breath hitching. 'Wait... I know you.' His eyes widened. 'You're the— you're Prince Rohan.'

Rohan inclined his head, calm and measured. 'Yes. Sheathe your blade. You stand among allies.'

The sword slipped from the soldier's fingers and struck stone with a hollow clang. His knees buckled as if the sound had cut whatever strength remained. 'Forgive me, my prince,' he said, trying to rise and failing.

'Rest,' Rohan said, firm but gentle, motioning him down.

The soldier sagged against the rock, staring past them toward the valley. 'I heard something behind me. Thought you might be...' He swallowed. 'Thought you might be what burned Steepmoor.'

'The Legion took it after we passed through,' Rohan said. His gaze dropped to the man's armor, to the battered crest. 'You're King's Guard.'

The soldier nodded. 'Silverfall. Captain Bluyr's command. We were first to reach Oxemount.'

Rohan's expression shifted, recognition cutting through the fatigue. 'I know Bluyr. We crossed paths north of Glimmerfell.' A pause. 'What happened to you?'

Behind the boulder, Niama and Kesaahn unrolled their bedrolls, keeping close enough to hear. Niama watched the soldier's hands as he spoke. They never stopped shaking.

His voice broke as he answered.

'We marched out certain of victory.' A bitter laugh escaped him. 'Twenty thousand strong. We joked. We wagered. Seven days north, banners high, songs in the ranks. We thought the Dark would flee at the sight of us.'

'When we first saw Oxemount, we felt untouchable.'

He faltered. 'Do you have water?'

Rohan handed him a skin. The soldier drank too fast, throat working audibly.

'Slowly,' Rohan said.

The man obeyed, wiping his mouth with his sleeve as he handed it back. 'Thank you, my liege.'

Rohan secured the skin. 'What followed?'

The soldier hesitated, breath shallow. 'The castle stood intact. But rumors spread fast. Guards spoke of things seen north of the wall. Shapes. Movements that weren't... right.'

'What things?' Rohan asked.

The soldier's eyes darted. 'I don't know. Whatever they were, men ran from them. Some deserted outright.'

Niama felt her chest tighten. She caught Kesaahn's eye. Neither spoke.

'That first night,' the soldier continued, voice fraying, 'I was posted to the wall. The Withered Peaks lay clear against the dusk. Then the light failed.'

'Shadows gathered where nothing should have been. They moved without sound. Took form where there should've been none.' His hands clenched in his lap. 'They watched us.'

He looked up then, eyes glassy with fear that had not dulled.

'And then... the wall screamed.'

He broke off, breath ragged, staring into the dark as if the mountains might answer him back.

He drew a shaky breath before continuing.

'It ran on all fours... then rose like a man.' His voice thinned. 'Its eyes—gods, its eyes—locked onto me. And even in the dark, I saw its face. A lizard's.'

Niama went still.

Kesaahn froze with a nut halfway to her mouth, fingers locked in place. Their eyes met for a heartbeat. Gauntillia.

'But it didn't attack,' the soldier said quickly, as if afraid of what their silence meant. 'It ran. Stopped. Ran again. Like it was measuring us.' His jaw tightened. 'I reported it. The sergeant told me to hold my post.'

His gaze dropped. 'Others began reporting the same thing. All along the wall.'

He rubbed his hands together, as though trying to warm them. 'After that, I only saw movement. Shadows. My relief came before dawn. I went back to camp.'

Rohan's eyes flicked to Niama, then Kesaahn. The resolve between them was wordless and hard.

'The horns woke us.' The soldier's voice grew distant. 'Orders came fast. We formed by the wall. The gates were far to our left. Torches burned, but the dark swallowed the light.'

'Then the ground began to shake.'

Silence stretched, brittle.

'Something struck the gates.' His breath hitched. 'Once. Twice. The wall trembled. Archers loosed fire into the dark. We waited.'

His hands clenched. 'Then the gates broke.'

He stopped, chest rising and falling as he forced himself on.

'For a moment... nothing.' His voice dropped. 'Then we heard it. Footsteps. Thousands.'

He shut his eyes.

'Men screamed. Officers shouted to hold the line. No one listened. No one could.'

Niama didn't move. Neither did Kesaahn.

'They came through the breach,' the soldier whispered. 'Creatures. Not men. Not beasts.' His face twisted. 'Nightmares.'

Niama's throat tightened. She forced the words out. 'What did you see?'

He looked at her, eyes glassy. 'Actari. Gauntillia. Hordes of them.' His voice shook. 'They moved faster than thought. Talons tore armor like cloth.'

His breath stuttered. 'They fed while fighting.'

The mountain wind sighed around them.

'I was ordered forward.' He laughed once, sharp and hollow. 'I charged. One hit me. Threw me down. I lost my sword.'

His hands trembled openly now.

'Others drew it off. I grabbed my blade. Stabbed it from behind when it turned.' His jaw clenched. 'It screamed. Fell. Dead.'

He stared at his hands as if seeing blood still there.

'I thought I would die.' His voice broke. 'Everyone did. And still they kept coming. It didn't end.'

Niama reached out before she thought better of it. Her hand closed around his wrist.

'You're alive,' she said quietly. 'That matters.'

The soldier nodded, though the terror in his eyes did not fade.

Above them, the wind slid along the mountain face, carrying the smell of smoke from the valley below.

And none of them doubted that what had broken Oxemount was still moving.

Niama passed the soldier a small portion of her remaining food. He took it with shaking hands and ate quickly, as if afraid it might vanish. The others drew closer, cloaks pulled tight against the knife-edged cold that slid down the pass.

Niama leaned in. 'What happened after?'

The soldier closed his eyes. When he spoke again, his voice was thinner. 'The fighting blurred together. I couldn't tell minutes from hours. Blood. Sweat. Rot. The screaming never stopped.'

He swallowed. 'Then the snow beasts came.'

Rohan stiffened.

'Huge,' the soldier said. 'White-furred. Horned. They carried clubs thicker than a man's body. They smashed through our lines. Men flew like dolls. One of them struck someone beside me. The body hit me full force.'

He touched his temple. 'I don't remember falling.'

Wind slid through the pass, carrying the smell of smoke from far below.

'When I woke, I was buried under the dead.' His breath hitched once. 'Blood everywhere. Animals were already feeding.' He shook his head, eyes glassy. 'I don't know how, but I crawled free. Took my sword. Ran. I didn't stop until the forest swallowed me.'

Rohan bowed his head, hands clenched together. 'So many,' he murmured.

Kesaahn broke the silence. 'What will you do now?'

The soldier straightened despite the tremor still in him. 'I'll return south. The King is gathering forces. I won't abandon the fight.'

The wind rose, sliding between stone and steel.

Rohan spoke without lifting his head. 'My father was killed in Dawnbury.' A pause. 'A few days ago.'

The soldier went still. The wind moved between them.

Rohan drew a slow breath, steadying himself. 'Silverfall will stand. My father would have seen to that. But we cannot return. Not now.'

The soldier's voice broke. 'My family is in Woodly. I have to go to them. I can't—' He stopped, shame flickering across his face. 'I can't leave them.'

Rohan looked up then. His gaze softened. 'You shouldn't.' He set a hand on the soldier's shoulder. 'Go to them. Keep off the roads. Take them south. Hazlehurst, if you can. From there, sail east.'

The soldier bowed his head deeply. 'Thank you, my liege.'

'Rest here tonight,' Rohan added. 'Take what we can spare.'

The soldier struck his arm across his chest in salute. 'I will not forget this.'

Later, Niama lay back on her bedroll, stone pressing through the thin fabric. Above her, the sky spread wide and cold, stars sharp and distant. They felt impossibly small against what lay ahead.

She watched them until her eyes ached, thinking of all that would be lost before this was done.

Far off, the wind wailed through the pass, a low, wandering sound that felt almost like mourning. For the moment, though, the night held. The stars burned clear and cold overhead.

Niama drew a slow breath, letting the thin air steady her.

The soldier shifted, armor whispering softly. 'Prince Rohan,' he said at last. 'May I ask you something?'

Rohan turned toward him, fatigue etched deep but his posture still firm. 'You may.'

The soldier hesitated. 'How did you come to be here? On this road, at a time like this?'

Niama watched Rohan carefully. His expression darkened, only briefly.

'We're seeking a way to stop what's coming,' Rohan said. 'There are forces moving in Atheron that cannot be met with steel alone.' A pause. 'That is all I can say.'

The soldier inclined his head at once. 'Forgive me, my prince. I meant no offense.'

'None taken,' Rohan replied. 'Questions are not a crime in days like these.'

The soldier relaxed, some of the tension easing from his shoulders. 'Then I wish you fortune,' he said quietly. 'We will need every scrap of it before this ends.'

They settled back into uneasy stillness. Cloaks were drawn tighter. Bedrolls shifted on unforgiving stone. The wind prowled the heights, carrying grit and cold with it.

Niama shivered despite the wool at her shoulders. The scent of earth lingered, mixed with the distant trace of smoke drifting up from Steepmoor. She tasted old water at the back of her throat, flat and bitter.

Eventually, exhaustion pressed harder than fear.

Her thoughts slowed. The stars blurred.

Sleep took her at last, thin and fragile, as the mountain kept its watch.

Morning spilled gold across the plateau, and Niama woke stiff and sore, the ground's cruelty pressed into her bones. She stretched slowly, easing the ache from her back. Nearby, Rohan was already on his feet, movements brisk, practiced, rolling his bedroll tight.

Storm clouds gathered along the horizon, dark and swollen, pushing inland with quiet intent.

Niama's gaze swept the camp. One shape was missing.

'I hope he reaches his family,' she said at last.

Rohan did not look up. 'So do I.' A pause. 'But hope is not always enough.'

She studied him. 'Why didn't you tell him what we're doing? About the prophecy?'

Rohan cinched a strap and exhaled. 'It wasn't mistrust.' His brow tightened. 'If he were captured, even by chance, we can't risk what he might give away. Not now.'

Niama nodded.

She packed in silence, the thought of the soldier lingering like an unresolved chord. The air smelled of damp stone and distant rain. Thunder muttered somewhere beyond the horizon.

A gust lifted her hair, cutting through the sun's warmth. She pulled her cloak tighter, fingers brushing worn fabric, grounding herself. For a moment, she imagined the soldier already far from here, moving fast, choosing roads no one watched.

Or lost.

The wind moved across the plateau, carrying grit and whispers. Niama tasted dust on her tongue and swallowed.

They shouldered their packs and turned back to the path.

Behind them, the plateau kept its secrets. Ahead, the mountains waited.

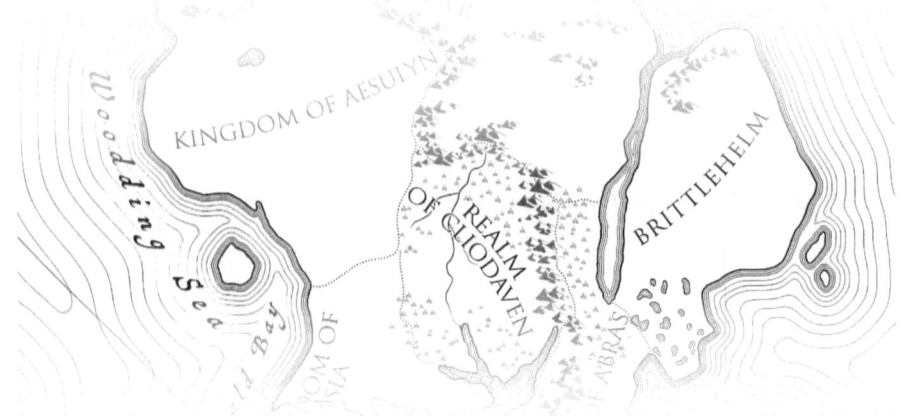

CHAPTER THIRTY-FOUR

The Cart

The group climbed the mountain's spine, bodies locked in stubborn rhythm with stone and slope. The terrain offered no mercy, each step demanding more than the last. Still, they pressed on. When at last they reached the crest, the world opened before them.

Green hills rolled outward, cut through by winding rivers that caught the light. Insects hummed. Birds called across open air. The sound alone marked how far they had come from the dead lands behind them.

Niama stopped, breath held. For a moment, weariness loosened its grip.

She drew in the scent of wildflowers and damp earth, clean and alive. The air tasted sharp and new. A smile touched her lips before she could stop it. This, she thought, was what the climb had bought them.

Below, Avonwich Lake flashed with sunlight, its surface broken by the slow movement of vessels. Barges and ferries traced familiar routes between the Wooding Sea and the Maidvern River, feeding trade into the heart of the land. Along the shore, Shaderock in Cliodaven and Riverhurst in Abras clustered like anchors, busy even from this height.

Beyond the lake spread the Dewforest, dense and sprawling. Rivers threaded through towering trees, the canopy breathing with quiet power. Even from afar, the place felt awake.

Northward, the Withered Peaks rose hard and pale, their snowbound ridges sharp against the sky. For centuries they had held the dark at bay. Now, as the legions moved, even stone felt uncertain. Niama's gaze lingered there longer than she meant it to.

Rohan wiped his mouth with the back of his hand. 'If the road holds, we'll reach Wyntown by evening. Athris willing.'

Niama nodded absently. Traveling with humans had taught her much. Some carried honor as naturally as breath. Others wore ambition like a second skin. Rohan belonged firmly to the first. His values sat close to those of the forest clans. Cooperation. Restraint. Defense only when forced.

Kesaahn shaded her eyes, looking west. Her hair caught the light, pale against the wind. 'It's been some time since I've walked Cliodaven,' she said, a note of memory softening her voice.

Niama turned to her. 'You know these lands?'

'Well enough.' Kesaahn nodded. 'The guild sent me there as an apprentice. The masters who dwell near the Dewforest taught me much.' Her expression sobered. 'Power gathers there easily. Too easily. Magic answers, but it always asks for something in return.'

She met Niama's gaze. 'The Fae guard their borders fiercely. We will need to tread with care.'

They began the descent toward the mountain's base, the road narrowing as it twisted downward. Gravel snapped beneath their boots. Wind slid cold through cloaks and seams.

Niama pulled her mantle tighter, teeth catching briefly on her lip. Beneath it, something stirred that had nothing to do with cold.

Anticipation.

Kesaahn walked beside her, expression closed and unreadable. Whatever stirred beneath her calm did not reach her face. Niama studied her quietly, sensing something steeled beneath the stillness. Not fear. Resolve. It steadied her. With Kesaahn and Rohan close, the road ahead felt survivable.

They followed the winding descent in measured silence until movement ahead caught Niama's eye.

A cart climbed toward them from below.

Rohan's hand drifted to his sword at once. Niama felt it too, the tightening in the air, and met Kesaahn's glance. The cart drew closer, revealing two men. One walked beside the horse, reins in hand. The other sat atop the cart, younger, watching them with open curiosity.

Rohan lifted a hand.

The cart halted. The horse stamped and snorted, leather creaking softly. The older man studied them with guarded eyes while the younger leaned forward to see more clearly.

Niama's pulse quickened.

The driver broke the silence with a broad smile. 'Good morrow. Not often we meet folk on this road.'

Rohan returned the gesture, polite but restrained, his grip still firm on the hilt. 'Good day. May I ask what brings you this way?'

The man's smile thinned. 'You may,' he said slowly, 'though I'm not sure why it concerns you.'

Rohan eased his stance, fingers loosening. 'No offense meant. We're travelers from the west. Bound for Cliodaven.'

The man studied them another moment, then nodded. 'Well then. Granth.' He jerked his chin toward the cart. 'And that's my boy, Frederick. We trade out of Wyntown. Heading for Steepmoor.'

He gestured to the bundled supplies lashed to the cart. The man was broad and weathered, his grey beard tangled by wind and road. Frederick sat bundled in layers, barely more than a boy, dark hair patchy on his chin in a valiant but failing attempt at a beard.

The horse shifted again, the scent of hay and leather hanging faintly in the air.

Niama watched them closely. Their hands were rough. Their eyes wary but not cruel.

Rohan's expression darkened. 'I'm afraid Steepmoor is gone.'

Granth stiffened.

'Swinish forces overran it yesterday,' Rohan continued, voice low. 'Fire took most of the town. Little remains.'

For a moment, Granth only stared. 'Gone?' he said quietly. 'There've been rumors. Strange things east of the mountains.' His eyes flicked to Frederick, then back. 'What of the people? We've friends there.'

Rohan's jaw tightened. 'We don't know their fate. Some fled south before the attack.' A pause. 'I wish I had better news.'

Granth exhaled slowly, grief and worry etched deep into his face. He ran a hand through his beard and glanced down the road they had come from.

Then, after a beat, he nodded once. 'Thank you for telling us.' His voice was heavy now. 'Better truth than hope built on lies.'

Frederick shifted in the cart, suddenly subdued.

Granth's expression softened, some of the tension easing from his shoulders. He looked between Rohan and his companions. 'Then perhaps I should know who I'm speaking with.'

Rohan offered a brief smile and introduced himself, Niama, and Kesaahn.

Granth studied them anew, his manner turning more measured. 'Two humans and an elf on this road is uncommon.' His gaze lingered on Rohan. 'What business brings you so far from safer paths?'

'We travel to Cliodaven by way of Wyntown,' Rohan replied. 'Kesaahn is a Magika seeking counsel from a Master within the forest.'

Granth's eyes flicked to Kesaahn's staff. He nodded slowly. 'I see.' He turned away with a weary sigh. 'No sense pressing on, then. Best we turn back ourselves.'

Rohan hesitated, then spoke. 'Might we impose upon you for part of the journey?' His tone was respectful. 'We've covered many hard miles. A cart, even briefly, would be a kindness.'

Granth turned back, a crease forming at the corner of his eyes as he smiled. 'I won't turn folk away without cause. You seem decent enough.' He gestured to the cart. 'Make yourselves comfortable. You'll have to shift a crate or two.'

The sun beat down despite the cold bite in the air. Rohan introduced Niama and Kesaahn more fully to Granth and Frederick as he rearranged supplies to clear space. Both men welcomed them readily.

'I'll ride up front,' Niama said, nodding toward the bench. 'I like to see the road ahead.'

Rohan and Kesaahn settled in the rear.

Niama climbed onto the worn seat, the cart groaning under the added weight. Granth glanced back with an approving grin. Frederick stared openly, wide-eyed.

She caught him watching. 'Is there something amiss?'

'N-no,' Frederick said quickly, looking away. His ears flushed as he fumbled with the straps at his side.

Granth clicked his tongue softly and urged the horse forward. Its dark coat gleamed as it moved, and the cart rolled on, wheels crunching against gravel in a steady rhythm.

Niama watched the road, letting the cadence quiet her thoughts.

After a time, she felt eyes on her again. She tilted her head slightly. 'You know it's impolite to stare.'

Frederick startled, gaze snapping away. 'I'm sorry. I didn't mean—'

Niama smiled and tapped his arm lightly. 'No harm done.' She offered her hand. 'I'm Niama.'

His face brightened. 'Frederick. But everyone calls me Fred.' He grinned. 'My father insists on the full name. Says it sounds refined.' He shrugged. 'I don't see it.'

Niama laughed. 'A pleasure, Fred.'

He shook her hand eagerly. 'Where are you from?'

'Mistwood,' she said, the name carrying warmth. 'A village tucked deep within Erbour Forest.'

Fred's smile dimmed. 'I've never heard of it. We've traded as far as Riverhurst and Glimmerfell, but never there.' His eyes lit faintly. 'I'd like to see it.'

'You should,' Niama said softly. 'We build among the trees. Wake to birdsong. Dine beneath the stars.' Her gaze drifted ahead. 'I miss it.'

The cart rolled on, the road stretching before them, and for a while, the world felt almost gentle again.

As Niama spoke of Mistwood, a familiar ache rose in her chest. Home-sickness pressed close, sharp and unyielding.

Fred listened intently, eyes distant.

'It sounds like a dream,' he said.

He was quiet a moment, watching the road ahead. When he spoke again, his voice had changed.

'My mother died of illness.'

He stared at his hands. 'Now it's just Father and me in Wyntown.'

A tear slipped free and tracked down his cheek.

Niama rested a hand on his shoulder. 'I'm sorry,' she said softly.

Fred nudged a loose pebble from the cart floor, watching it tumble down the mountainside. 'Father tried everything. Even went into the Dewforest.' His voice thinned. 'They said she couldn't be saved. Now I travel with him.' A small shrug. 'It's... something, at least.'

Their words faded. The cart rattled on, wheels grinding over stone and dust, the only sound daring to break the quiet.

Fred frowned. 'Can I ask you something?'

'Of course.'

'I heard someone talking about the Swinish.' His eyes lifted, uncertain. 'What are they?'

Niama drew a slow breath. 'Mercenaries. Leftovers from the Dark Magi-ka wars. Now they fight for darker powers.'

His face drained of color. 'Will they come to Wyntown?'

'I don't know,' Niama said honestly. 'But we'll be ready if they do.'

Granth spoke without turning. 'Enough of that, lad. Wyntown will stand.'

Relief flickered across Fred's face. 'Good.' He swallowed. 'I don't want our home to burn.'

After a time, Granth turned to face Frederick with a grunt. 'My turn's done.' He gestured Fred forward. 'These old legs have had enough.'

The cart rocked as positions changed. Niama smiled faintly, then stilled.

The motion.

The seat.

An old man beside her, long ago.

Cold crawled up her spine. She forced the memory away.

'You all right, lass?' Granth asked. 'Cold?'

'A little.'

He reached behind him and produced a thick wool blanket. 'Here. This'll help.'

Niama wrapped herself in it, the weight comforting. The scent of wool, hay, and horse sweat settled around her, familiar as a half-forgotten road. It reminded her of long journeys between forest villages, of nights spent listening to wheels creak under starlight.

'Thank you.'

Granth leaned closer, voice low. 'Since his mother died, I've kept him close. Too close, maybe.' He sighed. 'This land's changing. Darkness has a way of finding folk eventually.' His eyes stayed on the road. 'When it does, we'll head south. I've kin in Farmond. Might buy us time.'

Niama's fingers tightened in the blanket.

'We pushed it back once,' Granth went on. 'But I don't know if it'll bend so easy again.'

She met his gaze, seeing the fear he didn't bother to hide. Kindness was there too. And worry. Real worry.

Niama drew a steadying breath and nodded once, holding herself still as the cart carried them onward, down toward whatever waited next.

She wanted to tell Granth and his son that all would be well. That the prophecy would see them through.

She did not.

Doubt gnawed quietly. The darkness felt closer with every mile.

They rode on in silence, the steady clip of hooves and the creak of the wagon filling the space between them.

As the path descended, the air warmed. The bite of the heights faded, replaced by softer breath and leaf-scented wind. Niama slipped the blanket from her shoulders, grateful for the change. Wildflowers drifted on the breeze, their sweetness a clean counterpoint to stone and dust.

To the north, forest rose thick and shadowed, its canopy swallowing light. Rabbits flashed through the undergrowth, white tails vanishing as quickly as they appeared.

To the south, the land opened wide into gold fields and distant farms, cattle grazing beneath the sun.

Wyntown announced itself before it came into view.

The market's noise rose first. Voices calling. Metal clanging. Meat sizzling over open flame. Bread, warm and yeasted, cut through the air. Trade and life braided together in sound and smell.

Fred drew the cart to the market's edge, giving them space to dismount. They dismounted and bid Granth and his son farewell. The crowd surged and folded around them, color and movement pressing in from all sides. Niama took it in at once. Cookware ringing. Coins passing hands. Smoke and spice. Fabric dyed bright as fruit.

'Careful,' Rohan murmured.

Niama followed his gaze and felt her breath hitch. Two cloaked figures threaded through the crowd, their movement purposeful, faces hidden.

She caught Rohan's arm, urging him forward.

Kesaahn saw them too. Her jaw tightened. 'The Order is here.'

Niama's stomach dropped. If they were in Wyntown, the Order was tracking something. Possibly them.

They did not linger.

The inn rose ahead, its timbered frame worn smooth by years of use. Laughter and tankards spilled from the ground floor, blending with the street's din. Inside, they climbed to a cramped room on the second level. One window looked down onto the square.

Rohan dragged a chair beneath the door handle and wedged it tight. Wood groaned as it settled.

Niama went to the window.

The market churned below. Smoke curled upward. Meat crackled. Bread steamed. Her stomach stirred, but her mouth stayed dry. She gripped the sill, knuckles whitening as sound and color pressed in.

Rohan lit the hearth. Flame bloomed and steadied, warmth pushing back the dark. Light played across their faces, softening edges without banishing the tension.

Kesaahn sat on the bed and opened her satchel. One by one, she laid out dried leaves and bundled stems, precise and methodical, inventorying without a word.

They set watches and let the hours pass.

Outside, the market quieted. Voices thinned. Footsteps faded.

At last, exhaustion outweighed vigilance. One by one, they slept.

CHAPTER THIRTY-FIVE

Silenthollow

Night closed tight around the chamber, the last light fading into shadow. Niama sat on the edge of the creaking bed, eyes fixed on the narrow window overlooking the alley. A shape lingered there, its silhouette fused with shadow. At first she took it for torn cloth caught on the veranda rail. Then the figure shifted, a hooded stranger, face briefly lit by the ember of a pipe. The glow vanished. The figure did not move.

'There's someone watching,' Niama whispered. Her breath quickened, fingers curling tight. Had the Order found them already? No matter how carefully they hid, these people always seemed to close the distance.

'They've tracked us,' Rohan said, already packing. His voice was taut. 'Likely waited for us to cross the Orboros. We can't stay. We move now, before others arrive.'

Niama looked between him and Kesaahn, dread tightening her throat. 'Where do we go?'

Kesaahn rose. 'Granth,' she said. 'He may help us cross the river quietly. But we'll need to move unseen.'

The figure outside slipped back into darkness. Niama leaned her forehead against the cold glass, the chill grounding her as unease surged. With the watcher gone, the room felt no safer. If anything, more exposed.

'We don't have long,' Rohan said. 'Gather what you can.'

He eased the chair from beneath the door and turned the handle, wincing as the hinge complained. The hallway breathed rot and damp wood. He listened. Nothing. 'Clear,' he murmured.

Kesaahn lifted a hand. 'Wait. I'll pass more easily than you.' She adjusted her cloak. 'Magikas come and go here. I'll check the common room.' Her eyes met Rohan's. Understanding passed between them. 'I won't be long.'

'Be careful,' Rohan said quietly.

He shut the door behind her and leaned into it.

Wind rattled the window. Niama hugged herself as the weight of the mission pressed down. Her chest tightened. Breath came shallow, unsteady.

Her thoughts spiraled. Was Kesaahn walking into a trap? Had they already waited too long?

Rohan stood by the door, grip firm, knuckles pale. Niama watched the alley again, eyes tracking every shift of shadow. Outside, the wind rose, flinging grit and scraps through the darkness.

A soft knock struck the door.

Niama snapped toward the sound, muscles tightening. Rohan was already moving when a whisper followed.

'It's me.'

Kesaahn slipped inside, face pale, breath shallow. Rohan shut the door at once. They closed around her without speaking, waiting.

Niama loosened her grip on the dagger. Not fully. But enough.

'I spoke to the tavernkeeper's wife,' Kesaahn said. 'I pretended to admire a fabric I saw on Granth's cart.' Her hands shook as she spoke. 'She said only two people in town have it. A seamstress nearby. And an old man who lives with his son by the river.'

'Then we move,' Rohan said. He was already at the door. 'Now.'

They slipped through the empty tavern and out into the night. Wind cut hard as they ran, boots striking stone. They turned north, toward the river. The air carried salt and damp rot.

Mist thickened as they neared the house. Cold seeped into Niama's bones. Frogs splashed in the dark, the sound uneven and close. The building loomed ahead, roof sagging, chimney crooked against the sky. The door stood ajar. Smoke drifted weakly from within.

Wrong.

Niama's stomach tightened. She scanned the street, pulse loud in her ears.

Rohan slowed. 'We're being followed,' he murmured. He tipped his head toward a darkened stable. 'Hide there. I'll draw them out.'

They slipped around the rear of the structure. Darkness swallowed them whole, broken only by a flicker of torchlight. The stink of manure burned Niama's nose. She and Kesaahn crouched inside, weapons ready.

Rohan waited at the corner, pressed flat to stone. His knife caught the light once, then vanished.

Footsteps hurried closer.

Niama's mouth went dry.

The figure rounded the corner.

Rohan struck.

He surged forward, seized the pursuer, and slammed them into the dirt. His knee pinned their back. The knife hovered at the throat.

The stranger choked, coughing grit.

'Who are you?' Rohan said.

The body trembled beneath him.

'I mean no harm,' a voice gasped. 'Please. I'm a friend.'

A woman's voice.

Slowly, the hood fell back.

A girl lay in the dirt, wide-eyed and shaking.

Rohan eased back, blade still raised. Niama stepped closer, every sense sharp. Somewhere down the road, a dog barked once, then fell silent.

As the girl shifted, Rohan's sword lifted a fraction.

'Stay down,' he warned, the tip steady.

A horse snorted nearby. Leather creaked. The night seemed to lean in.

Niama clasped her hands together to still their tremor, eyes never leaving the stranger. Kesaahn moved in beside her, silent and watchful. Together, they hemmed the girl in.

'She sent me,' the stranger said quickly. 'To bring you to her.'

Niama's grip tightened on her dagger. 'Bring us where? And why?'

Kesaahn laid a calming hand on Niama's shoulder and stepped forward. 'Not where,' she said evenly. 'Who.'

The girl nodded once. 'Lady Armina. She requests your presence. In Silenthollow.'

Niama felt the name settle uneasily in her chest.

Kesaahn's posture eased a fraction, though her gaze stayed sharp. 'I know of her.' A pause. 'Why us?'

The girl's eyes flicked to Niama. 'Not you. Her.' She swallowed. 'She wants the elf.'

Niama stiffened. 'Me? Why?'

'She said you'd ask.' The girl's attention darted to the alley mouth. 'She also said time matters. You're being searched for. By more than one group.'

Niama's breath hitched. 'The figure at the window.'

The girl shook her head. 'Not me. I saw them too. They met others nearby.' Her voice dropped. 'We shouldn't linger.'

She looked up at Rohan. 'May I stand?'

The horses stamped again, breath fogging the air.

Rohan hesitated, then nodded. 'Slowly.'

The girl rose—and Rohan moved with her.

He slammed her gently but firmly into the wall, one forearm pinning her as his other hand searched for weapons. Steel chimed softly as he stripped several small knives from her belt and sleeves.

Nothing more.

He stepped back, sword still raised.

The girl rolled her shoulders, unfazed. 'You can keep searching me,' she said coolly, 'or we can cross the river before your shadows catch up.'

Niama blinked. A reluctant smile tugged at her mouth before she smothered it. Bold. Reckless. Or simply brave.

Rohan studied her, jaw tight. 'Don't mistake caution for insult. Lately, strangers come with blades.'

'Fair,' the girl said.

She reached into her pocket and drew out a ring. Gold. Heavy. Set with a dark red stone. A raven etched into its surface.

'This should help,' she said.

Kesaahn leaned in, breath catching. 'The raven seal,' she murmured. 'Skin changers.'

The girl inclined her head. 'Ammadella.'

The name settled between them, sharp and significant.

'If Lady Armina sent you,' Kesaahn said quietly, 'then we'll listen.'

Ammadella glanced toward the river, urgency tightening her expression. 'Then we should move. Now.'

Somewhere beyond the stables, footsteps shifted.

Niama stared at her. 'You're a skin changer?'

She had heard the stories. The magic folk of the Dewforest. Hunted nearly to extinction by poachers who feared what they could not control.

Ammadella's nod was small, weighted.

Niama exchanged a look with Rohan, then Kesaahn. 'How could you know we would come?' she asked. The question carried more unease than curiosity.

Ammadella's mouth curved faintly. 'The Lady sees far.' She met Niama's gaze. 'You will understand when you meet her. For now, we must move.'

Rohan slid his sword back into its sheath. 'Forgive the welcome. Caution has kept us alive.'

'I would distrust you if you were careless,' Ammadella replied. 'And yes, Prince Rohan. I know who you are.' She turned without ceremony. 'Follow me. I've secured a boat.'

They moved quickly, slipping through alleys and stands of scrub, taking paths that avoided lamplight. At the river's edge, Ammadella pushed aside branches to reveal a small skiff drawn up beneath reeds and shadow.

Together, they cleared it and eased it into the water. The hull scraped softly before floating free.

Rohan and Ammadella took the oars. Niama and Kesaahn crouched at the bow as the river swallowed the sound of the shore.

Moonlight fractured across the water. The far bank was invisible.

'Stay alert,' Ammadella murmured. Her gaze never left the dark ahead.

Mist drifted low, damp and cold. Niama pulled her cloak tighter, breath clouding the air. The steady dip of the oars became the only sound that mattered.

Wyntown fell away behind them, lights thinning until only the suggestion of a town remained. Far off, the bridge loomed, a darker shape against darker sky.

Rohan broke the silence. 'How much do you know of what we carry?'

Ammadella's expression did not change. 'Enough.' The oar dipped cleanly. 'The prophecy. The gods' light. The part you must play. And the cost.' Something old and tired touched her voice. 'We have seen this road approaching for many years.'

'Then why warn no one? People could have prepared,' Niama said.

Ammadella exhaled slowly. 'We tried.' Her voice dropped. 'Again and again. But Arghost listens to crowns and pulpits, not to those it once hunted.'

Rohan nodded faintly. 'Fear wears many disguises.'

'The past cannot be undone,' Kesaahn said. 'Only the path ahead shaped.'

The boat slid on, silent as a thought.

Niama glanced back. Nothing but mist and water.

'You should have forced them to listen,' she said, anger sharpening her words.

Ammadella did not look at her. 'They would not hear.' The oars whispered. 'We withdrew to survive. They named us monsters. Their priests taught it. Their hunters proved it.'

She paused, then added quietly, 'We give nothing now without reason.'

Her gaze shifted at last to Niama. 'But the Lady sees something in you. In all of you.' A beat. 'Truths you are not ready for yet.'

The boat cut onward through mist and moonlight, carrying them toward answers that promised no comfort.

Niama frowned. 'Truths?' She shifted to face Ammadella as the boat rocked gently beneath them. Water and pine scented the air, cool and clean. 'What truths?'

Ammadella did not look at her. 'Not mine to give.' Her tone was calm, immovable. 'When we reach the far bank, we rest briefly. Horses are waiting. Cliodaven will shelter us. Its wards still hold.' A pause. 'From there, Silenthollow lies only hours away.'

The boat slid onward, oars creaking softly. Ammadella leaned back and stared at the stars, their reflections trembling across the dark water.

'Do not mistake distance for safety,' she said. 'There are those who hunt what they do not understand. They will not hesitate.'

Time stretched. Arms were traded. Niama and Kesaahn took the oars while Ammadella and Rohan rested, the rhythm steady and unbroken.

Trees emerged ahead, first as shadow, then shape. Leaves whispered. Crickets sang. The shore was close enough now to taste.

Hope stirred.

Kesaahn glanced back. 'We're nearly there.'

Rohan shifted awake. Ammadella stirred sharply, breath catching as she sat upright.

'Keep rowing,' she said, already rising. 'I'll scout.'

Before Niama could speak, Ammadella moved.

Feathers burst where flesh had been.

A raven tore itself into the air, wings beating hard, the sound sudden and startling in the quiet night. It vanished into the dark above the trees.

No one spoke.

Niama's grip tightened on the oar. Awe crawled up her spine — and beneath it, something older. Recognition. The elders had spoken of skin changers in hushed tones, as though naming them too loudly might summon them. Now one had just sat beside her on a boat.

Moments later, wings cut the air again. The raven dropped onto the gunwale and, in the space of a breath, became Ammadella once more. She turned away as she dressed quickly, movements practiced, unembarrassed.

'We've drifted south,' she said at once. 'Not far, but enough. Adjust north.'

They did not question her.

The oars shifted. Water slapped harder against the hull as they corrected course, the boat responding at once. The river narrowed. The current tugged, then eased.

The shore drew closer.

The boat scraped against the bank and stopped. They disembarked quickly, hauling it clear of the water. Ammadella moved first, slipping into the trees with quiet certainty. The others followed close, the forest closing around them. Leaves rustled overhead. Crickets filled the dark with steady sound.

They emerged into a small glade.

Four horses stood tethered there, heads low, cropping grass as if nothing in the world were amiss.

Ammadella crouched by the firepit at its center and brushed ash aside. 'It's safe to light a fire here,' she said. 'The forest will not betray us.'

Rohan gathered fallen branches and kindled the flame. It caught quickly, light blooming—but stopping short. The glow held to the clearing's edge, as though an unseen boundary kept it contained. Beyond it, darkness waited. Yet the air felt calm. Guarded.

Niama frowned. 'You said powerful magic protects this place. What do you mean?'

Ammadella rose, her gaze steady. 'This forest is old. Older than most in Arghost.' She gestured to the surrounding trees. 'They are not merely alive. They remember.'

Rohan leaned closer to the fire. 'Remember what?'

'Their spirits are bound to Athris itself,' Ammadella said. 'Rooted in this place. Aware of everything that passes through it.'

Niama felt something stir at the words. Old lessons surfaced—stories whispered by elders beside quiet fires, half-myth, half-warning.

A breeze passed through the glade. Leaves whispered softly, as if in response.

Kesaahn broke the silence. 'Did these trees seed the forests of Arghost?'

Ammadella smiled. 'They did. Farther south, they mingled with other species, shaping the forests your people dwell within.' Her gaze flicked to Niama. 'They know the elves honor them.'

The fire crackled. Crickets sang. Smoke carried the scent of resin and wildflowers, the clearing wrapped in a rare stillness.

'All forests are linked,' Ammadella said quietly. 'Through the Light. They feel one another's loss.' Her voice tightened. 'Langmore suffers. Its pain echoes here.'

No one spoke.

Ammadella looked to Niama. 'That is why the prophecy matters. Whatever the cost.'

They laid out their bedrolls near the fire. Its warmth held steady, shadows gentle rather than threatening. Beyond the clearing, the forest was visible farther than Niama expected. Darkness thinned between trunks.

Soft lights drifted at the edge of sight. Pale shapes flickered, then vanished.

Niama watched them. 'What are they?'

'Wisps,' Ammadella said. 'Forest spirits. Curious. Watching.' A faint smile touched her lips. 'If they trust you, they'll come closer.'

More lights shimmered briefly, keeping their distance.

'We rest now,' Ammadella said. 'At first light, we ride for Silenthollow.'

They settled in.

Leaves whispered overhead. Crickets kept their steady rhythm. Smoke curled upward, carrying warmth and the scent of flowers. Wrapped in the quiet vigilance of the ancient trees, sleep came more easily than it had in days.

CHAPTER THIRTY-SIX

The Ithronel

N iama awoke with a start, something damp and coarse brushing her cheek. She blinked—and found herself nose to snout with a squat, pig-like creature, its snout pressed eagerly against her skin. She recoiled, but its tongue swept once more, leaving a slick trail before it squealed and bolted into the trees.

Chubby legs churned through the undergrowth. Hoofprints dotted the leaf litter. A musky, earthen stink lingered after it, unwelcome and unmistakable.

Still wiping her face, Niama shuddered. 'What manner of creature was that?'

'A grunter,' Ammadella said lightly. Her laughter rippled through the trees. 'Harmless. Merely curious. It seems you caught its interest.'

Niama grimaced, skin crawling as she scrubbed away the last of the slobber. If this forest welcomed her so freely, she wondered what else watched from the shadows.

Ammadella was already packing, efficient and unbothered. Niama watched her, thoughts drifting. Since leaving Mistwood, the world had widened at every step. Wonders. Horrors. Things her forest had quietly kept at bay. The realization settled uneasily. Home had been a shelter, not the whole of the world.

Kesaahn and Rohan stirred at last, drawn up by Ammadella's laughter. They rose stiffly, joints protesting, stretching until muted cracks marked the night's toll.

The forest breathed around them. Birds called from unseen branches. Leaves whispered as the breeze moved through. Damp air clung to skin and cloth, cool and alive. Underfoot, fallen leaves cracked softly, while hidden life skittered and fluttered beyond sight. The place felt aware. Watching. Not hostile—but awake.

They packed and mounted. Hooves struck earth in steady rhythm as they followed Ammadella deeper along the winding path, a narrow ribbon threading the green. Sunlight filtered through the canopy, scattering gold across moss and root. The air cooled their skin, leaving it faintly slick with moisture.

Rohan glanced sideways, eyes bright with mischief. 'I hear you've made a friend.'

Niama snorted. 'Regrettably.' She wiped at her sleeve, nose wrinkling. 'If affection tastes like that, I'd rather go unnoticed.'

Rohan laughed. His horse flicked an ear, as if sharing the joke.

Before long, the trees thinned. The path widened into a bare road. They urged their mounts faster, hooves clattering against packed earth and stone. Dust rose in pale clouds. Carts passed now and then, creaking between Wyntown and Silenthollow, drivers offering only brief glances.

By midday, Silenthollow emerged.

It did not announce itself. It simply appeared.

Dark structures rose from the earth as if grown rather than built, ebony walls crowned with moss and grass. Rooflines sagged and curved, softened by living green. Arched doors and windows opened like hollows in old trees. The roads did not cut the land but followed it, winding gently between trunks and roots.

Silenthollow did not intrude upon the forest.

It belonged to it.

Trees climbed skyward around the homes, their limbs knitting roof to canopy. Moss and vine spilled from every seam, leaves stirring to the wind's slow breath. Wildflowers sweetened the air, braided with birdsong so fluid it felt composed rather than random.

As they dismounted and led their horses along Silenthollow's winding paths, the mood shifted.

The villagers watched.

They were small folk, compact and wiry, hair knotted with twigs and leaf-fragments as though the forest had claimed them by habit. Pale skin and rounded noses gave them a uniformity Niama couldn't place. Their clothing was plain, woven from bark-fiber and undyed cloth. No blades showed. No tools either. Just eyes. Narrowed. Measuring.

Niama felt her unease sharpen.

Children peered from behind a low dwelling, eyes bright and unblinking. When Niama's gaze met theirs, they scattered, feet whispering over root and soil. A woman nearby ushered another group indoors, her movement brisk, protective.

'They won't harm you,' Ammadella said softly. She touched Niama's arm, steady and grounding. 'They're Fae. Wary of outsiders, but not cruel.' She inclined her head toward a knot of villagers murmuring together. 'Apart from the occasional trader, strangers rarely pass through here.'

'Fae,' Niama repeated, testing the word. She studied the village anew. Homes grown, not built. Paths shaped by footfall, not blade. An iridescent butterfly drifted past her face, wings scattering color like broken light. Wonder stirred despite herself. 'What are they, truly?'

Ammadella smiled. 'A forest-bound people. Secretive. Capable of mischief, rarely malice.' Her eyes flicked to Niama. 'Show respect, and they'll leave you be. Linger too long, and they may remind you whose home this is.'

She chuckled faintly. 'The last Fae to wander out did so by accident. Birch Flickerberry. Drank too much summer wine and fell asleep in a merchant's cart. Woke in Steepmoor.' Ammadella shook her head. 'Hasn't spoken of it since.'

They slowed as Ammadella gestured ahead. 'But we've arrived.'

The house at the village's edge stood larger than the rest, though it shared their living curves and moss-softened lines. Three ancient trees enclosed it like sentinels, roots lifting the earth around its foundation. Ammadella dismounted and tied her horse.

'Wait here,' she said, and slipped inside.

The others secured their mounts and remained on the path. Around them, the village resumed its quiet rhythms. No one approached. No one smiled. The sense of being observed did not fade.

Moments later, the door opened.

Ammadella stepped out with a tall woman beside her.

Dark hair spilled loose over the woman's shoulders, catching threads of green light as she moved. Her presence stilled the space around her, not by force, but by certainty. When she smiled, it was warm, practiced, and deliberate.

'Welcome,' she said. 'I am Lady Armina. You are safe in Cliodaven.'

Her voice carried an unfamiliar cadence, soft but assured. She wore a long blue dress trimmed in white, elegant without excess. As she approached, the fabric whispered against the road, the breeze lifting scents of wildflower, bread, and spice in her wake.

Niama felt the forest lean closer.

And for the first time since entering Silenthollow, the watching eyes did not feel hostile.

They felt expectant.

Niama found herself wondering how such an unassuming woman had come to live among the Fae. Lady Armina's presence was quietly disarming, her expression open, her eyes warm.

'Please,' she said, gesturing toward her door. 'Come inside.'

The rough-hewn wood creaked as it opened, releasing a wash of warmth scented with polished timber and fresh flowers. Ammadella followed lightly behind as Armina led them into a spacious sitting room. Plush chairs ringed a low table, shelves crowded with curious relics lining the walls. Firelight softened the room, shadows shifting across carved furniture worn smooth by age and care.

'Dandelion tea?' Armina asked.

They agreed at once. Ammadella poured, steam rising with a faint floral sweetness. Niama sipped, honey and bitterness balanced on her tongue as the fire illuminated the delicate carvings on the shelves. The room felt lived-in, ordered, quietly guarded.

Armina settled opposite them. 'You're likely wondering why I asked you here.' She lifted her cup. 'Arghost stands at a precipice. Your success matters more than you yet understand. You've gathered some of the potion's ingredients, I assume?'

'Yes,' Kesaahn said without hesitation.

Armina exhaled, tension easing from her shoulders. 'Good. Then you are not as far behind as I feared.' Her gaze sharpened. 'You met with the Seekers. Did they tell you why you require the God's light?'

Niama shook her head. 'Only that it will reveal the path to the staff.'

Armina's mouth tightened. She set her cup down. 'As I thought. They've sent you forward half-armed.' She leaned in, blue eyes steady. 'The Seekers hoard truth, even from those who serve them.'

She reached across the table and briefly covered Niama's hand. 'The potion is only the threshold,' she said quietly. 'What comes after will test you far more.'

The fire popped softly.

'You must descend into the mounds of the dead,' Armina continued. 'Deeper than any Dwarf has willingly gone. The air thickens. Light fails. Without the potion, you would be blind.'

Niama barely breathed.

'Athris set trials there,' Armina said. 'Not to bar the worthy, but to break the unfit. A Dark magika reached the staff once.' A pause. 'It could not hold it.'

Silence hung, heavy and deliberate.

'To reach the mounds, you must go west,' Armina went on. 'The main entrance was sealed long ago. But another path exists. Dangerous. Narrow. Easily missed.' She met their eyes in turn. 'In Barnrich Wood lives a Fae named Twig Olivethorn. He does not welcome strangers. But if he believes your cause true, he will guide you.'

No one spoke at once.

The fire burned low as the weight of what lay ahead settled fully between them.

'I fear the road ahead will be harsher still,' Lady Armina said. 'The mounds of the dead are steeped in corruption. Their soil was tainted by the Dark Magika, and what dwells beneath has long since abandoned mercy.'

'The withered men guard the staff. Once leaders. Once warriors. Now bound to decay and hunger, their bodies sustained by darkness alone. They do not sleep. They do not forget.' Her gaze held steady. 'Their purpose is singular. The staff must never return to the light.'

Silence pressed in.

'They are formidable,' Armina continued. 'Unyielding. But should you succeed, Arghost will owe you a debt beyond reckoning.'

Niama nodded once. She felt no comfort in the promise of reverence. Only resolve.

Armina lifted her cup, then set it aside untouched. 'There is one more truth you must hear.' Her eyes fixed on Niama. 'Only a descendant of the first race shaped by Athris may claim the staff. Any other would be consumed by its power.'

Niama's breath caught. 'Then where do we find such a person?'

The fire hissed softly.

Rohan and Kesaahn exchanged a glance.

Armina did not look away. 'You already have.'

The words landed with quiet force.

'Your people,' she said.

Niama looked at her, confused. 'From the village?' she asked.

'No, child,' Armina replied. 'Your real people, the Ithronel. They were born with hair the color of embers, as you were. They crossed the western seas and were among the first to walk Arghost when Athris gave it breath.' Her voice remained calm, deliberate. 'For a time, they lived in balance.'

She paused.

'Then Athris turned his hand to other creations. And the Ithronel felt abandoned.'

Niama did not move.

'Jealousy took root. It curdled into violence.' Armina circled the chair slowly. 'They struck at the newer races. When Athris turned from them entirely, they swore to undo his work.'

Niama's thoughts fractured. She had always known she was not born to Mistwood. But this—this reshaped everything.

Rohan and Kesaahn remained silent, faces drawn.

'It was then that Volthar, the Dark Magika, found them,' Armina said. 'He offered purpose. Power. A bargain.' Her tone hardened. 'Create a terror so absolute that even darkness would recoil. Do this, and be rewarded.'

Niama's fingers dug into the armrests.

'Blinded by envy and hunger, the Ithronel agreed.' Armina stopped behind Niama's chair. 'They forged a thing meant to unmake the world.'

Niama leaned forward, breath shallow, searching herself for some echo. Some recognition. There was nothing. Only dread.

'What did they create?' she asked.

The room seemed to draw inward.

'The Actari,' Armina said.

A chill ran through Niama, sharp and involuntary. The Actari. The memory surged unbidden: the thing on the road, its eyes too knowing, its teeth wrong. Her stomach twisted.

'No,' she said hoarsely. The cup slipped from her hands and shattered on the floor. 'That can't be true.'

'I'm afraid it is,' Lady Armina said. 'After Volthar fell, Arghost turned on the Ithronel. They were hunted without mercy.' Her gaze did not waver. 'Your parents fled east with you, hoping Aberon might shelter you. It did not. Mercenaries found them south of the Erbour Forest.' A pause. 'They killed your parents. You escaped into the woods. The hunt never truly ended.'

Niama lurched to her feet. 'No.' Her voice broke. 'The elders—did they know?'

'They did,' Armina said gently. 'And they chose mercy. They knew a child bears no guilt for ancestral crimes. They raised you to be better than the past.'

Niama stared at her. 'How could you know all this?'

'I am bound to the forest,' Armina replied. 'What the trees witness, they share.'

The words settled like frost.

Niama turned away, bracing a hand against a shelf. Her breath came slow and uneven. 'So much blood,' she whispered. 'What did it earn them? What kind of people become that?'

Rohan lifted his head at last. His face was hard, drawn tight with restraint. 'I don't blame you for what they did,' he said. Then, quieter, 'But my father is dead. And the Seer knew who you were. He gave you this chance to set right what should never have been broken.' His jaw clenched. 'Do not mistake that for forgiveness. If I had met you elsewhere, under different skies, I would have killed you.'

The words struck clean and deep.

Niama could not look at him.

Silence stretched, heavy and unforgiving.

Then Rohan turned and left.

'Rohan—' Kesaahn reached for him, then stopped. She set a hand briefly on Niama's shoulder before following him out.

The door closed.

Niama stood alone, the room suddenly too large, too empty. She felt hollowed out. Forgiveness, she realized, was not owed. It had to be earned. If it could be earned at all.

'You did not choose this,' Armina said. 'It chose you. And Rohan is grieving. Give him time.'

Niama swallowed. 'How do I undo what my people did?'

Armina met her gaze. 'You cannot undo it. You can only answer it.' Her hand settled briefly over Niama's. 'Restore what was broken. Prove that the Ithronel are more than their worst sin. That redemption is possible.'

Niama's hand closed around the medallion at her throat, grip tightening until her knuckles burned.

'Then tell me,' she said, voice steady at last. 'What must I do?'

Dear reader,

Thank you for reaching the end of *The Second Rising*.

Stories only live when they're read. Thank you for giving this one breath.

Finishing a book is a choice, and I don't take that lightly. Whether you raced through the final chapters or arrived here slowly, your time and attention matter. I'm genuinely grateful you chose to spend them in Arghost.

This story is only one thread in a much larger tapestry. There are other paths yet to walk, histories still buried, and consequences that will echo far beyond these pages. Niama's journey is far from over—and neither is this world.

If you'd like to stay connected, I invite you to join my mailing list at **www.derrenparsonsauthor.com**

Subscribers receive early news, behind-the-scenes insights, occasional giveaways, and a free ebook as a thank-you.

And if this story moved you—whether through enjoyment, frustration, or reflection—I'd truly appreciate a review. Reader feedback helps independent authors more than anything else, and every honest review makes a difference.

Thank you again for reading.

I hope our paths cross again soon.

— **Derren Parsons**

Facebook: AuthorDParsons **Instagram**: @derrenparsonsauthor
TikTok: @derrenparsonsauth **GoodReads**: Derren Parsons

With a deep sense of gratitude,
Derren Parsons

APPENDIX A: THE LINE OF THE LION

The Lineage of Kings

After the devastating great war, the once-thriving land of Arghost lay in ruins, its people struggling to pick up the shattered pieces of their lives. The air was heavy with the acrid scent of destruction, the ground stained with the blood of the fallen. Internecine conflicts and power struggles threatened to tear the land apart, and the prospects of lasting peace seemed remote.

But amidst the ruins and chaos, one young prince emerged, his voice a beacon of hope in the darkness. The Lion, they called him, a charismatic and visionary leader whose words stirred the hearts of the people. He promised a brighter future, one where all the tribes of Arghost could live in peace and prosperity. The hope he brought was a soothing balm to the wounded land, the sound of his voice like a refreshing breeze in the scorching desert.

Through sheer force of will and strategic prowess, the Lion succeeded in unifying the warring tribes under his rule, becoming the first King of Arghost. His leadership brought a newfound sense of order and security, a respite from the turmoil that had once reigned. The kingdom prospered, and the memory of the Lion remains strong to this day, an enduring symbol of courage, resilience, and unity.

The legacy of the Lion lives on, honored by the long-standing tradition of naming the first-born son of the reigning King 'The Lion.' The land of Arghost, once ravaged by war, has found new life and hope under his visionary leadership. The memory of the Lion is a testament to the human spirit, a reminder that even in the darkest of times, there is always hope for a brighter tomorrow.

The people of Arghost faced the challenging task of rebuilding their homes and communities, which had suffered extensive damage and destruction during the great war. The conflict had left a profound impact on the land and its people, who were struggling to come to terms with the loss they had endured.

Tensions rose between different tribes and factions as they competed for power and control in the aftermath of the war. Ambition and greed filled the void created by the conflict, and those with the desire to exert influence over the weakened and fragmented communities seized the opportunity.

These power struggles escalated into disputes and conflicts, and soon the different tribes were fighting each other for dominance. The once-united people of Arghost were now divided and torn apart by internal struggles, and the prospects of lasting peace seemed remote.

Rebuilding Arghost was not only a physical task but also a psychological one. The people struggled to come to terms with the trauma of the war and the divisions that had arisen in its aftermath. The journey to recovery was long and uncertain, but the people of Arghost were determined to overcome the challenges and build a better future for themselves and their descendants.

As the internal conflicts continued, the people of Arghost began to lose hope. It seemed their once-great land would never return to its former glory, but they remained determined to rebuild and overcome the challenges they faced.

The aftermath of the great war saw the various races of Arghost respond in unique ways to the widespread destruction and turmoil. Dwarves, renowned for their metalworking expertise and engineering skills, retreated to their mountain strongholds, withdrawing from the world and the ongoing conflict. The Namites, who called the deserts their home, returned to defend their southern borders against the invading humans, fighting fiercely to preserve their land and lifestyle.

Unfortunately, the asakal, a robust people who lived in the icy wastelands of the north, were entirely wiped out, leaving little trace of their once-thriving culture and society. Meanwhile, the humans spread across the plains and into the eastern mountains, setting up towns and outposts, constructing roads and bridges, and expanding their trade networks in a bid to exert their control over the newly conquered lands.

The elves, a secretive and reclusive people who lived amongst the dense forests to the south, sought refuge from the conflict and destruction that had beset the world. They were known for their peaceful and spiritual ways, as well as their connection to the natural world and reverence for the forest spirits. They withdrew even deeper into the forest for protection.

The violence and unrest that followed the great war lasted for centuries, but then a young prince from one tribe rose to prominence. This prince spoke of a brighter future, where all the peoples of Arghost could live in peace and prosperity. He was well known for his charisma and wisdom, and he quickly gained a large following among the disgruntled tribes. However, his vision was met with resistance from some of the other tribe leaders who were not keen on giving up their control. The prince was forced to fight these leaders, determined to bring unity and peace to the land.

Eventually, he succeeded in unifying the tribes under his rule and became the first King of Arghost. Known as the Lion, he was renowned for his wisdom and strategic prowess, and was loved by the people for his fairness and his willingness to listen to their grievances.

Under his visionary leadership, the King established a just and fair system of governance, working tirelessly to rebuild the shattered realm and bring hope to the people. The kingdoms of Arghost prospered during his reign, which lasted for many years, and he passed down the mantle of leadership to his son, who continued his legacy of peace and prosperity.

The memory of the Lion remains strong to this day. As a testament to his legacy, naming the first-born son of the reigning King 'The Lion' has become a long-standing tradition in Arghost. The title 'The Lion' symbolizes bravery, wisdom, and a commitment to peace and prosperity, and those who bear it are held in great respect and reverence by the people of the land.

King Magnus

However, not all rulers lived up to the legacy of the Lion. King Magnus was a cruel and ruthless king who was driven solely by his insatiable thirst for power and wealth. He was known for his cunning tactics and strategic mind, but also for his cold-hearted and merciless approach to ruling. Wars, both foreign and domestic marked his reign, as he sought to expand his kingdom at any cost.

King Magnus' most infamous war was against the neighboring kingdom of Abras. The conflict lasted for ten long and brutal years, causing immense suffering and loss of life on both sides. Despite the mounting casualties and the increasing financial burden on his kingdom, King Magnus refused to seek a peaceful resolution. He was determined to emerge victorious, no matter the cost.

In the end, King Magnus was killed in battle, but the damage he had done to his kingdom was already done. The kingdom of Atheron was left deeply wounded, both physically and economically, and it took many years for it to fully recover.

King Leif

King Leif, inherited a kingdom deeply scarred by a long and bloody war from his father, King Magnus. Determined to bring peace to his people, King Leif negotiated a treaty with the kingdom of Abras, which required him to pay a substantial sum of gold as reparations. This nearly pushed his kingdom into bankruptcy, but he was able to restore its economy, for some time at least, through wise financial decisions and a focus on agriculture and trade. In this way, King Leif continued the legacy of peace and prosperity established by the Lion.

Prince Leif's marriage to Lady Rowena, the second daughter of the King of Abras, was a strategic move that helped solidify peace between the two kingdoms. The alliance formed by their union strengthened the peace established by the treaty and brought prosperity to the region, as the two kingdoms were able to work and trade together. Lady Rowena was known for her intelligence and grace, and she quickly became a beloved member of the royal court. Her presence helped to heal the wounds inflicted by the war and bring a new era of peace and prosperity to the kingdom.

Unfortunately, towards the end of King Leif's reign, he began to exhibit traits similar to his father, King Magnus. In an attempt to rebuild the royal treasury after the financial strain caused by his father's war and the reparations paid to the kingdom of Abras, King Leif levied heavy taxes on his subjects. This caused widespread poverty and resentment among the people, who felt that they were being unfairly burdened by the prince's mismanagement.

Legend has it that King Leif suffered from seizures that sent him into violent fits, causing fear and unrest among his subjects. Towards the end of his life, he descended into madness, often running through the countryside while wearing only a cloak and claiming to be hunting goblins.

King Leif's descent into madness marked a sad end to what had once been a promising reign. Despite his early successes, his ultimate madness cast a shadow over his legacy, and many looked back on his rule with a mix of admiration and disappointment. The story of King Leif serves as a cautionary tale about the dangers of greed and power, and the importance of being mindful of one's actions and their impact on others. While he will always be remembered as a historical figure, the way in which his life ended has left a lasting impression on those who knew of him and his rule.

King Aethelred

King Aethelred was known for his weakness and indecisiveness. He struggled to make crucial decisions, constantly swayed by the opinions of his advisors, many of whom were corrupt and only sought to serve their own interests. As a result, his reign was characterized by mismanagement and economic decline, causing his kingdom to suffer greatly. In 5052, King Aethelred passed away, paving the way for his son, Prince Arcturus, to take the throne and usher in what became known as the Age of Kings.

The Age of Kings

This was a time of prosperity and growth, with the kingdom's economy flourishing and the people thriving. King Arcturus' leadership was instrumental in restoring the people's faith in the monarchy and fostering a sense of unity and purpose.

Despite his flaws, King Aethelred remains a noteworthy figure in the kingdom's history. His reign serves as a reminder of the importance of strong leadership and the dangers of being easily swayed.

However, the kingdom's peace and prosperity was not immune to outside threats. The Marauders, a group of raiders from the Western realms, were known for launching sporadic attacks, causing trouble and instability. But even these attacks failed to disrupt the peace and tranquility of King Arcturus' rule, as the kingdom remained strong and resilient.

Overall, King Arcturus' reign will always be remembered as a golden era in the kingdom's history, marked by progress and prosperity.

	Born (yr)	Died (yr)	Age at Death	Age at Lions Birth	Age at Coronation
Rohan	5149				
Rickart	5104			45	15
Annabelle	5118	5149	31	31	
Eadric	5057	5119	62	47	46
Adela	5067	5125	58	37	
Artucrus	5032	5103	71	25	32
Isolde	5034	5109	75	23	
Galen	5010	5064	54	22	42
Gwendolyn	5016	5076	60	16	
Athelred	4985	5052	67	25	49
Eleri	4991	5060	69	19	
Caius	4962	5034	72	23	22
Morrigan	4967	5042	75	18	
Edgar	4923	4984	61	39	39
Brienne	4943	5009	66	19	
Leif	4887	4962	75	36	34
Rowena	4905	4968	63	18	
Magnus	4864	4921	57	23	35
Astrid	4865	4926	61	22	
Orin	4834	4899	65	30	51
Giselle	4846	4896	50	18	
Roland	4812	4885	73	22	35
Isadora	4823	4893	70	11	
Benedict	4785	4847	62	27	49
Beatrice	4796	4853	57	16	
Charles	4762	4834	72	23	48
Gwendolyn	4772	4850	78	13	
Athur	4740	4810	70	22	29
Margaret	4745	4800	55	17	
Aric	4720	4769	49	20	52
Ursula	4725	4768	43	15	
Huxley	4700	4772	72	20	28
Joan	4704	4756	52	16	
Garret	4675	4728	53	25	40
Matila	4685	4722	37	15	
Ivan	4656	4715	59	19	42
Eleonora	4658	4723	65	17	
Blane	4635	4698	63	21	50
Edith	4638	4679	41	18	
Finnian	4613	4685	72	22	35
Ceclia	4605	4678	73	30	
Kael	4586	4648	62	27	-----
Isabella	4595	4656	61	18	

APPENDIX B: THE CATACLYSM

The clash of Dark and Light within the void was a cacophony of sound and fury, the deafening roar of battle echoing through the empty expanse. The darkness exuded a suffocating emptiness, a sensation of weightlessness and isolation that threatened to engulf everything in its path. In contrast, the light emanated a warm, comforting energy that filled the void with vitality and hope.

Over time, the power of darkness grew, gradually overcoming the light and inching closer to complete supremacy. In a last-ditch effort to avoid extinction, Light conceived the world of Arghost - a humble landmass surrounded by vast, untamed oceans. Infused with the pure energy of light, Arghost was intended to be a stronghold of its power - a place where darkness could not simply will its destruction.

The world was once a turbulent and unpredictable place, The waters boiled and churned, while the land was frozen and barren, a desolate wasteland where life could not take hold. As a result, life could not exist in such an inhospitable environment.

As the world of Arghost began to take shape, the once-turbulent waters settled into a gentle ebb and flow, the rhythmic sounds of waves crashing against the shore filling the air. The land itself was frozen and barren, a stark and inhospitable landscape that seemed incapable of sustaining life.

But as the power of light took hold, the world began to transform. The sound of towering trees bursting forth from the ground was like a symphony of life, the rustling of leaves and the gentle swaying of branches filling the air. The world was now alive with a vibrant energy, pulsing with the power of light.

And yet, the power of light was still volatile and unpredictable. When the great cataclysm struck, the sound of shattering earth was deafening, the ground trembling and splitting apart like a living thing in agony.

It was then that Athris, the master of light, acted. Striking the land with great crystals. The sound of his crystal-infused touch was like a musical chime, each crystal resonating with the power of light and radiating outwards, humming with a powerful energy that held the shattered landscape together. The sound of darkness receded as the crystals pulsed with light, keeping the encroaching darkness at bay.

But the darkness was not willing to give up so easily. It sent its minions to infiltrate the world of Arghost, to sow seeds of chaos and destruction wherever they could. And so began the eternal struggle between light and dark in the world of Arghost.

APPENDIX C: A BRIEF HISTORY OF TREES

The story of the trees in Arghost is a truly epic tale, spanning millennia of survival, evolution, and adaptation. The Seekers of Knowledge, the esteemed scholars of Arghost, meticulously chronicled the journey of the majestic trees. Piecing together a vivid account of their struggles and triumphs.

As the powerful Athris, the one true light, formed the world, he imbued it with his own power to keep the darkness at bay. The world was initially a tumultuous place, buffeted by harsh and unforgiving climates that made survival impossible. But eventually, the weather stabilized, and life emerged.

But soon things changed. The weather ceased its endless volatility, becoming more stable, albeit still harsh. It allowed for some very hardy beings to appear.

The very first life in the world was the trees, enormous trees that reached the heavens. Covered in dense foliage that contrasted the bleak landscape that sustained them. They were the guardians of the land, bringing light to the world and hope for its future.

In a world battling to keep the darkness at bay, the trees were a guiding light. They would move around the land seeking the comfort of the most amiable climates in which to thrive and produce their offspring. Their movements, although slow, were deliberate, as it took a great deal of energy expenditure to move even one inch.

The "Great Migration", as it was later called, was a staple of the world for many millennia. The trees grew to large numbers. Soon, other flora appeared, filling the landscape with beauty beyond measure.

But soon was the age of the Cataclysm. The world broke apart, and some trees became separated from the herd, forced to exist in climates that weren't overly favorable. To survive, they evolved over many years, new species grew that were more tolerant.

As time went on, the trees became tired and longed for a stable home. Many stayed where they were and just gave up, losing the ability to walk, settling into areas, and becoming dormant. Whilst others grouped together. Although no longer moving, they kept their abilities by staying in groups. Working together to protect themselves from other dangers that had arisen in Arghost.

One such place is the Dewforrest in Cliodaven.

The Dewforrest is a place of wonder and awe, a testament to the resilience and adaptability of the trees of Arghost. It is a place of renewal and rebirth, where the cycle of life continues uninterrupted, and the beauty of nature shines through in all its glory. As the sun sets over the Dewforrest, casting a warm and golden glow over the land, one cannot help but be filled with a sense of peace and contentment. Knowing that the trees are still there, silently watching over the world and guiding it toward a brighter future.

ABOUT AUTHOR

Derren Parsons is an Australian fantasy author and the creator of *The Chronicles of Arghost*, a series shaped by ancient myth, moral consequence, and the cost of power.

His work explores prophecy not as destiny, but as burden—focusing on characters forced to reckon with inherited sins, broken histories, and choices that cannot be undone. Alongside *The Chronicles of Arghost*, his published works include *Raven's Bane*, *Cryptic Dunes*, *The Magika Handbook*, and *The Jonathan Rourke Series*.

When not writing, Derren can usually be found refining worlds, untangling timelines, or quietly questioning whether any story ever truly ends.

You can learn more, join his mailing list, and explore upcoming projects at

www.derrenparsonsauthor.com

Have you read them all?

The Magika Handbook

A Comprehensive guide

The Magika Academy of the Arts Handbook is a vital resource for aspiring Magikas, providing important information on Arghost's flora and its properties. Students must treat the handbook with respect, dedicating time to studying it and internalizing its teachings.

To tap into the unique energy of Arghost's flora, one must embrace introspection, mindfulness, and a willingness to explore the unknown. Each biome on Arghost provides unique opportunities for discovery, but precision and mental acuity are necessary to blend the right plants in the right amounts. Becoming a proficient Magika requires years of focused, dedicated, and disciplined training, and success depends on one's abilities, resolve, and commitment to the craft. The handbook provides a starting point, but the true potential of magic is only limited by imagination and creativity.

Raven's Bane

Claws of Greed Spark a Battle: Wings of Love, a Revolution.

Seventeen-year-old Caelen's world is thrown into chaos when poachers invade his village, capturing his shapeshifter clan. With their very existence at stake, Caelen alone escapes the surprise attack. Determined to rescue his family, he ventures into forbidden human territory, navigating adversities and forging an unlikely bond with Leira, the poacher leader's defiant daughter.

Yet a darker threat is brewing. A ruthless sorcerer named Volthar has unleashed an otherworldly force to harvest Caelen's magical kin. As the fate of the realm hangs in the balance, Caelen and Leira lead a daring uprising against the spreading darkness. Outnumbered and outmatched, it will take every ounce of courage to save those they love and preserve the fabric of their world. But failure means annihilation.

Can star-crossed friends defeat an evil legion? Find out in this coming-of-age romantic fantasy brimming with forbidden friendship, shocking betrayals, and electrifying shape-shifter action.

Fate's Wager

Every Gamble Has Its Price.

When ex-soldier John's gambling debts embroil his family in a treacherous quest, he assembles a fellowship from his dark past—a cunning human, stalwart dwarf, fierce elven huntress, and twin Namites, jackal-headed warriors from a distant desert land. Bound by brotherhood forged through the calamities of war, they dare to pursue fabled treasure stolen by a legendary sea beast.

Braving untold dangers on land and sea, John's eclectic band of battle-hardened rogues must work as one to outwit ruthless brigands and monstrous jungle horrors in their drive to settle John's score. But as deception and betrayal threaten to tear the team apart, only their unwavering camaraderie can conquer the challenges ahead.

In this epic tale brimming with magic, mythic monsters, rip-roaring action, and sprawling world-building, one man's debt holds dire implications, forcing him to lead his team of damaged heroes on a breakneck chase that will either end a lifelong curse... or destroy everything he holds dear.

www.ingramcontent.com/pod-product-compliance
Lightning Source LLC
Chambersburg PA
CBHW030015180626
46810CB00001B/53